SAY MY NAME

ASHLEY JAMES

Say My Name Copyright © 2023 by Ashley James
All rights reserved. No part of this book may be reproduced in any form or by any electronic or mechanical means, including information storage and retrieval systems, without written permission from the author, except for the use of brief quotations in a book review.
This is a work of fiction. Names, characters, places, and incidents are either products of the authors imagination or used in a fictitious manner. Any resemblance to actual persons, living or dead, or events is purely coincidental.

Cover Design: Fortuitous Designer
Photographer: Xram Ragde
Interior Formatting: Wanderlust Formatting
Editing: Nice Girl Naughty Edits

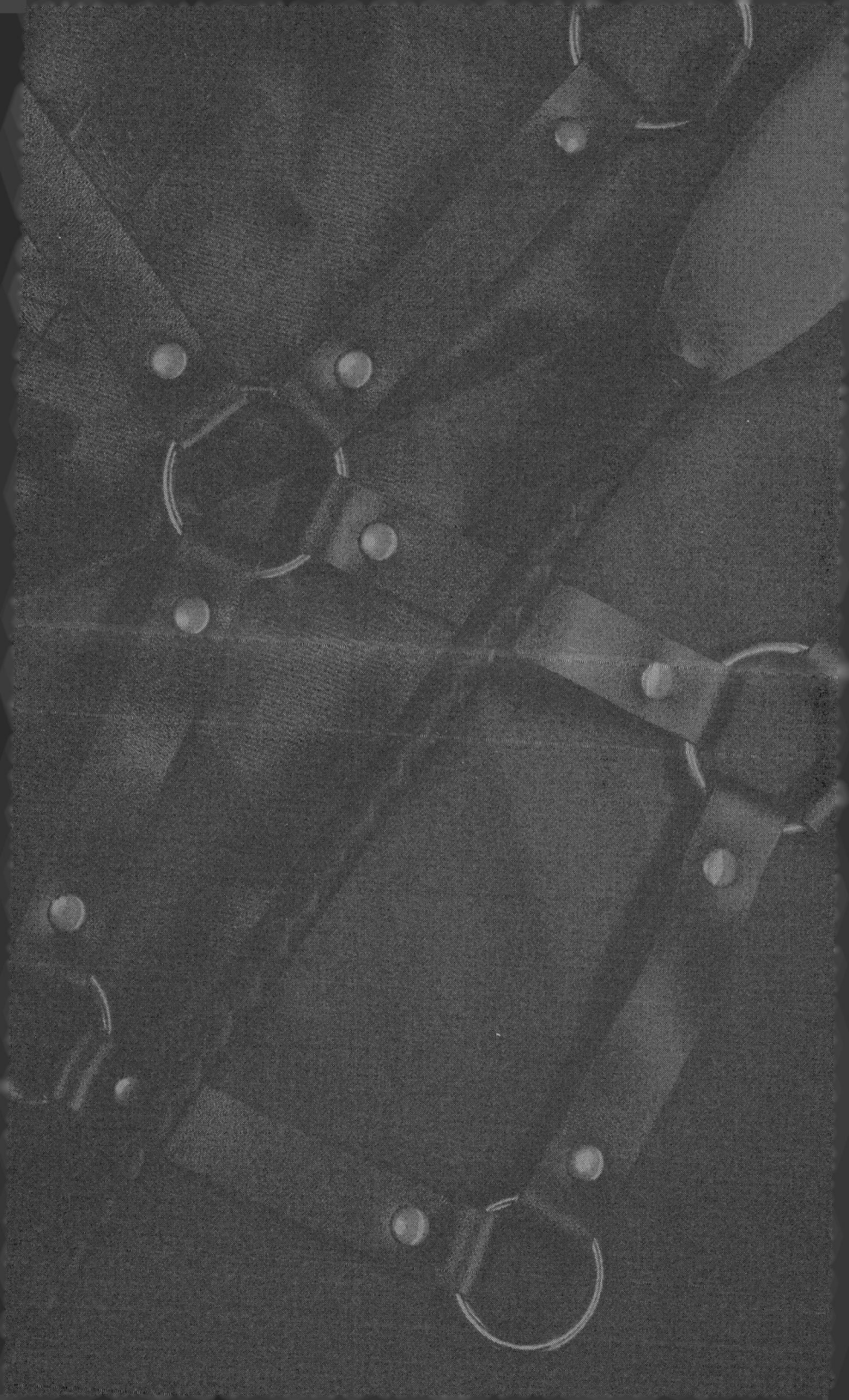

To Alex,
If it weren't for you, this story probably never would've even happened.
It's because of your undying love for Tony Troy and his HEA that we are here today.

And also to Mads,
Nobody loves Mateo the way you do—except maybe Travis.
Mateo loves you, cariño.

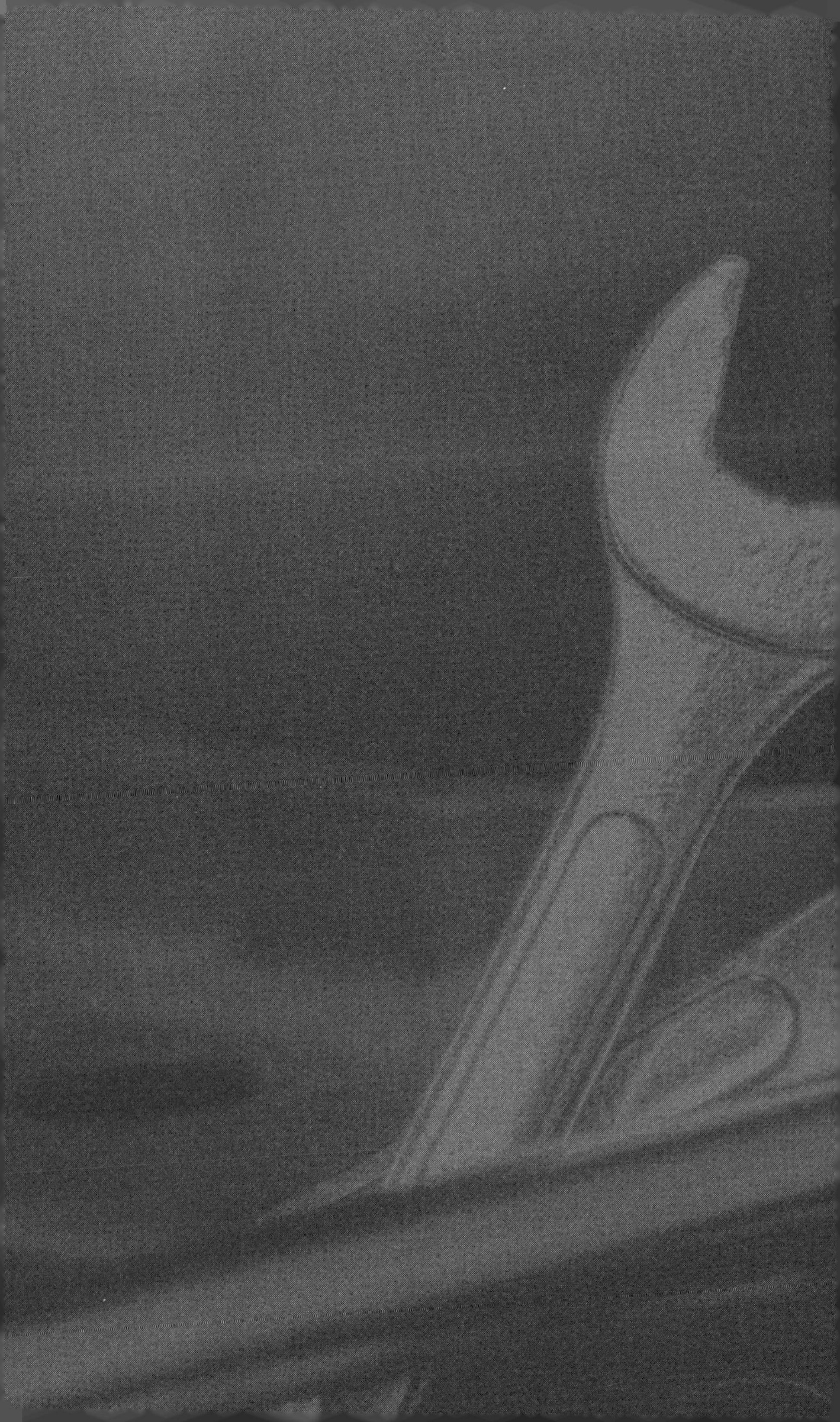

"In vain I have struggled. It will not do. My feelings will not be repressed. You must allow me to tell you how ardently I admire and love you."

—*Pride and Prejudice*, Jane Austen

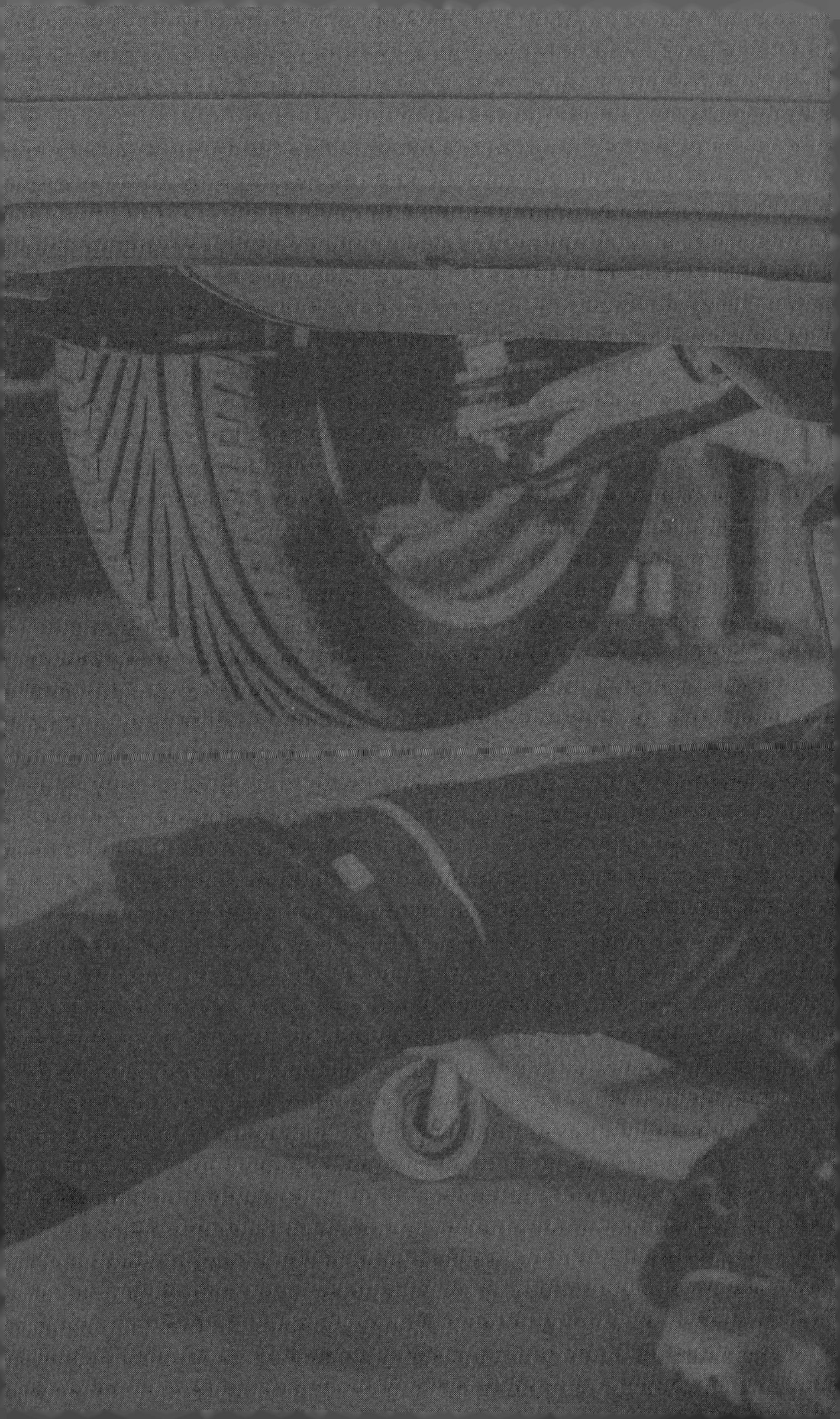

PLAYLIST

Theme Song:
"Fire Up The Night" — New Medicine

"Do It For Me" — Rosenfeld
"Tainted Love" — Marilyn Manson
"Prisoner" — Raphael Lake, Aaron Levy, Daniel Ryan Murphy
"Nails" — Call Me Karizma
"Rapture" — Underoath
"Chills (Dark Version) — Mickey Valen, Joey Myron
"Neon Grave" — Dayseeker
"Terrible Lie" — Nine Inch Nails
"Daddy" — Ramsey
"Feel You Out" — Landon Tewers
"The Death of Peace of Mind" — Bad Omens
"Vertebrae" — Allistair, Spencer Kane
"You Put a Spell on Me" — Austin Giorgio
"Breathe" — Kansh
"Hypnotize" — Flights Over Phoenix
"Gorilla" — Bruno Mars
"Control" — Puddle of Mudd
"Good 4 U" — Olivia Rodrigo
"Mine" — Sleep Token
"The Sex is Good" — Saving Abel
"Bad Decisions" — Bad Omens

Listen to the Full Playlist on Spotify

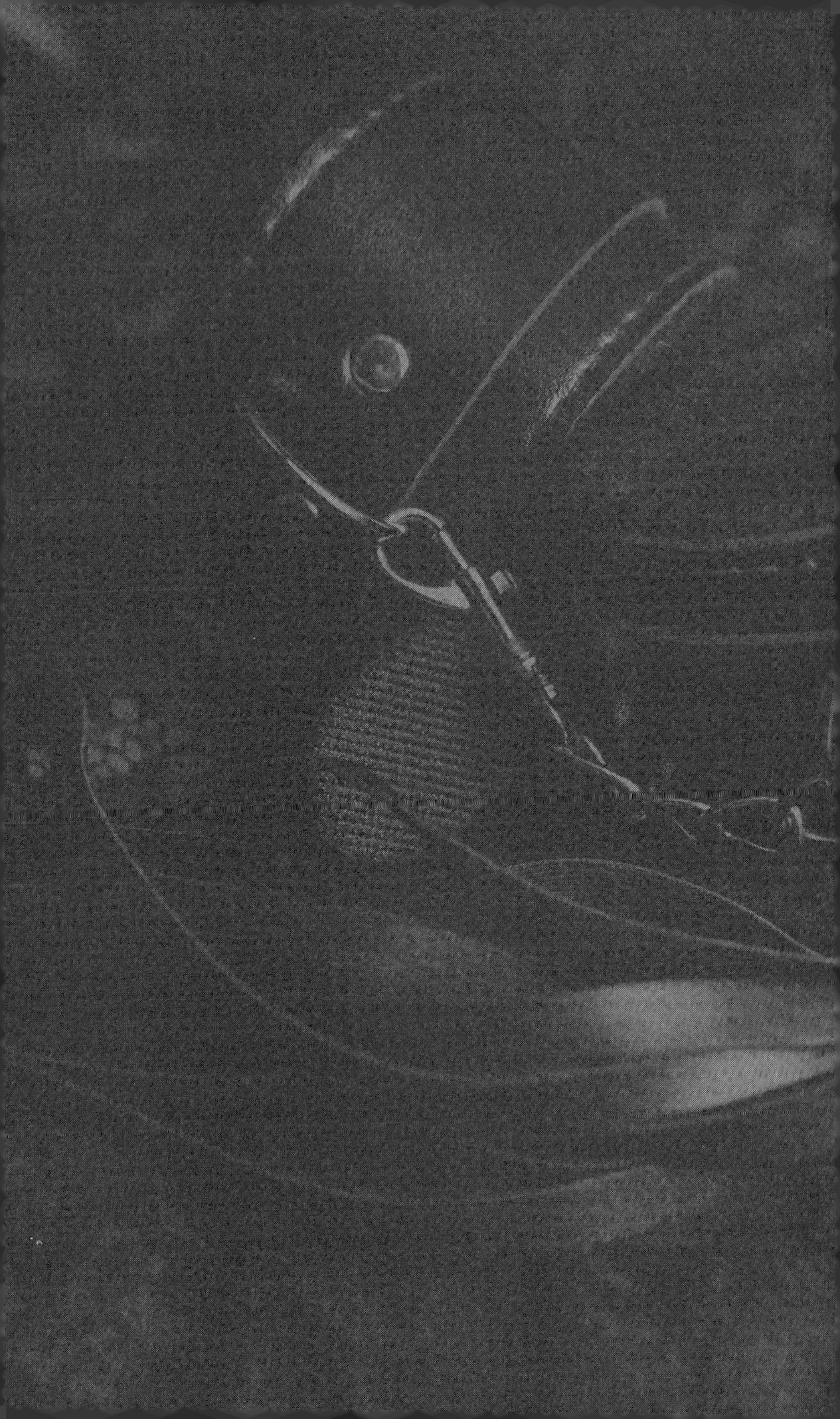

AUTHORS NOTE

THE BELOW MAY CONTAIN SPOILERS.

Say My Name was originally featured in the Anti-Valentine Anthology as a short/novella. Everything that was in the novella is included in this story but minor things have been changed/tweaked in order to expand their story into a full length, and for it to be cohesive and make sense timeline-wise. If you didn't read it in the anthology, don't worry, you aren't missing anything. This is a full, complete standalone.

This book contains a handful of kinks that may not be for everyone, as well as subject matter that may be triggering for some. Please see below for a list of kinks and potential trigger warnings.

This book features, but is not limited to, the following: Dubcon, Somnophilia, BDSM, Water Sports, Impact Play, Breath Play, Blood Play, Brief Mention of Conversion Therapy (not detailed), Religious Trauma (not detailed), Brief Mention of Homophobia, Brief Mention of Abuse from a Parent.

*The religious trauma, discussion of conversion therapy, homophobia, and abuse are all in the past but are briefly mentioned on page.

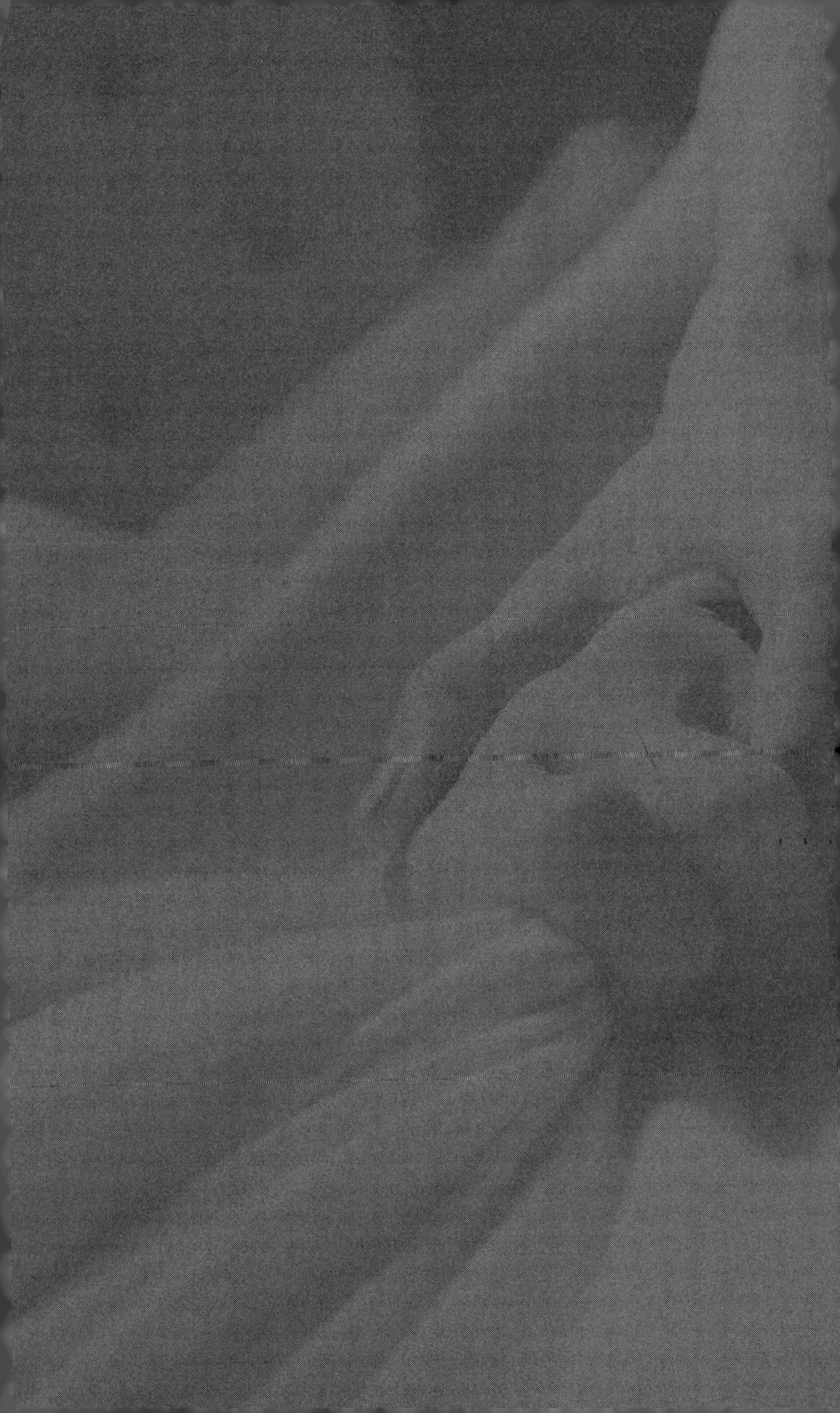

PROLOGUE

Travis

AGE 15

"Let's go, Jaguars, let's go!" A loud rumble can be heard around the court as students and parents alike beat their hands on the tops of their thighs as the Desert Creek High cheerleaders get us ready for our first home game of the season.

The first home game I've ever been to.

It's thrilling, witnessing the school spirit and the excitement. It's something you'd see in the movies. The girls down on the court are decked out in red, black, and white, with their pompoms, short skirts, and the paint streaking their faces. Their hair is big and bouncy, tied to the top of their heads, and the bows adorning each of their ponytails would look ridiculous if they were anybody but cheerleaders.

Basketball isn't my favorite sport in the world, but one of my friends, Dylan, is on the team, and it was an excuse to get out of the house and away from my mother's concerned eye for a few hours.

An elbow jabs me in the side, and my eyes drag to my left

to see Elliot, my best friend and the source of the jab. "Bro, do you see how hot Nia looks down there? I swear, she's been eyeing me all night."

A chuckle falls from my lips that I wipe away with my hand when his eyes narrow on me. He's crushing *bad* on Nia Hayes, Desert Creek High School's head cheerleader, a senior, and one of the biggest bitches I think I've ever had the displeasure of meeting in my life. She's also one hundred percent *not* into Elliot, much to his ignorance.

If I had to bet, I'd say her eyes were actually on Zuri Jordan, a junior, and our school's best softball pitcher, who's sitting a few rows behind us. I saw them making out in the alcove near the gym a few days ago, and by the looks of it, it didn't seem like it was the first time. Of course, Elliot doesn't know that, because it's not my place to out somebody and it's clearly not common knowledge.

"Yeah, man. Bet she totally wants you," I tease, bringing my attention back to the court as the players start filing out from the locker room.

We're playing Payton High tonight. They're from one town over, and a pretty big rival from what Dylan has told me. The gym smells of rubber, sweat, and teen spirit, sneakers squeaking and scuffing all along the court. I don't know how people sit through games hearing that all the time. It's obnoxious.

The game seems to start without a hitch. Not that I have any fucking clue what's going on. Both sides sink the ball into the hoop a few times, and we cheer. Not even halfway through, my phone buzzes in my pocket. Pulling it out, a text from my buddy, Jesse, has me swiping across the screen and unlocking it.

Jesse: Got the shit. Let me know when the game is over, and I'll meet you in the far right corner of the student lot.

Me: Sweet. Thanks.

Leaning toward Elliot, I whisper in his ear so only he can hear me. "Got the weed for tonight."

A straight, white grin stretches across his face, making his honey brown eyes squint. He got his braces off the summer before we started school this year, so his teeth look damn near perfect. With his fingers, he makes an 'okay' hand gesture before returning his attention to the court… or to the sidelines, where Nia is sitting with the rest of the squad.

Dragging my gaze around the gym, I take in how full it is in here tonight. I don't recognize anybody in the bleachers across the court, but that isn't unusual, since the away team's family and friends sit over there. It's nearly as packed as this side is. Payton High is in a wealthy town, and it shows. The parents all dressed to the nines, probably rich CEOs, lawyers, or doctors.

It's almost comical looking between the two sides of the room. Desert Creek isn't on the poverty line, by any means, but most households sit pretty comfortably right at middle class. Up until two years ago, my family was actually considered lower class until my mom got married to my stepdad, William Finch. He owns a string of restaurants that span across Washington and Oregon that seem to do pretty well. Moving in with him meant that my sister, Charlotte, and I could have cell phones like the rest of the kids at our school and finally afford dental insurance.

The side of the room I'm watching erupts into raucous cheer, letting me know they probably scored, and just as I'm about to divert my gaze to the court to see what's going on, someone in the crowd catches my eye and makes my breath catch painfully in my chest.

There's no way.

I rub my fists into my eye sockets, blinking and re-blinking to clear my vision, because there's no way I'm seeing who I think I'm seeing. My heart rate accelerates, and suddenly, I feel ten degrees hotter, sweat lining the back of my neck, coating the hair on my nape that I keep meaning to cut.

"Hey, man. You okay?" Elliot asks, pulling my attention away from the third row of bleachers almost directly across from me.

Glancing at him, I nod. "I'm fine."

"You sure?" His thick, dark, pierced brow arches. "You look like you've seen a ghost."

I have, I want to say. But I don't. Instead, I nod again. "Positive. I'm good." To emphasize how *good* I am, I hold up two thumbs like an idiot, only making both brows jump this time.

"If you say so," he mumbles before looking back at the court.

The rest of the game is spent with me stuck in my head, eyes glued across the room. Disbelief burning hot inside my gut.

When I was five, my father dipped. One random Tuesday morning, he got ready for work, per usual—showered, shaved, dressed in a suit and tie, went to the kitchen and poured his thermos of coffee—and left. Unlike every other Tuesday before, though, he never came home.

Well, maybe he got held up at work, I told myself as I laid in bed, peeking out the window in my room every five minutes to see if his car magically appeared in the driveway.

It didn't.

It didn't on Wednesday night either. Or Thursday. Or Friday.

By Saturday, I kind of gave up hope.

By Sunday, my Grandma Tillie came to get my sister and me. Mom was sick, or so I thought, and couldn't get out of bed. We stayed with my grandparents for over a week. At the time, it was fun. I was mostly able to keep my mind off the fact that my dad vanished, seemingly into thin air, and my mom must have had a pretty bad case of the flu. Or maybe, I wondered at the time, if she possibly got food poisoning from IHOP like I did the year before.

We didn't go to school that week, but we did go to the skate rink, the park, and a baseball game. It was a fun week, but by the time we came home, that spot where Dad used to park was still empty, as were my mom's eyes. Her light was gone.

And it stayed gone for many years following that week.

Everything changed after that Tuesday morning, when Dad went to work but never made it home. I thought he was dead until I was nine, when we were at the grocery store and my mom ran into his mom. I remember feeling excited that we saw her because I hadn't for quite some time. I pretended to read the label on the back of some soup cans while they talked. Mom asked how Logan was doing.

Logan was my dad.

That was the day I learned my dad wasn't dead after all. No, he wasn't dead. He just didn't want to be my dad anymore. It confused me, but more than that, it hurt. An ache formed in my chest that no amount of rubbing away would fix. It grew, it strengthened, and with it came a river of emotions, streaming out of my eyes and down my cheeks that night when I went to sleep.

As I got older, I thought maybe he was like those adults you see on TV who drink too much or who do the drugs parents and teachers tell you to say no too. Maybe he left because he was unwell, not because he didn't love me.

It's a lie I've held on to for years.

Until this very moment.

Because sitting in the bleachers, a court separating us, is a man with my same nose and my same blond hair, in a suit that looks more expensive than my whole wardrobe. He's sitting beside a pretty blonde woman with a cheerful toddler on her lap, who has bouncy blonde curls and dimples, and my same nose too.

It becomes abundantly clear that the dad who left my house that Tuesday morning for work and never came home didn't die. He didn't drink too much. He wasn't addicted to the drugs they warn you about in school.

No… that man was alive, and he was well, and he was sitting across the room with his new family, while his old family sat discarded just a glance away.

My chest tightens, my ribs constricting, threatening to squeeze my heart until it explodes. Air doesn't want to go into my lungs. The room spins.

It's hot.

So hot.

I glance over at Elliot to see if he thinks it's hot, but he's not even paying me any attention. He's cool as a cucumber. Understandably so, since his world isn't being rocked right now.

Bile churns in my gut, the taste rising in the back of my throat.

I need to get out of here, because I might pass out or barf, or worse, cross the basketball court and demand to know why he left me. Demand to know, once and for all, why I wasn't good enough, lovable enough, to stay.

The walls are closing in. I can't breathe.

I think I tell Elliot I'm leaving, but I can't be sure. My brain has short-circuited. By the time I burst through the double doors, down the hallway lined with red and black lockers, and out the main door, the chilly late fall air smacks me in the face, and it's like the floodgates burst open. I drop to my knees on the sidewalk, hands planting on my thighs as I stare at the concrete, vision blurry as moisture falls hot down my face.

I don't make a sound. Don't let a single whimper leave my lips. The tears come and come until there's nothing more left. Until my sockets have dried up.

Then, and only then, do I pull out my phone, shooting off a text to Jesse that I'm ready to meet up with him.

Tonight is about forgetting. Tonight is about forcing my mind to get so hazy, I don't care about what I saw.

And tomorrow... well, that's future Travis's problem.

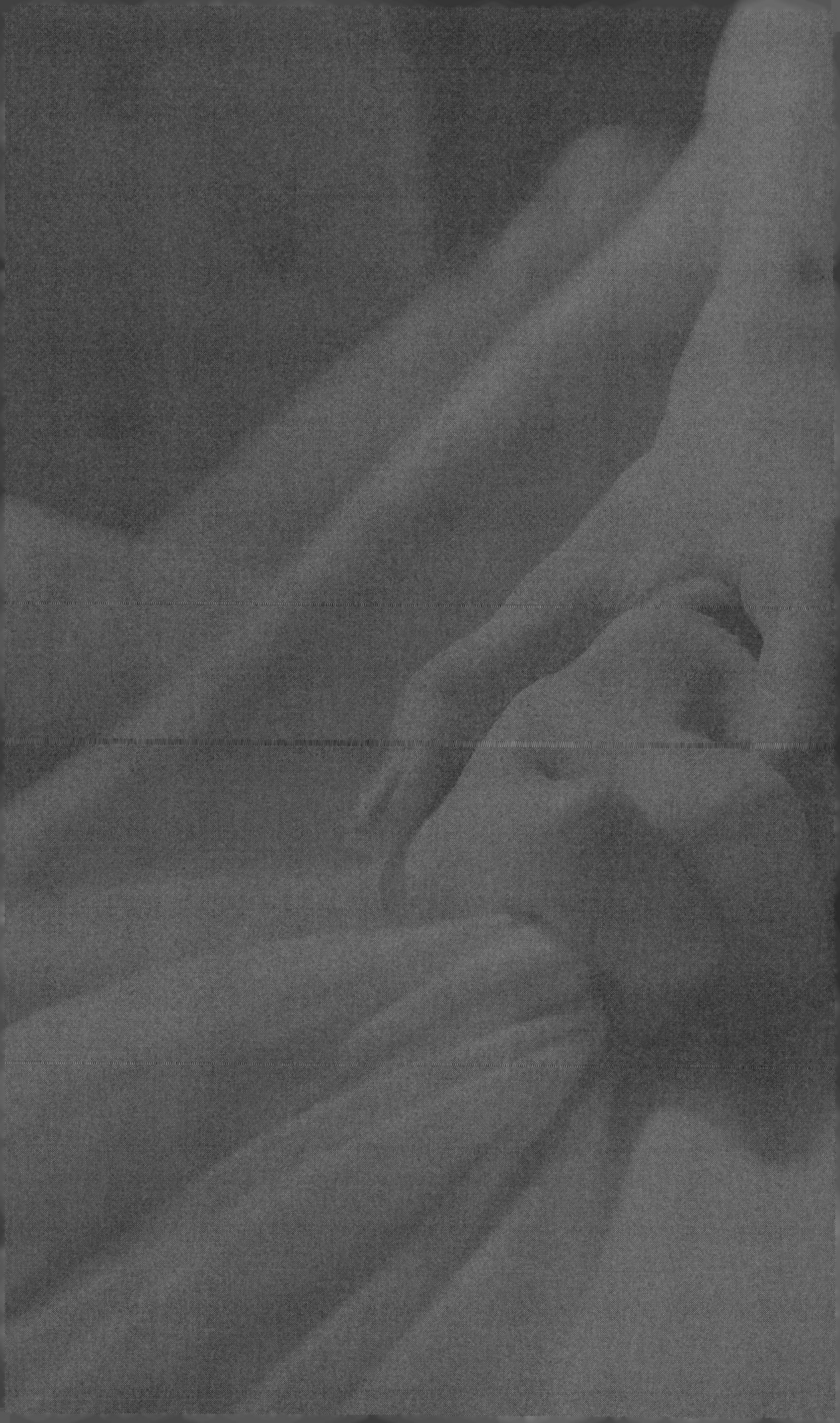

ONE

Travis

COLLEGE, SENIOR YEAR

Nathaniel: Sorry, babe. Won't be able to make dinner tonight. Someone called out at work, so I gotta cover the shift. Won't get off till 2. Will make it up to you. Xoxo.

Staring down at the phone in my hand, I try to block the lump of disappointment making itself known in my chest. It's not his fault he has to work, but fuck, I was really looking forward to our date.

It's our six-month anniversary, which I know seems like a silly thing to want to celebrate, but for me, it's a big deal. Nathaniel is my first actual relationship, so six months feels like a significant milestone. I really wanted to treat him to a nice dinner, then take him back to his place—because he lives off campus, while I live in the dorms—and *show* him just how happy he makes me.

I need to quit sulking. There are other nights we can do this. Like tomorrow or next weekend. It doesn't have to be today, I guess.

The door to my dorm shoves open, peeling my focus from my phone to my roommate, Xander, who's waltzing in. A boyish grin tugs on his lips, his already bloodshot eyes squinting as he sees me. "What's up, man?" He must notice my dreary mood because the smile slips. "What's wrong?"

"Nathaniel and I had plans to go to dinner tonight, but he has to work. I was looking forward to doing something tonight."

"Where does he work?"

"He's a server at the burger place a few blocks from campus."

Nathaniel is here on a partial scholarship, but his family doesn't come from a lot of money, so he works a few days a week to have extra cash.

"Well, shit, I'm sorry, Trav. But hey, I'm heading to that party the sorority is throwing tonight. Want to come? It's Friday, so may as well still make the most out of your night, even if it's not with him."

"I don't know," I mumble. "I'm not in the greatest mood. I probably won't be any fun."

"Oh, shut the fuck up," he drawls. "Let's smoke a bowl and head over. The weed will help get you out of your head. It'll be fun."

Glancing down at my phone and seeing no new texts from Nathaniel, I heave a sigh and agree. Xander rolls us a blunt that we smoke on the walk over to the sorority, and by the time we make it there, my mood is already improving. The house is overflowing with people, a damn near unlimited supply of liquor fills the kitchen counters, kegs line the backyard, and music blares and vibrates the walls.

We both grab a drink before heading out back. A few of our friends are out there playing a heated game of beer pong.

Party Up by DMX sounds through the Bluetooth speaker

they have on top of one of the kegs, a group of girls dancing to it on the grass, oblivious to everything around them. They're probably in the sorority, if I had to guess. Xander jumps in and plays the winners next. His partner is a guy in one of our classes who he's been trying to hook up with now for a few weeks.

I watch them while occasionally checking my phone. Nathaniel hasn't texted me, but then again, maybe it's busy at the restaurant. Deciding to be a nice boyfriend, I send him one.

Me: Hope your shift is going okay and you're making lots of tips. Miss you.

It's right there on the tip of my thumb to tell him I came to this party with Xander, but I don't. He can sometimes get jealous or upset if I spend too much time with Xander or if I go to parties without him. He knows I've hooked up with a handful of the people who frequently come to these types of things, and that makes him feel some type of way.

Nathaniel also thinks these parties are lame and a waste of time. He'd much rather stay in together or go out to dinner, just the two of us. Since we started dating, I've actually cut back on partying. Which, honestly, has saved me many hungover mornings, so I really should be thanking him.

I hit send on the message, shoving it back into my pocket before downing the rest of my drink. Catching Xander's eye, I let him know I'm heading inside for a refill. The house has gotten significantly more packed in the short time I've been outside, but that's not all that surprising, seeing as how it's only getting later. It's barely ten, and the bodies in here will probably easily multiply by midnight. This sorority in particular is known for its ragers.

Weaving my way through the crowd, I finally make it to the kitchen, and as I'm pouring the vodka into my solo cup,

I see him. *Nathaniel.* He's on the other side of the kitchen, more toward the dining room, standing around with all of his buddies and a few guys I don't even recognize, laughing and talking and drinking.

The blood in my body runs ice cold and a pit so deep and so sharp forms in my gut. *Why is he here? Did he get off early? Did he text me and maybe I didn't see it?* Grabbing my phone out of my pocket, I pull up our message, and nope. Nothing.

When I glance back up, he still hasn't spotted me. I watch him in his element for a moment. Maybe he's about to come find me. Maybe he just arrived and wanted to say hi to his friends first.

That's a logical idea.

He's not in his server's uniform, though.

Maybe he went home to change after his shift that must've ended early. The person who couldn't work, maybe they ended up being able to.

One of the guys I don't recognize leans in, whispering something in Nathaniel's ear. I can't make out what is said obviously, but whatever it is makes Nathaniel grin as he wraps an arm around the guy's shoulder, dragging him into his side.

The room goes silent. I can't hear anything, despite knowing the music is on and people are talking all around me. I can't hear anything other than the sound of my pounding heart in my ears.

Thump, thump, thump.

My throat goes dry, tongue stuck to the roof of my mouth as I watch him.

I should go over there. Say hi.

I'm sure there's an explanation.

Before I can even decide what to do, his eyes lift, scanning the room like he can feel himself being watched. They land on me, and the smile on his face falters for a single moment before he rights it. He doesn't immediately remove his hand from the other guy, but his body visibly stiffens as he takes me in.

We stay locked in this vortex of eye contact for a few beats before he *finally* drops his arm, saying something to the group of guys he's with—probably excusing himself—before crossing the room to where I'm frozen in place.

His signature pretty boy smirk—the same one he always flashes to get himself out of trouble or off the hook anywhere he goes—tugs on his lips as he stops only a foot or so in front of me. "Hey, babe," he nearly shouts over the music and the loud chatter that I surprisingly can hear again. "I didn't know you'd be here."

Yeah, clearly, I think, but don't say. "Xander invited me last minute."

"Did he?" he asks, his lip turned up almost into a sneer. Nathaniel really doesn't like Xander, and I don't get why.

I shrug. "Yeah, well, I thought you'd be at work, and he didn't want me to sit at home all night on a Friday."

"It was slow," he explains. "So, they sent me home."

And you didn't think to let me know? "Who's the guy you had your arm around?" I ask, hating how thick my throat feels.

Nathaniel glances over his shoulder. "Oh, him? He's just a friend from class."

"Looked awfully cozy with him before you saw me," I mumble so quietly, I think he won't hear me.

But he does.

"Don't be like that, Travis." His face falls. He almost looks sad. "You know it upsets me when you act like you don't trust me."

My chest squeezes, a pang of guilt hitting me right in the

13

heart. "I do trust you."

"It doesn't seem like it when you say stuff like that."

"I do. It's just…" It's just, what, Travis? Why do I always assume the worst at any given moment? "It took me by surprise seeing you here after you told me we couldn't hang out because you had to work. That's all."

"Well, I told you, babe. They sent me home. I thought you'd be asleep, and I didn't want to bother you."

"It's barely after ten," I argue. "When am I ever asleep that early?"

His gaze hardens as he takes a step back. "I told you what happened, and you're still acting like you don't believe me. I'm not doing this with you tonight, Travis. Let me know when you're ready to stop being such a drama queen."

"Baby—" I start to say, but he walks off, back to his group of friends, leaving me standing there like the cat got my tongue.

Why do I always do this? I always overreact and make him mad. Why can't I be a more laid-back boyfriend who trusts him effortlessly?

I fuck everything up. Always.

Scanning the room, I gnaw on the inside of my cheek as I consider what I should do. I know better than to try to argue with Nathaniel. It'll just make things worse. I consider going back outside to hang out with Xander, but my mood has plummeted, so he'll hound me to tell him what's wrong, and I'd rather not deal with that.

I should just go home. Maybe some sleep will be the best thing.

The walk home is only a couple of miles, but it's a little chilly. By the time I make it to my room, exhaustion has set in, mixing with the guilt and the anger toward myself. I always fucking do this.

Climbing into bed, it takes no time at all to fall asleep, and when I wake in the morning, I have a text from Nathaniel waiting for me.

Nathaniel: Sorry for getting so mad. But, babe, you know how it makes me feel when you do and say shit like that. Let's grab brunch in the morning, and forget it ever happened. Xoxo.

I let out a deep breath, feeling so much better. *He's not mad at me anymore.*

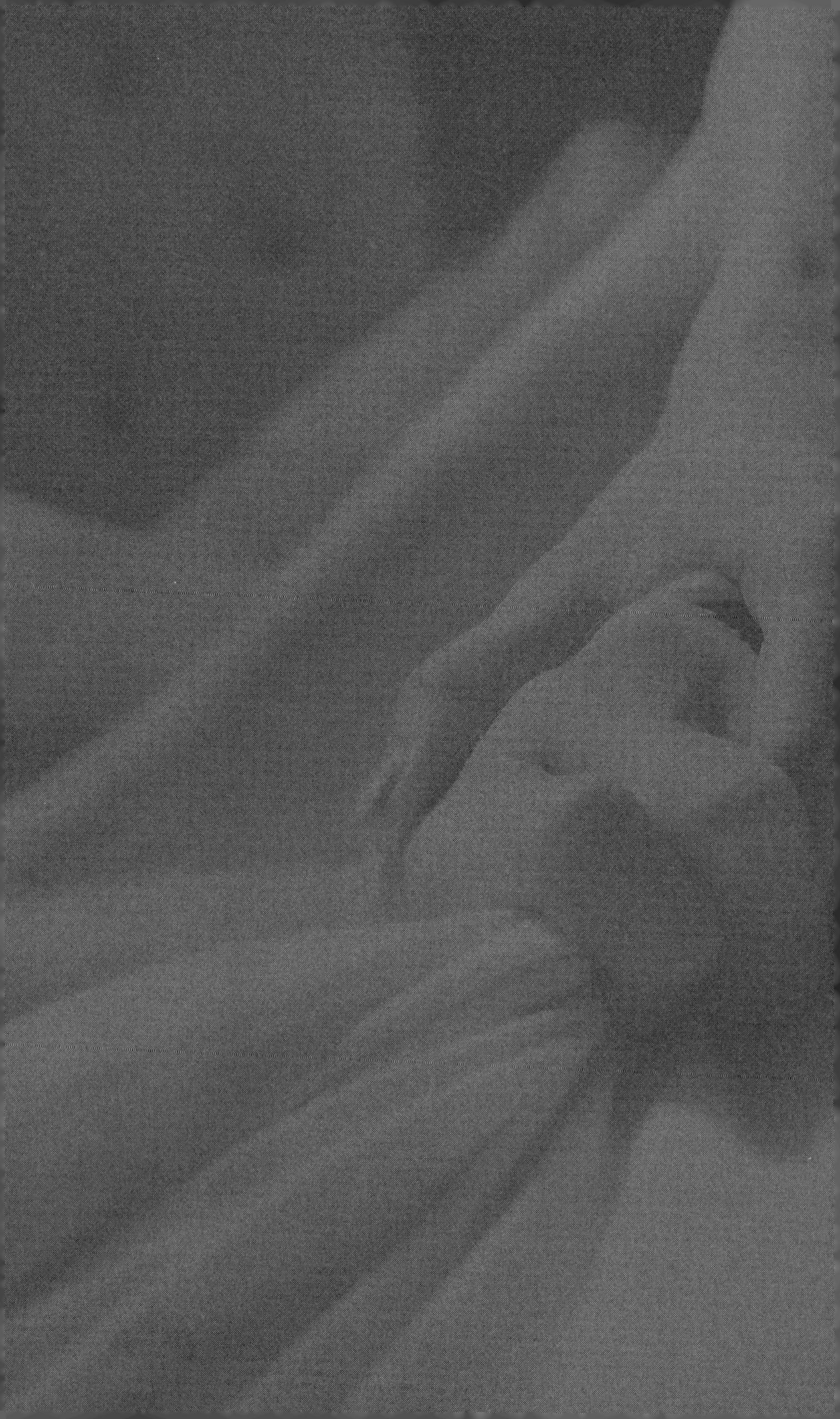

TWO

Travis

PRESENT

"Tonight's the night, right?" Raising my eyes from the computer screen I've spent the last several hours staring at, the spreadsheet morphing into something that doesn't even seem like English anymore, my gaze connects with Jasmine's smiling face.

A grin of my own tugs on my lips as I nod. "Yup, tonight!"

She squeals, taking a seat in the empty chair on the other side of my desk. "How are you feeling?" she asks, resting her chin on her palm. "Are you nervous at all?"

Before I can respond to her, Nolan, my other friend slash co-worker, rounds the corner, plopping down beside Jasmine. "Nervous about what?"

"Tonight's the night Travis proposes to his boyfriend," Jasmine all but squeals in Nolan's direction.

"Oh, shit." He drags his gaze over to me, a smile upticking his lips. "That's right. I forgot about that. Do tell."

"There's not really much to tell." I continue clicking away on my mouse, trying to hide the nerves that are eating away at me, because, *yes,* I am nervous, but I don't want them to know that. "He has to work late tonight, so I'm using it to my advantage, going home early, setting up, and having a nice dinner ready for him."

"What are you cooking?" Nolan asks.

"I'm not cooking shit," I reply with a chuckle. "Can't cook to save my life. I'm having his favorite Italian restaurant deliver before he gets home."

"Ahhh, I'm so excited for you, Travis," Jasmine gushes, her hands cupping her cheeks as she smiles so big, her eyes squint. "I know you've had your fair share of difficulties with Nathaniel, but it seems like things have been so much better since you guys bought the house, and if anybody deserves this, it's you."

Tipping his head in Jasmine's direction, Nolan says, "What she said."

"Thanks, guys. I appreciate that."

I've worked for Stratton Marketing since I graduated from college about four years ago. I started as an intern and worked my way up. Now, I'm one of their Senior Digital Marketing Specialists, along with Nolan and Jasmine. The promotion came a little less than a year ago, and with it came a pretty hefty raise.

Up until then, Nathaniel and I had been renting shitty apartment after shitty apartment. At the start of last year, he was also promoted at his job, but it was my promotion that got us to decide it was time to purchase a home.

That was an experience all on its own, buying real estate. It was something I never knew if I could do, but it was a goal and a dream regardless. Washington isn't exactly the most practical state to buy a home in, but the fact that we moved to a smaller town after graduation worked in our favor.

We were able to find a cute little four-bedroom house on a tiny bit of land within our budget. Our golden retriever puppy, Nova, loves the fenced backyard that none of our other apartments offered, and I was able to set up a home office in one of the spare bedrooms for the days when I work from home.

Truthfully, there have been many times in the span of my relationship with Nathaniel when I didn't know if we'd ever get here. We met in college, and basically had to learn how to be adults together. It was rough—downright brutal sometimes—going from never having an actual boyfriend to having someone I was suddenly living with and having to co-exist with.

But alas, here we are. Somehow, we've survived enough for me to spend what little I've saved up since buying the house on a ring I plan to give him tonight.

Jasmine and Nolan stay to chit-chat for a bit before they head back to their desks. Then my afternoon is spent in back-to-back meetings with potential new clients, allowing my mind to focus on something other than how nervous I am for how tonight will go.

It's around a quarter past four by the time I leave the office. After a quick stop at the store to pick up our favorite bottle of wine, I head home. We live about thirty minutes from my work with afternoon traffic. Not terrible. Nathaniel is usually off by four, but since he's working late, he shouldn't be home until at least six, giving me plenty of time to get the house clean and set up.

It's fall in eastern Washington, and it's cold as shit this year. But luckily, the sun is out, shining brightly, and giving the illusion of warmth. I soak it in with the heat blasting, and the music turned way up. The closer I get to the house, the more

19

the nerves in my stomach make themselves known. My hands practically tremble as I grip the steering wheel, and nausea washes over me in waves.

Sometimes, looking back on shit in hindsight, it becomes abundantly clear that the universe was tossing sign after sign in our direction. Trying to tell us something, trying to stop us from making terrible decisions. The types of signs that we reflect on after the fact, and think, *shit, I should've seen that coming from a mile away.*

This… Well, this is one of those moments.

As I pull up outside my cute little yellow house, the first thing I notice is the car parked next to the curb. I don't recognize it, but it must belong to the neighbors. The next thing I notice is my garage opener isn't in the car where it normally is. I got my car detailed at lunch today and must've left it in my office.

Grabbing the bottle of wine and my briefcase, I exit the car, locking it as I make my way along the path to the front door. With my keys in hand, I trudge up the two steps, but when I go to unlock it, I notice the door is slightly ajar. Not enough that it's obvious, but it's definitely not all the way closed.

My heart rate accelerates as I look around the neighborhood. My eyes immediately land on the car I've never seen on this block before. *What if someone broke into the house?* I was the last one to leave this morning, and I *know* I locked it when I left. I'm a freak when it comes to that kind of shit. I triple check the house is locked at night before going to bed.

Steeling my spine and blowing out a long, anxious breath, I push the door open, stepping over the threshold. Nothing looks out of place at first glance. Where's Nova, though? She usually always comes and greets me when I walk through the door. *That's odd.*

The kitchen comes into view first. Setting my briefcase and the wine on the counter, I continue through the house, not even bothering to remove my shoes. The dining room is empty and exactly how I left it this morning, same with the spare bedroom off to the right.

My hands are clammy, and my mouth is too dry to swallow as I turn down the hallway that leads to the other two bedrooms and the bathroom. What if somebody *is* in here robbing us? I'm not a fighter. What the hell am I going to do? I can't scare this intruder away.

Oh, my gosh, what if the burglar attacks me? *Kidnaps me?* Am I about to become another sad story on *The First 48*? Oh, fuck. I'm too young to die. I really hope it isn't a murderer down here.

Where is my fucking dog? Shouldn't she be protecting me from the Zodiac Killer lying in wait? *What if the axe murderer killed Nova?!*

Jesus, snap out of it, Travis.

Forcing my legs to work, I amble down the hall quietly. There's still no noise coming from inside the house that I can hear, but my neighbor is also currently mowing her lawn, so that could be drowning out any sound. Both the bathroom and my office are open, and nothing is out of order in either of those spaces, leaving only my bedroom. I stare at it, and I swear the hallway elongates before my eyes.

The closer I get, the more I notice. It's pushed shut, but not all the way. Our door is always left open. The grunting noises that can barely be heard over the lawn mower should've been a dead giveaway. Call it confusion or ignorance or what have you, but my feet carry me closer without a thought, and when I push the door open and the room comes into view, I've never experienced a shock like that. Whatever I expected to find on the other side of this door… *this* was not it.

There, maybe ten feet in front of me, bent over *our* bed with his pants around his ankles, is the man who should've been my fiancé by the end of the night. Behind him is somebody I've never seen before in my life. *He must own that car.*

The man railing my boyfriend from behind is *huge*. Tall, broad shoulders, muscular biceps. I can't see much else because he's still fully clothed. His arms are covered in black ink, as is his neck. I'll bet the rest of him is too. He's got a short, black, cropped beard and hair that looks perfectly styled. He's nauseatingly gorgeous, and when they both finally notice me standing in the doorway, a smug, arrogant grin tugs on his lips as he tightens his grip on Nathaniel's hips, doubling down on the dicking he's giving him.

Nathaniel, at least, has the fucking decency to look shameful. The color drains from his face, and his hands grapple with the sheets he's holding on to, almost like he wants to get up. But then… then the hard cock hanging down between his legs erupts. He comes with his wide eyes pinned on me, and I watch in horror as his lips part. He *moans*, and the guy behind him stills, grunting his way through what I know, with absolute certainty, is his own release.

The world feels like it slows down. It feels like it stops as I watch them orgasm together, both of them watching me—Nathaniel full of mortification, and the stranger full of what can only be described as haughtiness.

Nausea rolls in my gut, bile rising in my throat. I stand there for what feels like an eternity, but in reality, it's probably only been about a minute before my mind kicks into gear, and I see red.

"Travis, I—" Nathaniel starts to say, as the stranger pulls

out of him. He fumbles with his pants still around his ankles, but he doesn't have a chance to get anything else out.

Something dark and feral and bubbles over inside of me. Without thinking—without truly seeing either—I grab the object closest to me and chuck it in their general direction. It isn't until the object leaves my hand that I see what it is that I threw… an antique lamp Nathaniel's grandma gave us when we bought the house. It somehow misses Nathaniel entirely, connecting with the side of the smug stranger's head.

"Fuck you," I growl, pointing a finger at Nathaniel. Turning the finger on the man behind him, who's now bleeding from his temple, I add, "And fuck you too, whoever the fuck you are! I hope you need stitches, and I hope whoever does them botches it!"

It's then I hear it… paws sliding along the glass door. Nova. She's out back. Quickly rushing over to let her in, I hurry into the bedroom closet, grab a duffle bag, and faster than I thought humanly possible, I fill it with the bare necessities. Bag in hand, I find Nova's leash on the kitchen counter, attach it to her collar, and we leave. All before my pathetic now-ex-boyfriend and his fuck buddy have a chance to exit the bedroom. It's not until I'm a mile down the road that I break down. The lump in my throat tightens and the pressure behind my eyes gives way to a rainfall of tears pouring hot down my cheeks.

How could I have been so, so wrong about him? About us?

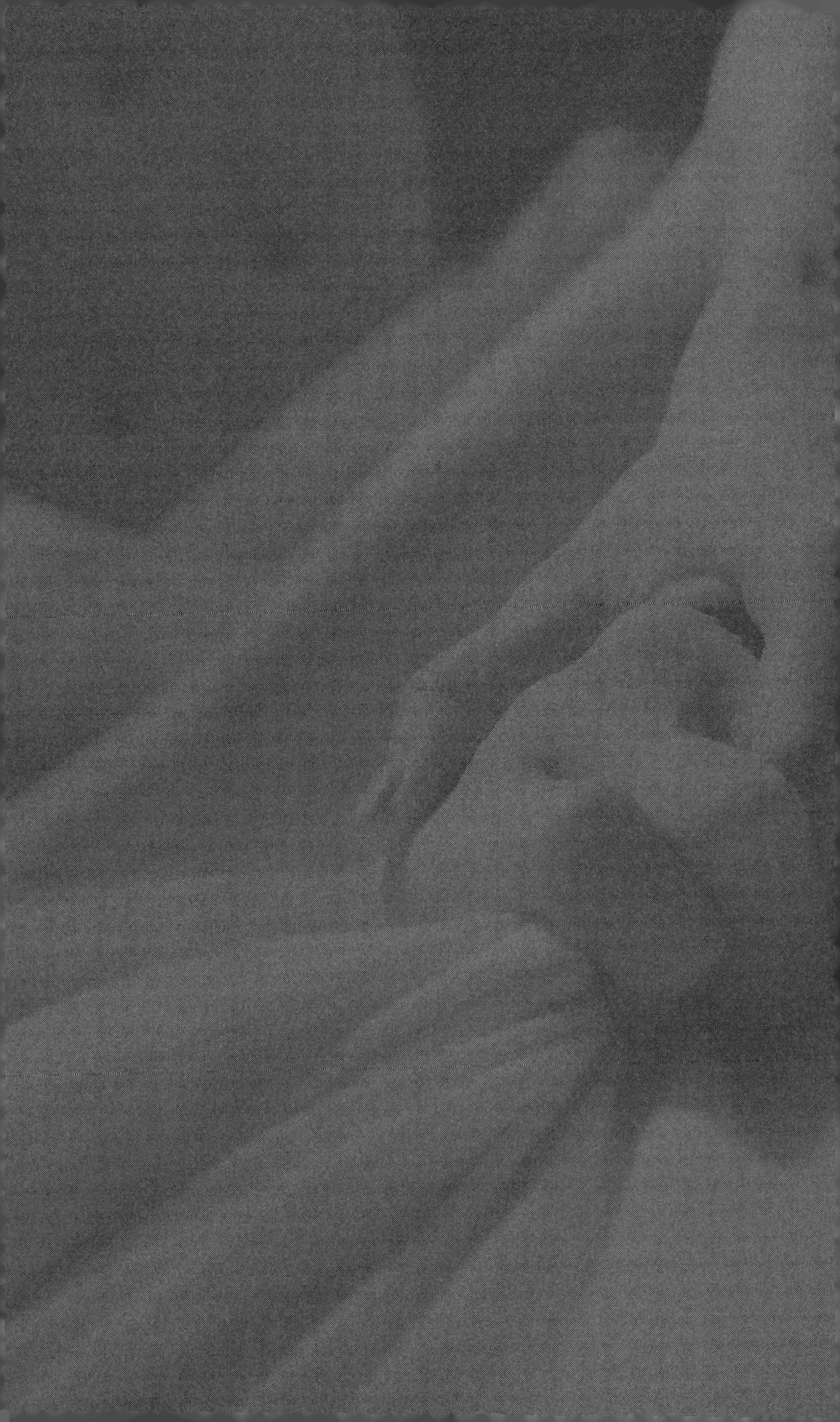

THREE

Travis

FIVE MONTHS AGO

"You're so fucking clingy, Travis. I can't do this anymore. You're always right there, up my ass, wanting more, more, more. It's suffocating. Let me live!"

Gaping up at the ceiling, I recount the fight Nathaniel and I had three days ago. The fight that started because he worked late *again*, and when he got home, all I wanted to do was cuddle on the couch with him and watch a movie. He wanted nothing to do with me, wouldn't even let me touch him. It blew up. The small argument exploded into something way bigger than it needed to be, and still, three days and a whole lot of space later, I don't understand why.

He said a lot of hurtful shit. Shit that cut me deep. Shit that's kept me up at night, wondering why or how I could've pissed him off as much as I did.

It was my last straw.

I can't keep doing this. Can't keep walking on eggshells. Can't keep wanting and needing more from him, while he pulls away further and further with each argument. I mean, shit, it's been three days since I left after the blowup, and went to Xander's, and he hasn't reached out to me at all. We've been dating for over four years, we own a home together, and he's just okay with not speaking to me for three whole days?

It's exhausting, this rollercoaster of emotions I go through with Nathaniel. He's so hot and cold. One day, he so obviously loves me. He'll cuddle with me, he'll have sex with me, he'll act like he gives a shit about my feelings. And then the next, it's like a switch is flipped. He'll work late, ignore me most of the day, and come home and act like I'm the biggest annoyance.

We've gone weeks without sex, or even kissing. Sometimes, it feels more like we're roommates than anything else. But again, then there will be periods when he's all over me, and can't get enough attention and love. It gives me whiplash. And I know if Xander knew the full extent of why I'm staying with him, he'd tell me to cut the ties and move on.

It's not that easy, though. I love Nathaniel. *So fucking much.* How do you spend years of your life with someone and *not* be consumed? I wish someone knew and would tell me, so I could stop needing him so much.

Clearly, he doesn't need me. He couldn't make that any more obvious.

A knock sounds at the door to the guest room I'm staying in. Xander must be home from work. I played hooky today because when my alarm went off this morning, I just couldn't fucking find it in me to put on a cheerful face and be a functional adult. So, I stayed home and smoked weed and felt sorry for myself.

"Come in," I call out.

Xan steps into the room, gaze falling to where I'm lying on the bed. "Have you been here the whole day?"

Crossing the room, he sits on the edge of the bed, the faint scent of marijuana wafting over to me. Xander partially owns a dispensary, so I feel like he always smells at least a little like weed at any given time.

"No, I've gotten up," I murmur, an edge of defensiveness to my tone.

"Want to come grab some dinner with me at the pub down the street?"

I should. It'll be good for me to get out and hang with Xander instead of sulking in this room that doesn't even belong to me.

Before I can respond to him, the doorbell rings, startling us both.

"I'll grab it," Xan offers, jumping up from the bed.

I sit up, looking around for my phone. He's not gone for more than a minute before I hear his footsteps padding across the hardwood floor toward this room, only this time, there's a second set.

Xander peeks his head in, an unreadable expression on his face. "Someone's here to see you."

My brows pinch together. "Me? Who?"

He steps aside, letting whoever it is walk by. As soon as he steps into the room, my heart palpitates, and my palms start to sweat.

"Nathaniel," I breathe. "What are you doing here?"

He scans the room, like he's taking it all in, before moving to sit on the chair in front of the desk. Xander's still at the door, and we make eye contact. I nod, silently letting him know it's okay. He gives me a terse nod of his own before leaving the room, shutting the door behind him.

"I miss you, babe." Nathaniel offers those words like they're the easiest thing in the world. Like we haven't spent the last three whole days in a fight.

Correction—we haven't spent the last three days fighting. We've spent the last three days not speaking at all.

"Yeah, then why did it take you so long to come here and say that?"

"Well, babe, I wanted to."

"But you didn't," I grit out, hating the sting behind my eyes and the lump in my throat.

"I wanted to give you your space, let you cool off." Leaning forward in the chair, he rests his elbows on his knees. "You know how you get when you're upset like that."

My heart thumps excessively, to the point it's hard to sit still. "You act like I overreact, Nathaniel."

His face softens; he gets this look to him whenever he's about to talk down to me. Speak to me like I'm a child. "Babe, you kind of do. Just…" Raising from the chair, he crosses the room in three large strides, sitting beside me on the bed. He slides his large, warm hand into mine, and I already feel my resolve slipping. "Come home, babe. We can figure this out. You know I love you."

I want to be strong. I want to stand my ground because I'm hurt. And mad. But he's touching me, his thumb brushing back and forth against the sensitive flesh of my wrist, and he's saying exactly what I want to hear.

He loves me.

But— "You say that, Nathaniel, but sometimes it feels like just words coming from you. You act like you want nothing to do with me sometimes. It hurts me."

"I'm sorry, okay? Work has been crazy, and I'm stressed out, and I've been taking it out on you, and that's not fair. I'm sorry, babe. You gotta believe me."

The back of my throat aches. I don't want to fucking cry.

"I don't know," I say. "Maybe we're no good for one another."

"Travis, don't say that." His voice cracks. *Maybe he really does love me.* "We're meant to be together. You're supposed to be my husband someday."

I don't say anything. I don't know what to say. My chest feels tight and warm, and I want to believe everything he's saying. I want to forgive him, and go home with him. Forget the last three days of misery I've caused myself.

He continues when I don't respond. "Come on, babe. I love you. Come home with me?"

Maybe I overreacted. Maybe I blew it out of proportion.

Nathaniel loves me. I know he does. He's stayed by my side all these years. He bought a house with me. We got a dog together.

He loves me.

He isn't my dad. He's not going to leave me.

FOUR

Travis

PRESENT

They say everything happens for a reason. That you're never given more than you can handle. To *trust the process*. Well, I don't know who *'they'* are, but *disrespectfully*, they can go fuck themselves.

Without lube.

Five years. Actually, five years and four months, to be exact.

That's how long I wasted my time on someone who, at one point, I thought I'd spend my life with. And by at one point, I mean, up until three days ago. Nathaniel Perry came gliding into my life on his magic carpet of lies and deceit during our senior year of college. One public speaking class and several late nights later, he had weaved his way into my heart, holding on for dear life with his promises of a future I so desperately craved. That, and his magical tongue. He knew all the right things to say to win me over. Knew all my insecurities and how to manipulate me.

Now, I admit, we moved fast; always spending the night at the other's houses, weekends frequently enjoyed on the lake or in the mountains, hikes at sunrise, and getting drunk under the stars while talking about the future. When graduation came, it was a no-brainer. We combined our savings for an apartment, taking that next step in our relationship without hesitation. The mundane, everyday tasks became thrilling; grocery shopping together, adopting a dog and bringing her on walks every morning and night, holidays with each other's families.

The first time we said *"I love you"* was shortly after we moved in together. Neither of us cooked. We were freshly graduated twenty-three-year-old guys who had spent the last four years drinking their body weight in cheap beer and surviving off Top Ramen and sub sandwiches. We wanted to celebrate getting our new place, so we decided to try our hand at cooking an extravagant dinner. The stove caught fire, the sprinklers in the entire complex turned on, and the fire department was called. It was a disaster.

We ended up getting takeout, grabbed a six-pack of beer from the convenience store, and laid blankets and pillows out on our teeny-tiny back deck, eating and drinking while searching for the Big Dipper and Orion's Belt. Despite the chaos of what had just happened, nothing had ever felt more perfect. The words tumbled out of my mouth before I could even process what I was saying, and he said them back like he meant them.

And for years, I believed him. For years, I had blinders on, desperately needing and wanting a love I thought he wanted to give me. I wanted it so badly, I ignored every sign trying to warn me. Because when Nathaniel was there, when he was *in this* with me, he made every single red flag look like Six Flags.

After picking the wrong guy over and over again all throughout high school and college, being second best or someone's *just for tonight*, finally finding someone who picked *me* and said all the right things felt like a breath of fresh air. It felt right.

The visual of Nathaniel getting plowed against our bed the other afternoon is burned into my memory, and no matter how much I try to erase it, it won't go away. After I grabbed Nova and a few of my belongings and hightailed it out of our neighborhood quicker than a crackhead running from the cops, I called my best friend from college, Xander. Thankfully, he lives a few minutes into town, and he let me crash with him. Which is exactly where I've been since.

Haven't gone to work. Haven't showered. Haven't really done anything except sulk in Xander's spare bedroom, questioning how I seem to have the worst luck when it comes to relationships and love.

Knock, knock.

Rolling over, I tug the blankets up to my chin, knowing Xander is coming in whether I tell him to or not. The white wood door creaks as it opens, his sock-covered feet barely making a sound as he crosses the room, then the bed dips as he sits on the edge. He doesn't say anything for long moments, probably wondering how best to deal with me.

I feel him scoot along the end of the bed until his back connects with the wall the bed is pushed up against. The distinct sound of a lighter flicking to life reaches my ears moments before the earthy scent of weed fills my nostrils.

"Sit up and smoke this with me," he grunts out in between hits.

Rolling my eyes, I do as he says, keeping the blanket on my lap as I rest my back against the wall opposite him. Xander hands me a lime green and blue swirl pipe, along with his red

BIC. His features soften as our eyes connect, but he doesn't say anything until I've taken a hit.

"Cash and I broke up before I moved here," he says quietly.

Xander moved from Pullman to Desert Creek a few months ago when he finished his grad program. Cash was his roommate all through the program, and they casually dated almost the whole time. I knew Cash from back when I went to Washington State University for undergrad. He was in the frat I went to frequently for parties.

Passing him back the pipe, I say, "Well, figured you guys broke up, but I didn't want to ask. Seemed like a touchy subject."

Xan nods, bringing the pipe up to his lips, lighting the bowl. "It kind of was for a while, but I'm over it now, I think." Smoke leaves his mouth in thick clouds. "But I just wanted you to know, that while Cash and I were never as serious as you and Nathaniel, I can still empathize."

"What happened?" I ask. "With you and Cash."

He waves me off like it's no big deal, but I don't buy it. "Cash was never in a place to be in a relationship. I knew it from the moment we moved in together as roommates. He was grieving the loss of… something. I didn't—and still don't—know what." Xander takes another hit, passing the pipe back to me. "It was your typical situation, where I'd hoped to be the one to fix him. I definitely liked him way more than he liked me, but it's okay. We ended shit civilly. He ended up moving to Texas after graduation anyway for a job, so it never would've worked."

"Damn. I'm sorry, that sucks."

He shrugs. "It is what it is."

When the weed's gone, I hand the pipe back to him. "Wanna get drunk?" I ask.

Xander busts out laughing at that, but nods. "Hell yeah.

Let's do it."

An hour later, we're six tequila shots deep while *Chokehold* by Sleep Token thumps through the speakers along the back wall of Xander's living room. We started playing video games, but those were long forgotten after about twenty minutes.

We're currently sitting side by side on his couch, music pulsing through us as we swap dating horror stories. Xander and I have been friends for quite some time now—we met during one of our very first classes freshmen year—but we've surprisingly never spoken about our dating lives all that often. Probably because we both have such terrible luck, so it's best if we don't share the details.

"Okay, okay, let me get this straight," Xander says, the words full of laughter. "You hooked up with not one, but *two* of Cash's friends… in the same year?"

"Yes. Fuck off." Even thinking about that time of my life makes me cringe. "It wasn't on purpose."

"Who was better in the sack?" Xander asks, waggling his brows at me.

A full-on belly laugh bubbles out of me at that question. "Well, I only actually slept with Branson. The other was barely foreplay before we were interrupted."

He rolls his eyes. "Lame. Who's got the bigger dick?"

I pin him with a *you can't be serious* look, which only makes him chuckle harder. Finally, I admit, "Aston. All the way. But Branson's pierced, so do with that what you will."

"I knew it!" Xander gets up and wordlessly goes into the kitchen, coming back out with two bottles of water, handing me one. "So, when you started dating Nathaniel, was there anyone in between him before graduation, or was he it?"

During our senior year, Xander and I drifted a bit. Not on

purpose and not because we valued our friendship any less, but because he was so busy with school and work, and he moved off campus, so we didn't see each other often.

"He was it," I admit after downing about half the bottle. "He gave me the attention I'd been dying to get for years. Why would I want to screw that up?"

"That's fair. Did you ever wonder if he wasn't being faithful recently? Or did this come as a total surprise?"

Dragging in a deep breath, I consider how to answer this without sounding like a fucking idiot who got played. It doesn't miss me that he said *"recently,"* because Xander knows better. "You know how when you're in the middle of something, it's easy to have blinders on? Like, it's easy to miss glaringly obvious red flags, because you're basically wearing rose-colored glasses, because what you have is everything you think you've wanted?"

He nods, and after what he told me about him and Cash, I have a feeling he understands a lot more than I used to think.

"If the last three days have showed me anything, it's that my blinders were firmly in place. We both know exactly who Nathaniel is to his core, but I think I wanted to believe he loved me so much, and I wanted to believe he wanted this future with me so bad, I tricked myself. I made myself see shit that wasn't there, the same way I tricked myself into ignoring shit that *was* there. I think, had I not been so desperate to get this life I've always dreamed of, I probably would've seen the situation for exactly what it was, and saved myself a lot of time… and money."

Xander's lips are pressed together, turned down into a frown, and I hate the pity I see on his face. "Fuck, I'm sorry, man."

"It's all good, Xan." Pulling out my phone, I check the time. "Don't you have work in the morning?"

"Yup."

"It's getting pretty late. Think we should call it a night?"

I hate how cut open and vulnerable I feel right now. Talking about Nathaniel does nothing but remind me that I should've known better. Guys like him don't settle down, especially not with guys like me.

Guys like me are the *just for fun* type.

The *make your ex jealous* type.

The *you're really fun and all, but I'm not looking for anything serious* type.

It's how it's always been, and how it'll probably always be. Never anybody's first choice. Ever.

"Yeah, probably should," Xander agrees, raising off the couch, grabbing the tequila and bringing it in the kitchen, while I grab the shot glasses and do the same.

As soon as I'm in my room—well, not *my* room, since I don't live here—the floodgates open. This is becoming a nightly occurrence… fucking cry about my pathetic life before bed. I hate it. I hate this reaction Nathaniel gets to pull from me, while he's probably not even the least bit bothered by our breakup.

For all I know, he's got someone over right now—maybe even the same guy from the other day—in our bed, rolling around in the sheets we bought together. The thought makes my stomach churn.

"Hey, man, did you—" Xander shoves the door open, standing in the entrance, brow immediately furrowing. Whatever he was about to say dies on his tongue as he sees me looking, I'm sure, like a fucking mess, with tear tracks and a snotty nose. "What's wrong?"

I sit down on the edge of the bed, a hiccup catching in my throat. "Nothing, I'm fine. I just do this sometimes lately."

Xander crosses the room, kneeling before me, his hands planted on my knees. "You know I'm here for you, right?"

I nod.

"I'm serious, Trav. Breakups fucking suck, and what you're dealing with is heavy. I know it's hard. It's okay to talk about it and get it off your chest. I'd never judge you."

Peering over at him, he's watching me carefully, and I can tell he means what he says a hundred percent. "Thank you, Xan. I really fucking appreciate that. And appreciate you letting me crash here."

"Dude, of course. What are friends for?" He stands, tapping my shoulder. "Now, come here. Hug it out."

Standing up, he pulls me into his embrace, and it feels so good to be hugged. Physical touch is my love language. Something about it always soothes me. I bury my wet face in his neck, trying not to cringe about the fact that I'm getting my snot and tears all over his skin. The hug lasts longer than it probably should, but I don't want to let go.

When we do finally pull away, it happens so fast. One moment, we've got our arms wrapped around each other in a friendly hug, and the next, my hands cup his face as my lips seal down onto his. I shouldn't do this. He's my best friend, and we've been drinking, but *fuck*, his lips feel so good pressed against mine.

My tongue swipes along the seam, and he miraculously opens for me, letting me slip inside and glide along his, despite his still-stiff body. Xander kisses me back only briefly before pulling away. His brows knit together, fingers coming up to brush against his slick lips.

"Trav—" He takes a step back, putting some much-needed distance between us. "You don't want this. I know you're hurting and want to take the pain away, but this isn't the way to do it. You'd wake up and regret it, and I can't let you do that to yourself."

"Fuck, I'm sorry," I mumble, hands thrusting into my hair as the room spins from the tequila. "I'm so, so sorry, man."

"No, don't even apologize. It's not a big deal. Just... get some sleep, okay?"

I nod, climbing into bed as he leaves the room, shutting the door softly behind him. Scrubbing a hand over my face, I groan into my palm. I can't believe I just did that. What a fucking dick move.

Pulling my phone out of my pocket, I have every intention of plugging it in to charge, and then pass out. But something larger than me is calling to me, telling me to do something I know I shouldn't do.

But I should.

I very much should.

I'm going to.

Pulling up Nathaniel's contact, I hit call. I bring it up to my ear and listen as it rings and rings and rings. Of course, he doesn't answer. He's probably balls deep inside some rebound. Someone who is better than me. Hotter than me. More laid back than me.

Someone who isn't me.

When his voice filters through the speaker, his voicemail picking up, I know I should hang up. In no universe is me leaving a voicemail for him a good idea. Of course, me being me, with the tequila clouding my judgement, I don't hang up. And when the beep sounds, letting me know the recording has started, I let it all out.

I tell him what a piece of fucking shit he is. How badly he

hurt me. How I thought we'd spend our lives together. I even tell him how that special thing he does with his fingers in bed that he thinks is sooooo good, isn't that good at all.

That part's a lie. Of course, it's that good.

By the time I hang up, moisture pools on my cheeks and I can barely breathe through the sobs. I plug the phone in, climb under the covers, and pass out. Not a single dream in sight tonight. I finally exhausted myself enough for true sleep.

FIVE

Travis

It's been a little over two weeks since my life was upended and me and Nathaniel broke up. I ended up taking an entire week off work to allow myself to just *feel* and to give myself time to grieve the loss of the future I thought I had.

That sounds horribly dramatic, but it's true. It feels like this whole life I envisioned was there one moment, and stripped from my fingers the next. As much of a douchebag as Nathaniel is, I still invested years into him, and into us, and to lose that feels like losing a part of me.

I'm stepping out of the office now to head back to Xan's. It's Friday, and I just finished my first whole week back since the split. To be honest, admitting to my coworkers what happened was almost harder than the breakup itself. I felt like an idiot. Not even two weeks prior, I was leaving work to propose to him, only to return after a week-long hiatus, cheated on and broken up. Talk about a fucking deep blow. The sad, pathetic part of me almost wanted to lie and say the proposal went great. Shit, I even considered telling them he fucking died.

Their looks of pity and the walking on eggshells are almost too much to handle.

Nova's been staying with my mom and stepdad since I moved out. I miss her a ton, and her cuddles would probably help a lot. Xander told me a few days after I got there that I could bring her to his house, but I didn't want to uproot her life more than I had to, and taking her from my old house to my mom's to Xanders, and then finally to wherever I end up after, seemed like too much for a dog. Plus, Xander has a bitchy little hairless cat that doesn't like anybody or anything. That seemed like a recipe for disaster since Nova loves everybody.

When I asked him why on earth he got one of those, he shrugged it off and said I wouldn't get it. *Whatever the fuck that means.*

Nathaniel never called me back after the ridiculous voicemail I left for him that night I kissed Xander. Not that I expected him to. I do hate how much I'd hoped he would, though. Not even necessarily because I want to take him back, but to feel like I had the upper hand for once. Like I had the ability to turn him down, to crush him like he's crushed me.

Maybe it's petty of me, or toxic, but I want to hurt him in the same way. But that'll never happen. Nathaniel has always had the upper hand in our relationship. Everybody always has the upper hand with me. I don't think I've ever been in a position to break anybody's heart before. Not that I'd want to, but still… always being the one hurt and left behind fucking sucks.

As screwed up as it sounds, I can't help but chronically compare every man to my father. And not in a fucked-up, incestuous way, but in a did he leave me for the same reasons they've left me type of way. My dad was the first man to ever break my heart, and goddamn, did it leave a lasting impression.

Because not only did he dip out on my mom, sister, and I, but he started a whole ass new life to boot.

I'll never forget the betrayal and the hurt I felt at seeing him with his new family across that basketball court in high school. The eye-opening realization that he didn't leave because he simply didn't want to be a husband and a father anymore. No, he left because he didn't want to be *my* father anymore. I've wondered on more than one occasion—usually after I've been screwed over or dumped or replaced for someone hotter, smarter, or all around better—if my love life would be any different had my father not abandoned me for some other family.

Xander's already home by the time I pull my car up to the sidewalk in front of his lawn. He texted me a few hours ago, letting me know he was cooking us dinner tonight. My appetite has been kind of shot lately, but surprisingly, my stomach is rumbling. Probably because it knows what a damn good cook Xan is. His mom is a chef for some majorly important restaurant in New York, and he's been cooking beside her since he was a little kid. It shows.

The house smells like oregano, garlic, and cheese as I step through the front door, and Xan's got music pumping through the speakers in the kitchen. Despite it being nearly freezing outside, the back door is open, and I can hear him singing along to the Sleep Token song currently playing. Bet he's even dancing to it too.

Xander is such a happy guy. It's one thing that drew me to him when we first met, because normally, I am too. When I'm not in the middle of a breakup and an existential crisis, I'm a glass half full type of person. We're both extroverted and enjoy being around people. It's something that made us fast friends. Lately, though, it's nauseating. I know he's been trying his hardest to give me space, but also to cheer me up. Somehow, it's all ended up feeling overwhelming and suffocating more than anything else.

I feel bad for getting so annoyed with him, because it's not his fault. He's been more than supportive and gracious through all of this. Giving up his spare bedroom for me. Cooking for me. Pretending he doesn't hear me sobbing at night through his very thin walls.

Rounding the corner, the kitchen comes into view, as does—yup, I was right—Xan dancing to the beat as he stirs sauce on the stovetop. He tosses a glance over his shoulder at me, a smirk tugging on his lips.

"What's up, man?"

"Smells fucking good." I tip my chin past him.

"It's only tortellini in a homemade five-cheese marinara sauce. Nothing fancy." He waves a hand before returning to the food. "How was work?"

I grab a beer out of the fridge, twisting the cap off and tossing it in the trash before taking a long pull. The crisp, amber liquid feels refreshing going down my throat. Wiping my mouth with the back of my hand, I grumble, "It was okay. Happy to be off for the weekend. How about you?"

"Not bad," he replies with a shrug, his back to me. "It was busy as fuck, though. I have to work tomorrow."

"On a Saturday?"

"Jordan is sick, so I have to cover." He glances over his shoulder, rolling his eyes. "Not happy about it, but whatever."

Letting him know I'm going to shower real quick before dinner, I head to the guest room, grab a change of clothes, then hit the bathroom. All in all, it only takes me about ten minutes before I'm all clean and back out in the dining room. Just in time, too. Dinner is done.

We both dish up, taking our seats at the table. Digging in, it's fucking delicious. An involuntary groan leaves my mouth as I shovel a bite in that's probably much larger than appropriate for table manners.

"This is fucking bomb, Xan," I tell him, taking a swig of my beer.

"Thanks, man," he says quietly. Based on his body language, I can tell there's something on his mind.

"Just say it," I blurt out, then set my fork down.

He peers over at me, something in his expression softening as he takes me in. "I love you, Trav, you know I do. But I think it's time I give you some tough love for your own good."

I have to fight not to roll my eyes. I knew this was coming sooner or later.

When I don't say anything, he continues. "It's been over two weeks now, and I think it's about time you let yourself start living again. Besides going to work, you don't do anything other than lay around."

There isn't an ounce of judgement woven between his words, and I love him for it. If anyone understands what it's like to always be an option, latching onto the first person who shows them the time of day, it's him.

Clearing my throat, I mutter, "I'm fine." The declaration is weak, and it's clear I'm *not* fine, but fuck, I don't want to admit that.

"You can't let him do this to you, Travis." My gaze lifts from the plate to meet his across the table. "For as long as I've known you, which at this point, is close to a decade, you've always settled, accepted the bare minimum from men. You gotta fucking stop that shit, man."

Letting out an exasperated sigh, he rakes his fingers through the mop of brown hair atop his head. "I don't know why you do this, or why you so clearly don't see your own worth, but it's time to stand tall, dust your damn shoulders off, and move on. And I don't mean with another temporary fix. You let Nathaniel walk all over you, and you were so in the clouds, you couldn't even see it. He'd constantly go out, stay out all hours of the night without so much as a heads-up text. He was always flirting with people right in front of your face, then gaslighting you when you confronted him. You deserve so much better. If there's anything I've learned in the past six months, it's that maybe it's best to leave college relationships in college. Live and learn."

Swallowing around the tightness in my throat, I listen to him tell me everything I should already know. *"You're a catch." "The right man will treat you with the respect you deserve."*

Blah, blah, blah.

I *know* I deserve better than what I accept.

I *know* I should be patient and wait for someone who is good for me.

But being nothing but second best your entire life, it's easier to accept simply having someone's attention, so you're not alone. It's easier to see the good in someone when they're rolling around in the sheets with you, looking at you like you're the only one they see, than knowing you're not good enough to be someone's first choice. Trust me, I did my fair share of sleeping my way through college. Grindr hook-ups, frat parties that ended with me sweaty and horizontal with someone who I meant nothing to… but it got old. I was trying to fill a void, trying to find love in the wrong places.

It was easier to take what I could get. It's why when

Nathaniel came around, I held on to him and was okay looking past his flaws—flaws I probably should've run from years ago.

"Listen, I talked to your sister."

"Wha—"

Holding up a hand, he continues, cutting me off. "She's coming over in the morning to pick you up, and the two of you are going to spend the day apartment hunting. And no, before you even try to say it, it isn't because I don't want you here. It's because finding a place for yourself will help you heal. It's the first step in moving on."

Pressing my lips together tightly to avoid saying something immature or bratty, I bring my attention back to my plate, suddenly not very hungry. I know he's doing this because he cares, and had I not been in the thick of my wallow-fest, I would probably thank him, but right now, the wound is still too fresh for me to even try to see things logically.

Eventually, I peer over at him, finding him still watching me. I give him a terse nod before we get back to eating.

Downtown Desert Creek in late October can be a frigid bitch. It hasn't snowed yet, but I know it's coming. Hot puffs of air form white clouds in front of me as Charlotte and I walk along the sidewalk.

"You want to talk about it?" My sister has always been too intuitive for her own good. That said, I do think Xander filled her in on my *situation*.

"Not really," I mumble, shoving my hands into my pockets. Why I chose to leave the house without gloves is beyond me.

In my peripheral, I see her glance over at me, but I don't dare look. She has this innate ability to get people to spill their guts, whether they want to or not. She's like a leopard—avoid eye contact at all costs or else she pounces.

"Okay, well, when you're ready," she mutters, but leaves it at that. "I found three nice choices for us to check out. They're all within a five-mile radius of your work, and not too overpriced."

We stop in front of a new looking white building. It's small, compared to other apartment complexes, sitting on the street next to a Dutch bakery and a Starbucks. Glancing over at Charlotte, her green eyes sparkle as she offers me a small smile, presumably meant to be reassuring.

The place isn't half bad. It looks clean and well kept. There're elevators, which is nice, since the available unit is on the third floor. It's got hardwood floors, with only carpet in the bedrooms—there are two—and the kitchen looks renovated, with granite countertops and stainless-steel appliances. Even the stove is gas powered, which is another plus.

"Whatcha think, Trav?" Charlotte comes up behind me, looping her arm through mine.

"It's nice." *It's not the four-bedroom house with a yard I just bought*, but I don't say that. "I'll take this one."

Her eyes widen. "Really? Don't you want to see the other two?"

"Not really," I resign. "This one's nice, and I'd rather get it over with."

What I don't say is this feels like giving up. Almost as if as long as I stayed at Xander's, I could pretend my long-term relationship with a guy I thought I was going to marry didn't fail. But I can't bury my head in the sand and stay ignorant forever. Xander's words ring through my thoughts. "*Step one to moving on.*"

So, squaring my shoulders and choosing to *move on,* we go back downstairs with the leasing lady, and I sign the lease with

plans on moving in next weekend.
    I can do this.

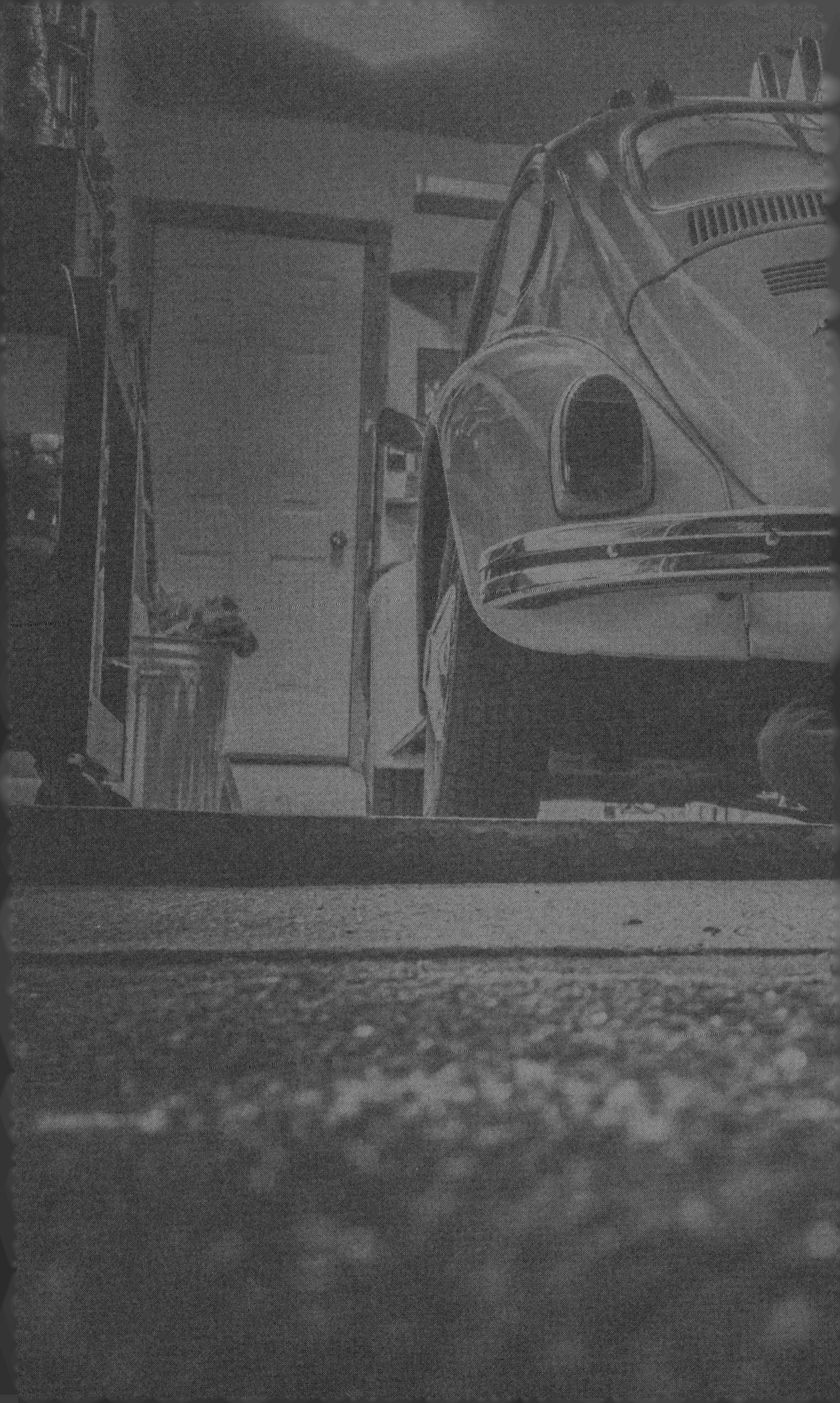

SIX

Mateo

Thursdays aren't usually this busy, but it seems like everybody, including their mothers and their grandmas, is in need of mechanical work today. From the moment we opened up shop this morning, walk-ins have been coming in steadily, on top of the appointments we already had scheduled.

Sweat lines my brows, more dripping down my back. My undershirt is stuck to my skin, and I can't fucking wait to rip this jumpsuit off when I get done. Wiping the back of my hand across my forehead, probably getting oil smeared all over, I bring my attention back to Mrs. Lawrence's Buick. It's about two years overdue for an oil change and a tune-up, but since Mr. Lawrence died a few years back, she's been kind of forgetful with maintenance.

Her nephew brought it in this morning after he noticed a smell coming from under the hood when he took it to pick up her groceries. It's about on its last leg.

Footsteps sound on the concrete floor, letting me know

someone is in the shop with me again. I can tell by the way they walk, it's my friend and co-worker, Miguel. That's confirmed when he pats me on the back and says, "Hey, *cabrón.*"

"What's up, man?" Shoving the rag into the back pocket of my jumpsuit, I brush my hands off. "Thought you were gone for the day already."

"Left my cell phone in the office," he says. "Hey, wanna grab a beer before I head home?"

"Hell yeah. I'm almost done with Mrs. Lawrence's car," I tell him. "Is Benny gone already?"

Benny, or *Benito*, is my uncle and the owner of this shop. Miguel and I have worked for him since before we graduated high school. I've been fixing up cars since before I could even drive one, so working for my uncle was always the plan. Aside from my sister, Benny is the family member I'm the closest to.

When I was kicked out of my house as a teenager, it was Benny I went and lived with until I turned eighteen and could afford to move out on my own. He's always been there for me, like this shop has always been here for me.

Miguel is like family to me. Everyone knows him as my cousin, but he's not actually my blood. We lived on the same block all growing up, and have been best friends since before I could remember.

"Yeah, he left about a half hour ago when I originally did. He's got a date." Miguel says the word *"date"* with a waggle of his brows, making me chuckle.

"Ah, okay. Well, give me like twenty minutes with this, and I'll be done. Want to head back to my place for beer instead, and I can grill us up something to eat?"

"Sounds good, Matty."

"I'm grabbing another. You need one too?" Miguel stops in front of my fridge, his hand on the handle as he glances over at me.

"Sure. Thanks."

I finish seasoning the steaks and head out to my back deck. The grill is turned on and ready to go, so I slap the meat down just as Miguel walks out, setting my beer beside me.

He rests his hip against the banister. "You never told me what ended up happening with that Grindr date from a few weeks ago."

Rolling my eyes, I groan, the sound morphing into a chuckle as I grab the bottle and down a couple swallows. "It was a fucking shitshow, man."

Arching a brow, Miguel asks, "How so?"

Miguel just got back into town from visiting his parents at the beginning of this week. He missed the mess that was my love life.

"The dude has a boyfriend." His eyes go wide, and I add, "Yeah, of the live-in variety."

"Damn." He blows out a breath, taking a swig from his beer. "How'd you find that out?"

"Oh, it's the best part. The boyfriend came home... while I was balls deep in this guy's ass."

My blood starts to boil even thinking about that day again.

Miguel cackles so hard, he's bent over at this hip, slapping a hand on his thigh. "Shut the fuck up," he says in between fits of lighter. "How does this shit always happen to you?"

"It does not *always* happen to me," I argue.

"You always pick the biggest douchebags to fuck. I don't

get it."

"Oh, because you always pick such winners," I toss back, rolling my eyes.

"So, what happened?" he asks, finally pulling himself together. He has fucking tears pouring from his eyes, for fuck's sake. "Wait a fucking second… is that where the gash on your forehead came from? Oh, fuck, pleaseeee tell me yes."

Yes, but I don't say it out loud. The stupid mark is finally almost fully healed. I'm surprised I didn't need stitches. That fucker got me good. Not that I blame him. If it were me, I would've done the same damn thing—or worse.

Opening the hood to the grill, I flip the steaks, my blood pressure shooting sky high from this topic. "Why the fuck did I invite you over again?"

That only makes Miguel laugh harder. "It is, isn't it? Oh, man, the boyfriend kicked your ass, didn't he?"

"He didn't kick my ass, *pendejo*. He got pissed after watching us come, then threw a fucking lamp at us, and it missed his boyfriend entirely and hit me."

Miguel snickers. "Was the sex at least worth the drama?"

Thinking about the question, the answer is there immediately—*no, it absolutely was not worth it*, but I don't say that. I don't know why. Instead, I shrug, bringing the bottle up to my lips. "It was fine. Nothing to write home about, but it was okay. Honestly, I think the hottest part was the pissed off boyfriend watching me finish."

"How the hell did you finish, knowing you're being watched by his boyfriend—literally caught in the act? My dick would shrivel the fuck up so fast."

Chuckling, I say, "Honestly, I think that's why I even came at all."

"You're such a fucking asshole," he quips, shaking his head. I mean, I can't exactly disagree. He's not *wrong*. But what I said was the truth, just not for the reason he probably thinks. The boyfriend was hotter than the dude I was buried inside of. He's someone I would normally go for had I met him out in public instead of in his bedroom... inside his boyfriend. Even one second of his furious gaze on me was enough to have me blow my load. I don't know if that makes me a masochist or a sadist... maybe both.

The steaks finish up, and I remove them from the grill before we head back inside to fix our plates. The conversation over dinner passes without issue. Miguel tells me about his kid's softball game, and the newest baby mama drama. Right after we turned eighteen, Miguel got a chick pregnant he was casually sleeping with. At the time, he wanted her to get rid of it, but now Izzy is his entire world.

Miguel leaves after dinner. He only lives down the block. Same with Uncle Benny. Miguel actually rents the little two-bedroom mother-in-law apartment behind Benny's place, just like he has for years.

Turning on some music, I do the dishes, cleaning up the kitchen before deciding to take a shower. By the time I get out, there's a message waiting for me on my phone. I roll my eyes when I spot who it's from, but ignore it for the time being until I get dressed.

Sitting down on the bed, I grab the phone, unlocking it, and pull up the message that's already grating my nerves.

Nathaniel: Had fun with you. Repeat?

It's not the first time he's hit me up since that day. I've ignored the other messages, but something feisty inside me has me typing out a response this time.

Me: What about your boyfriend? He joining?

Like he was sitting there with his phone in hand, waiting for my response, the text bubbles pop up immediately.

Nathaniel: Nah. We broke up. Just you and me. ;)

Huffing out a laugh through my nose, I lock the screen, tossing the phone on the bed. *Pass.* I'm too fucking old for drama like that. Especially from someone as mediocre as Nathaniel.

Raising off the bed, I walk over to my dresser, grabbing the clear red-and-white bong before reaching into the top drawer to pull out the wooden box I keep in there with my weed. I turn the overhead lights off, leaving the red LEDs placed around the room, taking a seat back on my bed as I load a bowl.

The first hit does wonders for taking the stress off my shoulders, and by the time I finish, my mind is nice and fuzzy, thoughts of my busy day and dumbass Grindr hook-ups nowhere to be found.

SEVEN

Mateo

"**H**ave you been here before?" I ask Benny, scanning the room filled with what looks to be college kids, but that makes no sense because the nearest college town is no less than forty-five minutes away.

"Once or twice," he says, glancing around the room too. "It's under new ownership, though, so figured we oughta check it out."

This week fucking sucked. Each day seemed to be busier and more grueling than the last. Kicking back and having a beer—or seven—with my uncle is just what I need.

"Why does everybody here look barely old enough to drink?" I ask Benny after the bartender drops off our drinks.

"Probably 'cause they are."

"How do you know that?"

"The new owner is offering cheap as shit drinks to anybody who can show a current college ID," he states, taking a sip of his beer. Benny isn't much older than me—only by twelve years. His parents had an oopsie. But raking my gaze over his face as he watches the crowd, his age is showing a little more these days. At almost forty, he's in pretty good shape, but his short beard is looking more salt than pepper lately.

He had to grow up a lot sooner than his siblings, my dad included. Being born to older parents, most would think he had it easy. Usually, the last born is the most spoiled, but that wasn't the case. My *abuelito* died of a heart attack when Benny was a teenager, and after he died, my *abuelita* just kind of gave up. They got married when they were barely teenagers, so they spent their entire lives together. He was her world, and without him, she didn't know how to manage.

Benny was working on cars for cash by the time he was sixteen, and helping pay the bills shortly after that. My father helped where he could, but he was raising his own family by that point, and money's always been tight where we come from. Benny opened *Benito's Garage* when he was twenty, and it's been his passion ever since.

I've always looked up to him. He's been there for me through thick and thin; something I can't really say for other people in my family.

"Is Miguel coming?" Benny asks before downing the rest of his beer.

Shaking my head, I say, "Nah. He's got Izzy this weekend." Guzzling down the rest of the contents in my bottle, I tip my chin toward his. "I'm going to get a refill. Want another?"

He nods. "You know it."

Weaving my way through the bodies lining the area, I make it to the bar, then pull my phone out while I wait for the bartender to get to me.

"Well, look who it is."

At the sound of the deep, gruff voice, my spine steels, veins filling with ice. Wearily glancing to my left, I already know who's waiting for me, but it's no less jarring to my nervous system when my gaze connects with a sinister pair of honey-brown eyes.

"Robbie," I grit out, keeping my face void of any emotion.

He rakes his gaze over my frame before landing on my face, a sickly sweet smirk that most would fall for—me included at one point in my life—sliding into place on his lips. "You look good, Mateo."

I don't return the compliment or thank him. His ego doesn't need that, nor is it my style to do so.

"Hey, guys, what can I get you?" the bartender asks, breaking our stare down.

"Two Coronas please," I reply.

"Make that three," Robbie interjects. "So, who are you here with?"

Dragging my narrowed gaze back to him, I say, "That's really none of your fucking business, now is it?"

He chuckles, the sound like nails on a chalkboard. It takes everything in me to not outwardly wince. Robbie is a part of my past I don't revisit... ever. He's someone I dated during a period of my life when I was lost and angry and easily manipulated.

Robbie is also the reason I haven't ever dated anyone since. He scarred me in ways I didn't even know I could be. Not that I'd ever let him—or anybody else—know that.

Hands raised in mock innocence, he whistles, that obnoxiously cocky grin never leaving his face. "So touchy, Matty."

My hand itches with the desire to clock him in the jaw for calling me that, and my skin crawls from being in his proximity.

The bartender comes back with our drinks, and I go to grab

my wallet out of my back pocket to pay and get the fuck away from him, when he has the audacity to put a hand on my arm, stopping me.

"I got it," he says smoothly.

"No, you don't. I'll pay for my own."

He reaches over, handing his card to the bartender. "I insist."

My heart is hammering in my chest, blood roaring in my ears. I shove my hands into my pockets to hide the fact that they're trembling. Robbie is the only person I've ever met who gives me a reaction like this, and I fucking hate it.

Standing here beside him, all the memories of us come trudging back, causing bile to rise in my throat as my stomach churns. I didn't even know he still lived in Desert Creek; it's been years since I've seen him.

The woman behind the counter hands him back his card, sliding the three beers across to us, and I don't think I've ever grabbed something so fast in my life.

Before I have a chance to walk away, though, he steps closer, lips right against the shell of my ear as he whispers, "I've missed you, Matty. What do you say we do some *catching up?*"

Grinding down on my molars so hard, pain radiates through my jaw, I don't bother looking back at him. "Fuck off, Robbie," I growl, putting one foot in front of the other, making my way back to where Benny's waiting for me.

I hand him his beer before chugging half of mine in one go.

"You okay?" he asks with clear concern. "You look like you've seen a ghost."

"Fine," I grit out, taking a deep breath to get my shit together. My pulse has gone haywire, and it feels like the air's been sucked out of the room. I need to get the fuck out of here. Finishing off the beer in record time, I set it on the table, standing up. "Think I'm gonna get out of here."

"What? Already?" he asks as his head rears back. "It's Friday night. Why are you leaving so early?"

"Meeting up with someone." It's the easiest and most believable answer that'll get me out of here the quickest.

"Oh, I see," he drawls, wagging his brows. "Go have fun, *sobrino*."

Pulling up my Uber app, I order a car, and thankfully, I don't have to wait too long for it to arrive. I'm on edge the entire time I'm waiting outside, thinking Robbie is going to come and find me.

Once I'm home, I strip out of all my clothes and climb under the hot spray of the shower, desperately needing to wash his presence off my body. I roll a joint after I get out, smoking it in the dark, under the covers on my bed. I can't remember the last time I've been this rattled.

Probably the last time I saw him.

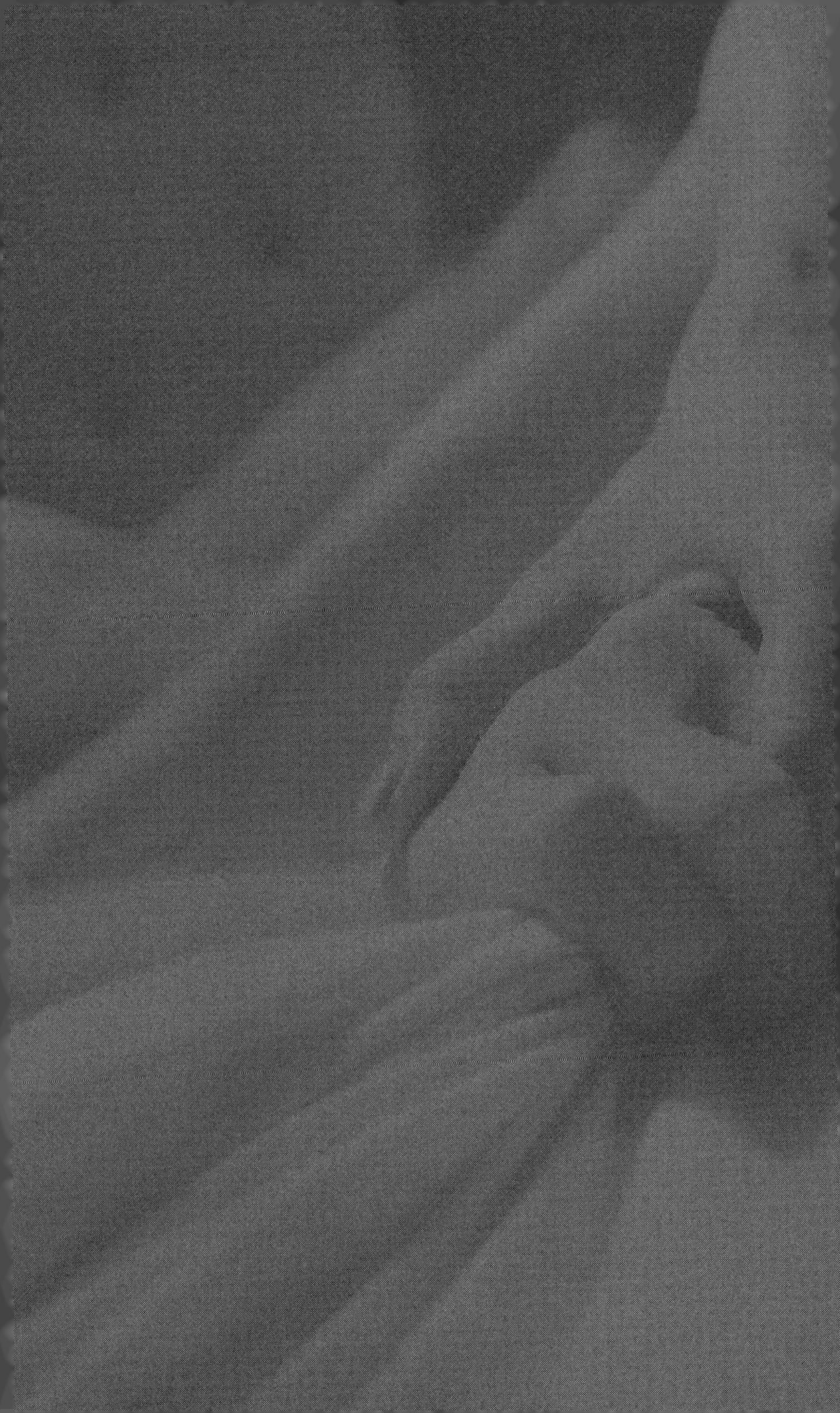

EIGHT

Travis

Every single time I move, I swear to myself it's the last time. It's such a tedious, exhausting task. It costs a fucking fortune for no goddamn reason, and if you aren't able to wrangle some friends into helping out, you have to shell out even more money for overpriced movers.

Thankfully, my sister, her husband, and Xan all offered to help me get moved into the new place. My mom and her husband are still puppysitting Nova while I get settled in. I can't wait to get her back once all this is said and done.

We're on our last load now, bringing it up in the elevator. Sweat lines my forehead, dripping down my nape, and my shirt sticks to my back as I set the very last box down in my unfurnished new dining room. The help is appreciated, but I can't fucking wait until they leave so I can take a shower.

Xander strolls through the place, looking in the cabinets and fridge in the kitchen, turning on the lights to all the rooms. "This place is nice."

"Yeah, it's not bad."

My mood's been shit all day, and I can't even pretend it's just from the stress of moving. I had to pick up the rest of my stuff from the house this morning. Nathaniel had never said anything to me about my ridiculous voicemail, so I figured when I texted him about coming to get my shit, he'd ignore me then, too.

He didn't. He was surprisingly nice—which is suspicious, all on its own—and he told me when I could come get my stuff, and said he wouldn't be there. Of course, when I pulled up, he was. Can't count on his word for anything, I guess. He wanted to talk, but I didn't. An argument started, excuses started rolling, and my temper steadily rose for the entire forty-three minutes I was there.

And yes, I counted.

Charlotte's husband, Greg, sets down a box labeled 'kitchen,' wiping his hands off on the front of his jeans. "That's it, man."

He's a nice enough guy. A firefighter. My sister met him at work some odd years ago when the elevator got stuck. He *"rescued"* her from death—her words, not mine. They got married a few years back in Tahiti. Nathaniel was my date. It was our first out-of-the-country vacation. He flirted with the venue's bartender that night. Should've been a bright red flag indicating what's to come.

Char steps up to me, a smile pulling at her lips. "Want us to order some Chinese?"

Shaking my head, I rake a hand through my mop of blond hair. I'm due for a haircut, but *priorities*. "Nah. You guys can go. Thank you for all your help. I'm going to shower, and then spend the evening unpacking."

"You sure?" With one thick, dark eyebrow quirked, she

studies me. Most likely seeing right through me. "I don't mind staying to help, baby bro."

Pulling her into a hug, I reply with as much gumption as I can muster up. "I'm sure. I'll be okay. You should enjoy what's left of your Saturday."

"Okay..." She grabs her purse and phone from one of the boxes in the living room. "Well, if you need anything at all, call me."

Don't get me wrong, I appreciate everything Charlotte's done to help me with the move, and how she's trying to be there for me, but she and I handle our emotions much differently. She likes to talk it out, while I usually prefer to take a bottle it up and pretend the problem doesn't exist. So, her efforts have wound up feeling suffocating. But I know she means well, so I make a mental note to take her to lunch to say thank you when I'm not so grumpy.

Fifteen minutes and one scalding hot shower later, I decide to grab some takeout. My stomach's grumbling, since I haven't eaten anything since last night. The chilly night air slaps me in the face as I step outside, heading down the block. Throwing my hood over my head and shoving my hands into my pockets, I make my way toward a Mexican place I know is down there. Temperatures have dropped, and tiny snowflakes cover the quiet streets in a thin blanket of white.

The restaurant isn't busy, most likely due to the weather, so I'm in and out relatively quickly. On a whim, I pop into the convenience store across the street from my place, grabbing a couple of six-packs for good measure. Getting drunk and unpacking go hand-in-hand, right?

Crossing the street, I pull open my building's door, shaking off my head as I enter. The snow's coming down thicker now. I wouldn't be surprised if it stuck overnight. My phone chimes in my pocket once I'm inside the elevator. Juggling the food and the beer in one hand, I take it out, swiping across the screen.

Nathaniel: Can we please talk? It meant nothing, and it's hardly something to lose so many years over.

And just like that, my blood pressure shoots through the roof.

Me: I'm good. Find somebody else to fuck over. Lose my number.

If it weren't for the fact that we had to figure out what to do with the house we own together, I'd block him completely. But we either have to sell it or, at the very least, get my name off the title. All of which requires me to communicate with him.

Not tonight, though.

It's so goddamn infuriating that he sent that and that he was trying to be nice and talk to me earlier. It's been weeks since I caught him getting fucked by someone else, and he hasn't contacted me once. Not that I wanted him to, of course, but fuck, it would've been nice to see some sort of remorse or effort. Losing years' worth of a relationship was clearly no sweat off his back.

And what? Did his Grindr options run out, so now he wants to crawl back to me? I don't fucking think so. I am *done* being anybody's back-up plan.

The elevator dings hitting the third floor, the doors sliding open. I climb out and hang a right, walking down the narrow hallway toward my unit. It's all the way at the end. As I get closer, I notice the neighbor directly across from me is outside—coming or going, I'm not sure. Even though I'm not in the socializing mood, I know I should do the nice, neighborly thing and introduce myself.

"Hey, man. I'm Travis, your new neighbor."

The guy, tall and built, glances over at me, and my veins turn to ice. Slightly bloodshot, hooded green eyes lock with mine. They rake boldly down my form before dancing their way back up. A sinful smirk tugs on the corner of his full, cherry red lips as he shifts, his whole body facing me.

I immediately regret being fucking neighborly.

"Hi, Travis." His voice is deep, raspy. Sexy enough to get under my skin and make me shiver. *This cannot be happening.* "So nice to formally meet you. The last time was a little… *rushed.*"

Rushed. Who the fuck does this guy think he is?

"Do you live here?" I snarl, taking a step back with a quickly pumping heart.

"Sure do, *neighbor.*" He practically purrs the last part, his accent making it sound like a dirty word.

How is it possible that, of all the places in Desert Creek I could've moved into—a town purposely *outside* of Pullman, where Nathaniel and I lived together— I picked the one across the fucking hall from the guy who helped upend my entire life just last week? What kind of cosmic joke is this?

Shaking my head in disgust, I turn with a groan, pulling out my keys to unlock my door. "Unbelievable."

As soon as I get the key into the lock, I sense him. The hairs on the back of my neck raise as he stands close enough that I can smell his spicy cologne and feel his hot breath on my skin.

"Mateo." That must be his name. I don't move, and I say nothing. "Welcome to the building, *cariño.* If you ever need *anything*—a cup of sugar, some flour, to let off some *steam*— don't be shy."

He steps back, cool air hitting my back in the absence of him. Only once I hear his door shut, do I exhale the deep breath I was holding. *Cariño*… what the hell does that mean? Pushing open my door, I kick it shut behind me, furious at his cockiness. How fucking dare he.

Does he have no shame?

He is caught with his pants around his ankles—quite literally—with my boyfriend, and he has the fucking *nerve* to make a pass at me. And that fucking smirk… so full of arrogance. I should've decked him right in his smug fucking face. A face that, of course, is full of sharp lines, high cheekbones, and ridiculously perfect features. Because why wouldn't he look like a fucking model?

With my appetite officially gone, I shove the food into the fridge before cracking open one of the beers I'm now even more thankful for. I wish I had gone to the dispensary this afternoon… could really use a fucking joint right about now too.

NINE

Travis

Mom: Okay, honey. See you when you get here. Drive safe. Xoxo

Turning my car on, I plug my phone into the charger as it connects to the speakers, and I turn on the heat, warming up the car. I am counting down the days until spring hits. A little warmth and constant sunshine will do wonders. The weathermen are predicting a long winter, though. *Cue eye roll.*

It's Sunday afternoon, and even though I didn't want to move a muscle after all the moving I did this weekend, I miss my pup so I'm about to drive to Pullman to pick up Nova—finally—from my mom's place. It's been too damn long without my dog, and I'll be happy to have her back. She hasn't seen the new apartment yet, obviously, but I think she'll love it. There's a little dog park around back, and there're a few really great trails nearby I can walk her on.

Nathaniel and I got Nova together, but she's always been more my dog than his. He didn't even want to get an animal at all until I put the idea in his mind, and practically begged him. I've always wanted a golden retriever, since they seem like the perfect family dogs. Growing up, my neighbor had one named Trixie. She was the sweetest dog I'd ever met. They'd let her come out front and play with me for *hours*. I'd walk her for them, and whenever they went out of town, I'd watch her. I wanted one of my own so bad, but my mom always said no.

Finding Nova was kismet. I searched all the shelters around here and came up with nothing. Not a single golden in any of them. Turns out, my boss's sister had one that was pregnant, and I was able to adopt one from her litter. Nova is barely a year old, but she's the sweetest pup I ever could've asked for. And she always seemed to prefer me to Nathaniel, which was a nice bonus. She must've seen what I couldn't.

The drive doesn't take too long. The two towns are only about twenty minutes apart, and there's minimal traffic with it being the weekend. Parking in my mom's driveway behind her Kia, I turn off the car and climb out. Her husband's truck isn't here, so he must still be at work. The front door opens, and my mom, all five-foot-one of her, stands on the porch, a blue-and-white apron wrapped around her waist as a flash of golden lightening zips past her into the yard. Nova's butt's wagging so fast, I'm surprised it doesn't fall off.

I kneel at her level, as she collides into me, knocking me onto my ass.

"Nova girl! Daddy missed you!"

Her big pink tongue licks every surface of my face in response, her tail whipping back and forth. Giggles from my mom sound from the porch, where she waits, watching us.

"Did you miss me, baby girl? Hmm? You happy to see me?" Her long, shiny coat is silky smooth under my touch, as I run my hand up and down her back, stopping to scratch at the spot behind her ear she loves so much. "Got a new house to show you, you know that? A nice, big place for just you and me, Nova girl."

Eventually, she calms down, lying on my lap right there in the middle of the lawn while I pretend the grass isn't damp beneath me.

"Come on inside, dear," my mom requests, her voice soft and welcoming. "Made some cookies. They're nice and warm."

Stepping into this house feels like stepping back into my teenage years. It looks almost the exact same as it did back then. Pictures of Charlotte and I line the walls, spanning from our early years until college. Pillows are everywhere—on the couch, on all the beds, the rocking chair, even on the floor by the couch. Candles are always burning, blankets drape over the furniture, knick-knacks decorate the space above the fireplace.

Cozy. That's how I would describe the feel of this house.

"So, how are you doing, honey?" she asks, gesturing with her hand for me to take a seat at the table.

"Not too bad." Not completely a lie. Today I really am *not that bad.*

Setting a plate of still-warm chocolate chip cookies and a glass of milk down, she takes a seat across from me, folding her hands in front of her. She's wearing her signature *worried mom* look, and I know she isn't going to let me off that easily.

That's confirmed when she sighs and says, "Honey, what happened with you and Nathaniel?"

There it is. I knew it was coming sooner or later. I can only brush her off for so long before she demands answers.

"Mom..." Raking my fingers through my hair, I go over in my head how best to say this to get her off my back. This isn't something I want to deep dive into, especially with her. "We just... We're in two different places, him and I. It never would've worked."

The wrinkles on her forehead deepen, her lips turned downward into a frown.

"It seems a little out of left field," she murmurs carefully. "You were about to propose, and then suddenly, you're moving out. What caused the switch?"

Moments like this, I wish Charlotte was the type of sister who's a blabbermouth. It seems like it'd almost be easier to have had my mom already hear this news from her, instead of me having to tell her. It's humiliating, and I don't even know why. It's humiliating to admit that I was so far off at gauging my relationship, that I was about to propose, and he was out cheating on me. How can someone misread a situation *that* badly?

Heaving a sigh, I mutter, "Mom, I don't really want to do this right now, okay?"

She watches me with that disappointed parent, pinched lip expression but, thankfully, lets it go. She easily transitions the conversation into one about her new hobby. She's picked up knitting, and apparently a couple of her friends from around town do it too. She shows me a hat she started working on last week, and it's actually coming along quite well.

Nova plays in the backyard with her dog while she makes us some lunch. We take it out on the back patio, enjoying the little bit of sunshine that's out today. It's still cold as shit, but she has space heaters out there which make it manageable.

Eventually, after we finish eating and I help her with the dishes, I pack up Nova's stuff, and we take off back to our new house. I have to go back to work tomorrow, and I'm nowhere near finished unpacking.. Not to mention, I'm nervous I'm going to run into *Mateo* again.

I still can't believe he's my next door fucking neighbor. The universe must really enjoy messing with me lately. I'm living proof of Murphy's Law right now—anything that can go wrong will go wrong. Story of my fucking life.

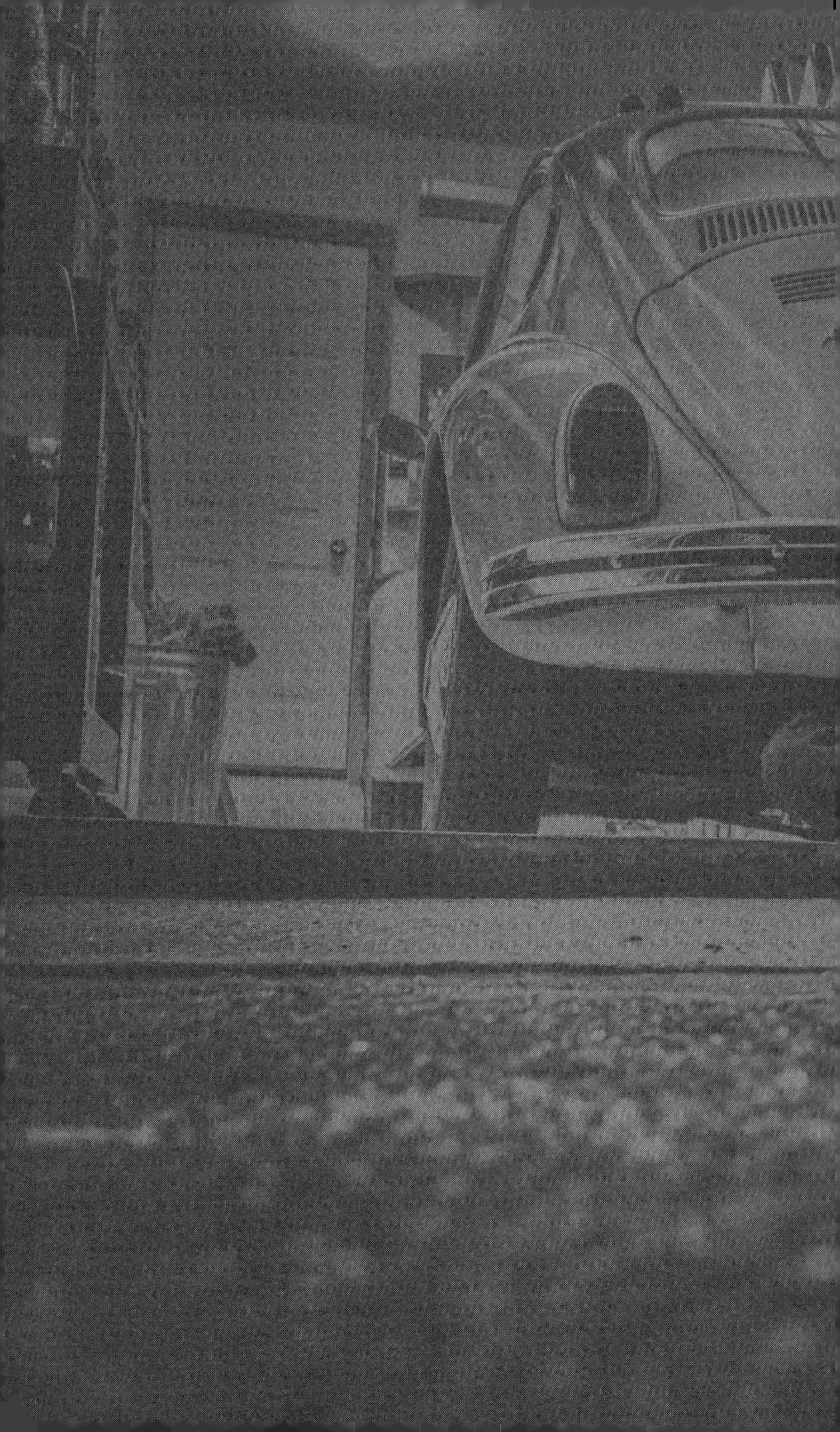

TEN

Mateo

"Hey, fucker. Brought you some coffee." Glancing up from the computer, where I'm ordering some parts, Miguel steps up to the counter, a drink tray with three iced coffees in hand. He sets them down, handing me mine.

"Thanks," I say, immediately taking a long sip off of it.

"Where's Benny?"

Before I can answer, footsteps sound from behind me. "I'm right here. You brought us coffee? What a good little errand boy you are."

Miguel rolls his eyes while I bark out a laugh.

"How'd the rest of your weekend go?" Benny asks me. "That hook-up worth ditching me for on Friday?"

"It wasn't bad," I lie with a shrug. "You'll never guess who my new neighbor is across the hall. They moved in on Saturday."

"Your hook-up from Friday night?" Benny drawls.

Shaking my head, I say, "No. Even better. Remember that dude I hooked up with who had a boyfriend?"

"Oh, fuck, they moved in across the hall, didn't they?" Miguel is practically jumping up and down with excitement. He loves drama, so long as it doesn't include him.

"Sort of. The boyfriend did."

Benny's eyes widen while Miguel's jaw falls open. I can't help the smirk that tugs on my lips. The entire situation is hilarious to me. Of course, this could mean a whole heap of drama that I don't want to deal with, which is the exact reason I ignored Nathaniel's last text message. But if I'm being honest, I'm almost excited to see how it plays out. Especially with how angry Travis looked standing in front of his door with his keys clutched in his fist and his dark brows furrowed.

"You're shitting me," Miguel sputters.

"I'm not. Swear."

"What are the fucking odds, man." He laughs.

"You should've seen his face when he realized who I was."

"He probably wants to fucking kill you," Benny spits out.

"I mean, I'd probably want to kill me too," I reply with a snort. "He's fucking hot, though." *Even hotter than I remember.* Probably because, the first time, my memory is a little hazy from getting clocked in the head with a lamp.

"Goddamn, here we go," Miguel mumbles.

Arching a brow at him, I scoff. "And what the fuck is that supposed to mean?"

"It means I know that look in your eye."

"What look?"

"The one that says you're about to make him your next victim."

I croak out a laugh. "You act like I'm a serial killer."

"Tell me I'm wrong," he challenges, eyebrow cocked.

The smile that splits on my face is so wide, I'm sure my eyes squint. "Listen, of course, I'd love to fuck him. You're not wrong there. He's very good looking. Way hotter than his boyfriend."

Now I really am wondering if I could get him to let me fuck him... I know his ex is a switch. It said as much on his Grindr profile. Is Travis a switch too...?

"Good luck with that," Benny snorts.

"What? You don't think I can?"

"Knowing you and your freakish luck, you probably could," he mumbles, rolling his eyes.

"Could be fun," I muse. "Hate sex is always the best sex." I shrug with a chuckle as someone steps into the garage, and we're forced to get back to work.

The day passes by easily enough. Snow is coming down harder as the hours progress, but it's nothing worth writing home about. The weatherman is calling for a pretty gnarly storm later on this week, but it's still too warm to stick.

I wish it would, though. It would get me out of the dinner tonight that I don't want to go to.

By the time the last car leaves the shop, it's dark out and I'm leaving later than I anticipated, meaning I don't have time to go home and change before heading to the restaurant. It takes me longer than usual to get there due to the condition of the roads. You'd think people would be used to this living here. It happens every single winter, but alas, here we are.

Pulling into the lot, I park next to a familiar Subaru that looks identical to mine except it's white, whereas mine's black. Hands still on the steering wheel, I let my head drop back onto my seat, eyes drifting closed as I force myself to take a couple of deep breaths.

It's one dinner. What could go wrong in the span of one dinner?

Turning off the car, I climb out, hitting the lock button on the key fob as I make my way inside. The restaurant is busy, and as the mouthwatering aroma of Italian seasoning wafts over me, my stomach grumbles, reminding me that I haven't eaten anything of substance since this morning.

Sweat lines the back of my neck, dread coating my gut as I stride toward the table where my family is waiting for me. I'm the last to arrive—not shocking.

My sister, Alondra—or *Ally*, as everyone calls her—spots me first, her dark brown eyes that match mine, lighting up as a smile splits on her face. "Matty! Finally, you made it!" She rises from her chair, coming over to wrap me up in a tight hug.

"Happy birthday," I murmur in her ear, finding instant comfort from her embrace.

Ally is six years younger than me, but we've always been fairly close as far as siblings go. When I moved out as a teenager, she would sneak my mom's phone at night after my parents went to bed, and would text and video chat with me, coming to sleep over at uncle Benny's whenever she could.

Scanning the table, my gaze connects with my mom's, a similar smile to my sisters on her face. "*Hola, mijo,*" she greets in her small voice.

"*Hola, Mamá.*" Ally returns to her seat to my mother's right, and beside her is her boyfriend. "Hey, Scottie," I mutter as I take a seat across from them. "How's it going, man?"

"Not bad, not bad," he replies with a kind smile.

Scottie reminds me of Kelso from *That 70s Show*. Like, there's not a whole lot going on up in his head, but he's a nice enough guy, and he treats Ally the way she should be treated. So, I can't complain. They've been dating since high school. She was the head cheerleader, and he was the class clown. Everybody was shocked when she brought him home.

The server comes and takes my drink order, dropping

off a few plates of appetizers they ordered before I arrived. When she steps away, Ally wastes no time showing me the diamond bracelet and matching earrings that Scottie got her for her birthday. He really does spoil her. For appearing like an airhead, he surprisingly has an impressive job and does quite well for himself.

"So, *mijo*," my mother says, glancing across the table at me. "How are you doing? I never see you anymore."

If there's one thing she's good at, it's guilt trips.

"Doing fine," I say shortly. "How are you, *Mamá*?"

She shrugs. "Oh, I would be doing better if you came around more."

"Work's busy," I lie.

"You seem to make time for your sister just fine," she argues, and she's right. Ally and I see each other at least once every other week. The difference is, Ally didn't turn her back on me when I was fifteen and outed, nor did she kick me out of my home at seventeen.

"*Mamá*, stop," Ally says, placing a hand on her arm. "Let's have a nice evening, yes?"

"*Sí*, it's just so nice to see your handsome face, Matty."

Something painfully similar to guilt swims in my stomach. There's a part of me—the little boy who wants his mother's love—that thinks I'm too hard on her. That it wasn't her doing, per se. And while that part of me *is* right, the side of me that holds the grudge and the hurt and the anger is also right, too.

Sure, when my parents found out I was gay at fifteen by my not-quite-boyfriend-but-not-quite-friend's blabbermouth of a dad, it wasn't my mom who beat the shit out of me with a belt and forced me to go to a church program they sold to me as a "*summer camp*" but was more like something out of a

79

horror film. And yeah, when I ran away from the camp and went back home, it wasn't her who kicked me out in the dark of night in the pouring rain because *"no son of mine is going to be a mamabicho."*

But she also didn't do jack shit to stop him either, and that's just as unforgivable in my book.

Growing up, Ally and I were all the other had. When I was seven and Ally was just a baby, our sister, Marisol, died from the chicken pox. She was three years younger than me. You'd think losing one child to an illness would be enough to make you cherish the kids you still have, regardless of their sexual orientation, but what the fuck do I know?

If it weren't for Ally being so close to my mom, I'd probably never see her. And I can't fault her for having a relationship with her own mother. It's not like she knows the details of what went on with us, nor do I ever want her to know. It's not her burden to carry, and I refuse to let her take on that weight.

Thankfully, she can sense the tension and does what she does best… filling the silence with her chatter to avoid any lulls where Mom has the opportunity to guilt trip me some more. It's a miracle I make it out of the restaurant in one piece.

The drive home is a blur, the snow having since stopped. There's not even a trace of it on the ground anymore. Maybe there won't be a storm after all.

Strolling through the lobby of my building, the elevator doors are sliding shut as I approach, so I pick up the pace. They're old and slow as fuck, and I know if I miss it, I'll be waiting at least five minutes for the next.

"Hey, hold the door, please," I shout, speeding up into a jog. Thankfully, a hand slides out, stopping the door just in time. "Thanks," I murmur as I round the corner into the metal box, only for my eyes to collide with an icy pair of blues, attached to just the person I'd love to run into on an elevator. "*Hola, cariño.*"

I can't explain why I want to fuck with him so much. He's just so... animated, wearing his every emotion right there on his pretty face. Seeing him has my pulse racing, my body temperature rising. Just like when I saw him in the hallway when he introduced himself to me, I want to mess with him, rile him up. It's like his anger ignites something inside of me that I can't explain.

The scowl on his face is instant as he narrows his eyes, stepping back into the far corner like I carry some communal disease he doesn't want to catch. Which... is fair, I suppose. It only makes my grin stretch wider.

"Cat got your tongue?" I ask, pushing the button to our floor.

"Fuck off," he grumbles.

Just to fuck with him, I stand right beside him, despite there being space. He smells sweet, like caramel, and masculine all at the same time. Leaning in, I say right in his ear, "You know how fucking hot you look all angry like that?"

Head whipping to the side, fire burning through the iciness of his gaze, he shoots daggers at me, full lips pressed into a thin line. "You think you're so fucking funny, don't you?" he snaps, voice laced with venom. "Bet you're real proud of yourself too, huh? Fucking someone else's man. What a macho man you are."

A better man would probably point out, once and for all, that I didn't know he had a boyfriend. But where's the fun in that? It would likely stop this push and pull I can't seem to get enough of.

The grin on my face widens before I blow him a kiss. He scoffs as the doors slide open. Without even looking back, he scurries off the elevator as I call after him, "Goodnight, *cariño!*"

Fuck, riling him up sure did a number on improving my mood.

ELEVEN

Travis

This day couldn't get any worse. Since the moment I woke up this morning, the whole day's been screwed. My coffee spilled all over my lap as soon as I sat at my desk; thankfully, I had a change of clothes in my car, then two of my clients canceled on me with zero explanation, and I realized halfway through my morning that I forgot my lunch at home. Left it sitting right on the counter, where it's doing me no good.

I've also been majorly in my feels over the last few days. I was brutally reminded that it should've been mine and Nathaniel's dating anniversary yesterday when a watch I had ordered on backorder for him months ago showed up at my work. It was a slap in the face I didn't need, and the cherry on top was running into Mateo in the hallway last night—*again*—when I got home from work.

It happens *all the time*, and I swear, he's standing in the hall, *trying* to run into me. Of course, that's absurd and awfully vain of myself, but I can't help but think it. I've never ran into any of my neighbors as much as I do him. Though, maybe I did, and I didn't notice as much because I didn't loathe the very sight of them the way I do him.

It's like running into *Mateo*—even his name infuriates me—paired with the delivery of the gift that was meant for a boyfriend as a way of saying *I love* you and *Happy Anniversary* set off a bunch of lovely reminders of all the shit I've gone through these last few months. A stinging flashback of how fucking stupid and naive I was to stay with Nathaniel.

It seems like whenever you get cheated on, you can't help but look inward, try to pick apart what it is about *you* that made them cheat. What *you* could've done differently to have kept them from wandering. Why is it, whenever you're disrespected in a relationship, your first thought *isn't* what the fuck is wrong with *them*, why was it so easy for *them* to lie and deceive you?

No, the first thoughts are always centered around how it could've been your fault. What could *you* have done differently to keep them from straying. At least, that's how it is for me. How fucked up is that?

All I've wanted since I was a kid is somebody to love me, to pick me, to choose me, like I'm Meredith fucking Grey out here. I've never cheated or played somebody, never ghosted anyone. I'm always honest and upfront, even if it's uncomfortable. Yet, time and time again, I land here. Nathaniel is my most recent and most painful, but he certainly isn't the first.

And something tells me he won't be the last.

It's as if no matter how much I want love, I want a family, I want it all, I have a permanent sign on my forehead, begging assholes to fuck me over.

I need to get over Nathaniel and what he did to me, but I don't know how. No matter how hard I try to not think about him, to not dwell, he's always right there, in the forefront of my mind. No amount of work hides my feelings, and no amount of booze drowns out his face—or the memory of him bent over the bed for another man. It's been almost two months since I caught him in the act... you'd think time would start healing those wounds already.

Thrusting my fingers into my hair, I sit back in my chair, letting my head drop back. Heaving a shaky sigh, I decide my best course of action is to run and grab some lunch. Maybe some fresh air and time away from the office will help reset my day.

I highly doubt it, but one can hope.

After I bundle myself up in my coat, hat, scarf, and gloves, I grab my wallet, keys, and phone, leaving my office, and heading downstairs. The storm they keep warning us about has to be hitting soon. The flakes are thicker, the wind has picked up, and it's finally starting to stick. I fucking hate this time of year. I hate the cold.

I was born in the wrong state, I swear.

Thankfully, my car is a beast and handles this god-awful weather like a champ. Turning up the heat and the music once I'm settled behind the wheel, I take off in the direction of a sandwich shop on Crawler Avenue. The condition of the road and the other cars around me surprisingly keep my mind from wandering into unwanted territories.

Taking a right, I pull onto Crawler, keeping an eye out for a spot to park along the curb. Fucking hate parking around here. What the hell ever happened to parking lots?

Jesus, I'm annoying even myself with the poor mood I'm in today.

I find a spot about a block away from the sandwich shop, and weave my way in, but not before slipping on some ice and hitting the curb. It's surprisingly busy inside, but I'm able to be in and out in less than fifteen minutes. Damn near freezing my balls off, I walk back to the car, stopping dead in my tracks as I approach it.

"You gotta be *fucking* kidding me." The tire that hit the curb when I parked is flat. My head drops back onto my shoulders as I stare up at the sky. "Anything else you'd like to fucking throw my way today?"

Letting my eyes close, I drag in a deep breath, exhaling through my nose. I repeat the process a few more times before finally pulling out my phone. Knowing I don't have a spare with me, I call the nearest shop, and they let me know they're sending a tow truck, but it'll be close to half an hour before they can get there.

Great.

Climbing back in the car, I turn it on, cranking the heat before sending a text to my team, letting them know I'll be late coming back from lunch. With nothing else to do but wait, I eat the sandwich I now regret coming here to buy. It's good. Not good enough to buy a whole new fucking tire, but whatever.

After what feels like an eternity, the truck finally pulls up, so I turn the car off and get out to meet the guy. His door opens, and he hops out, and I swear to God, I'm being punked. There's no other explanation for it.

"You must be fucking joking," I grumble under my breath as none other than Mateo, the man I apparently can't fucking stay away from, stands before me in his oil-stained coveralls, minty-green eyes, watching me with pure amusement.

"*Cariño,*" he purrs in that annoyingly sexy voice of his. "Fancy meeting you here. Car trouble?"

"You're a tow truck driver?" I ask stupidly, crossing my arms over my chest.

"I'm a mechanic," he corrects. "Who just so happened to be driving the tow truck you needed." Mateo smirks, all his teeth on display. They're such nice teeth too.

"Can we just get this over with, please? I need to get back to work."

He glances down at my deflated tire. "What? You don't know how to drive in the snow?"

I roll my eyes. "Fuck off."

Mateo chuckles, scribbling something on his clipboard before passing it to me. "Read through here, initial here, here, and here, and then sign at the bottom."

Instead of waiting for me to do as he asked, he turns and starts working on getting my car loaded onto the truck.

Once I finish signing, I tuck it under my arm and watch him work. It's annoying how attractive he is. Nobody should look that good in a pair of dingy, oily coveralls. They're rolled up once at the bottom, showing off his clunky black lace-up boots. The top button is undone, revealing the black shirt he's got on underneath. A pair of black sunglasses sits on the top of his head, despite there not being a wink of sun anywhere in sight, and his hair is perfectly gelled back, not a stray piece out of place.

"Alright, come on," he says, rounding the driver's side of his truck. "Hop in, I'll drive you back to wherever you need to go."

Huffing out a laugh, I stay rooted in place. "I'm good."

He rolls his eyes, backtracking to come stand in front of me. "Get in the fucking truck, *pendejo*," he growls. "I'm not about to have you sue my shop for walking in the freezing weather. It won't kill you to let me drive you back to work."

This day could not get any fucking worse.

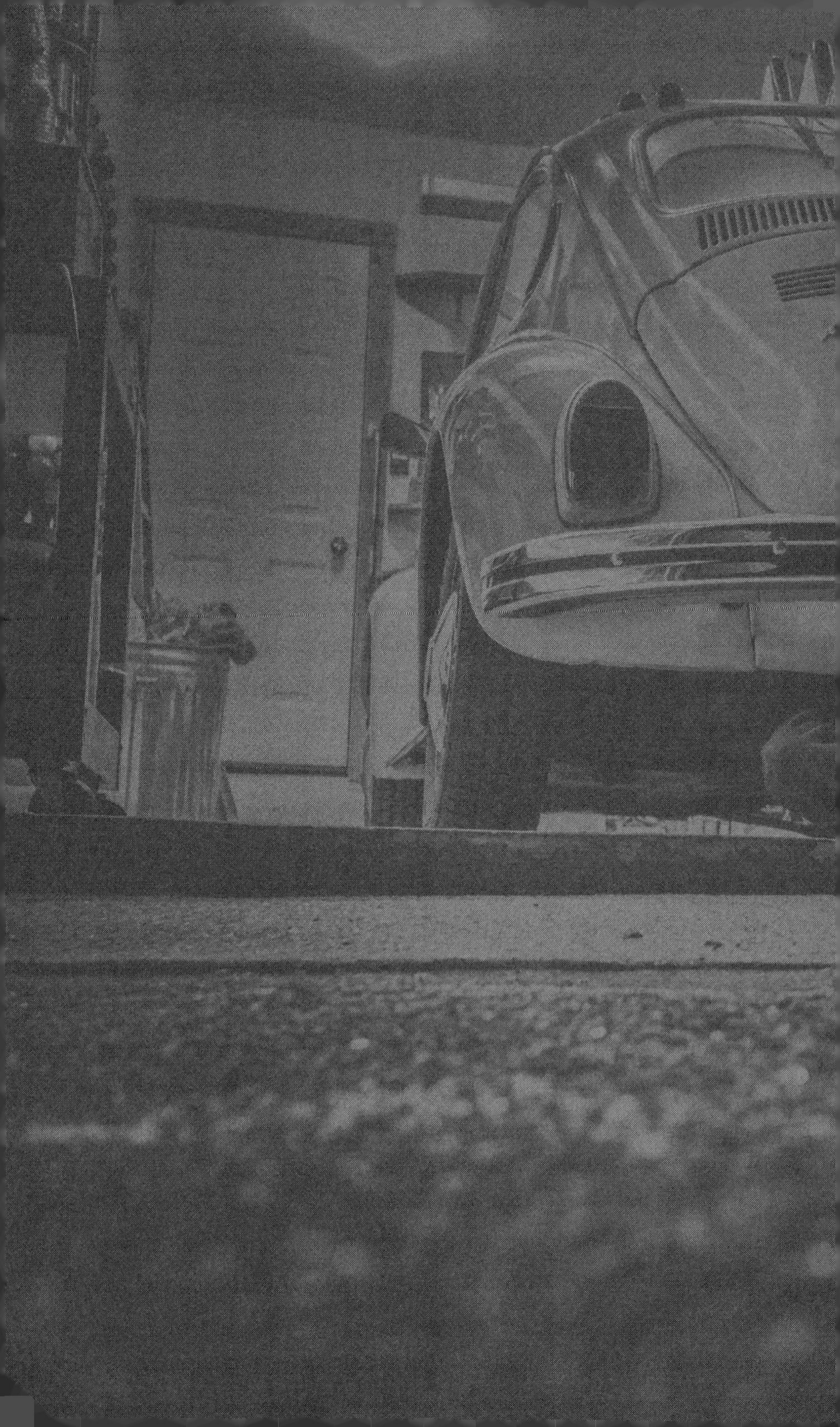

TWELVE

Mateo

"Hello?"

"Hey, you busy?" Ally's voice is chipper in my ear as I'm walking through my apartment door.

Kicking off my shoes, then hanging my keys up, I say, "Just getting home. What's up?"

"Scottie and I are getting married!"

I choke on my own spit, coughing and quickly clearing my throat, not at all expecting that to come out of her mouth. "Holy shit, sis. When did that happen?"

"Last night. We went out for our anniversary dinner, and he had a whole thing planned." Her voice cracks.

"Congratulations, Ally. I'm so fucking happy for you."

"I, uh..." She clears her throat. "I want you to walk me down the aisle."

My throat fills with emotion. My sister always reserved that for our father, but when he died from a heart attack five years ago, she lost that dream. "Of course, I will, Al."

It's a bitter thing, seeing how much Ally cares for and

misses our dad. I can't wrap my head around how the same man who beat me and sent me away as a teenager for being gay is the same man who adored and spoiled her. I'm happy for her, that she got the love she deserves, but it doesn't make it any less of a tough pill to swallow. It's like we had completely different childhoods living under the same roof.

"Thank you, Matty. We're having an engagement party next month. Please come."

"Is Mom coming?" It's a fucking stupid question.

"Of course, she's coming." She says it with an airy laugh, trying to lighten the mood. Even through the phone, I know she can sense my unease. "Matty, you gotta let this go. She's trying to accept you."

"Ally, don't," I warn.

Yanking open the fridge, I grab a beer, twisting the top off, and downing a few swigs.

"Mateo, it's been years," she pleads. "Can we please put all this behind us?"

I know she means well, that she isn't trying to be insensitive. "You have no fucking clue about the shit they put me through, Alondra."

"So, tell me," she shouts into the phone, followed by an unmistakable sigh. "Just talk to me for once about it, Mateo."

Pressure builds behind my eyes, and it pisses me off even more. Running a shaky hand through my hair, I grab the bottle, downing what's left of it before tossing it in the trash. That's not going to do it tonight.

"I gotta go, Ally." My voice comes out dry. Clearing my throat again, I try to muster up as much pep as I can manage as I add, "Congrats on your engagement. I'm so fucking happy for you." I fail, of course, sounding despondent instead of genuine.

Not bothering to wait for a response, which would most likely turn into an argument, I hang up the phone, tossing it onto the counter, and reaching into the freezer to grab the tequila. Foregoing a glass altogether, I twist off the cap, taking a pull, and then another.

With the bottle in hand, I amble into my room, heading straight for the window. It's too damn cold to go outside, but I need to smoke, so this'll have to do. I grab the pack of smokes out of my pocket, placing one between my teeth. Igniting the red lighter, I hold it to the end of the cigarette until it glows in the dark room, toxic smoke filling my lungs.

I don't know why I've never told Ally what went down with me and my parents and that fucking camp. It's like no matter how much I hated them, I just couldn't do that to her. I couldn't destroy the stars in her eyes that she had when she looked up to them. They don't deserve her love, but she doesn't deserve to have the image of them shattered either. I guess, in my own fucked-up way, I was—*am*—trying to protect her.

And trust me, I want to look past it all. I want to be able to look at my mom and not rage inside. But I just... can't. I can't look at her and forget everything that happened.

I can't forget the way they locked me in a room at that camp, and starved me for days, giving me only enough water to keep me alive.

I can't forget the hateful speech they tried to preach to all of us, going on and on about God's will, and how we're supposed to be made in his image, and bullshit about how we're sinners, and going to Hell. Yet, their entire program was based on bigotry and abuse.

And above all, I can't forget the way my own goddamn mother stood there and watched as her husband beat me when

I got home. She watched and did *nothing* to stop him. To help me. I can't forget it and, frankly, I don't fucking want to. I don't want to forgive. She doesn't deserve my forgiveness.

I'm not a what-if type of guy. What's the fucking point, am I right? Dwelling on what could've been doesn't change the present, it doesn't change what's happened. But every now and again, I do wonder what my life would've been like had my parents been a bit more accepting. What the rest of my adolescent years would've looked like. Would my relationships have been a bit healthier? Would I hold on to less anger inside of me?

Who fucking knows.

I lift the bottle to my lips, filling my mouth with the chilled, smooth liquid. It burns as I swallow, and I fucking relish it. Tears spring to my eyes as I down a little more, replacing the lip of bottle with my cigarette.

Forcing myself to drag my thoughts away from my fucked-up family, my mind shifts to this afternoon. To the call the shop received about the flat tire and the tow needed. To how I showed up, only to find an angry Travis shooting daggers at me when he realized it was me who needed to help him.

Fuck, that was rich.

Highlight of my entire week.

Now, listen, I can understand—and even respect—why he's so pissed. I would be too, I'm sure. But he's directing his anger in the wrong direction. Frankly, it's about damn time he gets over it, too. Watching him seethe as I loaded his car onto my truck was fucking satisfying. Then, on the drive to his office, watching him sit as far away as humanly possible was even better.

Fuck... The way the scent of him filled the cab of my truck, intoxicating and fresh. It was a shame his work was so close to where I picked him up from. I shamelessly spent the entire rest of the afternoon social media stalking him in between cars. Even went as far back as his college days on his Instagram.

Inhaling one last drag off the cigarette, I put it out in the ashtray before taking another pull off the tequila bottle, wiping my mouth with the back of my hand as I wonder what that little angry fucker is up to. Bet he's sitting in his apartment, envisioning killing me. The thought makes me snort out a laugh as my feet carry me into the hallway.

I'm at the front door, pulling it open before my tequila riddled mind can even try to tell me it's a bad idea. My fist comes up, pounding on his door, probably harder than necessary, but it does the trick, because a moment later, he's standing in front of me in a pair of plaid pajama shorts and a white tank top.

A large ball of fur steps up beside him, my gaze dropping to take in the creature I vaguely recognize from the day I was at Nathaniel's house. He immediately put the dog out back.

Dropping down into a squat, I hold out my hand for the dog to sniff me. "Hi, puppy."

The sniffs quickly turn into licks before he or she lets me pet them.

I glance up at Travis, finding him watching us intently, an emotion passing through his features I can't quite figure out. "What's his name?" I ask.

"*Her* name is Nova."

"Nova, you're such a pretty girl, aren't you? Such a good girl too, huh?" Her tail wags rapidly back and forth as she licks the side of my face.

Standing at my full height again, a smirk slides on my lips as I lean against his door frame, crossing my arms over my chest. He takes a step back, looking equal parts disgusted and furious. "*Cariño,* looking all kinds of cozy, aren't we?"

"What the fuck do you want?" he spits out.

"Just wanted to make sure my neighbor made it home safely," I reply in my sweetest voice. "You know, since your car is still in my shop."

As luck would have it, the tire he needs, we have to order, and he also somehow fucked up the entire wheel when he hit the curb. *But he insists he didn't hit it that hard.*

When he doesn't say anything, I continue. "You know, if you needed a ride to work in the morning, so you didn't have to drive your rental in the snow—since we both know that isn't your strong suit—I could take you. I'm nice like that."

He huffs out a laugh. "I'd rather fucking walk, but thanks."

"Aw, come on, Travis. You can't still be mad I fucked your boyfriend, can you? How long has it been?" I rub a hand over my mouth to try to hide my grin when his eyes narrow on me.

"You're such a fucking prick, you know that?"

I shrug. "I've been told."

"And you, what? Find enjoyment out of ruining people's lives?"

Rolling my eyes, I say, "Don't be so dramatic, *cariño.* You forget, we fucked the same man. I know he ain't that fucking special in bed. I did you a favor." With a smirk, I add, "You're welcome."

Blame it on his speed or the alcohol running through my system, but I don't see it coming when he shoves me out of his doorway, slamming the door in my face. I stumble back, nearly losing my footing, but a laugh escapes me anyway.

He's so fucking easy to piss off.

THIRTEEN

Travis

Fuck! Those twelve beers I pounded last night are coming back to haunt me. It doesn't help that the daylight is pouring in from my bedroom window because I forgot to close my curtains last night before passing out. I didn't do a damn thing last night besides get shitty drunk and feel sorry for myself. Vaguely, I remember downloading Grindr. I don't even know why, because a random hook-up is *not* what I want. The app was deleted an hour after it was downloaded, anyway, because I stumbled upon Nathaniel *and* my annoying fucking cocky neighbor on there.

Must be how they met.

It's actually infuriating how good-looking Mateo is, and he knows it, too. He's Mexican or Puerto Rican, or something similar. His perfectly dark, bronzed skin tells me as much, as does his accent. He probably bags a lot of ass that way. He talks to them in his deep, sultry voice, rolls his Rs in that undeniably sexy fucking way, and suddenly they're rolling around for him.

Asshole.

It's not only his voice that he's got going for him either. It's his eyes… they're so bright, yet pale. Almost mint green. And it's also the tattoos. They cover both arms and snake up his neck. He even has some on the side of his head, where it's buzzed short. I just know if he were to take his clothes off, they'd cover every inch of him. He was mostly dressed when I walked in on him in my house—my *old* house—so, that doesn't tell me much. His beard is short and thick, perfectly manicured, just like his eyebrows. There's a hoop in his nose, and his lips are plump, the bottom one more so than the top, and prominently red. *Kissable.*

It's no wonder Nathaniel fucked him. He's the poster child for tall, dark, and handsome. How could I ever have competed with all *that*?

My blond hair is chaotic, never sitting right. I'm sure if I glanced in the mirror right now, it'd look like I stuck my finger in a light socket. And my eyes are plain blue. Which yes, a lot of people *do* seem to like blue eyes, but they aren't a shimmering mint fucking green that practically radiates off tan skin. And speaking of skin, mine's about as pale as it can get without being translucent. I'm nearly as tall as Mateo, only an inch or two shorter, but where he's all beefy and built, I'm lanky and lean. Now, for the sake of being fair, I *can* admit, I'm not totally out of shape. A vague six-pack is visible, and my pectorals *are* nice. But still, he's… absolutely everything I am not.

What the fuck am I doing? Comparing myself to a fucking douchebag? This is pathetic. And it's not even the first time I've caught myself doing it since moving in here and realizing he's my neighbor.

Rubbing both my closed eyes with my fists, I roll out of

bed and immediately regret doing so. My head throbs, like someone's playing ping-pong inside my skull. Except the ping-pong balls are rocks. My throat is so dry, if I don't guzzle some water soon, I'll probably turn to dust.

After taking the world's longest piss, I pad out into the kitchen. Nova's nails click along the hardwood floor as she waits, not so patiently, for me to give her food. Once that's done, I refill her water before deciding I need some for myself too. I don't feel like dirtying up a glass, so instead, I turn the faucet back on, sticking my mouth under it and drinking straight from the source. I've got back-to-back meetings at work today, but I don't fucking feel like going.

So, I'm not going to. Today seems like the perfect day to play hooky.

The grumbling of my stomach reminds me that I never ate last night. It also reminds me of the Mexican food I have in the fridge. While I heat up the chicken enchiladas with beans and rice, I scour the apartment for the phone I've seemed to misplace. It wasn't on my bed or on the floor beside it when I woke up, either. I need to let my boss know I'm taking a sick day, but it'll have to wait.

The microwave dings after a minute and a half, and I give up. I can find the stupid phone later. The aroma coming from the kitchen smells so fucking good; I'm practically salivating by the time I walk back in there. Thank God they provided plastic silverware, because I do not feel like going through my boxes to find mine.

Not even ten minutes later, I'm shoveling in my last bite, and just as I figured, it was fucking delicious. Tossing the garbage in the can beside the counter, I meander into the bathroom. May as well take a shower before I get to my day of moping and day drinking. Flicking on the light, I notice my phone sitting on the counter.

Hmm. That's where that went.

Opening Spotify, I turn on my playlist, moving to start the shower. *Love Note* by Whynotcordell starts playing, the room quickly filling with steam and the slow beat of the song. Ridding myself of my clothes, I kick them into the corner before stepping under the stream. The hot water feels good on my achy muscles as I hang my head and let it beat down on my body for a few minutes.

For a brief moment, I allow my mind to wander to everything that's happened in the last few months. At how different my life is now than it was then, when I thought I was about to get engaged. It's crazy how things can change in the blink of an eye. How a future you were so sure about can fade like it meant nothing. I'm sure in a month or two, I'll realize it was for the best, but for now, it still fucking hurts. No matter how much I'd like to pretend it doesn't.

Turning the water off, I climb out, toweling dry, before rummaging through a box in my room for some clean clothes. I end up settling on a pair of white sweats and a black tee. Unpacking my clothes hasn't been high on my radar lately. I guess I could spend today doing that.

But… some more beer *would* make the task a little easier, right?

Yeah. And besides, I need to take Nova potty. I haven't done that yet—way to go me—and she'll probably appreciate a walk.

Finding some socks, I pull them on before pushing on my black Nikes. My black puffer coat is draped over the back of my couch, so I slip into that and grab the keys off the counter, shoving them into my pockets. I gotta admit, it's awesome having a convenience store across the street. Almost everything I could need is within walking distance, which is even nicer since gas prices are atrocious. Once I have Nova's leash attached to her collar, we leave.

The hallway outside my apartment is quiet, not a soul in sight. Stepping into the elevator, I press the main level, reaching into my pocket for my phone. Only... *shit*. I must've left it in the bathroom. The doors slide closed, and I start my descent. Oh well, I'll only be gone ten minutes at most. I still need to text my boss too.

Once I reach the bottom floor, I step out, noticing the lobby as dead as my hallway. *That's weird.* Where is everyone? The answer quickly slaps me in the face, though, when I round the corner and get a good look at the outside.

Shiiit...

It's a fucking blizzard out there. The light snowfall from the last week has clearly picked up its speed, hitting us with the storm the weatherman kept warning us about. There's gotta be at least six or more inches in front of the door, and it's coming down *hard*. I can't even see across the street. I can't see *anything* other than white.

Knowing Nova needs to use the bathroom, we go outside anyway. Thankfully, she does her business quickly, probably not wanting to be in this shit for any longer than I want to.

A quick glance across the street shows the store is closed. Guess I'm not getting beer after all.

Heaving a sigh, I spin on my heel, heading back toward the elevator. When I get up to the third floor, I stroll down the hallway, thankful I don't run into douchebag Mateo again. Twisting my door handle, I curse when it's locked. My old place, the door wouldn't lock unless you did it manually with the key, but this one locks automatically—something I keep forgetting. Which seems like a safety hazard, if you ask me, but what do I know? Grabbing my keys out of my pocket, I fish through them, looking for the new house key.

Throwing my head back, I groan audibly because, *of fucking course*, I forgot to grab them when I left.

Fuck, fuck, *fuck!*

And my goddamn phone is inside too.

"Fuck!"

At the sound of a door opening, my spine steels, and I refuse to turn around. I already know who is standing there behind me, probably looking smug as fuck.

"What's got you shouting out here, *cariño?*" His voice is full of gravel, like he just rolled out of bed. It has no right being as fucking hot as it is.

Still, I don't turn around. "Nothing you need to concern yourself with," I growl.

I feel, more than hear, him step closer to me. He smells faintly of marijuana and cedar. His warmth radiates off him, wrapping around me like a blanket I don't want. A brown, heavily tattooed arm rests on the door beside me as he brings his lips right beside my ear. "What's wrong, baby? Locked out?"

Spinning around, I shove him, finding sick satisfaction when he stumbles. "Get the fuck away from me," I snarl.

The sound of his gruff chuckle washes over me, goosebumps forming from head to toe at the sound. "Oh-ho, he's *feisty* again today." Similarly to last night, Nova prances around at my feet until Mateo bends down to pet her. He talks to her in a baby voice that should be obnoxious. No, it *is* obnoxious. Standing, he backs up, resting his shoulder against his doorway. He crosses his arms over his broad chest—something he did against *my* doorway last night, and it's no less hot now than it was then. "You call the landlord yet? A locksmith?"

"Not that it's any of your business, but I left my phone inside." His grin grows, dimples poking out and taunting me, further inflating my annoyance. "I was only planning on running to the convenience store before I realized the weather."

"You know, I *do* have a phone you could use if you ask nicely." His eyes darken as he drags his gaze over me once more.

"Oh, how fucking generous of you," I deadpan, rolling my eyes.

He shrugs. "I can be," he chirps, throwing me a wink.

"Yeah, well, thanks, but no thanks. I'd rather ask one of the other neighbors."

Spinning on my heel, I head down the hall, determined to get back into my apartment as fast as possible to get away from this asshole.

"Three out of the four other apartments on this floor are vacant," he calls out after me. "The fourth belongs to Ms. Sheri Lee, retired nurse and widow who spends every single winter in her condo in Arizona."

God-fucking-damnit.

Slowly and begrudgingly, I turn to face him, my scowl deepening as his smirk spreads. "You may as well suck it up, *cariño*, and use the damn phone."

I *hate* that he's right. What am I going to do? Be stubborn and sit outside my apartment until the snow clears? That could be days. But the thought of using anything of his, taking him up on any offer he has, makes my blood fucking boil.

Stomping over to him, I hold out my hand, palm up. "Fine," I grumble as he slaps it into my hand.

"Atta boy." He shakes the hair on my head messily, and if I

101

wasn't already irritated, that would surely do it. "Maybe you're not so stupid after all."

"You're a fucking prick, you know that?"

"I do know that, baby. But one day, you'll find it endearing. Trust me."

"Stop fucking calling me baby and whatever the fuck cariño means." Of course, I butcher the pronunciation of that word, saying it much less sexy than it sounds rolling off his tongue.

Based on the way his lip tugs into a crooked grin, I'd say he noticed. "Just make the damn call, you stubborn fool."

Ten minutes later, I've called every single locksmith within a twenty-mile radius. Every single one saying they can't make it out due to the weather conditions. To make matters even better, my landlord—who lives in the building—just so happens to be out of town this week.

This can't be fucking happening.

The icing on top of this snow-covered cake is that the window in the hallway is broken, so it's probably close to twenty degrees where I'm standing, and not even the puffer jacket is keeping me warm. At this point, call me Count fucking Olaf because this is a series of unfortunate events if I've ever heard of one.

Dragging my gaze back up to Mateo, I hand him his phone, already knowing what he's going to say next. And I fucking hate it.

"You could come inside and wait out the storm." He motions to his apartment. "I don't bite... hard."

"Please!" I cough up a laugh. "Like I would ever have *sex* with you. Do I look that desperate?"

The humor in his expression vanishes, replaced by anger as he stalks toward me, backing me up against my door, boxing me in with his arm as his other hand wraps around my throat, squeezing just enough to startle me. "Let's get one thing straight, *estúpido*... I said you could come inside and *wait*. I said *nothing* about *fucking* you." He steps back just enough to give me a once-over with a disgusted look in his eyes and a curl to his lip. "And I'd say you are, in fact, pretty desperate, so maybe don't bite the hand that fucking feeds you, boy."

Swallowing around the lump in my throat, I avert my gaze, feeling like a fucking idiot. He squeezes my throat a little tighter, my eyes snapping to meet his.

"How about we try this again with some manners this time, shall we?" His hands are removed from my body, and he takes a step back, putting some much-needed distance between us. "Would you like to come inside and wait out the storm, or would you rather sit out here and catch hypothermia?"

Clearing my throat, I run a hand through my hair. "Uh, sure. I'll come in," I say, barely above a whisper. "Th-thanks."

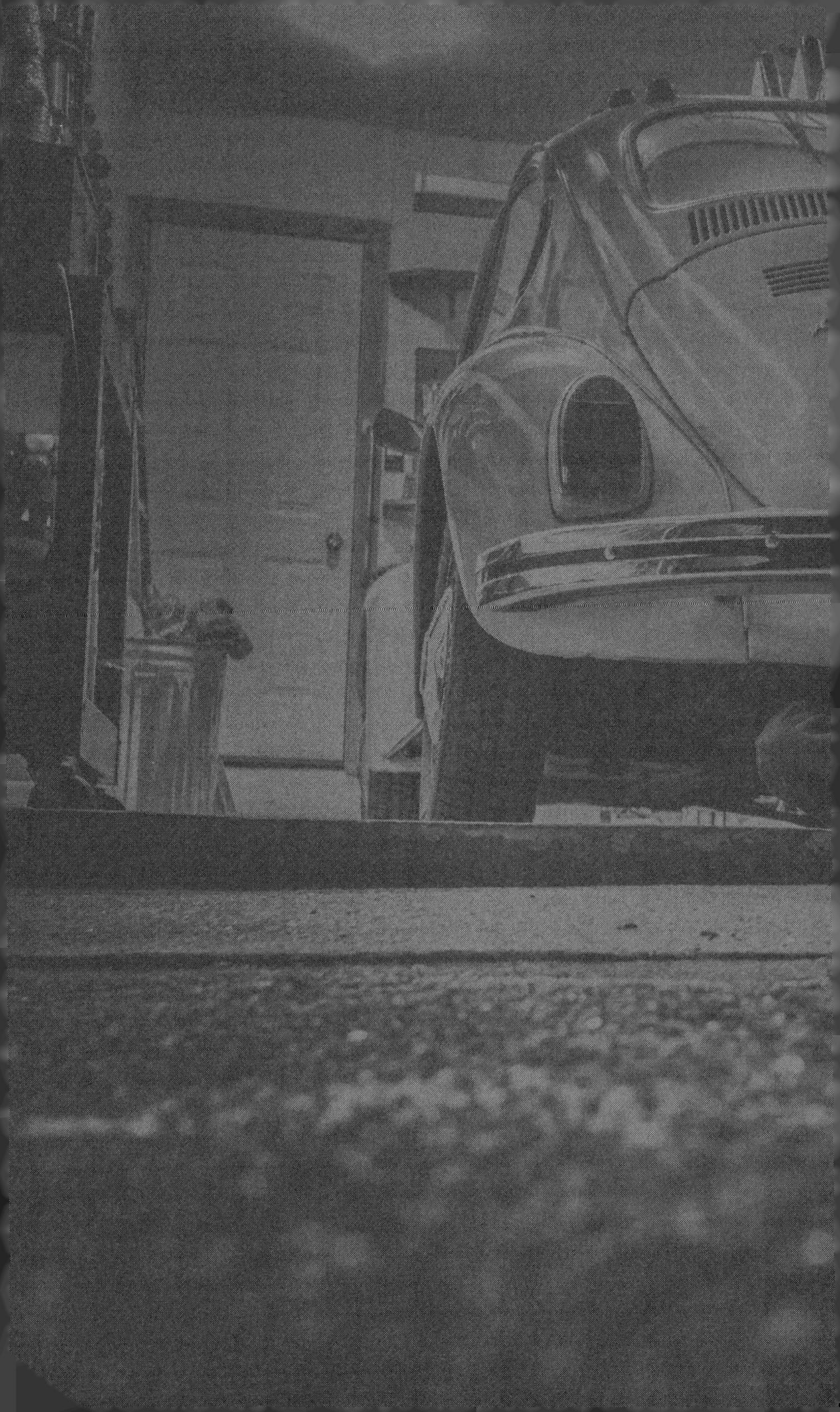

FOURTEN

Mateo

Like a hawk hunting his prey, my eyes never leave the sight of Travis as he wanders around my apartment, nervous and uncomfortable. It's been ten minutes, and he hasn't sat down once. I'd be lying if I said I wasn't thrilled by the fact that he's locked out of his place and had no choice but to come into my house. *The enemy.* I know that's how he views me. It's in the way his eyes narrow as he takes me in, lips pinched into a thin line. The way he not-so subtly scoffs or groans under his breath anytime I speak to him.

Not that I blame him, but again, he's throwing his anger in the wrong direction. When I met Nathaniel on Grindr, I had no clue he was in a relationship. I may be a dick, but I don't frequently make a habit of fucking men who aren't mine to take.

One thing's for sure… I'm going to enjoy fucking with Travis while he's here. We're trapped. Why not have a little fun? Sauntering into the kitchen, I pull open the fridge, glancing over to where he's pacing in front of my couch. "Want something to drink?"

His head snaps up, like he's lost in thought and forgot where he was. The scowl that's ever-present around me slides firmly into place as he stops pacing, arms crossed over his chest. "No, I don't want anything to drink," he huffs.

Shrugging, I chuckle as I reach for a beer. "Suit yourself, man." I twist off the cap, tossing it in the trash as I bring the bottle up to my lips, letting the crisp liquid fill my mouth. Maybe it'll help clear up the fucking hangover and piss-poor mood I woke up with. I guess the conversation with my sister is still weighing on me because I'm feeling more snarky than usual.

"Does she need something to eat?" I ask, nodding toward the golden ball of fur that's made herself right at home on my couch. I already gave her a bowl of water as soon as we got back in here. "I don't have dog food, but I have some leftover rotisserie chicken."

Travis looks at me from across the room, his pacing halted, an expression on his face I can't quite read. "I fed her before we left the house, so she's good for now. But thank you."

Nodding and setting the bottle on the counter, I amble across the space into my bedroom. This entire situation could use some weed, and I'll bet he won't turn *that* down. I know he smokes. There was a bong on the coffee table when I came over to fuck Nathaniel, and he told me it wasn't his. Figured he had a roommate. I grab the red-and-black box off my dresser. It's ugly as sin, but it belonged to my grandma before she died.

After plucking out one of the Js I rolled this morning and a lighter, I make my way back out to the living room. His eyes—pale blue and narrowed—track my every move until I'm right in front of him. With the joint between my teeth, I flick the striker until the flame ignites, holding it on the end of the rolling paper until it glows red.

The earthy, sweet taste of marijuana sits heavy on my taste buds as I take a couple of hits, holding it out for him. "Want some?" Exhaling the smoke, I can't help the grin that forms on my lips. He *wants* it, but he also wants to say *no*. An internal war with himself I love to see. "Come on, *cariño*. It's just some weed. It'll help you relax, so you're not such a buzzkill."

His grimace deepens as he takes it from me. The black polish on his nails is chipped and worn, his cuticles picked at. Taking a hit, his nostrils flare, accentuating the black hoop in his left one. It's fucking hot. *He's* hot, and as his pale pink lips purse around the filter, a sudden image of how he'd look with those same lips wrapped around my cock flashes in my mind.

Shit, he'd look fucking pretty like that.

We pass the weed back and forth for a while until it's almost gone, nothing on my mind except that thought. It'll probably be somewhat of a challenge at first. He thinks he hates me after all, but hate sex is always the best, isn't it? Taking one more hit, I stroll into the kitchen, putting the joint out and throwing it away, before grabbing my beer off the counter.

I plop down on the couch, my gaze sizing him up. "You need to relax, man."

He glares at me, the blue of his irises now accompanied by red as the effects of the weed become evident. "Don't tell me what to fucking do, *man*." He mocks the last word, and I can't help but chuckle.

Standing to my full height—which truthfully, isn't *much* taller than him, but I have a couple of inches on him—I step closer, hand wrapping around his throat as I push him until his back hits my wall. The air is knocked out of him, and I feel his Adam's apple bob as he tries to swallow beneath the constriction. I'm walking a dangerous line right now. He could decide to deck me in the face. But if I'm right—which I think I am—he wants this. Even if he doesn't *want* to want it.

With my grin wide, I decide to test my luck. Channeling all my frustration from the call last night into this, I bring my mouth right by his ear, feeling a shiver rack through him. Keeping my voice low, I ask, "But what if I want to tell you what to do, baby?" Goosebumps erect over the flesh on his neck as I continue. "Want to know what I think? Don't worry, I'll tell you," I taunt. "I think you *need* someone to tell you what to do. I think you *crave* it, giving up control."

Pulling back, but not removing my hand from his throat, I run my gaze over his face. There's a faint pink splashed on his cheeks and his bloodshot eyes are heavy. Once again, his hands come to my chest, shoving me away, but this time, I'm prepared for it. I don't move.

"You have no fucking idea what you're talking about, asshole," he snarls.

A smirk pulls on my lips before I run my tongue along the bottom, relishing the way his eyes track the movement. "It's no wonder your man cheated on you," I growl, taunting him. Begging him to take the bait. "You're fucking bitter and boring."

His eyes narrow, lips parting like he wants to give me a rebuttal, but he remains quiet.

"Maybe if you let yourself have some fun, you'd feel better." Stepping back, I shamelessly drag my gaze down his body before meeting his eyes once more. An idea forms in my mind. It's crazy, but again, we're trapped, so why not? "Let me make you come, *cariño*. Bet you'd be in a better mood."

This time when he shoves me, I let him. The thrill pulsing inside me at his fury is undeniable. My dick's already so hard inside my pants, and we've barely gotten started.

"I'm not boring or bitter," he barks, stepping closer to me, a finger shoved toward my face. "You're just a fucking asshole who doesn't understand boundaries." When I say nothing back, simply smiling, he continues. "And you're not even that attractive. I doubt you'd be able to satisfy me, anyway. Guys like you are always selfish."

There's so much I could say, but I don't. Instead, I just reply with, "Prove it."

He swallows hard. "W-what?"

"Let's prove how much I *can't* satisfy you, Travis." I push my hands into my jeans pockets as he stands there looking wildly uncomfortable. "Let's see if you're right. You aren't," I add. "But we can humor you for the sake of being fair."

He shuffles anxiously on the heels of his feet, the entire space quiet save for the ticking arm on the analog clock behind him. "How would we do that?"

Watching his blue eyes dilate, I know I've got him. I know I'm not crossing a line—well, I *am*, but it's at least one he *wants* me to cross. So, I continue. "Let me make you feel good." *Come on, cariño. Give in. Give it to me.*

His brows pinch together. "That's all?"

"That's all," I repeat. "*But* we play by my rules. This is my house, my bet. We do things my way, got it? But if I'm right, and you enjoy yourself, you have to let me take you out sometime."

"Like a date?" he balks, eyes going wide and round. "Why would I do that?" He crosses his arms over his chest, but the temptation is clear as day in his eyes.

"Why not? Are you scared?" I taunt as I reach down and adjust myself, his gaze zeroing in on it.

"I'm not fucking scared."

Stalking toward him, I back him into the wall once again,

my hands not touching him. "Prove it, then, *cariño*. Prove how not scared you are." Our faces are mere inches from each other, his breath fanning my lips, chest rising and falling in rapid succession. I know if I touched his chest, his heart would be pounding beneath the surface. "*Submit. To. Me.*" The words come out as a thunderous growl, snapping his resolve as his lips crash against mine.

FIFTEEN
Travis

His lips *devour* mine, hungry and ardent. His tongue annihilates all logical thinking. And when his hard, muscular body presses against mine, pinning me farther into this wall, an electric current sets off in my veins, demolishing any reserves I may have had minutes ago.

This is a *terrible* idea. Probably one of the worst I've ever had. But where has playing it safe ever gotten me? So, for tonight… just this once, I'll make a deal with the devil. I'll play his sinister games and reap the benefits. It's my turn to be selfish. I've always been the one used up and thrown away, but this time, I won't be disposable. This time, when I get mine, it'll be *me* deciding to walk away.

I'm pulled from my thoughts when sharp teeth chomp down on my bottom lip hard enough to draw blood, a hiss escaping me a second before Mateo's tongue glides across it soothingly. When he pulls back, the grin curled on his lip—slick with our shared saliva and my blood—is half smile, half threat.

He uses the pad of his thumb to wipe his lip off, sucking it clean seconds later as his dark, tumultuous eyes lock on mine, one perfectly manicured brow arched in question. "I take that as a yes, then?"

Despite being harder than I've probably ever been in my life, I roll my eyes, groaning. "*Fine*," I grit out. "But only this one time. After the snow melts and I go home, we pretend this never fucking happened."

His bright eyes fucking *gleam* with arrogance as he watches me. "Oh, baby, it's cute that you think you'll be able to walk away from me once we're through." Bringing our bodies flush again, he nips along my jaw before he continues. "I'll be your worst goddamn nightmare, your new drug of choice, *cariño*."

His words send a shiver down my spine as my cock throbs behind my sweats.

Reaching up and threading his fingers through my hair, he yanks my head back, exposing my neck to him. His teeth sink into my flesh as I cry out, my hips instinctually thrusting forward to meet his. My skin feels like it's connected to a live wire, everywhere he touches lighting up in response. A low groan bubbles out of me as he sucks on the spot he just bit, both elevating the pain and undoubtedly leaving a mark.

Should I care? Yes, probably.

Do I care? Not one bit.

When he speaks again, it's throaty and hoarse. "I'm going to *cut* you open, wring you dry, and when you finally manage to escape my claws, you'll be crawling back, *begging* for more. You'll leave here a fucking fiend for the way I'll make you feel. I promise you that."

My mouth's so dry, I don't think I could talk even if I knew what to say. He uses my silence as an invitation, though, sucking my bottom lip into his mouth before thrusting his tongue inside, licking along my own. I groan as I feel the barbell running through his tongue, and the way it feels tangling with mine.

I wonder where else he's pierced...

One minute his lips are wrecking me, and the next I'm left standing there, head in a cloud as he saunters into a room, presumably his bedroom, leaving me to follow.

Stumbling inside and shutting the door to keep Nova out, my jaw drops, taking in the space before me. It looks like I've walked into a dungeon. The entire back wall facing me is painted black. In front of the wall is his *massive* four-post, king-size bed. It's medieval style, tall—nearly as tall as the ceilings—and made of dark wood. There's a built-in shelf above the headboard, tall enough that it wouldn't bother you if you were sitting up, that's holding black and red candles, all various levels of melted down. Unlit. The bedding is crimson and black, and in front of the bed is a black leather chest full of God knows what.

My gaze slides anxiously from the bed to where he's standing in front of a dresser made from the same wood as the bedframe. His grin is depraved and full of mischief, dimples poking out, only adding to his sex appeal. Reaching a hand behind his head, he pulls his shirt off, letting it fall to the floor beside him. His entire chest is covered in ink, all black and shade, and he has two tiny bars running through his nipples.

His body is *cut*. Sharp, defined lines, deep divots making up his eight-pack, and the V that disappears behind his pants leaves little to the imagination. My mouth waters as I take him in.

"Get undressed, *cariño*." His instruction snaps my gaze back up to his face as I swallow around the lump in my throat. When I make no attempt to move, he growls, "Don't make me tell you again."

With shaky fingers and trembling limbs, I pull my shirt off before pushing my sweats down until they pool around my ankles. Kicking them off to the side, I clasp my fingers in front of me, feeling insanely awkward as I stand here waiting for the next order from the dungeon master.

He quirks a brow at me. "Those, too. Off." He indicates to my black boxer briefs. I shuck them down, despite him still wearing pants. He drags his greedy gaze down my body until he lands on my cock, which is jutting out, hard as a rock. The urge to cover myself is strong, but I ignore it.

I'm confident in what I have, despite the feelings of nervousness rushing through me now.

Seeming satisfied with what he sees, he tips his head in the direction of the bed. "Climb on up, boy." He strolls over at the same time, holding a lighter to the candles. I don't know if he's setting the mood or what, but I've never had a hook-up light candles for me before.

It's kind of unnerving.

"Let's get a few things out of the way," Mateo states, pinning me with a hard stare. "Communication is important, especially during something like this. If you're, at any point, feeling overwhelmed and you need me to slow things down, you say *yellow*. And if, at any point, you need me to stop, you say *red*. Am I making myself clear?"

Safe words? Why the hell would we need safe words?

"When I ask you a question, I expect an answer."

I nod, stunned silent.

"I need to hear you say it, *cariño*."

Licking my lips in an attempt to wet my severely dry mouth, I mutter, "Y-yellow means slow, red m-means stop. I got it."

"Good boy," he mutters. I hate the appreciative twitch my cock does at those two words.

Next, he opens the chest, tossing various leather straps onto the bed as my pulse goes into overdrive. "What the fuck are those for?"

Instead of answering me, he stands, rounding the bed on my left side. He grabs one of the straps before running a large, hot hand up my calf. He squeezes, raking his nails down the flesh, then wraps the strap around my ankle and connects it to the bed. Effectively restraining me.

"Uh, no," I sputter. "You aren't tying me to your bed, Mateo."

He smirks, tightening the strap. "Say my name like that again, *cariño*. It turns me on when you're all growly."

"Fuck off. I'm serious. You're not tying me up."

"Yes, I am." He arches a brow as if he's challenging me to defy him. "*My. Rules.* Otherwise, you know your safe words."

Not waiting around to see if I'm going to argue with him, he does the same to my hand before moving around to the right side of the bed and doing the same over there. When he's done, I'm starfished across his bed, completely exposed.

Yet, despite how insanely vulnerable I feel, my cock is still throbbing and leaking a puddle all over my stomach. I don't think I've ever wanted someone to touch me so badly in my life.

Mateo crosses the room and grabs something off his dresser before walking over to the light switch by the door, flipping it off. At the same time they turn off, red LED lights illuminate the room. He must have strip lights along the floorboards and underneath the bed. Between those and the candles, the entire room is glowing in an erotic red.

Next, he pulls his phone from his pocket. The sensual beat

of *Chills* by Mickey Valen and Joey Myron reverberates through speakers placed around the room that I can't see. Grabbing something out of his back pocket, he tosses it bedside me—a bottle of some sort—before shoving his pants down and climbing on the bed, still sporting his red briefs.

Clearly, that's his favorite color.

He positions himself between my *wide fucking open* legs, uncapping the mystery bottle. For a minute, I think it's lube until he pours a generous amount onto my left thigh. *Massage oil.* A pineapple aroma floats up, meeting my senses as he begins rubbing it in. His touch is firm as he runs his hands up and down, dipping underneath my leg to spread the oil back there. When he applies pressure behind my knee, it feels like a direct line to my groin. My cock drips, and I bite down on my bottom lip to stifle a groan.

Moving on, he switches legs, focusing on my right. This is sensual as fuck, despite him never actually touching me anywhere sexual. He takes his time, ensuring he gets every inch of my legs before moving to my abdomen. Straddling my lower thighs, he's careful not to graze my cock, and I know he's taking sick satisfaction in watching me squirm. He pours a small amount onto my chest, setting the bottle beside us before working the oil into my skin.

His face is completely unreadable. If it weren't for his endlessly dark, blown-out eyes, I would think he was totally unaffected. The air in the room is thick, the constant eye contact between us heady. Every sense, every nerve ending in my body, feels like they've finally come alive. It's visceral, the way he's making me feel.

His fingers circle my nipple at the same time, tweaking and making me cry out. That has his eyes darkening even further, hips rolling on top of me, the very tip of his erection brushing against mine. My eyes roll back at the feel of him.

"You're so pretty, *cariño*." The rough gravel of his voice sends a shiver down my spine as his devilish eyes, sinful and gleaming, devour me. I can't tell if he's being sarcastic or genuine, and right now, I don't think I care. "I bet you bleed pretty. I bet you cry pretty, too." His body towers over mine now, full, cherry red lips brushing against my ear. "And I bet when you're turned inside out and fucking *ruined* for me, you'll be the prettiest fucking mess I've ever tasted."

My entire body is coiled tight, like a hair-trigger ready to explode. I'm desperate for him to stroke me, to fill me up, and I'm almost to the point of begging.

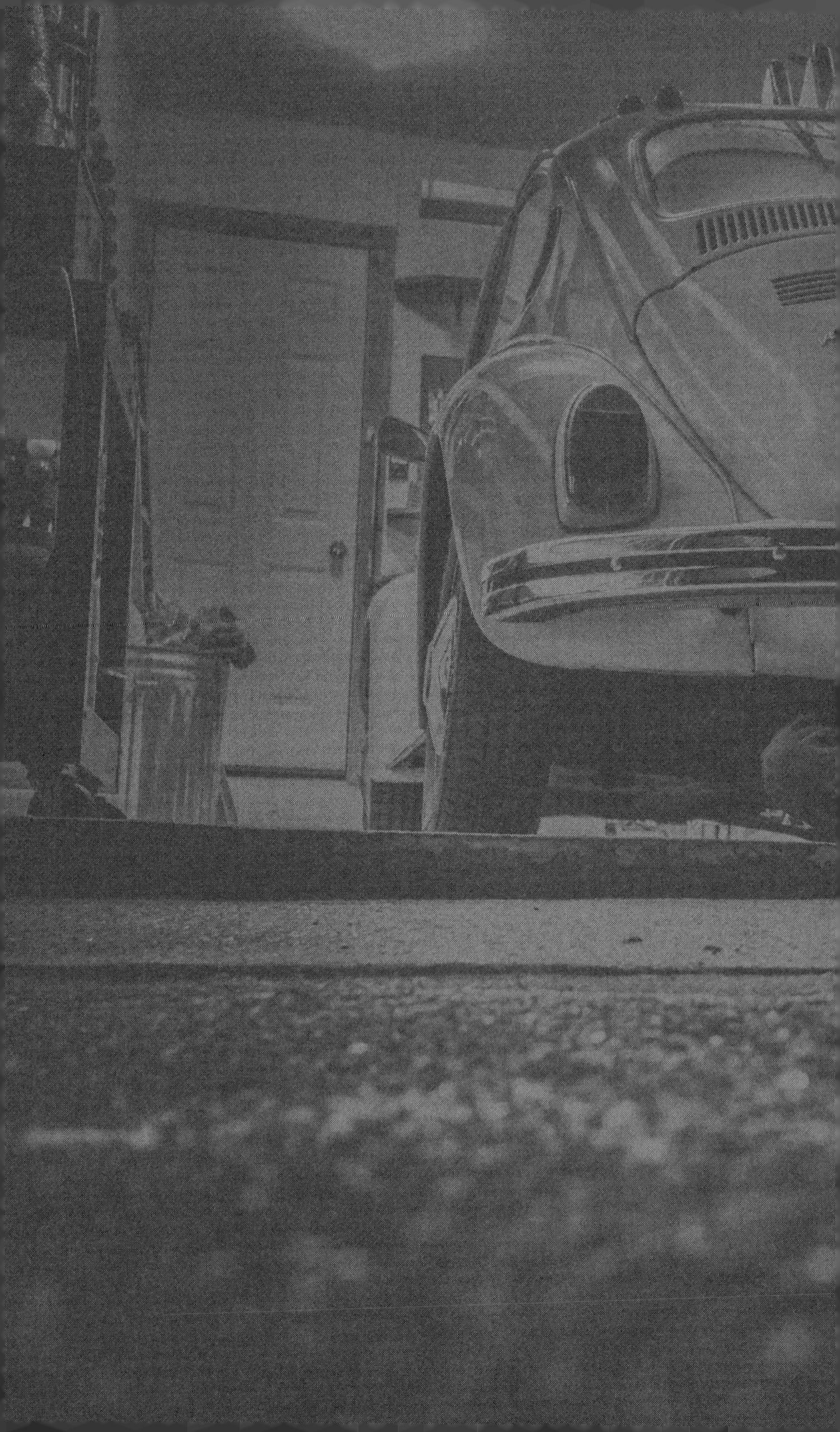

SIXTEN

Mateo

He's putty underneath me. Body eager for release. Just the way I want him.

Terrible Lie by Nine Inch Nails fills the air, accompanied by Travis's breathless pants. Watching him writhe with my hands roaming his body is almost too much, but I don't let it show. I've thought about having him like this since the very moment I laid eyes on him. He's even more stunning than I imagined. His body is beautiful; a pale blank canvas with long limbs and smooth skin. God, he'd look so fucking good marked up by me. Something I plan to do in spades. Leave bruises, cut him open and watch him bleed, have him begging for mercy.

"You like this, *cariño*?" I purr, inching my hands closer to his red, throbbing cock. "Look at how you shake for me, baby." Leaning down, my lips hover over his. "Like a pathetic, needy slut," I spit out, flicking my tongue inside his mouth before sitting back.

Baring his teeth, he shakes his arms, testing the straps.

"Fuck you," he grits, I'm sure wanting to appear angry and volatile, but between his heaving chest and his pitch-black eyes, I see right through the act.

"You want me to touch your cock?" My fingers walk along his pubic line, his stomach dipping, ab muscles tensing. He glares at me, a sadistic laugh bubbling out of me at the sight. "Beg me, cariño. Beg me to wrap my oiled up, slick palm around your throbbing cock. Beg me to slide my fist up and down, *up and down*, while you lose your mind. Or better yet... beg me to fill up your tight little cunt while you cry out my name."

His eyes turn into angry slits as he tugs on the restraints again. "Fuck you," he repeats. "Take these fucking things off me, asshole. I'm not begging you for shit."

A grin slides onto my face that I'm positive looks demonic as I lean forward, left arm resting beside his head, while my right cracks down sharply against his cheek before gripping his face in my palm.

His blue eyes go wide as he stares at me, stunned silent.

"We're gonna have to teach you some manners, *cariño*." I rub the affected cheek while simultaneously rolling my hips into his, causing him to groan. "But don't worry, baby. I can be patient."

Prisoner by Raphael Lake, Aaron Levy, and Daniel Ryan Murphy filters through the speakers. The bass thumps sensually as I climb off the bed, never taking my eyes off Travis while I push open the chest, pulling out more fun toys he's probably going to have a conniption about.

He really does look so damn *beautiful* right now, helpless and immobile, spread wide open, giving me a delicious view of everything I plan to destroy by the end of the night. His skin is pulled taut and flushed pink, beads of sweat glistening under the glow of the red lights. My teeth ache to sink into his perfect complexation, marking him for anyone to see. Marking him as *mine*, because if he thinks this is truly just tonight, he's got another thing coming.

Wild, cautious eyes track my every move as I climb back on the bed and position myself over his thighs again. His cock ruts out at my proximity, the tip slick with his evident arousal. My mouth waters with an undeniable need to taste him—taste how much he wants me, how much his body goes against his mind.

Travis glances down at my hands, swallowing hard, his Adam's apple bobbing. "The hell is that?"

"You need to learn to be quiet, *cariño*." Without another word, I lean down, my tongue flicking out against his left nipple. It tightens under my mouth, and when my teeth graze along the sensitive flesh, he gasps, back arching off the bed.

"*Mateo...*" My name is a breathy moan that he probably doesn't even realize slipped off his tongue. My cock twitches at the sound.

Using my teeth to tug just hard enough to bring some pain, I pull back, placing one rubber-tipped clamp on the swollen bud as his eyes fly to mine, lips parting with a hiss. I repeat the same process on the other side before pulling, not so gently, on the metal chain the clamps are connected to, causing his upper half to lift slightly off the bed. When my lips meet his, I feel it everywhere. His tongue slips into my mouth, brushing against mine as I release the chain, letting him fall back onto the bed.

One hand crawls up to his neck, wrapping around and squeezing *just* enough while my other slips between us, taking his silky, hard length in my palm. He's burning hot to touch, whimpering into my mouth as I stroke him. Ripping my lips away, I work my way along his jaw, nipping as I go, until I reach his neck. Flicking my tongue against his earlobe, I can't help the smirk that slides into place as I feel him shiver beneath me, goosebumps popping up on his flesh.

He's *so fucking* responsive. I can't get enough.

I run my thumb over his slit, gathering his precum and smearing it around before bringing it up to my mouth. He watches in rapt silence as I slip it past my lips, sucking it clean. His masculine, salty flavor seeps into my taste buds, and I want *more*. I need to taste more of him. Feel his weight against my tongue. Watch his face go lax from the pleasure *I* bring him.

Needing all of that and more, I slide down his body, positioning myself between his legs as the song switches to *Feel You Out* by Landon Tewers. I wrap my lips around his flared head, running my pierced tongue along the slit. His thighs tremble, breathing labored as he gazes down at me, a fervent type of hunger dancing in his eyes.

He moans softly as I take more of him into my mouth until my nose is brushing against the short blond hairs at the base. The clean, lightly musky scent of him surrounds me, my own cock throbbing painfully. The desire to sink into him, take him, and make him wholly *mine* is strong. Too strong.

But not yet.

I swallow around his length before wrapping one hand around his shaft, bringing the other up to toy with his balls, and hollowing my cheeks. My mouth glides easily up and down his cock, sucking hard, and bringing him closer to the edge. It doesn't take long to feel him swell in my mouth. Removing my hands and mouth from him, I sit back on my haunches, chuckling when I see the annoyance on his face at the loss of an orgasm. His brows pinch tightly together as he narrows his baby blues at me.

"You're such a fucking asshole." He drops his head back,

staring up at the ceiling.

Grabbing the oil from beside me, I uncap it, smiling. "We've already been through this, *cariño*. Get used to it."

Slick fingers find his crack as I use my other hand to spread his cheeks open. He shivers when the tip of my finger presses against his pink, puckered hole, but he bares down, letting me slip right past the muscle into his tight, hot channel. Gasps quickly morph into moans as I work my finger slowly in and out of him, only pausing to add a second digit into the mix.

My fingers crook, grazing that spot inside him that immediately glazes his eyes over. Supple lips part as sexy little cries fall from his mouth. Under the red glow, it's hard to see clearly, but the pink splash staining his neck and cheeks is evident, giving way to how much I'm affecting him.

"Tell me how much you hate me, *cariño*." I slip a third finger into his hole, using my other hand to wrap around his cock, still hard as steel. "Tell me how much you can't fucking stand me, baby, while I have your body trembling with need from only my fingers. *Tell. Me.*"

He says nothing. There's nothing he could say. Not anything truthful, anyway. Sure, he *wants* to hate me. Wants to place his anger somewhere. The thing is, though, he could've told me to stop at any time. But did he? *No.* Because he wants this just as much as I do. The only difference is, I'm not afraid to admit that.

So, he may not *like* me, but his body sure does.

"What's the matter, baby?" I taunt. "Don't like how well I know your body already? Don't like how good I make you feel? Makes it pretty hard to hate me, huh?"

"Fuck you," he growls as he thrusts his hips into my fist.

"Look at you... writhing pathetically on the fingers of a man who fucked what was yours." My fist tightens as I jack him hard. "You're right on the edge, about to come like a little fucking whore for a stranger you claim to fucking hate."

He grits his teeth, but otherwise says nothing.

"You know what, though?" Withdrawing my fingers, I climb up his body until I'm sitting on his chest. "You don't fucking deserve to come. You haven't *earned* it... yet."

My fingers thrust brutally into his mussed-up hair, gripping painfully and yanking his head back until he has no choice but to look at me. With my other hand, I pinch his chin between my thumb and index finger, his lips parting.

"Now, open your fucking mouth," I growl, and much to my surprise, he listens. Leaning closer to his face, the spit falls past my lips, onto his tongue as I let go of his chin, pushing my briefs down. I pump myself a few times before smearing my precum on his lips. His tongue darts out, cleaning the mess immediately.

Pushing past his lips, I shove my cock far enough into his mouth, he gags. Tears spring to his eyes, and *fuck*, it's a heady sight. "That's it, baby," I coo, rolling my hips so I'm fucking his face slowly. "Cry for me, *cariño*. Choke on me."

Both my hands move to cradle the back of his head as I use his hot, wet mouth. His bloodshot eyes peer up at me, and mine down at him, as I watch myself disappear between his swollen, red lips.

"Your mouth feels so good wrapped around me, baby." My palm cracks down on the side of his cheek as I thrust myself deeper, a smirk pulling on my lips as I further taunt him, because I simply can't fucking get enough of his lust-fueled anger. "Almost as good as *he* felt."

He glowers, eyes shifting into thin, angry slits as he yanks on the restraints to no avail. Part of me wonders if he'll try to bite down on my dick. He tries to turn his head, but I tighten my grip, not giving him even an inch of budge.

"I don't think so, *cariño*," My hips snap a little harder, pushing a little deeper, tears streaming steadily out of his eyes now. Reaching behind me, but never taking my eyes off him, I grab the chain connecting the nipple clamps, tugging roughly. He cries out around my cock, eyebrows pinching together in pain. "You're not finished until I say you're finished. Now, *suck me* like you fucking mean it, and maybe I'll consider letting you come."

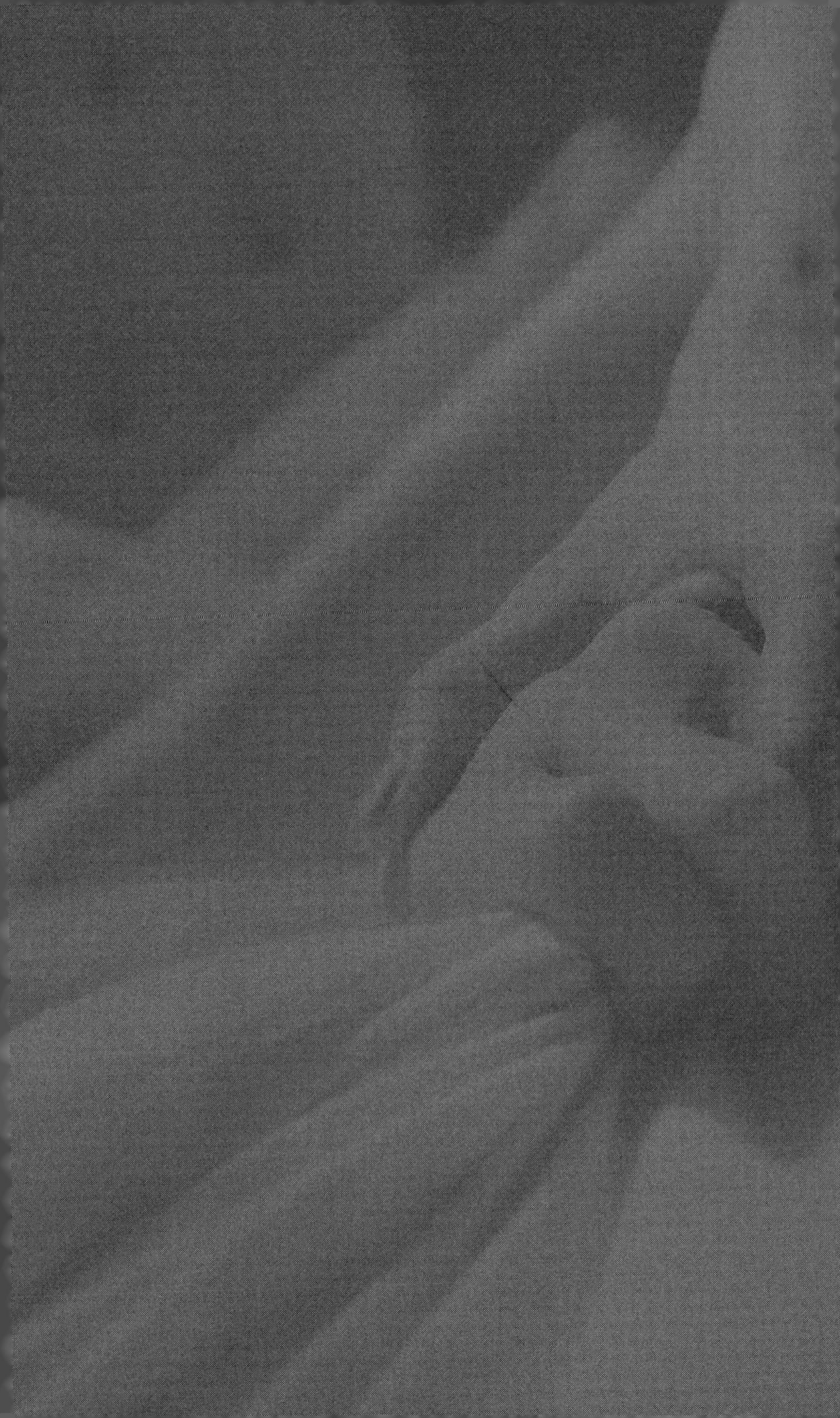

SEVENTEN

Travis

There hasn't ever been a time in my life when I can remember being so unequivocally *pissed off* and turned on at the same time. I'm so fucking horny, I can't think straight. I've been denied *two* orgasms, and now my throat is stuffed full of *him* while my nipples are on fire as he tugs painfully hard on the clamps.

And I want to complain about it. I want to say I hate it.

But I don't. Not even a little bit.

Every sense is doused in Mateo. I see, smell, taste, touch *all* of him. He's lodged so far into my throat, cock so fucking thick it barely fits. Spit is seeping out of the corners of my mouth, eyes watering, nose running. He's everywhere. It's like he knows exactly what I want—what I need—without me even having to tell him. He's the big, gruff, dominating type I love to submit to.

And *Christ*, it's fucking annoying. It would be easier if he was shit in bed. It would make hating him easier. As it is right now, I'd probably do just about anything he asked me to do if it meant he'd put his hands back on my cock again. It's still so hard, it's got its own heartbeat, and I'm restrained, so I can't even touch myself.

The hold he has on the chain has lessened as he continues to pump into my mouth, the pain easily turning into scorching hot pleasure. He tugs gently, the clamps having an unforgiving hold on me, and I can't even help the way my eyes roll back as I moan around him. The throaty, husky sound of *his* moans meets my ears, causing my eyes to snap back open, landing right on him. The sound sends warmth through my already feverish body, and my mind suddenly hyper focuses on getting him to moan like that because of *me* again.

His gaze on me, from where he is towering over me, makes my blood pump harder in my veins, sending my nerve endings blazing. Under the red glow, his eyes appear black as he watches me suck his cock. His lips are parted, the silver of his tongue ring glinting in the candlelight. The tendons in his neck are pulled taut, chest muscles flexing with each brutal thrust.

"*Fuck*, you look so good taking my cock. Such a *good fucking boy.*" His brows pinch together, teeth biting down on his bottom lip. He wraps a hand snug around my throat, squeezing enough to cut off some of my air supply as his huge cock cuts off the rest. "I wanna come down your throat, make you swallow me down while you fight for air."

His words shouldn't turn me on, shouldn't saturate my veins with a salacious need I don't quite understand, but they do.

"But this time..." he says, his voice strained as he continues to pump into me. "This time I want to fill your *tight fucking cunt* with my cum until it's dripping out of you, and you're nothing more than a *sloppy. Fucking. Slut.*"

He pulls his cock out of my mouth, leaning down to crash

his lips against mine, tongue diving in mercilessly. It's quick and messy, and when it's over, he cranks my head toward him as he growls into my ear, sending a wicked chill down my spine. "*My* slut."

I don't know which part I should be more concerned about; the "*this time*" part, indicating he thinks there will be a *next time*, the "*my* slut" part, or the part where he just assumes I'm a bottom—that there'd be no way someone like *me* would do the fucking. But as he positions himself between my legs, the realization hits me that I'm too fucking gone to care. The shame and regret will probably hit later, but that's future Travis's problem.

This is the first time I'm getting a good look at Mateo's cock, and *fuckkk* me, it's nice. It's dark and thick—*so* fucking thick—and his glistening tip pokes out from his foreskin. He's bigger than me, by at least a couple of inches, and I know with absolute certainty, he's going to fill me so fucking good.

He grabs the bottle of oil from the bed, pouring some in his hand before slathering it along his shaft. When his cock is lubed up enough, he brings slick fingers to my hole, pushing a thick digit past the tight muscle, a hiss escaping me at the intrusion. He wastes no time working a second finger in, grazing my prostate as he works me open.

"I'm going to fuck you now," he purrs. "You're gonna take *every. Single. Inch*, and you're going to thank me for it when I'm done. You'll beg me for more."

With his face cast in shadows, under the red glow of the candles, he looks like Satan himself. Like he crawled his way from beneath the crust of the earth to break me down and tear me apart. Trepidation buries itself deep in my gut as I swallow over the unease balling up in my throat. Letting him fuck me is a *bad* idea.

I know it is.

But as he grabs my thigh in a bruising hold, lining himself up, I don't stop him.

I don't want to.

And when he pushes inside, filling me fuller than I've ever felt, all logical reasoning as to why this is a terrible idea vanishes. The ache as he stretches me is overwhelming, my chest rumbling with a low groan as he pumps in and out of me, giving me no time to adjust.

I'd expect nothing less from him.

"*Fuck, cariño...*" The blunt tips of his nails dig into the meaty flesh of my thigh, the bite of pain only adding to the full feeling of his cock in me. "Your pussy's so *tight*, baby. You feel so *good.*"

My face heats at his fucked-up praise. I desperately wish he'd touch me, stroke me.

He pulls all the way out before reaching up and gripping my chest, slamming back into my ass hard enough to knock the wind out of my lungs.

"*Fuck,*" I moan, wishing I had my hands to wrap around him.

"You like this, *cariño?*" His nails dig in deeper. I know he's going to draw blood soon, but I love it. The pain mixed with the pleasure, it's euphoric. "You like the way my cock makes you feel?"

Words are lost on me. I can do nothing more than nod my head feverishly, breathless moans falling off my lips as he plows into me at a vicious pace. My head's light, body trembling. There's an inferno flowing through my veins, my mind and body at war with each other.

"T-take... take these off." My arms yank on the straps

restraining me to the posts on his bed. They've gone numb. "P-please."

His fingernails rake down my chest, beads of blood popping up in their wake. Hissing through gritted teeth, I watch as his gaze zeroes in on the mess he's made. His near black eyes flit up to mine, a menacing smirk on his face. "Look at you bleed for me, *cariño*. So beautiful... so *delicate*."

Leaning down, he runs the flat of his tongue along the length of one of the cuts, a deep groan rumbling from his chest. I can feel the vibrations pouring into mine. The way he looks—hair hanging in his eyes, dark gaze locked on mine, as he laps up the blood on my pec from the gash *he* created—is driving me wild. It's too much. It's monstrous and lewd. And I can't get enough of it.

"Mateo," I whisper breathlessly. "Take these off, please. I need to touch you." The words leave my lips on a plea, and whatever he sees in my gaze is enough, because the next second, he's reaching up, undoing the leather strap, and letting my arm fall before moving to do the same to the other. "My feet. Get those, too."

As soon as I'm free of all restraints, without a second thought, I grab his face, pressing his lips to mine. He moans into my mouth as he slips his tongue inside, the metallic taste of copper heavy, rolling his hips harder into me at the same time. *The Death of Peace of Mind* by Bad Omens is the background noise to the clashing of our bodies, sweaty and slick.

He burrows his face into my neck, nipping and sucking all over. I'm going to look like a crime scene by the time this is over, but I don't care. I flip us, so I'm on top of him. He grabs hold of my hips, nails biting into the skin as I grind on his lap. The position makes my eyes roll back as it pegs that sweet spot inside me over and over.

"Fuck... *fuck*, I'm close," I breathe. One hand wraps around my cock while my other one stays planted on his chest, holding me up. "I have to come! Please, *please*... have to come."

Before I even process what's happening, he's flipped us again, him towering over me as he grips the headboard with both hands. The cords of his muscles protrude on his forearms, sweat dripping from his forehead as he slams into me with malice. His teeth are bared, the wild look in his eyes purely animalistic as he pushes us closer to the edge.

I pump myself in time with him, wrapping one hand around his thick, tattooed arm. I'm so, *so* close, I can feel the heat building at the base of my spine. "I'm... fuck, I'm gonna come!"

With one hand still gripping the headboard, he wraps the other around my throat, squeezing and cutting off my air supply. It sends me over the cliff. Jaw slack and my eyes rolled back, I cry out, despite no sound escaping, as my cock pumps out thick ropes, coating my chest in my release. My head swims, lungs aching with a need to fill, but the wanton desire coursing through my body in waves is unparalleled.

When he finally releases me, I drag in gulps of air, my hands flying up to thread through my hair. With two thick fingers, he runs them through my release, shoving them into my mouth. The salty flavor of myself paired with the way his fingers taste is enough to make me come again.

Mateo's movements start to get jerky, and I know he's close. I'm suddenly desperate to watch him come undone with my name on his tongue when he does.

"Say my name," I beg. My legs wrap around him as he drops his face near mine. "Say my name when you come. My *real* name."

He takes my lips in a bruising kiss, unadulterated need pouring into me as he thrusts his tongue into my mouth. With his forehead rested on mine, his dark, hooded gaze locks on mine. "I'm gonna come," he pants. "Travis... *fuck*, I'm coming. *Travis... cariño...*" He stills, emptying himself inside me. I'm all too aware that he's inside me raw right now... something I *never* do.

Resting on top of me for a few minutes, he finally pulls out, removes the clamps from my nipples, and rolls off me. Now that the moment is over, I'm left feeling incredibly awkward. Like I should go home... but I *can't*. He saunters into the bathroom, coming out a moment later with a washcloth. Sitting on the edge of the bed, he lifts my leg slightly, bringing the warm, wet cloth to my hole and cleaning me up.

The gesture is soft and unexpected, but during all of this, we never make eye contact. I can't tell who's avoiding it more, me or him.

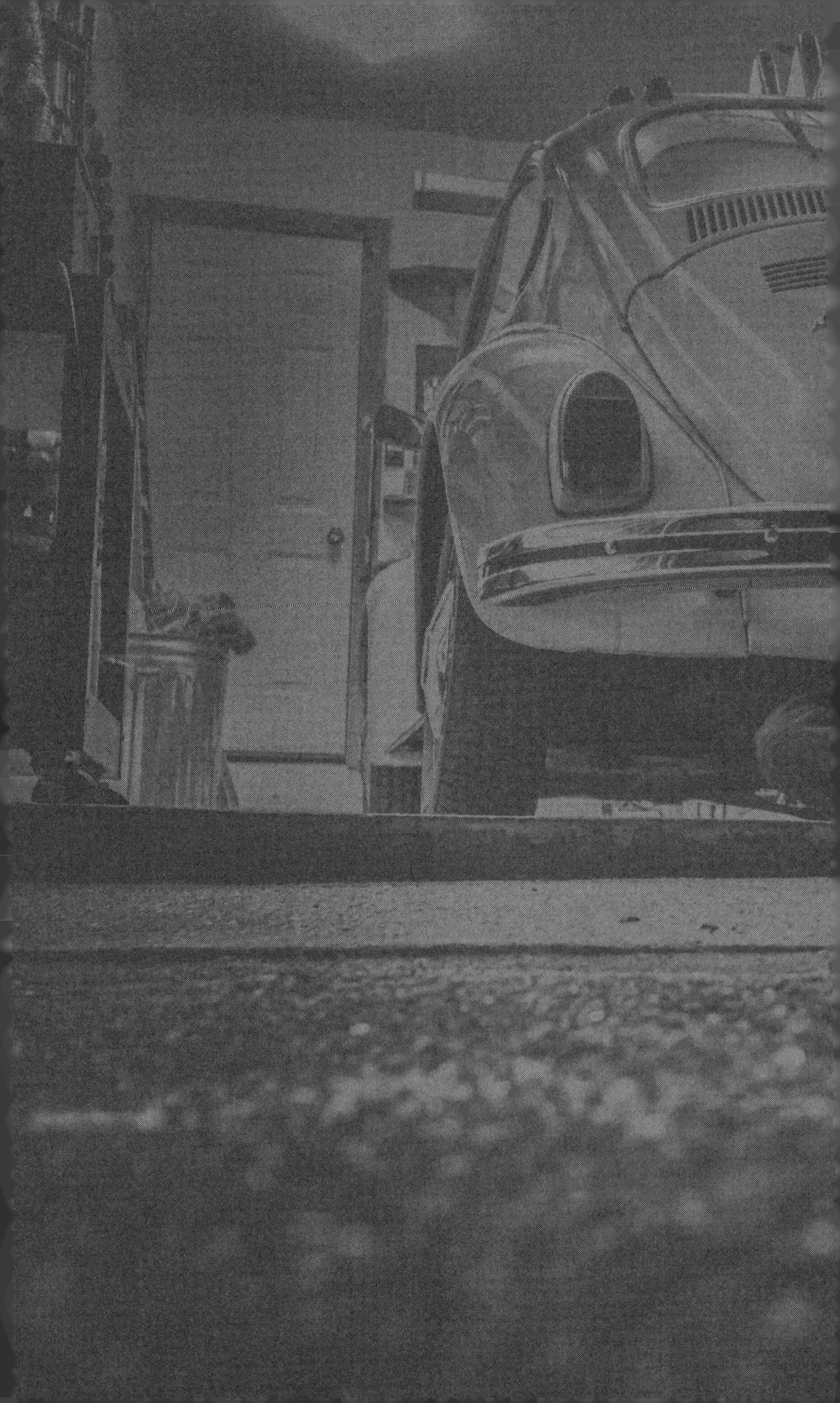

EIGHTEN

Mateo

After I cleaned us up last night, I got Nova some more water and dished up the leftover chicken before climbing into bed. Travis was already passed out by the time I got back, and he drifted onto my side of the bed throughout the night, curling up next to me and nuzzling his face into my neck. He probably doesn't even know he did it. I'm up—wide awake—before he is. Flashes of last night come back in heavy waves, crashing into me, causing all the blood in my body to fly south. Travis bared to me. Restrained. So, so fucking needy. The way he was so compliant, so eager, so willing to bend to my will. It was the hottest sex I've had in too long.

I wasn't always so aggressive in the bedroom. As a teenager, and even in my early twenties, I was pretty timid. Too shy to voice what I really wanted. I was never ashamed of my sexuality, despite my father's attempt to do just that, but I think a part of me was afraid to give life to those desires in my head—the ones that needed *more*. More than soft and sweet. More than vanilla.

Not that there's anything wrong with vanilla, it's just not the flavor for me. And ironically, it took me leaving a really shitty relationship, where I often felt inferior, to finally find my voice, and discover my true likes in the bedroom. It's how I started to crave control in the bedroom, and I've never looked back.

Glancing to my left, he's sound asleep, lips parted as soft snores reach my ears. Blond hair that's wild and tousled sticks up every which way. My eyes dip lower to his bare chest. He didn't put a shirt on before falling asleep, so his creamy complexion, marred only slightly by the nail scratches and bite marks *I* gave him is on display.

Reaching below the covers, I palm myself over my briefs, squeezing myself almost to the point of pain. This erection needs to go away. I know full well I shouldn't act on any of the desire coursing through my blood.

I shouldn't.

But I'm going to.

Scooting a little closer, careful not to disturb him *yet*, I place my hand on his firm stomach, trailing my hand lower until it slips under the covers. My fingers curl around the thick ridge of his cock, a smirk sliding into place when I find him already hard.

Wonder what he's dreaming about behind those fluttering eyelids.

Making myself as light as can be, I shimmy down the bed until I'm almost eye level with his hips. He stirs a little, letting out a sleepy sigh, and as if his body can sense what I want to do, he shifts over until his front is turned ever so slightly toward me, giving me better access.

Slipping my fingers under the waistband of his boxers, I shove them down enough to let his beautiful cock spring free, my own twitching behind the confines of cotton. The pretty pink tip glistens as the sunlight beams in from the open window. Using the flat of my tongue, I swipe up the precum leaking from his slit as his hips thrust up a little. I glance up at him, seeing he's still sleeping.

I close my lips around the flared head, flicking my tongue gently along the underside. He tastes faintly like the pineapple oil I used on him last night and a mouthwatering musk that's all him. It's intoxicating. Hollowing my cheeks, I mold my tongue around him, sucking hard as he stirs a little more. His hand absently reaches for *something*—if I had to guess, probably his cock—but when his fingers thread into my hair, I feel his body jerk as he lifts himself onto his elbows. With him still in my mouth, I peer up at him from beneath my lashes. He moans softly when I twirl my tongue, and when he speaks, it's thick and raspy from sleep.

"That goddamn tongue ring." Grabbing a fistful of my hair, he shoves me farther down until there's nothing more for me to take. "*God*," he groans, deep and low. "It was only supposed to be one time."

I pull off him, a smirk tugging on my wet lips as I replace my mouth with my hand, pumping him hard and slow. "Come on, *cariño*. You didn't *really* believe that, did you?"

He grumbles, as if it physically pains him to be unable to deny himself me. Bright blue eyes gaze at me while he watches his cock disappear into my mouth. He bites down on his bottom lip, the act causing my nuts to ache. "Fine," he finally mutters. "But once the snow clears, that's it. I mean it."

That's what he thinks. He's fucking out of his mind if he thinks I'm walking away after getting a taste of this.

Chuckling, I tell him, "Sure, whatever you say. You're not

getting rid of me that easily, boy."

He huffs, lying flat on his back. "Now, come fuck me already."

Shit, you don't gotta ask me twice.

I roll over, sliding off the bed, and open the chest in front. Rummaging through the junk in there, I grab the bottle of lube. As soon as I drop the bottle onto the bed, I get rid of my briefs, letting them pool on the floor as I climb back over him. He's already gotten himself completely naked, his heavy eyes watching me as he runs his closed fist up and down his shaft.

Positioning myself between his spread thighs, I slather my cock, drinking all of him in. "Need me to fill you up again, *cariño*?" My words are taunting as he chews on his bottom lip some more. "Pull your legs back for me, baby. Let me see that pretty pink pussy."

His face flames as he averts his gaze, sliding his hands behind his knees and pulling them toward his chest. I don't know why Travis being shy is so endearing, but it is. Makes me think of all the ways I can corrupt him and push him out of his comfort zone.

My oiled-up finger drops to his hole, slipping inside with ease. We didn't shower last night, and he's still slick with my cum and worked open from that. "You're so wet for me already, baby."

"Oh, *my God*," he groans, tossing his head back. "You're so fucking vulgar. Must you say shit like that to me?"

Throwing my head back, a deep belly laugh rumbles out of me. Gripping myself at the base, I line myself up. "What's the matter, *cariño*?" I sink into him in one go, his eyes widening as he fists my sheets, a cry falling off his lips. "You don't want to hear how tight your little cunt is wrapped around my cock? How you're still wearing my cum from last night, and how I can feel me inside you with every thrust?"

His hands fly up, covering his face as he grumbles incoherently. Glancing down, I'm mesmerized as I watch my dick be swallowed by his tight fucking hole. It's such a beautiful sight to see. It's rimmed red and still slightly swollen from last night, stretched wide to adjust to me, and he takes me *so well*.

My hand wraps around the back of his thigh, pushing until it's practically resting on his chest, my other hand planted beside his head as I fuck into him hard. When he finally removes the hands from his face, he looks so fucking gone. His pupils devour his irises as he gazes up at me, brows pinched tight, and jaw slack.

"Your cock feels *amazing*." His words come out breathless, and it's like music to my ears.

When he wraps a tight fist around himself, a growl tears its way up my throat as I slap it away, replacing it with mine. Jacking him firm and fast, I ask him, "You wanna come, baby?"

"Yes... *yes,* please."

Molten lava pools in my groin with an overwhelming urge to come, but I stave it off, wanting him to go first. "Come, then," I grit out. "Milk my cock, *cariño*. Put that hole to use."

He spills onto my hand, his eyes slamming shut, lips parting as the most beautiful moan rolls out of him. That's all it takes for me to follow right behind him, a shudder tearing through me as I empty deep inside him.

Pulling out, I revel in the way my cum drips out of him. It's *filthy*. He pulls the covers over him as I climb out of bed, heading to the bathroom for a rag. Like last time, I clean him up, then me. He watches me while I do it, an unreadable expression on his face.

I swat at his ass once I'm finished. "C'mon. Time for a shower." Heading toward the door, his voice stops me in my tracks.

"What?" he scoffs.

Making sure to wipe the grin off my face, I turn to face him. "You know... shower. Shampoo, body wash. Get clean?"

Not giving him any more time to protest, I spin back around and walk into the en-suite. After turning the water on, I grab two plush deep red towels out of the closet, setting them outside the shower. Finally, after a few minutes of me wondering if he's going to ignore me altogether, he pads into the bathroom, barefoot and still naked, looking less than amused with me.

I chuckle, reaching over to pinch his cheek. "Aw, cheer up, *cariño*. You're always so serious. Maybe you could keep a man if you let loose every once in a while."

His face screws up. "Fuck you, Mateo. God, you're such a fucking—"

"Asshole," I finish for him, deadpan. While I can admit, I haven't exactly been forthcoming with the truth about Nathaniel, and my lack of knowledge that Travis even existed, he hasn't exactly made any effort to hear my side either, choosing to judge without all the facts. It's something I didn't expect to annoy me so much, which makes fucking with him that much more fun. The thought of telling him *has* crossed my mind, but ultimately, I've decided against it.

At least for now.

For one, there's like a ninety-nine percent chance he wouldn't believe me anyway, so what's the point? And for two, hate sex is fucking phenomenal, the best there is, and as much as Travis insists that was an isolated incident, I very much plan on continuing to fuck him. Even though I don't know Travis *that* well, I know him enough to know if he found out, it would naturally soften his opinion of me, thus taking away the *hate* in hate sex.

All in all, it's better if he continues to think he hates me.

"Get in before my patience wears thin, and I beat your ass raw with a paddle to teach you a lesson."

His eyes darken at the same time he rears back, like he doesn't know if he should be turned on or offended by that. Regardless, he steps under the stream, with me following. The hot water feels exceptional on my tired and achy muscles, and it's an added bonus that he looks fucking delectable, dripping wet in front of me.

With his hands clasped in front of him, shoulders hunched over, unease radiates off him. He picks the weirdest times to be awkward. I can be three fingers deep in his ass while he's restrained to my bed posts, but a shower is too much?

"Turn around," I instruct him as I reach for the shampoo bottle.

Narrowing his eyes, he glances down at my hands before dragging his gaze back up to meet mine. "Why?"

I roll my eyes. "Can you just do what you're fucking told?"

Still look skeptical, he purses his lips, slowly spinning until I'm left with a fantastic view of his tight ass. I have to resist the urge to bend down and bite a chunk out of it.

Closing the distance between us, I set the bottle down before lathering my hands up, bringing them up to his scalp. His whole body stiffens the moment my fingers slide into the strands, and I have to hold back a laugh.

"Why are you washing my hair? You don't need to wash my—"

"*Fuck*," I groan. "You're *impossible*. Will you please shut the fuck up and let me take care of you for five fucking minutes. Then you can go back to hating me after."

He huffs his annoyance, but says nothing else as I get to work, massaging his scalp and cleaning his hair. Eventually, he relaxes, his head lolling back, eyes closed. After I'm done with hair, I move on to his body, which makes him stiffen all over again, but in a completely different way. I drop to my knees to get his legs and feet, his cock jutting out in front of my face, taunting me. His cheeks are bright pink as he gazes down at me, lip pulled between his teeth.

Standing back at my full height, I bring my hand to his stiff length, washing the one area left. His bright blue eyes flutter closed, a content sigh coming from him as I half stroke, half wash. I pull away, letting him rinse the suds off on his own, putting a little bit of space between us. We *just* had sex; there's no reason why I'd need to take him again so soon. But the erection I'm sporting would disagree.

That's nuts.

Once I'm done with him, I tell him where he can find a change of clothes, and he gets out, letting me wash myself. Alone with my thoughts, I'm not quite sure what to make of this *situation* I've gotten us into. I'm no stranger to casual hookups, nor am I a stranger to the type of aftercare that is needed afterwards with my tastes. But I can't help but notice how different this feels than it usually does. Normally, this part feels like a *going through the motions* type thing, where I can remain pretty detached. This, though… I don't know what I'm feeling, but it's certainly not that. All I know for sure is I wouldn't mind one bit if this storm kept on for a few more days…

NINETEEN
Travis

T he last twenty-four hours have been… interesting, to say the least. Mateo is *infuriating*, and even more so since he can work my body over like a puppeteer and I'm his marionette. I need the snow to melt *now*, so I can get a locksmith here and I can go home. Being in his proximity is fucking with my head.

He's a smug bastard, and no matter how good he makes my body feel, I can't get the image out of my head of him railing Nathaniel, and the cocky look on his face when I caught them. Like he found great satisfaction in ruining a relationship. And I know, I know, Nathaniel is more to blame than Mateo, but it isn't Nathaniel I'm trapped in this house with, forced to spend dreadful time with. So, it's much easier to place my anger with Mateo at the moment.

Now, I'm standing in his room, freshly fucked *and* showered, wearing *his* clothes, staring out the window at the winter fucking wonderland happening outside. The snow has at least stopped, but none of it seems to be melting. Who fucking knows how much longer I'm going to be trapped here. The sun needs to come out and wipe this shit away, and fast.

I don't even know how much time has passed since I've been standing in here. I vaguely heard Mateo come in and get dressed before leaving the room. Thankfully, he didn't say anything to me, and just let me be. That shower was *too much*. The way he washed my hair with delicate fingers, and scrubbed my body down, making sure to take his time and get every single inch of flesh. *God*, it felt so fucking good, and he knew it too with the way my cock bobbed in front of his unreadable face.

The aroma of something I can't quite place meets my senses. It's food of some sort, and my stomach grumbles as I smell it, reminding me that I haven't eaten in far too long. Another inconvenience due to this goddamn snowstorm from hell. After contemplating starving myself in favor of hiding out in this room for as long as I can, I decide food is more important to me than holing up, so I begrudgingly pad out to the living room, where I see Mateo in the kitchen, *Neon Grave* by Dayseeker playing softly, while he cooks… something. I'm still not sure what. The faint earthy scent of marijuana mixes with whatever he's cooking, letting me know he probably smoked while I was getting dressed.

At the sound of my bare feet on the hardwood, he glances up, his usual unreadable expression plastered on his face. "You finally decided to come out," he deadpans.

Deciding to ignore his statement, I sit down on the stool at the bar. "What are you making?"

"Breakfast burritos and hash browns. I took your dog to use the bathroom downstairs a minute ago. She does not like the snow. And I got her some more chicken." He doesn't look up from his frying pan as he speaks to me. "How do you take your coffee?"

I hate the flutter in my stomach that comes from hearing him take care of Nova. It's such a small gesture, but he didn't have to do it. Hell, he didn't even have to let us in his house at all.

"I don't." When he snaps his head up to look over at me, I clear my throat. "Uh, I mean, I don't like coffee. Water is fine."

"Are you a child? Who doesn't like coffee?"

Scoffing, I reply, "No, I'm not a fucking child. It just tastes like shit, asshole."

When he smirks, his teeth practically sparkle and his dimples poke out, and I have to look away for fear of my stupid knees giving out on me. He has no goddamn right to be *that* gorgeous.

He points the spatula in my direction and chuckles. "God, you're hot when you're feisty."

"Fuck off," I growl.

Clutching his chest, he bows his head. "I'm hurt. So hurt."

"You're fucking ridiculous." I roll my eyes, turning to walk toward the couch.

"You'll love it one day," he quips.

"Doubtful." I try my best to keep my tone neutral, but I don't miss the way he's insinuated more than once that this won't be the only time between us. Glancing to my right, the sun is finally shining through his giant open window. "Can I use your phone?" I ask him, wanting to try the locksmith again.

"It's on the counter."

When I reach the counter, he grabs the phone, pulling it toward him, throwing me a shit-eating grin. "You can use the phone on one condition." He arches a brow while he waits to see what I say back.

He's so fucking annoying. Making a show of dramatically rolling my eyes, I cross my arms over my chest. "And what's that?"

Tapping his index finger to his lips twice, he says, "Give me a kiss."

A laugh claws its way up my throat. "Ain't no fucking way."

He shrugs, pocketing the phone, returning to cooking. "Then no phone."

"Mateo, *come on*. I need to call a locksmith and get home."

"Then kiss me, baby." He peers at me from under his lashes. "It's not like you haven't had my whole ass cock in your mouth already. One kiss, one phone call."

Amusement dances in his eyes as I narrow mine at him before throwing my arms in the air, groaning loud enough that you could probably hear it from my apartment. "You're so fucking *impossible*." Rounding the bar, I hold out my hand. "Fine. *One* kiss."

I lean in, lips puckered, but he backs up. "Ah-ah," he says in a chastising way. "A real fucking kiss, *guapo*."

Cool. Another fucking word I don't know the meaning of.

"Whatever," I mumble. "Let's get this over with so I can make the damn call already."

A faint smirk ghosts his face as he wraps his hand around my neck, pulling me into him. His eyes dip down to my mouth as his pink, pierced tongue glides across his full, red lips before his gaze connects with mine again. My heart hammers behind my breastbone, blood roaring in my ears as his lips press down on mine.

Mint toothpaste with a shadow of sweet marijuana comes to life when his tongue slips past my parted lips, dipping into my mouth and licking all over. A moan falls from me without my permission, the sound causing him to growl into my mouth as his fingers tighten ever so slightly on either side of my esophagus. The feel of the ring through his tongue as it tangles with mine causes my body to warm all over from the memory of that same barbell dragging along the underside of my cock.

The kiss lasts less than a minute, but when we pull apart, my head feels light and woozy. I don't understand how he affects me so much. It's maddening.

Handing me the phone, he smirks. "See, was that so hard?"

"Yes," I huff, walking away as I look up a locksmith. It rings a few times, and much to my surprise, they answer.

"Jefferson Locksmith. How can I help you?"

I have to force myself to not jump with excitement. "Yes, hi. I'm locked out of my apartment. I live on 35th and Freely. Are you able to get out this way and help me?"

"I can send someone out, but it'll be at least an hour till they can get there. What's the address and your phone number?"

"It's 3542 Freely Place, and 555-435-7640."

"Alri—"

"Oh, wait!" I cut him off, realizing I gave him *my* phone number, which I don't have. Turning to face Mateo, I ask him, "What's your phone number to give to this guy?"

Not even looking up from what he's doing, he says, "555-230-6557."

Repeating it back to the guy, he assures me someone will be out within the next hour to hour and a half. The relief I feel hanging up that phone is insane. I can't wait to be back in my own house, and away from Mateo and his devil dick.

Speaking of Satan, as soon as I lock his phone, he's strolling over to me with a plate full of burritos that smell divine and a giant glass of ice water. "Eat up." Shoving it into my chest, he walks back to the bar to dive into his own.

We eat in silence, the only noise coming from the speaker currently playing *Vertebrae* by Allistair and Spencer Kane—

one of my favorite songs. Which further annoys me.

After we finish, he takes my plate and loads everything into his dishwasher. The air's tense, but I think it's just me being awkward. Once he's done, he sits in the chair across from the couch I'm sitting on. His house is decorated nicely, which, for some reason, surprises me.

"So, what do you do for work?" The question catches me off guard. I glance over at him, blinking, but saying nothing for a moment.

"Are we on a fucking date now? What's with the small talk?"

He holds his hands up. "I'm just trying to pass the time. Relax. It's a simple question."

"I work for a marketing firm. Social media marketing for Fortune 500 companies."

"Cool, cool."

This is stupid. "So, you're a mechanic?" I don't know why I phrased it as a question. We both know I know he is.

He nods, thankfully not calling me out for being awkward as fuck. "I work at my uncle's shop in town."

I nod my head, unsure of what to say from here. Small talk is the *last* thing I expected to be doing with him, and that says a lot, considering this entire predicament has been one off-the-wall experience after another.

"How long were you and what's-his-fuck together for?" he asks, breaking our current round of awkward silence.

I can't help but laugh at the question, and this entire situation. "Almost five and a half years."

Mateo's eyes narrow. "Where'd you meet?" He's got both elbows propped on the chair, hands crossed over himself, watching me like I'm a science project he's trying to figure out.

"Why the fuck do you care?" I spit out. "Like seeing what

kind of damage you did to your fucking conquests?"

Face unreadable, he breathes a sigh through his nose. "Where'd you meet?" he repeats, completely ignoring me.

"College," I reply, rolling my eyes. He's really fucking annoying. "We went to Washington State together and met our senior year."

"Did you love him?"

"What kind of fucking question is that?" I scoff. "Of course, I loved him."

"Did you, though?" He sits forward, elbows on his knees. "Or did you just like the idea of him? Of what he *could* be?"

"Fuck off," I bite out. "You don't get to sit there in your ivory fucking tower, psychoanalyzing me and my relationship—a relationship *you* helped destroy, I might add."

"No, I'm serious, Travis." *Travis.* "Five seconds in that guy's presence and I could tell he wasn't shit. Not someone you do long term with. And you, my boy, seem like someone who wants to do long term."

"What the fuck do you know about long term?" I hate how defensive I feel right now, vulnerable, like all my flaws and insecurities are on display where he can see them.

"I'm just saying..." He shrugs. "You deserve someone who wants what you want."

"What? And that's you?" I laugh, immediately feeling dumb for saying that, because why the fuck would I assume he meant him?

"Maybe." His eyes darken, not a smirk in sight on his usually cocky face. His stare is so intense, I have to fight to not squirm underneath it. My mouth dries, and I try to swallow against the lump that's formed in my throat. Suddenly, the air feels thick for an entirely different reason.

Surely, he doesn't mean that. He's just trying to fuck with me... right?

Before I have a chance to respond, a knock sounds at the door, startling me and effectively breaking the bubble we've built. We both stand, watching each other for a moment longer before he turns, heading for the door. With his hand on the knob, he glances behind himself at me. "Don't forget our bet... you owe me, *cariño*."

He pulls the door open a second later, a short, stocky man standing in front of us. "Locksmith?" the man says.

Pulling my gaze away from Mateo, I regain my senses. "Uh, yeah. That's me. It's across the hall."

I follow the man out into the hall, Nova trotting right beside me, as he gets to work. Mateo stays put in his doorway while the man fiddles with mine. It only takes a handful of minutes before the apartment door pops open, and as I'm entering my house, I turn around and glance at Mateo, a signature cocky smirk on his face.

The first thing I do once inside is plug my phone into the charger. When it powers on, I scroll through all my missed notifications. My sister and Xander have sent several, but it's the text from an unknown number that catches my eye and has me opening it before all the others.

Unknown: Soon… we're going out. Don't even think of telling me no. A bet's a bet, cariño.

For a second, I'm confused about how he got my number, and then it hits me… I gave it to the locksmith over the phone. *He memorized my phone number.*

My stomach flutters, and I roll my eyes despite the stupid smile forming on my face. Nothing good is going to come from this. I just know it.

TWENTY

Mateo

It ended up raining overnight. Woke up this morning, and it's like the snowstorm never even happened. Fine by me... I fucking hate the snow anyway. Walking into the shop, I flick on the lights, heading into the office to crank the heat. It's so damn cold in here, I can see my breath in front of my face.

I'm usually always the first one to arrive. Miguel and Benny are slower starters, whereas I like to get up and get moving right away. I've been this way for as long as I can remember. In high school, I'd get up a few hours before school to run and workout. I still do that, but it's too damn cold right now, so I've been pushing it off for later when it warms up. The gym is about a mile from my house, and when it's not literal freezing temperatures outside, it's usually no problem for me to jog there before work.

Stepping into the garage, my eyes find Travis's car, and thoughts from the last few days come rushing back, a smirk sliding into place. The sex with him was some of the best I've had, and I'm antsy for a repeat. Something tells me he isn't going to make it easy, though.

I turn on some music and get to work. Miguel and Benny show up about an hour after I do, and we're all busy enough that we don't get a chance to shoot the shit at all until it's late afternoon, and finally time to eat lunch. We ordered pizza because none of us brought anything, nor did we want to leave to pick anything up.

"So, my neighbor locked himself out of his apartment the day the storm started," I say nonchalantly as I shove another piece of pizza into my mouth.

Miguel drops his slice, knowing gaze meeting mine. "Oh, yeah? Which neighbor?"

"The one across the hall."

"You mean the one who hates you?" Benny asks.

I nod, my smirk growing. "That's the one."

Miguel laughs like he already knows what's coming. "What did you do?"

"I did what any good neighbor would do," I murmur with a shrug. "I invited him in to wait until a locksmith could make it out."

"There's no way he took you up on that," Benny scoffs.

"Oh, but he did." I always feel a sick sense of pride whenever I accomplish something—or someone—either of them thinks I can't. There are very few—if any—things I've set my mind to and have been unable to attain. I get what I want, and people doubting me only makes me want it more.

"Oh, boy," I hear Miguel mumble under his breath as Benny groans. "Do tell."

"It was no big deal," I say nonchalantly. "He came in, used my phone, but the locksmiths were all closed due to the snow. We smoked a little weed, we made a bet." I shrug. "No big deal."

"What was the bet?" The question comes from Miguel, but they're both watching me.

"That I could make him come."

Benny throws his hands in the air, rolling his eyes. Miguel chuckles.

"You fucked him, didn't you?"

Grinning, I say, "Of course, I did."

Miguel steps up, high-fiving me. "That's my boy. How was it?"

Something washes over me at the question. Something like... protectiveness. Which makes no sense. Of course, I want them to know we fucked, but for some reason, I'm not dying to tell them *all* the juicy details. It feels personal, like I want to keep that part of him all to myself.

So, instead of delving it all up, I say, "It was as good as I knew it would be."

That seems to appease him, because he slaps me on the back before we all get back to work. My mind frequently goes back to Travis and this need to see him again. Have a repeat of the other day. A repeat of yesterday morning before he went home.

I wonder how hard it's going to be to talk him into it. I know he wants it, but he's stubborn.

"Heard your sister's getting married." Benny's voice pulls me from my train of thought. He's working on an old Chevy a few stalls down.

"Yup. Scottie's giving her that dream wedding she's always wanted."

"Do we like him?" Miguel asks.

I wipe the sweat off my brow with the back of my wrist. "Yeah, he's cool. Treats her well, makes her happy."

"I don't know him that well," Benny interjects. "But he seems nice enough. She said you're giving her away?"

"Yeah. I don't know anything other than that, though. She called me a few nights ago to ask if I would, then we got into it a little about mom, so I got off the phone." I close the hood to the car I'm working on. "You going to the engagement party she's having?"

"Yeah, I'll go," Benny confirms.

"Miguel?"

"If I'm invited, I'll come. I can probably bring Izzy too."

"Cool. Should be fun," I lie.

The truth is, I'm dreading it. Not because I'm not happy for Ally, because I am, but because it's a situation where I'm forced to be around people I have no interest in being around. And not just my mom.

Which, yes, she's a huge stressor for me. But more than her, it's Robbie. He and Scottie are cousins, so I know he'll be there. That didn't even hit me until after I got off the phone with Ally. She knows we dated, obviously, and knows we broke up, but doesn't know all the details about how fucked up our relationship was, and how messed up I was coming out of it.

Aside from recently running into him at the bar, I've done pretty well at avoiding seeing him altogether since the breakup, and I'd prefer to keep it that way.

Robbie and Scottie aren't close by any means, but their parents are. There's just no way he won't be there. His mother would never allow him to miss it. The thought alone of having to see him at this thing is enough to have lead knots twisting in my gut. And knowing it won't be the only time I'll have to see him, too, makes it that much worse. There's still the actual wedding, and any other wedding-related event there may be.

Lucky for me.

The rest of the day goes by quickly, but not without

distraction. My mood soured after all thoughts of Robbie, my mom, and engagement party. Regardless, I'm able to wrap up my work and leave the shop a little early. By the time I get home, I'm in serious need of a shower, a bowl, and a beer. So, I do all of that, in that order.

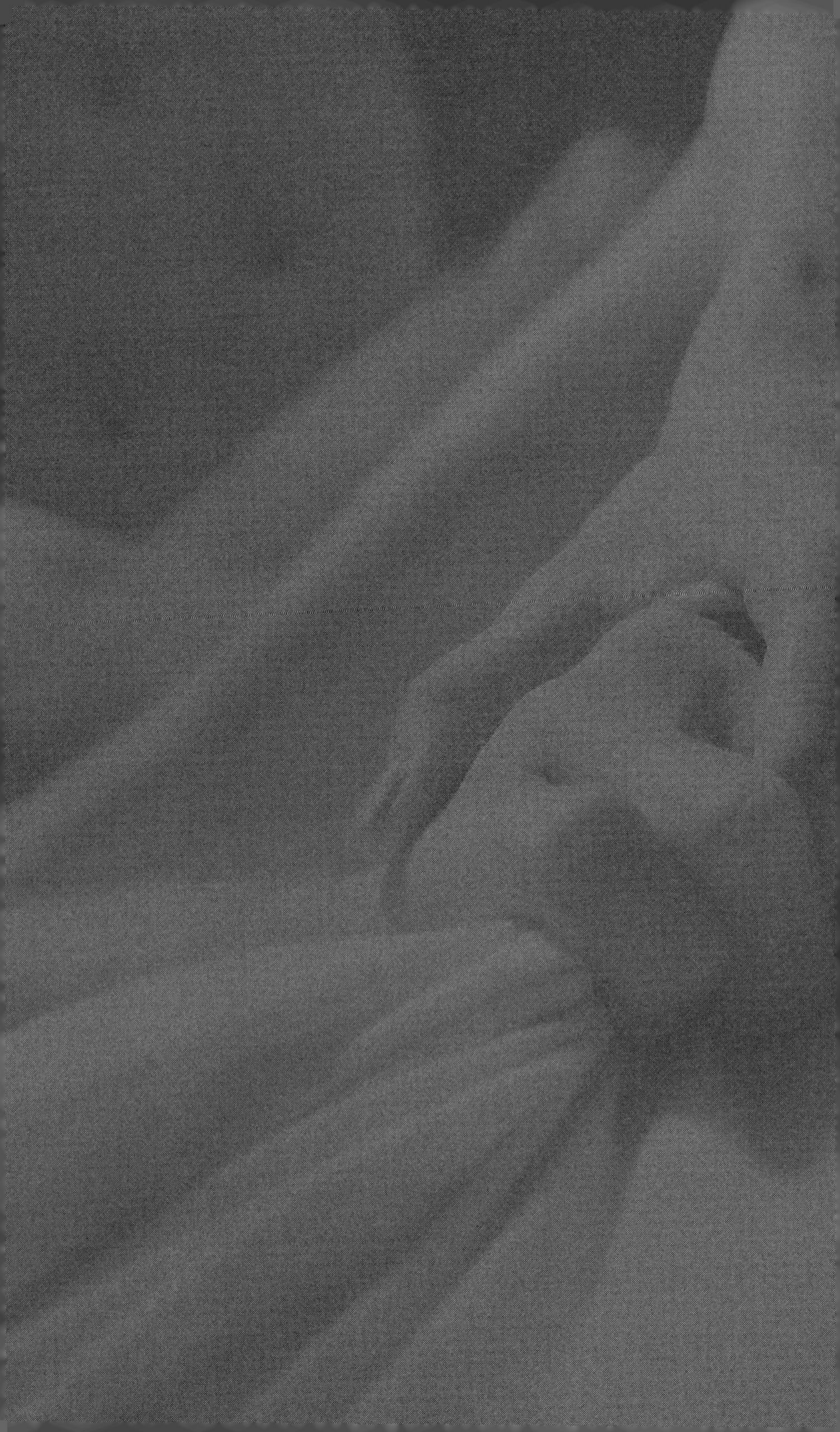

TWENTY-ONE
Travis

This morning has been non-stop crazy since the minute I walked into my office. The phone's been ringing off the hook, I've sat in meeting after meeting full of unorganized people, and there's construction going on in the next building over that can be heard obnoxiously loud at my desk.

It's almost noon now, and I finally have a single free moment to call over to Benito's Garage to check on my car. There's no way it's not done by now. How fucking long does it take for one tire to be delivered?

After pulling up the phone number on my computer, I dial, bringing the phone to my ear. It rings several times before finally connecting to the voicemail. I hang up and try again. Same thing.

Taking a quick glance at my calendar and confirming I don't have another meeting until two, I grab my keys and head out. If they won't answer, I'll just go down there in person and ask. Maybe they're so busy working on my car, they can't hear the phone.

I park out front, walking in through the wide-open garage. My eyes flit to the office, but I don't see anybody in there. Music's playing loudly toward the back of the area, so I walk back there. The upbeat tune of Olivia Rodrigo's *Good 4 U* is playing. Kind of surprising. Not exactly the type of music you'd expect to hear in an auto garage.

As I get closer, I can see someone bent over the hood of an older Honda Civic. I have a view of their backside, but I can tell based on body type alone, even through the navy-blue coveralls, it's Mateo. His foot's tapping along to the music, and when I scan the room, I don't see anybody else. *He thinks he's alone.*

Leaning against the doorframe, I fold my arms over my chest and allow myself a moment to watch him. Watch as his foot continues to tap to the beat. Listen as I swear I hear him singing along to the lyrics. Observe him in his element.

I have a hunch I'm watching a side of Mateo he doesn't let many people see. The man doesn't strike me as the type to let his guard down. He seems to present this strong, iron-clad front. He's confident, borderline cocky, and sure of himself.

He quite literally seems to be everything I am not.

Like he knows what he wants, and has no qualms about going after just that and getting it.

So, watching him dance and sing along to pop songs, where anybody could see him, has me feeling like I'm witnessing a rare sight.

It's probably why I haven't let him know of my presence yet.

The song hits the last bridge, and now I definitely know he's singing along. He gets a little louder as Olivia gets a little madder, and by the time the final chorus hits, he's grabbing the tool closest to him and using it as a microphone as he belts out lyrics about being a *damn sociopath.*

I have to bite the inside of my cheek to keep from laughing, the smile on my face painfully wide as I clap my hands together in a slow, dramatic fashion. Mateo startles, his back immediately going rigid as he lowers the tool, slowly turning around.

"When's the tour?" I tease, stepping farther into the space.

The scowl on his face deepens, his eyes narrowing on me. "What the fuck are you doing here?"

"Clearly watching the show," I drawl.

He tosses the tool on the cart beside the vehicle, tugging a dirty rag out from his back pocket, wiping his hands off. His face is unreadable, like always. "I don't know what you're talking about."

"Uh-huh, whatever you say, Olivia."

"Can I fucking help you?"

It's weird being on the other end of this. Normally, it's him annoying the shit out of me, and me angry.

"I'm checking on my car," I say. "I tried calling, but nobody answered. Now I know why."

"Nobody answered because I'm *busy*, and the only one here today. Your car will be ready by Friday."

"Friday? That's two days away!"

"Way to state the obvious, *cariño*." He rolls his eyes.

"It's a fucking tire, Mateo. What could possibly be taking so long?"

"It's called the weather, dipshit. It's been delayed. Take it up with mother fucking nature."

Mateo turns his back on me, returning his attention to the Honda he's working on. My blood boils. He's so fucking infuriating.

Groaning, I mutter, "It better be ready by then, Mateo. This is bullshit. Fixing a tire shouldn't take this long."

"You're awfully grouchy," he says, the words coming out muffled since his back is still to me, but I don't miss the playfulness in his tone. "Sounds like you need to be dicked down again, *cariño*." Glancing over his shoulder, with eyes full of cockiness and mischief, he adds, "You should stop by my place later on. Could help you with that... again."

He winks, and my stomach lurches, his mood today throwing me for a loop. "Not a fucking chance, asshole."

Storming out of the garage, I climb into the rental car, turning it on. I drive off the lot quickly, steam practically billowing out of my ears. He's such a fucking prick.

And the worst fucking part is that there's no part of my body that wants to turn him down. Every fiber of my being wants to take him up on his offer and let him work my body over again with his magic.

It's nauseating how much my body wants him.

But I *refuse* to fall for his voodoo again. I meant it when I said the snowstorm was the one and only time that would be happening.

TWENTY-TWO

Mateo

"Yo, grab me another beer while you're up there," I shout to Miguel's back as he weaves his way through the crowd toward the packed bar.

It's Friday night, and I'm so fucking happy to be off for the weekend. It's been one hell of a week. I don't know what it is about the first of the year, but it always brings in a mess of car trouble. Probably has to do with the holidays, and people neglecting their car maintenance in favor of paying for it all.

Miguel and I are meeting our other friend, Doran, here to kickback and have a few beers. Doran actually owns this bar with his husband, and the three of us all met back in high school.

He and his husband just got back from a trip to Europe for their anniversary. Been married six years now.

"So, how was the trip?" I ask him over the music playing.

Doran glances up from his phone, a smirk playing on his lips. "It was fucking great, man. Definitely recommend."

"Where all did you go again?"

"London, Paris, Rome, and Amsterdam."

"Damn, sounds like a good fucking time."

"What's new with you?" he asks. "Heard you got the shit beat out of you by someone's boyfriend mid-fuck."

Miguel steps up to the table, three beers in hand, glancing between a laughing Doran and a glaring me.

"What the fuck did you tell him?" I spit out, rolling my eyes. Turning my attention back to Doran, I say, "I didn't get the shit beat out of me. It was a lamp… got thrown at my head."

Doran grabs his abdomen, head thrown back onto his shoulders as he barks out a laugh.

"Oh, fuck off. Both of you." I look away, the ghost of a smirk playing on my lips. It is a little comical if you think about it. Especially considering who my neighbor is now.

Speaking of my neighbor, my mind drifts back to Travis. He occupies the space a lot lately, I won't even lie. I'm craving more of him, and it's like the more I want, the more he pushes away. It's been a little over a month since we hooked up during the snowstorm, and he's played an impressive—and infuriating—game of hard to get ever since.

We see each other in the hall of our building often, after work and shit, but aside from simple pleasantries, he won't give me the time of day. And when I say *simple* pleasantries, I mean it. I've tried to be the nice, friendly neighbor and everything, and still… nothing. Same thing when I try to text him. The fucker has a lot more willpower than I thought he would, and it's not working in my favor. In fact, it's slowly driving me fucking insane.

I'm getting antsy and impatient to not only have him underneath me again, writhing and begging, but also to spend time with him in general. Even if we did something boring and mundane, like watch a fucking movie together or walk his dog. I can't explain this desire to simply be near him, clothed or not.

Hanging out isn't usually my cup of tea, but it's like the more Travis ignores me, the more I want to have him in any way that I can.

Who the fuck am I lately?

I down the rest of my beer before pulling my phone out of my pocket. Knowing I probably shouldn't, as he'll probably ignore me, I do it anyway.

Me: Cariño…

Me: What are you doing?

Peering over at my friends, I raise off the chair, stretching my arms over my head. "I'll be right back. Getting another. You guys want one?"

They both nod.

Travis doesn't have his read receipts on, so I can't tell if he's read it or not. It's been a few minutes, and nothing. No text bubble popping up with an incoming text, no response. Nothing. It's infuriating.

The bartender takes my empty bottle, walking away to retrieve me three more. While I wait, I send off another text. Because why the fuck not.

Me: Oh, come on… no need to ignore me. What do you say I come on by, and we have a repeat of before?

"Here you go," the bartender says. Dragging my gaze from the screen up to her face, I grab the beers.

"Thanks. Can you just put these on my tab?"

"Name?"

"Mateo Rojas."

She taps a few buttons on the screen before nodding. "You got it."

My phone vibrates in my hand as I walk back to our table, a swirl tickling my gut with anticipation. As soon as I set the drinks down, I unlock the phone, disappointment clouding my mind when I see the text is, in fact, not from Travis, but my sister.

Ally: Can you come over tomorrow and help me build a bookshelf?

I roll my eyes before typing out a response.

Me: Why can't Scottie help?

Ally: He's out of town this weekend with his cousins. Besides, I can build shit without my fiancé helping me, Matty. I'm a strong, independent woman.

Me: Yeah? Then why are you asking me if you're so strong and independent?

She sends me three eye rolling emojis, and a laugh escapes me because I can see the exact expression on her face right now.

Me: Fine. What time?

Ally: Yay, thank you! How's ten?

Me: Damn, why so fucking early?

Ally: Because I want to get it done, and I have plans in the afternoon.

Me: You owe me.

I switch back to my message with Travis, annoyed to still find no response. What could he possibly be doing on a Friday night that he's too busy to reply to me? And more importantly, why wouldn't he want to take me up on my offer for a repeat?

We're two people who found great pleasure in the other's bodies… why not take advantage of that? Who fucking cares that I fucked his boyfriend. It wasn't on purpose.

Not that he knows that.

But that's beside the point.

Pissed off, I lock the phone, setting it face down as I bring my attention back to Miguel and Doran. They're talking about some club Doran and his husband went to in Amsterdam. We end up getting a couple of rounds of tequila shots and a few more beers as the night progresses.

At close to midnight, I'm feeling tipsy and horny, so I excuse myself to the bathroom. I still have no fucking response from Travis, but that's about to change if I have any say in the matter. I'm done with his silence. The stalls are all empty when I step inside. I take the one farthest from the door, locking it before pulling out my phone.

With my free hand, I slide the zipper down, flicking open the button to my jeans. My dick's already half-hard by the time I pull it out, fully stiffening after a few tugs. Opening the camera app, I snap a picture of my cock at a nice angle, attaching it to my text thread with Travis.

Not bothering to add a caption, I hit send before taking a quick leak. By the time I wash and dry my hands, I have a response.

Bingo.

Travis: Does that work for you often?

Me: It did this time.

Travis: No, it didn't.

Me: It got you to respond to me, cariño. Seems like a win to me.

Travis: Don't you have a relationship to destroy?

I like when he's feisty.

Me: I'm coming over.

Travis: No, you're not.

Me: Oh, yes, I am. I miss that sweet little tight cunt of yours. And I know you miss my cock filling it.

Travis: Good God. You're delusional.

Me: Be there in 20.

Travis: Mateo. No!

Locking my phone, I shove it into my pocket as I leave the restroom to tell my friends I'm heading out. I order an Uber that only takes a few minutes to arrive, and almost exactly twenty minutes on the dot later, I'm raising my fist, knocking on the door that's across the hall from mine.

Just as I'm about to knock a second time, he pulls the door open. Travis stands before me in nothing more than a pair of flannel pajama pants. I shamelessly drag my gaze down his frame. His chest is bare, nipples quickly pebbling at the cool breeze coming in from the hall window that's still broken. Even his feet are bare.

When my eyes find his again, they're narrowed on me, the blue looking icier than usual. "I fucking told you to not come over here."

Shrugging lazily, I say, "Yeah, but we both know you don't mean that."

Just then, his dog peeks her head out of the door, tongue hanging as she eyes me excitedly. I lean down, petting her head a few times, and she practically preens under my touch. She really is adorable.

Travis sighs heavily. "Mateo, it's almost one in the fucking morning. You're not coming in. I'd like to go to bed, so just go home."

Rolling my eyes, I stand, becoming eye to eye with Travis. "You can pretend all you want that you didn't love what I gave you that night—and the next morning—but you can only deny it to yourself for so long before you crack, *cariño*." My voice is low as I bring my body nearly flush with his. I don't miss the way his breath hitches, or the way his eyes drop to my mouth. "You can run, baby, but you can't hide."

His jaw clenches, but he says nothing. Dragging another greedy gaze down his body, I smirk before turning and unlocking my apartment. I'm horny and pissed he didn't cave, but I meant what I said... he won't be able to deny it forever. And I've got all the time in the world to wait him out.

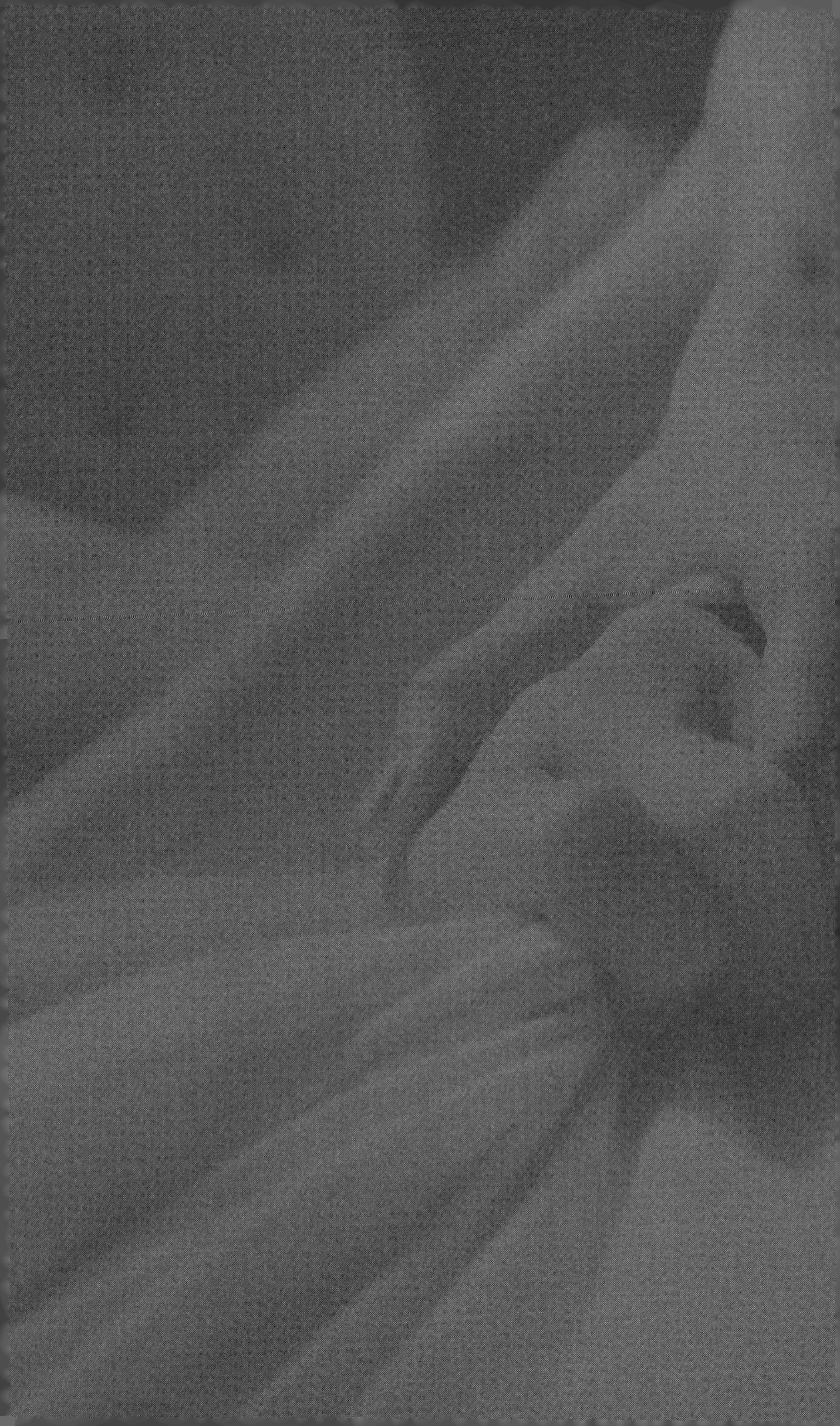

TWENTY-THREE

Travis

Tiffany's Table is one of the best brunch spots in Desert Creek, which really doesn't say much since it's such a small town and the options are pretty slim, but it's still delicious. In the spring and summer, they even have Sunday drag brunch events that are always a blast.

Me, Xander, and Charlotte all make an effort to meet for Saturday brunch at least once a month. So, that's where we are now, circled around a table overlooking downtown with bottomless mimosas, fruit, and pastries.

Bringing the flute up to my lips, I take a long sip, wishing this had more champagne and less orange juice. "When do you leave, Char?"

"On Monday," she replies, not bothering to look up from her phone where she's probably texting her husband. Those two are practically attached at the hip; I'm always half expecting him to show up to brunch one of these days, even though it's strictly only been Xander, Charlotte, and me for as long as I can remember.

My sister is flying to Las Vegas for a few days for work. Some conference. I'm jealous she gets to escape this frigid weather, even if only for a few days. The snow, thankfully, hasn't returned, but it's no less freezing.

"Is Greg going with you?"

She shakes her head, finally meeting my gaze. "No. He has to work. It'll just be me and my assistant."

The server comes and takes our orders, bringing over another round of drinks.

"Anything new with you?" I ask Xander, who's been quieter than usual.

He shakes his head. "Nah, not really. Just work. One of the donors came in the other day. It was the first time I've met him."

Xander partially owns a weed dispensary, along with one of his long-time buddies. Aside from their share of ownership, there're also a couple of donors who basically fronted the rest of the money but don't take part in any of the running the business. There're tons of fees and licenses required to run such a business, and between Xander and his partner, they couldn't do it on their own. It's basically a small handful of rich ass investors paying into the business.

Xander knows one of them well since it's his aunt. But the other two have been silent donors, up until now, I guess.

"Oh, yeah? How'd that go?"

He shrugs, taking a drink from his mimosa. "It was okay. We were slow when the guy showed up. He didn't specify who he was, although it was kind of obvious. He was driving some top-of-the-line Tesla, dressed to the nines in a suit that looked tailor made, and he screamed money."

"What do you think he was doing there?"

"Who knows," he mutters. "Checking in on his investment,

I'd imagine."

"Was he friendly?"

Shaking his head, he says, "No, not really. I mean, he wasn't rude or anything. He just didn't say much."

"So, how do you know he was a donor?" Charlotte asks as she pops a strawberry into her mouth.

"When people pay, they have to show their ID," he says. "Well, they show ID at the door too, but I wasn't at the door when he entered. But I was the cashier who rang him out, and saw the name on his license. It looked familiar, but I couldn't place where I knew the name from. Not until I got home that night and went through all the paperwork."

"What did he buy?"

"Some chocolate edibles."

"Hmm, interesting," I murmur. "Wonder if he'll stop by again."

"Speaking of interesting," Charlotte says, a smirk playing on her lips. "Mom mentioned something about how you locked yourself out of your place during the snowstorm last month?"

Great, here we go.

Glaring at her, I say, "Yup."

"Weird that I've talked to you several times since then, and you've never mentioned that."

Xander chuckles beside me. "What the fuck did you do?"

Both of them probably have an *idea* about why I didn't mention it, because they both know who my neighbor is, but fuck me, I didn't want to explain this to them. I wasn't even planning on telling my mom, but it kind of slipped out when I was on the phone with her last week.

"It's not a big deal." *Lies.*

"So, you were able to get back into the house right away?" Charlotte asks knowingly.

Rolling my eyes, I mumble, "No."

Xander smirks. "Do tell, Travis."

Internally groaning, I take another sip, trying to buy myself some time while they both stare at me impatiently and expectantly. Finally, heaving a sigh, I mutter as nonchalantly as I can manage, "I had to wait out the storm at my neighbor's house. My phone was locked inside my apartment, and when I was able to use my neighbor's phone to call a locksmith, they were all closed."

Charlotte and Xander glance at one another, then back at me. My sister arches one of her perfectly manicured brows, looking at me like I'm full of shit. "Neighbor, huh?"

"Yup."

"Would this be the same neighbor you caught with his pants around his ankles at your old house?"

I roll my eyes. "Fuck off. You know the answer is yes."

"You fucked him, didn't you?" Xander asks at the exact moment our server walks up with our food.

Her eyes widen, flitting between the three of us. "Alright," she blurts out awkwardly, her face turning several shades of red. "Here we go. Is there anything else I can get you guys?"

Xander chuckles.

"I think we're good," I mutter. "Thank you."

She practically runs away. Not that I can blame her.

"Way to go, big mouth," I say with a laugh as I plop a hash brown bite into my mouth.

Xander pins me with a stare. "Answer the question, Travis."

When I don't immediately respond, Charlotte chimes in. "Oh, my gosh. You did, didn't you?"

"Yes, okay!" I blurt out much louder than I intended to. "We slept together! It's not a big deal."

"Travis…" Charlotte says my name like she's so disappointed in me.

"Charlotte, don't," I warn. "It shouldn't have happened. It was a moment of weakness, and it won't be happening again. I don't need your lecture."

"I just worry about you is all," she says softly. "I'm not trying to lecture you."

I glance over at Xander. He's eating his food, not saying a word, but I know he wants to. He wants to lecture me probably as much as Charlotte does. Tell me how I deserve better, and how I'm supposed to be putting myself first. I don't want to hear it. I'm mad enough at myself after sleeping with him—and enjoying it as much as I did—I don't need it from them too.

Charlotte exhales heavily. "Have you heard from Nathaniel at all?"

I consider lying, but what's the point. "He's tried contacting me a couple of times since the split."

"What does he say?"

"That he wants to sit down and talk about everything."

She worries her bottom lip for a moment before replying. "You wouldn't ever get back together with him, would you?"

"Fuck no!" I snap. Suddenly, I'm regretting coming to this damn brunch at all. "No, Char, I wouldn't," I say with much less anger. "I may be an idiot, but I'm not *that* much of one."

"You're not an idiot," she insists. "You just want to see the good in everyone. That's not always a bad thing."

It's fucking infuriating to see the way people look at me sometimes. Like Xander and Charlotte, for example. I know they both love me and want what's best for me, but sometimes it's very clear they think I'm stupid. Like I make terrible decisions when it comes to my love life. Which okay, I kind of do, but Jesus.

Just fucking once, I'd like to not make the wrong call. I'd like to pick the right, good, nice person. I'm always the guy people say *"I told you so"* to, and I'm tired of it. Sleeping with Mateo was foolish. It shouldn't have happened, and all it's done is make me feel even weaker than I already did. Even though I've ignored every invitation from him, that doesn't seem to matter in the grand scheme of things to people. And now, sitting here, with Charlotte, who's giving me her sad, *I want to help him* eyes, the anger stews inside of me, bubbling over.

She must take a hint, though, because she changes the subject, and we're able to make it through the rest of our meal without bringing me, or my pathetic love life, back up. I've never felt more relieved than I do when I step inside my apartment later.

Nova trots up to me, tail wagging, tongue sticking out, happy as a clam to see me.

"Hi, sweet girl!" I get down on her level, petting her head as she tries to maul my face with kisses. "Should we go for a walk?"

Her ears perk up and she jumps back, prancing on her toes at the word *"walk."*

"I'll take that as a yes." Her leash is on the kitchen counter from when I used it last night. Grabbing it, I hook it onto her collar and head out. We take the elevator down to the bottom level and, thankfully, nobody else is in there. The building seems pretty quiet and empty right now, which is fine by me.

I'm still in a piss-poor mood from my sister's questions at brunch. Being alone, with just my pup, is probably a good idea.

But of course, the universe has other plans for me when, on my way through the lobby toward the front door, I spot somebody I definitely do *not* want to see right now. A sinister smirk slides on his devious lips when he spots me.

Mateo's walking toward the elevators, obviously just coming home, but when he gets near me, he turns, so now we're walking the same direction.

Why wouldn't he?

"Hello, *cariño*," he greets in a too-sultry tone that makes my heart race and my blood heat. I hate it. When I don't respond, he glances down at Nova, sticking his hand out for her to sniff. "Hey, pretty girl."

My gosh, why does the voice he uses to talk to my dog have to be so fucking hot? He's so annoying. And Nova eats it up too. She loves the attention.

Trust me, girl. I get it. Don't let him fool you, though.

"Where are we going?" he asks as I push through the heavy glass door that leads to the sidewalk.

"*We* aren't going anywhere," I correct. "Nova and I are going for a walk."

He chuckles. I don't know what's funny, but okay. "I'll come with you guys. I drank too much last night, and could use the exercise."

"Oh, is that why you showed up at my front door in the middle of the night after sending me a shitty dick pic?" I scoff.

Mateo gasps, clutching his chest like I offended him. "That was not a shitty dick pic," he growls. "That picture was hot as fuck, and you know it."

"Whatever you say," I grumble, rolling my eyes. It was *not* hot, and I most certainly did *not* jack off to it before bed last night. Nope. Definitely didn't do that.

We're halfway down the block, and it's becoming painfully clear he literally meant that he was joining us.

Great.

"Did you have a thrilling night in?" Mateo asks after several minutes of silence.

"It was fine."

"Could've been better."

He is unbelievable. "You're awfully fucking full of yourself, you know that?"

Holding his hands up in mock innocence, he says, "I'm just saying."

"How could it have been better, Mateo? Hmm?" I glance over at him, finding an unsurprisingly unreadable expression. "By accepting your invitation to come over and fuck me?"

Mateo's brows pinch together. "Yes," he says, like it's the most obvious answer. "I don't get why you're fighting it. We had fun together, didn't we?"

My eyes roll so hard of their own volition, and I groan. "That's not the fucking point."

"Then what is?" he asks dryly. "That you clearly are a masochist who gets off on denying yourself of a good time instead?"

"Oh, my fucking God." Stopping mid-step, I turn to face him, the urge to deck him in his smug face growing stronger. "You act like you're God's gift to man, and that we should all just be falling at your fucking feet, begging you to fuck us all. News flash, you're fucking *not!*"

Tugging on Nova's leash, I begin walking, but back toward the apartment this time.

"Where are you going?"

"Back to my fucking house."

"Your dog didn't get a very long walk."

Fucking kill me now.

"Not your concern," I grit out. Not even three seconds later, he's sidled back up beside me. "Can you take a fucking hint?"

"Well, *cariño*, I live this way too."

"Stop fucking call me that!"

"Why?" he asks, bringing his body impossibly closer to mine. "Because it turns you on, and you don't like it?"

Scoffing, I say," It doesn't turn me on."

It does.

"Oh, is that right?" Without warning, he shoves me into the nearest wall, slamming his mouth down on mine before my brain even has a chance to catch up. When my lips part in protest, he uses it as an invitation, slipping his tongue inside, brushing up against mine. My traitorous body vibrates with need, a pathetic fucking moan bubbling up my throat.

Mateo tastes like nicotine and mint, and the feeling of his hard body pressed against mine is intoxicating. *And infuriating.*

After way too long, my mind finally catches up, hands going to his chest and shoving him away. I wipe my lips with the back of my hand, feeling all sorts of disheveled. Glancing down at Nova, she's sitting there like this is any other day, like her owner wasn't just *assaulted*. Okay, maybe that's a bit much, but still. The smirk on Mateo's face is cocky when I look back over at him, the sight making my blood boil further.

"You're such a fucking dick! Just because I slept with you when I was *trapped* and had nowhere else to go doesn't fucking mean I'm going to drop my pants every fucking time I see you." Taking a step away from the wall, I put some much-needed distance between us before adding, "You're a piece of shit, and that is never going to happen again. Leave me the fuck alone, you fucking asshole."

Thankfully, and surprisingly, he doesn't follow when I storm away. Or if he does, he keeps his distance, because I'm able to make it back to my apartment without another word.

Unfortunately, that kiss, and the way his body felt pinning me to the wall, stays in my mind on repeat for the rest of the night.

TWENTY-FOUR

Mateo

Nathaniel: Hey, man. You free tonight? We should grab a couple drinks. Maybe have a repeat of last time? ;)

Glancing down at the phone in my hand, I can't help but roll my eyes. This has got to be, like, the fourth time he's texted me to hook up since it happened the first time. And every single time, I've ignored him. It's been *months*.

I really should just block him. And you know what? I'm going to, but be it my shit day or my general annoyance with him, I'm responding before doing so.

Me: Nah, bro. I'd be perfectly fine never being inside you ever again. Lose my number.

Hitting send, I promptly block him.

"Damn, who are you texting that has you looking like that?" My gaze lifts from my phone, connecting with Miguel's.

"That dumb fuck, Nathaniel," I grumble.

"You're still talking to him?"

"No. We hooked up the one time and haven't since."

"And what's going on with your neighbor?" he asks as he closes the hood of the car he was working on.

"Not shit," I say honestly, much to my annoyance. He's a stubborn fuck. Although, at the question, the kiss from the other night crosses my mind. It was much too short for my liking, but goddamn, it was good.

Miguel watches me for a moment, like he's trying to get a read on me. I don't know what he sees, but after a few beats, he shrugs and changes the subject. "You going to that thing Doran's hosting at the bar this weekend?"

I nod. "Yup. You?"

Doran and his husband are having a huge cocktail hour party at their bar to celebrate their anniversary. They do it every year, and it's always fun. Tons of people from the town come, and the food's always incredible.

"Yeah," he confirms. "Wanna ride together? I have to drop Iz off with her mom at noon, but I can pick you up after?"

"Works for me," I grunt out, bringing my attention back to the truck I'm working on.

Benny is out today—caught the flu or something. He's been sick as a dog since yesterday morning. So, Miguel and I work in comfortable silence together the rest of the day.

On my way home, I stop at the restaurant down the street to pick up some dinner. I grab a beer out of the fridge once I get home, sitting at the table in the dining room, and dig in. I'm fucking starving. After I finish eating, I force myself to go to the gym for a couple of hours, needing to get back into that routine. I let myself slip almost every winter, and it's a nasty habit.

It's a little after eight by the time I make it home again. After a *long*, hot shower, I change into some comfy clothes, and park my ass in front of the TV. A few mindless hours of Netflix will do the trick. Restlessness courses through my bloodstream tonight, and I'm not sure why. Nothing has been different about my day, yet I feel unsettled.

At about a quarter to eleven and three re-run episodes of Shameless later, my phone dings with a text message. I'm taken aback when I see who the message is from… and what it says.

Travis: Hey, are you awake?

A smirk slides across my lips, a rush of excitement coursing through my blood, as I type out a response.

Me: My, my cariño… did you really just 'you up' text me?
Travis: Obviously.
Me: Well then, obviously I'm awake.
Travis: What are you doing?

Since when does he not only text me in general, but do small talk?

Me: Watching TV. You?
Travis: Are you alone?

What the fuck?

Me: Uh, yes?
Travis: Can I come over?

My dick twitches at the question. Ain't no fucking way Travis, of all people, is hitting me up at eleven o'clock on a weeknight for a hook-up. *Especially* after the way he went off on me in the middle of the sidewalk a few days ago.

There's also no fucking way I'm turning it down, though, either.

Me: Sure.

All I get in response to that is a series of thumbs-up emojis. *Alright.*

I have time to walk into the kitchen and grab another beer, popping the cap off, and taking a sip before the sound of knuckles rapping on my door pulls my attention. Striding across the room, I pull it open, finding Travis standing on the other side, hands shoved into the pockets of his dark denim jeans, bloodshot eyes lifting from the ground up to meet my gaze.

"Well, this is a surprise," I grunt out, stepping to the side to let him in.

The sweet, earthy scent of marijuana wafts in after him, explaining the bloodshot eyes, and his body language is stiff. He stops in the hallway right inside the door, slowly turning to face me. He doesn't say anything.

"So, what are you doing here?" I ask, leaning my shoulder against the now closed front door, folding my arms over my chest.

His pretty blue eyes drop down, checking out what I can only assume are the muscles popping out from under my t-shirt before he finds my gaze again. His tongue swipes across his lips, wetting them, and he runs his fingers shakily through his hair. He's clearly nervous, shifting his feet as he looks between me and the door, like maybe he's considering making a run for it.

I don't have a fucking clue what's going through his mind right now, but something clicks into place in his eyes—resolve, maybe—and he takes two steps toward me, erasing the distance. He's so close, I can smell the beer on his breath and feel the shallow puffs of air fanning my face as his chest rises and falls rapidly.

"Just this once," he breathes against my lips, and before I have a chance to ask what he means by that, he's slamming his mouth down onto mine, shoving my back against the door. His lips are feral, his tongue hot and hungry as it thrusts into my mouth, licking all over, arms wrapping around my neck as he brings our bodies flush.

It takes my mind a moment to catch up, but once it does,

my hands find purchase on his hips, holding him close as I slant my mouth against his, letting him deepen the kiss. I can feel his length swell against my thigh as my own dick goes rigid behind my pants, a smile pulling at my lips as I continue to kiss him, feeling victory at him showing up here. I fucking throb for him, the sensation only heightening when he drags his hands down my chest, groping my muscles, teeth nipping down on my bottom lip.

Travis pulls away suddenly, eyes wild with desire. His fingers brush over his spit-slick lips, and he looks almost confused as he pulls his hand back, glancing at the digits like they hold all the answers as to why he's here and why he just mauled me against my front door.

"What the fuck are you doing?" I ask after several long moments of stifled silence.

"I, uh…" Travis clears his throat, gaze meeting mine. "I went out with some friends for drinks after work."

"Um, okay?"

"Sometimes, when I drink, I get a little… you know."

I bite down on the inside of my cheek to keep from laughing. "No, *cariño*, I don't know. Enlighten me. Sometimes, when you drink, you get a little… what?"

He shrugs, probably trying to appear nonchalant. "Horny," he mumbles.

Elation fills my veins, almost as much as the arousal does.

"So, you came here to what? Have me make you come again?"

His cheeks flame red, and he rolls his eyes.

"I'm gonna need an answer, *cariño*. Otherwise, it's late and I have to work in the morning."

Travis groans. "Are you always this fucking insufferable? Yes, okay! I came here because I thought we could hook up."

Huffing out a laugh through my nose, I say, "Well, all you had to do was ask, baby." I take a step toward him, closing the distance once more before lowering my voice and saying, "So, ask. *Nicely.*"

I wish I could snap a picture of his face right now. He's beet red, discomfort and embarrassment rolling off him in waves. A better man would put him out of his misery, just give him what he wants... but I certainly never claimed to be a better man, and I plan to watch him squirm as long as I can.

"Please..." He whispers the word. "Will you fuck me?"

"Aww, you can do better than that," I reply with a grin. "Drop down to your knees, *cariño*, and beg me like I know you can."

His eyes narrow into fiery blue slits as he clenches his jaw. "I'm not doing that."

The smirk on my face brightens, probably bordering on maniacal as I shrug, reaching for the knob behind me. "Okay, then have a good night."

I don't even get the door cracked before his knees collide with the hardwood floor. "Fine!" he blurts out. "I'll do it."

Arousal and something like pride swells in my chest cavity as I drop my hand, glancing down at him waiting. Travis awkwardly walks over on his knees until he's directly in front of me, his fingers going to the waistband of my pants. I hear—and see—him gulp loudly before he peers up at me beneath his thick, curly lashes. He's chewing on his bottom lip and his cheeks are a vibrant shade of red. Disheveled, it's a good look on him.

Travis tugs the front of my pants down just enough to pull my cock and balls out as he finally seems to find his voice, and says, "*Please*, Mateo..." He swipes that damn tongue across his lips as my stiff length springs free. Wrapping a surprisingly steady hand around me, he continues. "Please fuck me."

Keeping my face neutral, I mutter, "I don't know. What happened to me being a piece of shit, and you saying this'll never happen again?"

I can see the exact moment Travis fights to not roll his eyes. This isn't easy for him, but I fucking love it. "I was having a bad day. I didn't mean it."

"Oh, so you *don't* think I'm a piece of shit?"

Heaving a sigh, he squares his shoulders. "No, I *do*. You're just a piece of shit with a great dick."

Laughter bubbles up my throat at his response.

Well, there's something to be said for brutal honesty, I suppose.

"You're not wrong," I say, breath hitching when he starts to stroke me. "But you *did* say, and I quote, *that is never going to happen again*."

"Okay, and tomorrow we can go back to that and pretend this never happened too." His full lips brush against the side of my shaft as he gazes up at me, eyes full of want. "Please?"

I watch as he wraps those same lips around the tip, chest rumbling as I feel the swirl of his tongue brush over the slit. He sucks on the crown gingerly, never taking his eyes off me. My hands clench at my sides as I pretend to think over his offer. Me fucking him was never a question. The minute he came in here, throwing himself at me, it was a yes. But hearing and seeing him beg is too good to pass up.

After a couple of minutes, I step back, removing myself from his mouth. "Alright, up." I tuck myself back into my pants, brushing past him farther into the house, leaving him to follow.

This should be interesting.

Bypassing my bedroom entirely, I continue on down the

hall until I get to the last door on the left. Pushing it open, I flick on the light switch. It turns on the lamp in the corner, covering the space in a deep red glow. He steps in behind me, nearly running into my back, and when I glance over my shoulder, his eyes are scanning the room.

"You must be joking," he states, walking around me and into the room. "How is this room even more of a sex dungeon than your bedroom?"

Glancing around, I try to look at the room through fresh eyes. The bed in the middle is a wooden four-post just like the one in my room, only smaller, and black and red candles line the shelves hanging at various levels on the wall above it. To the left, there's a swing made up of leather straps and a velvet seat that has my mind swirling with ideas for him, and to the right, there's a red-and-black leather St. Andrews Cross. A long, black massage table sits by the window, and there's an assortment of fun *tools* hanging from the wall.

Dragging my gaze over to a wide-eyed Travis, I smirk. "Get undressed, *cariño*."

That sentence and the scene unfolding before me gives me a wicked sense of deja vu to the first time I had him in my house, ready to bend him to my will.

Travis is frozen in place as he stares at me. "Don't make me ask you again," I warn. "Get undressed."

Crossing the room, I reach into the chest in front of the bed—similar to the one in my room—and take out a thin, clear bottle of lube. After tossing it on the bed, I turn around, pleased to find him undressed down to his navy-blue briefs. He looks unsure of himself, his right arm folding over his chest, fingers wrapped around his left upper arm.

"We gotta loosen you up, *cariño*," I tell him, crooking my

finger and using it in a *come here* motion.

Travis stops in front of me, his breath coming out in shallow pants, his dick stiff behind the thin piece of cotton. I wrap my palm around the back of his neck, hauling him into me. His apprehension is potent as my lips move against his, the lust barely overshadowing the tension in his body. He sighs into my mouth as I suck on the tip of his tongue, his body molding against mine.

Wrenching my lips away, I give his shoulder a quick shove, pushing him onto his knees. He peers up at me beneath his lashes, chewing on his slick, swollen lip. Desire prickles every inch of my body, my need for him thrumming through my veins, igniting a burning inferno, making it hard to take my time.

Reaching lower, I push my pants down enough to free my aching cock. It bobs long and heavy in front Travis's face. His pupils blow, and he licks his lips at the sight of me. I'm not even sure if he's aware he did it.

Wrapping a fist around myself, I give a squeeze at the base and say, "You want this, you little cock slut?"

It's there in his eyes, the urge to be stubborn and say no, but he can't. His need for me to own him, to destroy him, to give him what I know he's been craving since the first time, outweighs his need to fight it.

Instead of replying, he simply nods, chewing on the inside of his cheek, his dick hard and dying to be touched.

Bringing my glistening tip up to his juicy, full lips, my pulse quickens as I watch his pink tongue dart out, lapping up the evidence of my arousal, moaning at the taste of me before enclosing me in his hot, wet mouth once more. *God,* he looks fucking stunning down there on his knees, lips wrapped around my cock, body practically trembling with need.

"That's it, *cariño*..." Bringing my hand up, I fist his short dark blond strands, forcing myself deeper into his mouth. "Get me nice and wet, baby. Suck me good, like I know you can."

I lodge myself throat deep, my eyes rolling back as I feel him retch around me. Eyes filling up with moisture, a single tear streams down his cheek as his face reddens. Travis's palms come up to my thighs, but he doesn't push me away.

No... he fists the material of my pants, holding me closer. He gasps for air when I withdraw, dragging the length of my cock along his tongue. Spit drips out of his mouth, his swollen lips a bright red that suits his pale skin so fucking well.

I let him suck me a little longer before pulling back completely. Tipping my chin to the left, I say, "Up. Over there."

Travis turns his head, following my gaze before glancing back at me. He swallows hard before standing and obliging. Grabbing the bottle of lube off the bed, I meet him over there. He's standing in front of the swing awkwardly, like he doesn't know what to do.

"Well, what are you waiting for?" I ask. "Get up there."

He gawks at me for a brief moment, the refusal right there on the tip of his tongue, I'm sure. I bite the inside of my cheek to hide the smile trying to break free when he heaves a sigh, climbing into the swing. It has a maroon tufted seat that is large enough to fit his entire torso and his ass, with two foot holes. Of course, his stubborn ass doesn't put his feet in them until I instruct him to.

God forbid he does anything without being asked.

Bringing a slick finger to his tight pink hole, I watch a shudder rumble down his spine as a whimper falls from his lips. He lets out what I can only describe as a sigh of relief when the digit slips past the muscle, getting sucked into the velvety warm channel.

"You're so tight, baby," I groan. "Gotta relax for me."

I withdraw the finger, only to go back in with two this time. Leaning over, I run the flat of my tongue along his sac as I crook my fingers, grazing the spot inside of him that has him crying out. Goosebumps line Travis's flesh, and his thighs tremble as I work a third finger in, stretching and getting him ready to take my cock. I can't hold on much longer. I need to be inside him *now*.

"I knew you wanted this again, *cariño*." Removing my fingers from him, he gifts me with another desperate whimper. Chuckling, I soak my cock in lube, smearing it around, getting it nice and slick before I line myself up. "You can deny it to yourself all you want, but you can't lie to me."

Sinking inside of him is wicked. It feels wrong, but so damn right. Knowing he can't help himself... knowing that he fought this, tried to deny himself, but in the end, the body gets what the body wants. Knowing Travis will probably wake up in the morning and hate himself for giving in—and not only giving in, but *initiating* the very thing he swore he didn't want—it shouldn't make my chest swell and my black heart beat to a different drum, but it does.

He's squeezing the life out of me by the time I seat myself fully. Face contorted into a grimace, hands white-knuckling the straps on the swing. He's falling apart. I fucking love it.

My hands wrap around the handles above his head, using them to pull his body off my cock, only to impale him again. The air leaves his lungs as he throws his head back.

"*Fuck!*"

"Yeah, that's fucking right, *cariño*. How does it feel to finally give in again to what you hate yourself for wanting?"

Using the swing as leverage, I'm pumping in and out in earnest now, the slick sound of our skin slapping together filling the sex-infused air. With each thrust comes an animalistic growl from me, and a whimper from him. It's easy to get lost in him, get lost in the way he feels around me, the way I know I'm making him feel.

Our bodies move together in such perfect synchrony, his body inviting me in and constricting as I leave. The push and pull between us is electric, and when we finally give in to the desire, it's explosive.

Travis is writhing on this swing as our bodies collide savagely. Perspiration pours down my forehead, a thin sheen lining the back of my neck. I want my mouth on him, I want to taste his sweat, I want to *mark* him, but I can't when he's in this swing.

It's a great contraption for fucking, but not so much if you want to be *close*.

Pulling my dick out of him, I could laugh at the disgruntled noise that claws its way up his throat at the loss of fullness. His brows pinch tight, and I swear to God, his lip pops out into a small pout.

"Get the fuck up, *cariño*," I order him, backing up and giving him the space to do so. I've never seen him move as fast as he does right now, out of the swing in the blink of an eye. He steps up to me, and I don't know who moves first, but our lips collide before my brain has time to catch up. His tongue, dripping with need, shoves into my mouth, his hands coming up to cup the back of my head, and when I reach down, palming the backs of his thighs, he doesn't need any further instruction, he hoists himself up into my arms.

I walk us over to the wall, pressing his back up against it as

I reach down and line myself back up. There's nothing gentle about what comes next. He curls his arms around my neck, holding on tight as I pound him up into the wall. My lips find his throat, nipping and sucking along his Adam's apple, moving over to do the same underneath his ear.

His moans are loud, filling the room, and they only get louder the more I mark him. It's like he gets off knowing that come tomorrow, he won't be able to deny what happened, because the proof will be littered all over his neck.

Working my way up, my hungry lips find his, and as soon as my tongue tangles with his, I know I won't last much longer. Heat pools low in my spine, spreading and multiplying as his hole constricts around my cock. A second later, he cries out into my mouth, and I feel his release coat my stomach. I pump into his tight ass once more, twice more… three times, and I'm spilling inside of him, throwing my head back as my eyes roll. It's his turn for his lips to latch onto my throat, sucking, nipping, licking—heightening my orgasm as I groan harshly.

As the last drop seeps out, I bury my face in the crook of his neck, my breathing ragged and shallow. Exhaustion is quick to take over, and suddenly, the thought of carrying him over to the bed and passing out beside him sounds like the only thing I want to do.

I step back, letting Travis down. It hits me that his mind isn't where mine's at. It's obvious in the way he won't look at me.

"You can sleep over if you want, *cariño*."

He scoffs. "I live three feet from your front door; I think I can manage to make it home."

In the span of two minutes, he's fully dressed, walking out of the room without so much as a backward glance. Not a single word or a goodbye before he's gone.

The bitter feeling swirling around in my gut isn't one I'm used to, nor do I understand where it's coming from. He came over and did exactly what I wanted, finally succumbing to this thing between us, so why am I so... *angry* that he left?

TWENTY-FIVE

Travis

Xander opens the door to my car, sliding into the passenger seat. "What's up, man?"

"Hey, how's it going?"

As soon as his door closes and his seatbelt clicks into place, I put the car back in drive and take off. We're going to an anniversary party for Benton, one of Xander's friends. It's at some bar he owns with his husband. If I'm not mistaken, Xan met this guy at work, and he's a regular customer.

"I bet this place will have some delicious fucking food," he murmurs, pulling out a joint, placing it between his lips, and lighting it. He rolls his window down a crack, taking a couple of drags before passing it to me.

"What type of food is it? It's a bar, right?"

He nods, taking another drag as I hand it back to him. "Yup. But the event is being catered. I think it's a taco bar if I'm not wrong. His husband is Hispanic, so it's, like, the *good* tacos."

Xander grins, smoke billowing out as he does.

Taking one last hit, I pass it back to him and he puts it out.

We fall into a comfortable silence as I focus on the drive. The place is only across town, so it won't take too long.

In my periphery, Xander glances over my way. "So, that investor guy—*whoa*, what the fuck is that on your neck? Is that a *hickey?*"

Shit.

It's been a few days since my poor, drunken mistake, and most of the marks have faded, but one in particular under my ear is seeming to stick around for the long hall.

Ignoring his question completely, I change the subject back to him. "The investor guy, what?"

"Wha—No, I don't think so. You're not getting out of this that easy."

"Yes, I am. The investor guy, what?"

Xander grumbles loudly, and I know if I looked over, he'd be rolling his eyes. He hates when I do shit like this. He's so talkative and open, and it always annoys him how closed off and private I am. "Fine, you pain in the ass, but we're getting back to you eventually. He stopped into the store again yesterday."

Glancing over at him, my eyes widen. "No shit? Did he introduce himself this time?"

"Not until I called him out."

That makes me laugh. "What did you say?"

"He was browsing our selection, asking me question after question about the different strains, which is fine, lots of people do that. But finally, I asked if he was quizzing my knowledge because he is one of the investors and he wants to make sure I know my shit, or if he's genuinely wanting to know."

"And?"

"He chuckled a little, and said maybe a little bit of both."

"At least he's honest," I say.

"At first, I didn't know if he knew I was one of the owners or not, but then I figured, nobody is going to invest in a company and not know exactly who the owners are."

"So, did he buy anything?"

I take a left, pulling into the parking lot of the bar. The lot if pretty full, so we must be some of the last ones to arrive. Checking the time on the dash, we aren't late.

"Yeah, same thing he bought last time."

It's not hard to find a spot, despite how busy it is. Putting the car into park, I unbuckle. "You think he'll be back?"

"I'm sure he will. I just don't know why. It's kind of intimidating."

We both climb out, and I lock the car, as we head inside. "Do you know anybody besides Benton?" I ask Xander.

"His husband's come into the store with him a few times, but other than him, no."

The aroma of Mexican food wafts over to us as we enter the threshold. My stomach growls, it smells so fucking good. The area is dimly lit, LEDs all around, mixed with the natural light pouring in through the windows. Tall, circular tables line the center, booths around the edges of the room, and the actual bar over on the far right. It looks like a nice place. Bet it looks even cooler at night.

Xander bumps me with his elbow. "There's Benton and his husband. Let's go say hi."

I follow his gaze, my heart thrashing in my chest as I locate where he's looking. "You must be fucking joking," I mumble under my breath. I'm surprised Xan even heard me at all.

"What's the matter?"

Huffing a laugh through my nose, because *what are the fucking odds?* "See that guy standing next to them? The one in the black-and-white striped short-sleeve?"

"Yeah…"

"That's Mateo."

Xander's jaw drops open as his head snaps in that direction. "No, it is not."

"Yes, it fucking is."

And as luck would have it, that would be the exact moment that fucker's bright green eyes would scan the room, landing right on us. Well, on *me*.

"Shit," I hiss right as Xander busts out laughing. "Is something funny?"

He stops laughing momentarily. "Um, yeah. You. Him. All of this."

"Real fucking nice," I scoff. "Wait, where are you going?"

"To go say hi to Benson and his husband. And apparently meet your new boo." Xander stops in his tracks, leaning in to add low enough for only me to hear him, "And I can see why you can't stay away. He's fucking hot."

This cannot be fucking happening.

Waking up the morning after we… *hung out*, I was so pissed at myself. When I'm sober, I can't fucking stand the guy. He's an annoyance to the largest degree, and there shouldn't be any reason I can't stay away from him. Like, why would someone feel the urge to hang out with someone they can't stand? But drunk or high Travis apparently can't seem to grasp that concept. It's like my inhibitions leave the room—leave the whole damn building—when I get a substance flowing in my veins. I become immune to my ability to… well, be immune to Mateo.

A cocky fucking smirk is plastered on his face, only growing the closer we get. The men next to him—Benson and his husband—seem to be unaware of what's going on around them. They're too busy conversing about something together.

I'm a little surprised when we stop in front of the three of them, and Mateo has yet to say anything sarcastic or dick-ish. It's like he's waiting to see what I'll say. Or maybe his friends don't know what an enormous jackass he is.

"Hey, Benson. Hey, Doran," Xander says, slapping a hand on one of their backs. "This is my buddy I was telling you about, Travis."

Five sets of eyes look at me, one stronger than the others. The man, who's slightly shorter than everyone else, extends an open hand for me. "Nice to meet you, Travis. I'm Benton, and this is my husband, Doran."

They're an attractive couple, to say the least.

"Nice to meet you both," I murmur. "And happy anniversary."

"Thank you, and thanks for coming." Benton offers me a warm smile before adding," Oh, and these are our friends, Miguel and Mateo."

I can feel more than see Xander beaming beside me. And the way Mateo's eyes are glued to the side of my face is unnerving. *Do I pretend we don't know each other? That this is the first time we're meeting?* That seems like the safest option without having to explain anything.

Too fucking bad that choice is taken from me when Xander blurts out, "Oh, these two know each other," dragging a finger between the two of us.

Mateo's eyes glint with amusement, while I am wishing for the ground to open and swallow me whole.

"We're neighbors," I grit out.

That makes the man beside Mateo—Miguel—huff out a laugh. My gaze darts to his, but he's already looking at Mateo. "*This* is your neighbor, Matty?"

"Matty?!" My hand comes up to cover my mouth, because I

didn't mean to blurt that out. But *Matty?* That's his nickname? Mateo scowls at me, while Miguel and Xander laugh. Poor Doran and Benton stand there looking between us all, clearly missing what's so funny. This is a disaster.

After a few minutes of awkward small talk, I'm able to excuse myself to the bar to get a strong drink. Probably not the smartest idea, but I don't have many of those anymore.

Luckily, the place is pretty full, so we're able to mingle with other people, while Mateo does the same. Throughout the entire event, though, I can feel his intimidating gaze on me, dark, heady eyes following my every move. It's unnerving, and I tell myself I hate it, the way he watches me, but I'm not very convincing.

Xander and I have just finished eating what is probably our sixth taco each, when he leans in, a knowing smirk on his face. "The hickey's from him, isn't it?"

Knew this was coming.

"I'm not doing this."

"But I'm right, aren't I?"

"Xander," I warn, the edge clear in my tone.

He grabs us each another beer, handing me mine as he takes a sip of his. It's an IPA of some sort. I wonder if it's made locally.

"Matty," Xander says with a chuckle. I can't tell if he's saying it more for himself. "Funny nickname for such a large and in charge man."

"Mmhmm."

"Do you remember that time you hooked up with Branson Adler, and he didn't know your name, so he would call you Tony-Troy?"

Narrowing my eyes at him, I grind my molars. Xander cracks up laughing, clearly finding himself so funny.

"Who's Tony-Troy?"

Blood turning ice cold, I turn my head, gaze colliding with a familiar pair of mint greens. How I missed him walking over is beyond me.

"No, I must've forgotten that memory," I deadpan, ignoring Mateo completely.

But of fucking course, I remember that one time I hooked up with a hot-ass guy only to hear from friends after the fact that he gave me a fucking nickname because he couldn't be bothered to remember my name in the first place.

Definitely a core memory.

A highlight of my college career.

And if that one fucking nickname doesn't perfectly describe my dating life as a whole... fine enough to hook up with, but not good enough to remember. *Sounds about right.*

"It's a name someone from college gave to Trav—" Xander blurts out before I smack him in the chest with the back of my hand. "Ouch!"

"It's none of your fucking business, *Matty*."

Admittedly, I take a bit more satisfaction watching his jaw clench together at the sound of his nickname than I should. Keeping my gaze trained on his face, I refuse to let it travel down to take in the way that shirt fits him perfectly or the way his arm muscles bulge through the sleeves. Will not trace his tattoos that enhance those same arms either, admire the way the veins and tendons line his deep brown flesh. And I definitely won't be dropping my gaze farther to check out how well his pants fit his body, the way there's probably a bulge in the crotch because his dick is so fucking massive, it can't be hidden, or the way his tight ass is probably hugged perfectly by the material.

Nope, my eyes will stay locked with his because that is the only safe option.

His gaze drops from mine, though, to my neck, looking at what can only be the not quite faded bruise he left there while he was buried deep inside me the other night. Everything comes rushing back in this moment, feeling his heavy stare on my marred skin.

I feel the way his hands felt on my body. Tight on my hips, around my throat, in my hair.

I feel the salacious way his massive cock moved inside me, dragging along each and every nerve ending, setting my blood ablaze. Every stretch, every burn, every potent shot of pleasure.

I even feel his hot breath fan my overheated, sweat-slick skin.

I feel it all. Every last unforgettable sensation. My pulse races in his proximity, and the way he's now watching me, you'd think he could read my mind. I hate this. Hate what he does to me, how he makes me feel, how my body can't seem to get on the same page as my mind.

My skin is crawling. I gotta get out of here. "As fun as this is, we have to go," I blurt out, sneering at Mateo.

"Uh, we do?" Xander looks and sounds confused. I throw him a look that I hope says *just fucking go with it*, but I don't think it comes across clearly.

"Yes. Bye, *Matty*."

The universe must be at least a little bit on my side because the whole way back to my house, Xander doesn't say anything. He must be able to sense the turmoil bubbling over inside me. We already had plans to hang out at my place, and I've behaved weirdly enough for one day, so I'm not about to cancel our plans. Then Xander will really force me into spilling my guts.

And I'm nowhere near ready for that. He would never

judge me—we've all made stupid choices—but I don't know... I think a major part of me knows it'll probably happen again, and I'm not ready to admit my fault like that.

Once inside my apartment, I turn on some music while Xander rolls a blunt. He's a fucking pro, and he's lighting it up a few minutes later. *Holding Me Down* by Picturesque bumps through the speakers in my living room as he passes it to me. Placing the grape-flavored wrap between my lips, I inhale slowly, letting the smoke dance down my throat, expanding my lungs. My head feels light and fuzzy by the time I exhale through my nose.

We both sit kicked back on opposite sides of my small couch, passing the blunt back and forth as the room fills with clouds of smoke and music. The tension is growing thicker. I'm not even surprised when Xander finally breaks the silence.

"You don't have to tell me anything you don't want to, and the marks on your neck may not even be from him, but if they are, please be careful."

I glance over at him but don't say anything. My throat's thick with emotion I'm not prepared to feel.

He scrubs a hand down his face, blowing out the smoke from his hit. "You deserve more than to wind up with just another Nathaniel. Yeah, Mateo is hot, but he's clearly a fucking asshole. I don't want to see you end up hurt all over again. You haven't even given yourself a chance to get over what you lost with Nathaniel."

"Thanks," I breathe. "I'll be okay. I know exactly who he is, and he's not somebody I want to be with, so no worries there."

It's the truth. He isn't somebody I want to be with. Yes, I'm sexually attracted to him, but it's nothing more than that.

It can't be. That's a disaster and a heartbreak waiting to happen.

"He was staring at you the entire time," he says, barely above a whisper. "You know that?"

"He was not," I scoff.

"Oh, yes, he was." Xan laughs. "Couldn't take his eyes off you. He's trouble, man. Please be careful."

"I said there's nothing to worry about, Xander," I insist. "I mean it."

Holding his hands up innocently, he says, "Okay, okay."

Xander kicks it for about another half an hour before one of his co-workers picks him up. They're all going out for one of their birthdays. We smoked another blunt before he leaves, so now I'm nice and toasty.

Getting dressed in pajama pants after taking the world's hottest and longest shower, I amble out into the kitchen, grabbing a bag of spicy Dorito's and a couple of bottles of water before parking my ass in front of the TV. Putting on another episode of Shameless, I pull my phone out, not even paying attention to the show as I scroll aimlessly through social media.

A hard knock on the front door pulls my attention, my eyes lifting to glance at the time. *That's weird. Xander must've forgotten something.*

Raising off the couch, I cross the room, pulling open the door to come face to face with... not Xander.

"What are you doing here?" I ask, leaning my shoulder against the doorframe, folding my arms over my chest. My heart hammers behind my ribs as I take in the man before me. The man I didn't expect to see again tonight.

Minty green eyes give me a quick once-over before meeting my gaze. His features are soft, his usual malicious smirk nowhere to be seen. "Can I come in?"

"Why?"

"Because I'm home alone, and I'm guessing you are too. And I thought maybe we could keep each other company." He shrugs, his eyes filled with lust and insinuation. "Go back to hating each other in the morning," he adds.

Huffing out a snort, I throw back, "Hating each other? What the hell do you have to hate me for?"

He smirks, the sight causing my stomach to flutter. I hate it. "You know what I mean, *cariño*."

Be it the fog the weed has my brain blanketed in or the spell his magic dick seems to have me under, I become hyperaware of the fact that zero part of me wants to turn him away, despite knowing I'm doing nothing but proving Xander right. Taking a step back and to the side, I let him in for what will more than likely be a huge fucking mistake.

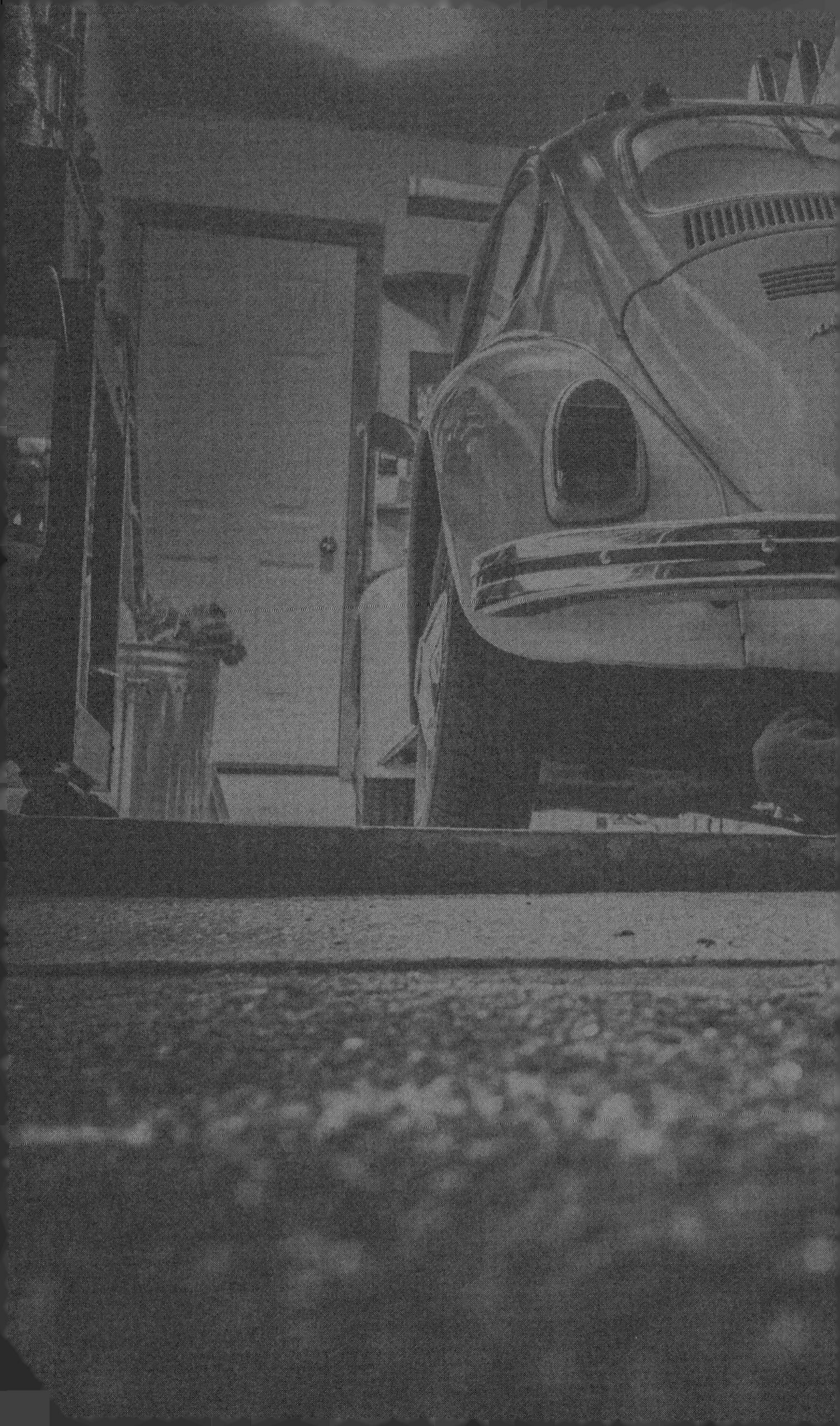

TWENTY-SIX

Mateo

After the pissed off way Travis left the bar earlier, I figured he'd rather deck me in the face than let me into his house, but alas, here I am, standing in his entryway mere inches from him. He's half naked, wearing only a pair of purple and black pajama pants, his chest bare and smooth, pale, milky skin with barely-there muscles pulled taut, rippling with tension.

"What gives you the right to show up at my house like this?" he asks with a sneer.

"Why not?"

"Because I told you last time—"

"Yet, you let me in anyway," I counter. "Why do you think that is, *cariño*?"

He scoffs. "Maybe because I didn't want to argue with you in the hallway, where anybody could hear. That's a little rude and disruptive."

A smirk pulls at my lips. "Oh, *all* the many neighbors we have on this floor?"

He opens his mouth like he wants to say something, but eventually snaps it shut.

I take a single step forward until I'm standing nearly flush with him. His breath hitches. "Can we skip this bickering foreplay for once and get on with it already?"

Without waiting for a response, I haul him into me by the back of his neck, our lips colliding brutally. He gasps and I slide my tongue in, sweeping along his. He tastes of weed and something else I can't quite place. His plush lips, the feel of his trembling body against mine, and the sound of his inhibitions leaving on a soft mewl being pushed into my mouth has my blood heating.

Coming here wasn't my plan. I left the bar and came home with every single intention of going into my house and calling it a night. When I got to the hallway between the two apartments, there wasn't a thought as I raised my fist and knocked on his door. It was automatic. A subconscious impulse of my unabashed desire for Travis.

For the past several days, mostly since we hooked up again, I've been trying to pinpoint what it is about him that has me so out of my mind. It's never been like this for me. Since Robbie—and hell, even before him—I was fine being alone. Fine with meaningless hook-ups and one-night stands. I've never yearned for the feeling of someone beside me, never itched to have someone's flesh against mine as I slept. Yet, the other night when he left after we fucked without so much as a second thought, I felt a gnawing ache in my chest. A bitter taste on the back of my tongue.

It stung.

Lips still locked, I wrap an arm around his middle, walking us backward into his living room. His ass hits the back of the couch, and I use my hands on his hips to lift him up. Travis's legs wrap around me, his arms going around my neck as he slants his head, opening wider for me.

We kiss like we may never get the chance to ever again, and hell, we might not if his stubborn side gets his way. But if this really is the last time, I'm not wasting it. Wrenching my lips away from his, trailing along his sharp jawline, I take the lobe of his ear between my teeth, tugging and nipping. Travis groans, his hands gripping my shirt tightly.

Next, I nip at his neck, sucking on the salty flesh, marking him exactly how I know he loves. For someone who swears he can't stand me, he sure loves to wear the evidence of me being here. Seeing the hickey on his neck earlier at the bar that I knew I gave him lit my blood on fire. Because I've never been much of a feelings or relationship guy after the trainwreck that was Robbie, possessiveness has never been my thing... but with Travis, it's ferocious.

Not only do I want to own him behind closed doors; I want the entire fucking world to know he belongs to me.

I want to piss on his leg and mark my territory for everyone to see.

"Mateo..." My name leaves his lips on a breathless moan as he tips his head back farther, silently begging me to keep going.

Lapping over his Adam's apple, it rolls under my tongue as he swallows thickly, his body vibrating against mine.

"What do you need, *cariño*?" I ask against his throat.

"You," he admits easily, much to my surprise. "I need you. I need it all."

Pulling back and meeting his baby blue gaze, I push a stray strand of dirty blond hair out of his eyes. His cheeks are flushed, his lips swollen, and he's looking up at me, letting me see just how badly he wants me right now. It ignites a throbbing type of yearning inside me.

"Let's go to your room," I murmur before placing one last kiss upon his lips.

The layout of his apartment is exactly like mine, but I let him lead me to his room anyway. It isn't until we step into the room that I remember he has a dog. She's lying on a huge navy-blue bed on the floor in the corner of his bedroom.

Travis whistles, waking her up. "Nova, out, baby."

"You don't have to kick her out. She was sleeping."

"Trust me, she'd wake up, and then it'd be weird." He glances at me over his shoulder. "She's got a big bed in the living room, so she'll be fine."

I chuckle. "Yeah, okay."

Travis closes the door once she leaves, resting his back against the tall wood. A mixture of nerves and arousal dance over his features as I close the distance between us. Threading my fingers through his on both hands, I raise them above his head, pushing them into the door as I press my body into his.

He's already hard, but so am I.

Our lips mold together, moving hungrily. My tongue slashes into his mouth, the taste of him exquisite. I can't get enough. It's too much. *It's everything.*

Switching the hold I have on his wrists to one hand, I bring my other down to his throat as I pull back, giving him a once-over.

"*Hermoso,*" I breathe, my chest tight, throat dry.

I walk us over to the bed, where I sit on the edge, patting my thigh. Making a kissing noise, I order him, "Come, puppy." I can't even get the two words out before I'm laughing, his eyes narrowing into slits.

It doesn't deter him, though. He climbs in my lap, our lips finding each other again. It's passionate, the way we consume each other right now. Slipping my hands into the back of his pants, a grin slides onto my lips when I realize he's going commando. I palm his tight, firm globes, squeezing and massaging them as his hips undulate into me.

"Go lie on the bed," I growl. "I need to taste you, *cariño*."

A shudder runs down his spine as he bites down on his bottom lip, climbing off my lap.

Standing up, I add, "Lose the pants too."

"So bossy," he grumbles, but I don't miss the slight smirk trying to break through.

Reaching into his pocket, Travis grabs his phone, tossing it onto the bed before shoving the fabric down. Kicking it off to the side, he crawls onto the bed, turning music on before getting settled.

The sensual beat of *You Put A Spell On Me* by Austin Giorgio filters through the sexually charged air of this room, and I'm frozen in place as I watch him peer over at me, one hand wrapped around his dick, the other reaching down, cupping his beautiful pink balls. The sight sparks something dark and feral and *needy* inside of me.

Climbing on the bed on all fours, crawling over to him, I position myself between his spread open thighs, lowering myself onto my stomach. I wrap an arm around one of his thighs, lowering my lips onto his heated flesh. The ghost of a moan leaves his lips while I run the flat of my tongue along his skin, inching closer to his center.

Travis's hand moves leisurely up and down his shaft, fingers dancing along his sac. Part of me wants to stop and watch, absolutely mesmerized by his unabashed toying, but another *larger* part of me needs to taste him like my lungs need oxygen. Nuzzling my nose into the crease between his groin and his leg, I breathe in his fresh, musky aroma, my head growing dizzy and my mouth watering.

Everything about him has my body operating on overdrive. His scent, the way he feels, the sounds he makes, the way he's *still* playing with himself shamelessly, even as my tongue drags along his balls. He moans, the sound throaty.

I want more of that noise.

I *need* more.

My tongue trails down farther, licking along his taint before dipping into his crease. I nip sharply at his flesh, sucking on it hard enough to pull a gasp out of him before flicking my tongue over it soothingly. I relish the way his gasps morph into groans, like he isn't sure how I make him feel.

Just as my tongue swirls around his hole, Travis's phone starts vibrating incessantly like a call is coming in. He grabs the phone beside us, quickly silencing it. The music comes back on, and I dive in. I spread him open with my hands, pushing his legs back onto his chest, closing my lips around his hole, sucking.

Travis lets out a long, low rumble as he pushes himself up onto his forearms, letting his head drop back. "Fuck, Mateo…"

My name on his lips is a firecracker set off in my bloodstream.

His body quivers with need, legs coming down to sit on my shoulders, thighs squeezing the sides of my head. He cries out as my stiffened tongue slips through his tight muscle, fucking him with it while my hand comes up to stroke his cock.

I'm fucking insatiable when it comes to Travis. My tongue can't move fast enough, can't lap up his flavor quick enough. I want him every single way I can have him all at once; a ravenous type of hunger claws at my insides, fighting to break free for him.

And the way he wants to hate me? It makes the craving even more ferocious. I wasn't lying earlier when I referred to our bickering as foreplay. I get off on it as much as it infuriates me. He awakens something inside of me, and as much as I've tried to chalk it up to simply enjoying the chase, I think it's time I admit that it's more than that.

This thing with Travis isn't just about the chase. About scoring. Because if that was the case, I've already scored, I've already caught my prey. It's more than that, and truthfully, I'm not sure how I feel about that.

I'm pulled from my thoughts and the heavenly sound of Travis moaning my name when his phone goes off *again*.

"Who the fuck keeps calling you?" I growl, demanding an answer like I have any right whatsoever.

Travis grabs the phone, glancing at the screen before heaving a sigh. He takes entirely too long for my liking to respond to my question, so I sink my teeth into the part of his ass that meets his thigh. He jerks back, gasping. "Ow, you fuck! It's Nathaniel."

Nathaniel? Why the fuck is he calling him? My jaw aches as I grind down on my molars, my blood pressure skyrocketing as I try to make sense of this.

"Why the fuck is he calling you?" I snarl, clearly unable to keep it cool.

He shrugs. "Fuck if I know."

"Does he do that a lot?"

"Like, a few times a month," he states, like it's no big fucking deal.

Multiple times in a row? Huffing out a snort through my nose, I say, "What? Are you getting back with the guy?"

"Um, no?" His brows knit together as he phrases it like a question. A beat passes, and his eyes widen. "Wait, are you *jealous*?"

I watch as he chews on the inside of his cheek, trying to hide a smirk. It fucking pisses me off.

"No, I'm not fucking jealous, *pendejo*," I growl. That's fucking ludicrous.

He snorts out a laugh. "Whatever you say, Mateo." He wraps a fist around his softening cock, stroking himself lazily. "Just because he calls doesn't mean I answer. I have no desire to speak to him."

Damn fucking right. That guys a fucking douchebag.

"Give me your phone."

Confusion clouds his features, his hand stalling. "Why?"

Because I fucking said so," I rumble, extending my hand toward him palm up. Travis narrows his eyes on me for a moment before doing as I ask. Turning on the screen, I pass it back, grumbling, "Unlock it."

Once I have the phone in my hand unlocked, I find that stupid fucking prick's contact, pulling up a new message.

"What are you doing?" he asks, tone full of skepticism.

"Don't you worry about a thing, *cariño*. Just lie on back and let me take care of you while we send a little clip to this douchebag, letting him know how much you *don't* miss him."

"A video?" he croaks, looking and sounding horrified.

"Nah… just an audio clip." I smirk, turning on the record button and setting it down beside us, wasting no more time spreading him open for me and diving back in. A moan hiccups out of him as he falls onto his back, hands gripping the sheets.

My tongue delves out, lapping up a hot, wet trail from his hole all the way up to his balls. Sucking one into my mouth, I peer up at him through my lashes, loving the lust-drunk expression on his face. His lip is tucked between his teeth, biting down so hard it's nearly white.

Shaking my head, I say, "Uh-uh. Let me hear you, baby."

For good measure, I nip at the skin just underneath his ass cheek, pulling a beautiful yelp from him before I return my attention and my tongue to his tight, fluttering hole. I can't wait to sink my fucking cock into it soon. It's practically begging me to with the way it constricts and pulses around my tongue.

I wrap my hand around his length, squeezing at the base before I stroke, continuing to loosen his ass with my tongue. He cries out, a slick hand coming up to fist the strands atop my head.

"Oh, fuck," he cries out hoarsely. "Like that… yes, fuck, like that." The smile that slides on my face against his skin is involuntary, but I can't help but get harder at the fact that the phone is catching all of this. My chest swells even further when he adds, "Bite me again… I want the pain too."

Little fucking masochist.

Well, shit. Who am I to deny him?

Sinking my teeth into the firm flesh of his ass cheek, I stroke him faster, swiping my thumb over his weeping slit, spearing around the stream of pre-cum leaking out. I suck the reddened flesh into my mouth for a moment before pulling back and grabbing the phone. Ending the audio, I glance up at Travis, whose heavy, blown-out eyes are already on me.

"I'm going to hit send, *cariño*, unless you tell me not to."

My heart thumps erratically in my chest as I wait on bated breath for his response. Even though I may be an asshole, I'd never send something like that if he truly didn't want me to. But I'd be lying if I said I wouldn't be disappointed if he said no.

"Do it," he says, voice throaty. "That was fucking hot. Send it and fuck me already. I'm done dealing with Nathaniel."

Heat pools low in my groin as my finger punches down on the send button. He's right, it was fucking hot, and now I need to get inside him *now*.

Tossing the phone onto the bed beside us, I crawl over him. "Lube?" I ask, my mouth a hairsbreadth away from his.

Travis's eyes dip to my lips before coming back up. "Nightstand."

Quickly grabbing it, I return to the spot between his legs, but he stops me before I can bring slick fingers to his crease. My eyes lift to meet his questioningly, but I don't say anything.

"Let me fuck you this time."

I don't know what I expected him to say, but it wasn't *that*.

"No."

His brows pinch together. "No? Are you a strict top?"

"Yup." Probably ignorance, but it never crossed my mind that Travis would ever want to top. It's something we should've talked about, but I truly don't think either of us expected us to wind up here, fucking multiple times.

In his stubborn brain, he probably genuinely thought the snowstorm was going to be the only time.

He looks perturbed, like he wants to argue it, or at the very least, discuss it further. Travis must see something in my features, though, because he thankfully drops it, lying back and widening his thighs to give me better access.

My dick's gone soft after that, but it doesn't take long for me to stiffen back up once I'm a few fingers deep into his tight ass. He squirms and moans, chomping down on his lip as his baby blue eyes bore into me.

A deep ache buries itself in my loins. The idea of waiting another second longer to sink into him is impossible. Slathering my cock with the cool gel, I line myself up to his entrance, pushing inside. I'm not gentle and I'm not slow, but the way his features morph into one of rapture as he lets out a low, gravelly moan tells me he prefers it this way.

If there's one thing I've learned about Travis so far, it's that he craves the pain right along with the pleasure. The hand on the throat, the smack on the ass, the edging and tempting, he's desperate for it all. Which works out perfectly because I enjoy dishing out the teasing and the pain.

From the few times we've wound up in bed together, it would seem we're a perfect match; sexually, at least. The way his body moves with mine, the way it opens up so easily for me, the sounds I'm able to pull from his body like he's an instrument I know how to manipulate naturally.

My mind drifts back to all the toys I have in my room, and I can't help but wonder if he'd ever let me use them on him. Sure, he put up quite the protest about the leather cuffs at first, but it was glaringly obvious he ended up liking it.

Sitting back on my heels, holding his hips in a bruising grip, I begin to pound into him recklessly. His perfect pink balls bounce with the impact and his jaw seems to be permanently dropped open for the time being as he cries out, moans getting louder and louder as the tip of my cock grazes along his prostate. His chest glistens with sweat as he white-knuckles the sheets below.

Glancing down, my balls throb as I watch my dick disappear in and out of his tight fucking hole. It's a heady sight. Sordid and lewd.

"Just a pretty, tight little cunt," I growl, tracing along his stretched hole with the pad of my thumb as my cock continues to plunge in and out. "Do you like when I destroy your tight pink pussy, *cariño*?"

Travis whimpers but says nothing.

Wrapping my hand around his throat, I squeeze the sides tight enough to cut off the airflow a little, but mostly to get his attention. "Answer me when I ask you a question, *cariño*."

"Yes... yes!" he gasps, rolling his hips up to meet me thrust for thrust.

I grunt, the sound feral and animalistic. "That's fucking right. You love what I do to you, baby. You love the way I make you feel. You can pretend to hate me all you want, but it's my cock, my fingers, my tongue, *me*, that's making you rip at the seams. I want you to remember that the next time that fucker calls or texts you." My thrusts become harder, the slap of our slick skin reverberating through his room. "I want you to remember this moment, and every other, when you're even thinking of being with anybody else, *cariño*. I own you. I make you feel this way."

The last part is snarled through gritted teeth, the honesty behind the words shocking me a little. Sweat pours down my back, coating my hair, and the organ in my chest is pounding so hard against my ribs. My head's light. I feel high on Travis, and Travis alone.

He thrusts both hands into his hair, eyes rolling back. "Fuck, Mateo... *oh, God*."

"Fuck, yes, baby," I growl. "Let me hear you scream for me. Give it all to me. Don't hold back."

"Shit... Mateo, ahh. Fuck, I'm gonna come," he cries out.

The hand around his throat tightens a bit more, one of his hands coming down to grip my wrist as he dips his chin, lust-drenched gaze connecting with mine. His lips part, jaw dropping moments before his dick erupts, spilling his release all over his stomach.

"Mateo... *Mateo*..." My name plays on a breathy loop off his tongue as I work him through his orgasm. He's squeezing my cock so tight, he's practically strangling it, his hole constricting with each spurt of cum.

It takes no time at all for me to catch up, following suit, spilling into his tight, spent cunt. My release plunders through me, taking me with such force, tears spring to my eyes by the time I drain myself into him. I let out a guttural roar, my muscles tightening, my jaw clenching.

That's the hardest I've come... I think ever.

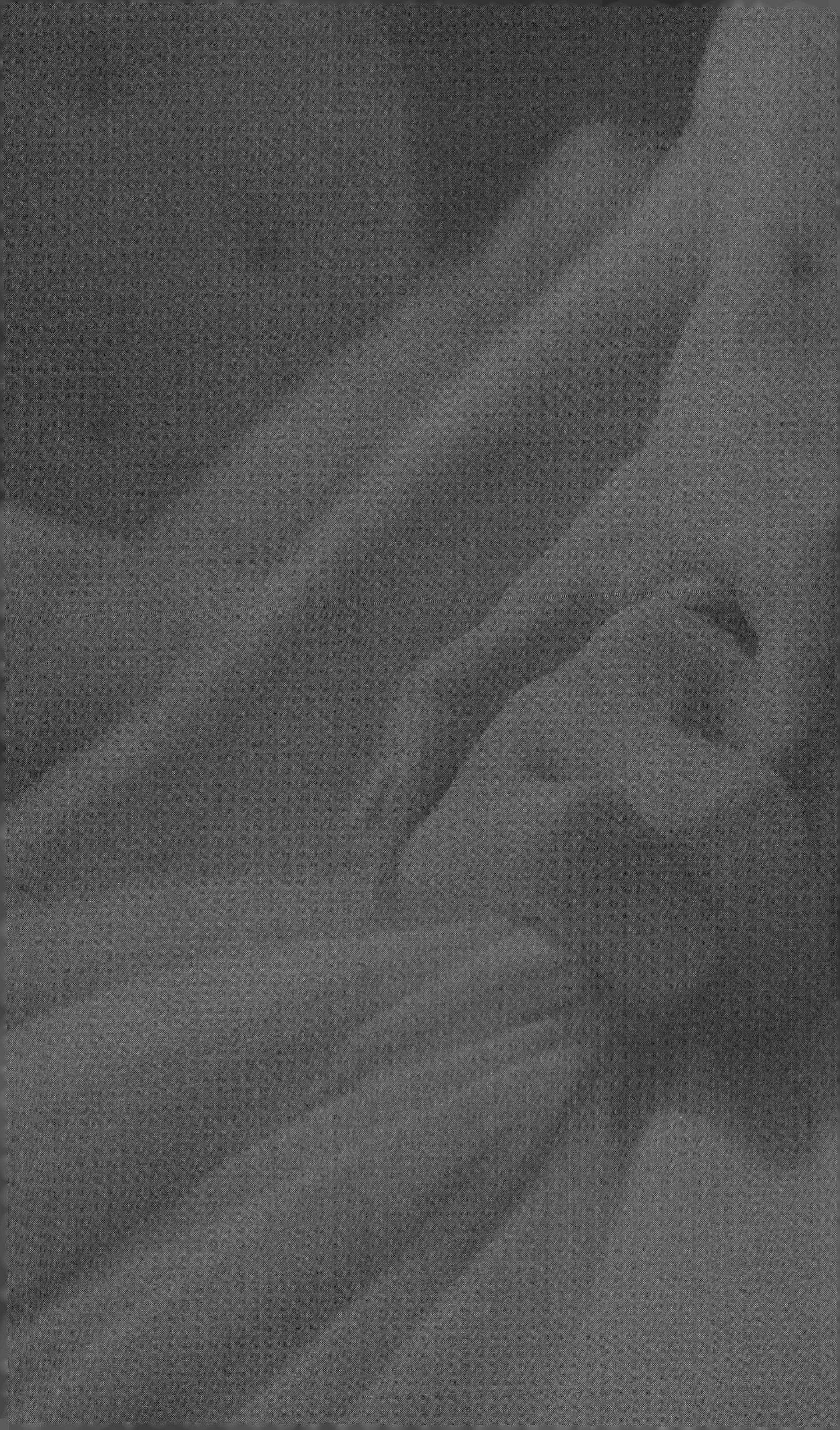

TWENTY-SEVEN
Travis

Stepping under the hot stream, my shoulders release from my ears, my muscles relaxing almost immediately. I let the water fall over my face, my eyes closed as I try to gather my bearings. The large, overpowering body asleep on the left side of my bed is currently haunting me. I don't know why I let him sleep over, nor do I know why he wanted to.

I'm confused. So fucking confused.

Why can't I seem to stick to my guns around him? When he isn't near me, I have no problem setting boundaries and sticking with them. But him standing anywhere in my vicinity? I'm helpless to his magic. No matter how much my mind knows I need to keep my distance, every other part of me craves him like a feint. It's like his minty green eyes and huge devil dick have a kill switch for my brain.

Why else would I have let him not only record that audio yesterday, but send it to Nathaniel? I'm not the type of person to do petty shit like that, but he brings out that side of me. And I don't know whether it turns me on or terrifies me. It's not like Nathaniel doesn't deserve a little retaliation for what he put me through...

Another thing my mind keeps replaying from yesterday is how adamant he was about not bottoming. Which, yes, I've been with plenty of men who are strict tops, so that doesn't bother me. I love to bottom. But I don't know... something about it just feels off with him. The way he tensed up at the mere question, and how clearly closed off he was to the discussion.

I want to ask him why, but I'm not sure it's my place.

What *is* my place in all this with him anyway? I keep saying and insisting this'll never happen again, only for it to happen again... and again.

The bathroom door pushes open in my periphery, grabbing my attention. This apartment has a glass shower, so I can see everything out there and Mateo can see everything in here. His eyes shamelessly rake down the length of my body, stopping to unabashedly check out my cock, which is now thickening under his gaze. Even through the fog and the glass, I don't miss the sexy smirk that slides on his face when his eyes finally land on mine.

Of course, I take my time checking him out too. He's in nothing more than a pair of maroon briefs. They hug his thick thighs and his massive bulge in a mouthwatering way. His chest is bare, save for the miles of black ink covering every inch of flesh, and the two silver bars pierced through his deep red nipples.

The weight of his stare on my body, and the way I know I affect him, it's a powerful feeling. Mateo sits on the corner of the sink, his fingers gripping the edge as his eyes never stray from me.

An overwhelming sense of confidence and boldness washes

over me, and when the object in the corner of my shower that I completely forgot about until right this moment catches my eye, a wide grin pulls on my lips.

Glancing back over at Mateo, I reach over, grabbing the eight-inch suction cup realistic dildo from where it was sitting on the shelf. Beside it is a bottle of lube, so I grab that too. Coating my fingers with the gel, I bring them to my hole, inserting one, then two, while Mateo watches in rapt silence.

It doesn't take much for me to work myself open since he was inside me not even a full night's sleep ago. I pour a generous amount onto the thick toy, spreading it around. Lifting my eyes to meet his again, I place my foot on one of the lower shelves, opening myself up further as I bring the blunt tip of the dildo to my entrance.

I bite down on my lip as the toy inches its way in. Mateo's chest rises and falls rapidly as he continues to watch me, his gaze alternating between the silicone dick pumping in and out of me and my face. Letting my eyes drop for a single beat, I can tell he's hard. Extremely so. That fact urges me on, giving me more confidence.

It hits me as I'm fucking myself for Mateo's viewing pleasure, that not only is it a strong, heady feeling having his eyes on me, but despite the fact that I wish I didn't, I enjoy it too. I enjoy his desire for me. I get off on the way he talks to me when we're in bed, the way he man-handles me. His asshole personality turns me on, even though it shouldn't. Even though I wish it didn't. This, right here, is setting my blood ablaze. I can't get enough of his attention.

A deep, throaty groan rumbles from my chest as the toy grazes that sweet button inside of me. It sends an electric jolt through my body, and my legs tremble from the sensation as I let out a breathy, "*Fuck...*"

Mateo swallows hard, his Adam's apple bobbing in his throat. His hands are gripping the edge of the sink so hard, his knuckles have blanched. I wrap a hand around my throbbing cock while my other continues to fuck my ass with the toy. My back rests on the cold tile wall, the temperature a stark difference to the inferno inside of me.

He watches without moving for much longer than I thought he would, but eventually, he shoves his briefs down, stepping out of them and kicking them to the side, before stalking toward the shower with arousal and mischief dancing in his eyes. Mateo rips the door open, nearly off the hinges, as he steps inside, crowding the tight space with his massive body.

"You drive me crazy, *cariño*. You know that?"

I smirk. "I could say the same about you."

His rough, calloused palm wraps around my stiff length. I gasp, but it's cut off by his mouth covering mine, tongue driving inside. My back slams into the wall, the chilly temperature no less jarring than it was earlier. As always, his free hand slides up to my throat, wrapping around and squeezing. I'll probably never admit this out loud, but I kind of love it. The possessiveness of it, it swirls something dark and potent in my gut.

Mateo rips his lips from mine, using his thumb to tip my chin up, forcing me to meet his gaze. His eyes flutter all over my face, and he looks like he wants to say something, but he doesn't. He simply continues to stroke me roughly, inching me closer to the finish line. The eye contact is heady, his hand gliding just right up and down my shaft. The act feels too intimate, but I can't seem to force myself to break the eye contact.

My heart hammers in my chest, and I can't catch my breath. He keeps up a relentless pace for several minutes, but when his wrist twists, I'm done for. My eyes slam shut, but only briefly, because he squeezes my throat in a silent attempt to get my attention. As soon as my eyes fly open, they lock with his while he gives me a terse shake of the head.

"Eyes on me, *cariño*. You look at me while I make you come, you understand me?"

"*Fuckkk...*" is all I get out before my release barrels through me, making my legs tremble. It pulses out of me in spurt after spurt after spurt. It feels never ending, as does his dark, salacious gaze on me. He sees right into my soul. Sees what he does to me. Sees this hold, this spell, this absolute smoke-filled daze he has me in.

My body turns boneless. If it weren't for his grip on my throat, I'd no doubt collapse. I'm wrung dry, but despite coming ten seconds ago, I'm still so turned on as I glance down and see his thick, long, rigid cock pointing right at me. Like it's choosing me.

Like *he's* choosing me.

Reaching up, I wrap my hand around his wrist, removing his grip from my throat. I sink down, my knees colliding with the shower floor as I peer up at him beneath my wet lashes. My hand shakes, for what reason, I'm not sure, as I wrap it around his dick, my fingers not even touching with how girthy it is. Honestly, I've never been with someone with as large of a cock as Mateo has. It's as impressive as it is frightening.

My tongue darts out, lapping up the warm, salty moisture pooling at the slit, enjoying the way he clenches his jaw as to appear unfazed. When I pull back, jacking him off, I watch his eyes peruse over me appreciatively.

"Look at you," he says in an almost coo, voice rough and deep. "Marks all over your neck and chest because of me. I know if I were to turn you around, you'd have them on your ass too."

"Do you like that?" I ask, letting the tip of his cock trace my lip. "Me being marked by you?"

"Of course, I do. You're *mine*," he snarls. Mateo clamps down on his teeth as soon as the possessive word leaves his mouth, like maybe he didn't mean to say it.

But he *did* say it, and I heard it… twice. Once earlier, and once right now. And fuck, it wakes something up inside of me. The raw, carnal ownership. Fire licks my veins, rolling through my entire being as something strong and unlike anything before takes over.

He wants to own me, to mark me and make sure everybody knows it's *him* doing it, and in this moment, on my knees before him, in one of the most submissive positions there is, I realize I want that too. To be wanted so wholly, they want the world to know.

Looking back on this moment, I don't think I'll ever truly understand where this next suggestion came from, or what the hell came over me to even think this was a good, sane idea. Placing a soft kiss along the side of his dick, I pull back, peering up at him, and say, "So mark your territory then."

His brows knit together as he tries to make sense of what I'm saying, but it doesn't take long for something to click and his signature cocky smirk to spread on his full, red lips. "Are you suggesting what I think you're suggesting, *cariño*?"

Biting down on my bottom lip, I nod, keeping my hands clasped together in my lap.

His eyes darken, and he wraps a tight fist around himself. "You're sure?"

I nod again. "Do it. I want you to."

Mateo's smile widens, his bright white teeth on display as he breathes out a laugh. "You're just full of surprises, aren't you, baby?"

My dick is already starting to get hard again, watching him tower over me, his cock in his hand. The water sluices down his muscled chest, streaming onto me as he places a flat palm on the wall behind me, and a different, slightly warmer liquid begins to mix with the water. My pulse races as it covers my chest.

The way he's looking down at me right now, the heat in his gaze, the way his lips are parted just enough for me to see the silver ring glinting through his tongue. The adoration. The desire.

He finishes, the act itself only taking several seconds at most. Mateo strokes himself, running water over his cock before bringing it up to my lips. I open up automatically, groaning when the weight of his length glides over my tongue. Bringing his hand to the back of my head, he fists the strands, sinking deeper until he touches the back of my throat and I gag.

Pulling back slightly, he lets me gulp in a lungful of air before he slides in all the way again. Tears spring to my eyes, my chest aching with the need to breathe, but the way he's looking at me is *everything*. I don't think I've ever had someone look at me the way Mateo does.

Both of his hands are now gripping my head, holding it in place as he fucks me throat deep. His grunts are guttural.

Mateo looks like a wrecked God towering over me, owning me, while I can do nothing more than sit here and take it. Take all that he's giving me.

And I do.

I want it all.

A full-body shudder races through him as he pulls out of my mouth, his large hand fisting his massive length, stroking himself feverishly. His teeth are bared as he pumps himself, his hand still gripping the back of my head.

Mateo lets out an even deeper groan as his hot cum jets out, splashing my face and my neck. My hands are pressing on his thighs, and I can feel them quake as he works himself through his release.

He lets go of his spent cock, running his fingers through the second mess he's made on me, shoving his fingers into my mouth until I can taste nothing more than his flavor. I swallow every drop, and when he slides the digits of my mouth, strings of spit and cum still connecting us, he yanks me up by my throat, crashing his lips down on mine. He kisses me until I'm breathless.

Until I don't even know what's happening.

He kisses me until the water finally runs cold.

He kisses me until a longing ache forms in my chest, telling me I never want him to stop.

TWENTY-EIGHT

Travis

Mateo went home after we got out of the shower. That was almost five minutes ago, and I'm still sitting on my bed in nothing but a towel around my waist. I think I'm in shock… Yeah, this could definitely be characterized as shock. Or maybe I experienced an aneurysm and lost function in the rational, sane part of my brain. That has to be it, because why else would I have not only let what just happened happen, but also *instigate* it?

I can't even pretend I was coaxed into it or pressured. No, it was wholly *my* idea to have Mateo *piss* on me like I'm some fucking city fire hydrant and he's a dog.

Nova is standing in the doorway to my room, staring at me with eyes full of judgement like she knows what I just did. Like she can sense that he marked his territory on her owner.

"What the fuck." Scrubbing a hand down my face, I try to figure out which part disturbs me more; the fact that I let him—*asked him*—to give me a golden fucking shower, or the fact that I enjoyed it as much as I did. Honestly, it's probably the latter. *Why did I like it so much?*

My throat feels tight, shame sitting like lead in my gut as I force myself off the bed to get dressed. It's late morning by now, and I haven't even taken Nova for her walk yet. My whole day is off kilter because of this now.

As I'm tugging my t-shirt over my head, a knock sounds at the door. I glance behind me at Nova, like she would know anything. Her fuzzy ears lift and flop back down as her tail wags a little.

"Who is it, girl? Is it for you?" She, of course, says nothing. "Maybe it's Hank, your doggy boyfriend." Her head cocks to the side at the name. Hank was the name of the dog that lived next door to us when we lived in the house with Nathaniel. He's this adorable black and white mutt, and his nose had a spot on it that made it look heart shaped. They used to love playing together.

A knock sounds again. "C'mon girl," I say, patting the side of my leg. "Let's see who's here, and then we can go for a walk." Her ears really perk up for that.

Strolling across the apartment, I glance out the window in my living room, seeing the sun shining. Getting to the door, I pull it open, my heart palpitating in my chest. "What are you doing here?"

Mateo holds up a joint, his eyes gleaming. "Wanna smoke this with me?"

He says it so nonchalantly, like he didn't just piss all over my chest and then subsequently come all over my face.

I can't help but wonder if he's ever done that before. Given someone a golden shower. He didn't seem to be too shocked by the idea, and he went along with it easily enough. *Why does the idea of him doing that with someone else make my stomach churn?*

Remembering he asked me a question, I shake my head. "Can't. Going on a walk with Nova." And as if to further prove my point, I reach behind me toward the coat rack hanging on the wall in the hallway, grabbing the pink leash hanging there.

"I'll come with you," he states effortlessly with a shrug. "Let me grab my coat."

Not bothering to wait for me to agree to him coming along, he spins on his heel, heading back into his apartment across the hall, leaving me standing there, dumbfounded.

What the fuck is happening?

He comes back out a moment later, a black puffer coat and a matching black beanie on. "Ready?"

"Uh…" My brows dip inward as I slip my arms into my coat. "I didn't say you could come."

"Don't be fucking weird," he scoffs. "It's a walk, *cariño*. I'm not asking for your damn hand in marriage. Let's go."

He's so bossy.

Why is that hot? It should be repulsive.

"And give me her leash." Mateo grabs it from my hand. Clearly, he's not bothering to wait for approval on anything today.

Quickly shoving my feet into my shoes, I shove my keys and my phone into my pocket, and we leave. It's hellaciously cold outside. I should've taken a page out of Mateo's book and grabbed a hat.

"Where do you normally walk her?" he asks as soon as we're on the sidewalk in front of the building.

Pointing to the left, I say, "There's a trail a bit down the road this way."

The sidewalks are crowded on both sides, which is unusual for this time of day. But if I'm not mistaken, there's a car show this afternoon a few blocks up, so that's probably where everyone is headed.

Neither of us says anything for a few minutes as we walk. He's got his dark, tattooed hand wrapped once around Nova's leash as she walks beside us. I can smell his rich cologne from here. It's annoying how good it smells.

We make it onto the trail. I love this place; it's the perfect walking area. It's covered in trees, so even when it's hot out, I'm sure it'll be nice and cool. I've run into a lot of other dog owners on this trail too.

Mateo clears his throat after a while, and I feel more than see him glance over at me. "So, I'm cashing in on our bet."

Snapping my head in his direction, I ask, "What bet?"

"The one from the snowstorm," he grumbles. "The date."

"You can't be fucking serious."

"A bet's a bet, *cariño*. I won fair and square. Time to pay up."

Annoyance flares in my chest as I roll my eyes. "What did you have in mind?"

I can't believe I'm even entertaining this.

"My sister, Ally, is having her engagement party this Saturday. You'll be my date."

"What?" My voice goes up at least two octaves, my chest tightening. "I'm not meeting your fucking family."

"Yes, you are," he replies sternly, leaving no room for argument. "A deal's a deal. It's a couple of hours, free food, and free booze. I think you'll survive."

"Why not bring someone who actually wants to go with you?"

"Because it's a week away, and I don't feel like finding someone."

"So, why bring a date at all?"

"Why do you ask so many fucking questions?" he retorts. His body visibly stiffens as we walk, and there's a bite to his words that wasn't there a moment ago.

"I'm just trying to make sense of why you would bring some random dude to meet your family."

"None of your fucking business, okay? Will you just do it?"

It's right there on the tip of my tongue to say no. Truthfully, I'm under no obligation to hold up to my end of the deal if I don't want to. It was a dumb bet anyway. But there's something about the faint sense of desperation to Mateo right now, how he's almost pleading with me in not so many words, that has me folding.

"Fine," I mumble. "What time is it, and what do I have to wear?"

"It starts at six. It's at her fiancé's parents' house on the other side of town, so we'll leave around five-thirty. You can wear slacks and a button-down shirt. It doesn't have to be overly fancy or anything."

"This better not be awkward," I grumble.

Mateo's body language is so different than it was a few minutes ago. The shift is obvious. His words are clipped, shoulders are damn near up to his ears, and his knuckles are white from tension as he holds Nova's leash. There's clearly more to the story and more on why he is having me come, but I don't have time to analyze it any further.

"Travis?" A voice I'd recognize anywhere reaches my ears as a hand comes to my shoulder from behind, stopping me in my tracks. Ice runs through my veins as I turn around, coming face to face with the jackass who broke my heart. "Thought that was you. Hey."

The easygoing grin on his lips pisses me off. Like running into each other is a joyous event. It's not.

"Hi, Nathaniel."

Nova, the traitor she is, wags her tail and rubs her head against the side of his leg. He reaches down to pet her as I glance over at Mateo, who's looking at Nathaniel with angry, narrowed eyes. His jaw is clenched, nostrils flared.

My heart is hammering, and it feels like someone is squeezing the shit out of my lungs. I can't seem to breathe deep enough. The very last thing I want to do is be in Nathaniel's presence. *Especially* with Mateo. The images of him railing Nathaniel over *my* bed flood into my mind without my permission, and I have to swallow against the bile threatening to rise in my throat.

I need to get out of here. I consider making a run for it, just darting away, but it hits me that Mateo is still holding on to Nova's leash. I can't leave her here with them. So, instead, I blurt out the first question that comes to mind. "What the fuck are you doing here, Nathaniel?"

He doesn't even live here. He lives in Pullman, in the house we bought *together*. I've never seen him randomly frolic around Desert Creek. *Ever.*

Nathaniel stands back up from petting Nova, gaze connecting with mine. His irises are a menacing shade of green that I used to think were sexy. Now all I can think about is how they're ugly as shit compared to the mint green of Mateo's.

What? No. I shouldn't be thinking that.

"I'm in town for the car show," he says plainly. His eyes drop to my neck at what can only be the hickeys, and I see the exact moment he spots them. Anger flares wickedly in his features as he lifts his gaze back up to my face before realizing I'm not alone.

It's at this moment, I realize how close Mateo now is to me. He must've shifted closer at some point in the last minute since Nathaniel approached us. Our shoulders are brushing.

Nathaniel huffs out a laugh, but there's nothing of humor in the sound. "What are you doing with him?" The question comes out cold.

I can feel the rage radiating off of Mateo. "That's not for you to worry about, now is it, *cabrón*?"

My body is frozen in place as I drag my eyes from Mateo to Nathaniel at the same moment he glances back at me, then down to my neck, then back at Mateo, his eyes narrowing into thin slits. "It was you, wasn't it?" He doesn't bother clarifying; we all know what he's referencing.

Mateo takes a step forward, stopping right in front of Nathaniel. The way his body is positioned, he's acting almost as a shield to me. He's taller than Nathaniel by at least a couple of inches. Looking down his nose at him, I can't see his face, but I can hear the ice in his voice when he says, "Yeah, it was. What the fuck are you going to do about it?"

My eyes widen at that, glancing around the area to make sure nobody is watching. Palms slick with sweat, I wipe them on the front of my pants as my heart pounds, blood roaring in my ears.

"You fucking asshole," Nathaniel grits out.

"I'm sure it was surprising hearing sounds like that coming out of Travis," Mateo growls. "We all know you could never pull anything like that from him. But don't worry, I know how to take care of him like you never could."

I really should break this up before it gets nasty. Say something... anything. Or even just walk away. But I can't. It's like my body is frozen in place, my thoughts a complete blur. My chest aches with my lung's inability to seem to work.

Nathaniel grunts, stepping up to Mateo, their chests fully

touching now as they puff them out, glaring at each other. I have never seen Nathaniel get into a physical altercation with anybody in my life. He's almost as non-confrontational as I am, and that's saying something. But looking at him now, he's *pissed*.

"You got a lot of fucking nerve, asshole," he spits out through gritted teeth.

"Okay, that's enough," I grunt, stepping around Mateo, and coming face to face with Nathaniel. Finally, it's like time catches up with me, and my mind remembers how to work. "If anyone here's got a lot of nerve, I'd say it's you."

Nathaniel blinks at me a few times. "Excuse me?"

Mateo grabs onto my arm, trying to pull me back behind him, but I shake him off. I need to do this. Need to say this.

Dragging in a deep breath, I square my shoulders, making sure to look Nathaniel in the eye. "What you did to me was fucked up, Nathaniel. I gave you *everything*, I was always there for you. I forgave you more times than I can even count, even when you didn't deserve it. You knew how much I wanted a future with you, and you led me to believe you did too. And instead of just being a fucking man, and being up front with me, you act like a fucking coward and bring someone into *our* house, and let them screw you in *our* bed."

My chest is heaving, my heart pounding so hard, I can't even tell how cold I am. The adrenaline coursing through me gives me the courage to keep going.

"I deserved better than that. Better than you." I point my finger in his direction. "When I caught you with Mateo, it fucking broke me. It made me question what was wrong with me, what I did to make you do that." Huffing out a humorless laugh, I glance over at Mateo for a moment before continuing, eyes locked back on Nathaniel's. "What you did isn't a reflection on me. There's nothing wrong with me, and everything wrong with you. So, yeah, you have a lot of nerve showing up in this park, acting like everything is okay."

Nathaniel's gaze bounces between Mateo and I for a moment, almost like he doesn't know what to say. I expect him to argue or deflect, do his typical gaslighting bullshit he knows so well. Instead, he cocks his head and asks, "So, you what? Decided to hook up with him as payback?"

I want to say I'm surprised. That him painfully missing the mark of what I was saying is shocking. It isn't. "Did you even hear what I said?" I ask, my voice cracking. I hate it.

Mateo shoves me out of the way again, and this time, I let him. Getting right in Nathaniel's face, his eyes narrow as he bares his teeth to him. "It's okay to be a little jealous," he drawls, sounding as cocky as ever. "I probably would be too if I heard what you did. You know he moans so pretty for me, and *mmm*, he tastes so fucking goo—"

It happens so fast. Before Mateo can even finish his sentence, Nathaniel's fist connects with Mateo's jaw, his head jolted to the side as he stumbles into me. Bringing his hand up to his jaw, he rubs as he smiles wickedly at Nathaniel. The punch didn't even faze him.

"Is that all you got, *pendejo*?" Mateo then grabs Nathaniel by his shirt with one hand, his fist colliding with Nathaniel's nose, blood spurting out on impact. The sickly *crunch* sound is unmistakable. My hand flies to my mouth as I gasp, stepping back.

Nathaniel drops to the ground like a bag of potatoes, Mateo wasting no time climbing over him and punching him again… and again.

Finally, after several hits, my brain decides to work again, as do my limbs. I grab onto Mateo's shoulder, pulling him off of Nathaniel. It takes a few tries, as he's *much* stronger than me, but eventually, he stands up, moving back, his head twisting to meet my gaze. His eyes are flared with anger and there's sweat glistening on his forehead.

One look down at Nathaniel and it's clear Mateo rocked his shit, even with only a few punches. There's blood smeared on his face, his right eyebrow is now busted open, and his shirt is stretched all to hell on the front.

"God, what the fuck is wrong with you two?" I shout, picking up Nova's leash from where Mateo dropped it on the ground before he lunged at Nathaniel like the Hulk. Her ears are back, her eyes wide, but other than that, she's silent. "What is this? Some dick measuring contest? You're both fucking pathetic."

With Nova in hand, I turn and walk away, leaving them both there to calm down… or kill each other. One of the two would be fine with me, honestly. Vaguely, I hear Mateo call out my name, but I ignore it. I can't deal with his macho bullshit right now.

By the time we make it home, I'm so confused by how I'm feeling. On the one hand, I'm fucking pissed that Mateo thinks he needs to stand up for me, *or* that he has any right whatsoever to claim me as his. But on the other, it was undeniably hot as fuck to have him fight Nathaniel because of me. It was possessive and animalistic and downright sexy. It turns me on.

But Christ, I shouldn't be turned on by such levels of caveman behavior, especially from someone who has no business claiming me.

What the hell is wrong with me?

TWENTY-NINE

Mateo

Me: Don't think because you've ignored me all goddamn week that you can get out of the engagement party tonight. I'll be at your door to pick you up at 5:30 sharp, cariño.

Hitting send, I lock my phone, setting it on the counter before stripping out of my clothes and climbing under the hot spray of the shower. I'm all fucking sweaty because I just spent the last two hours in the gym, blowing off some steam on the basketball courts with some buddies.

Travis and I haven't spoken since the fight with Nathaniel last weekend. I sent a text the other day, but when he didn't respond, I decided to give him a little space. *Space* isn't exactly my forte, but he's pissed, and I guess I get it, to an extent. Honestly, I don't know what came over me on that trail when we were walking Nova. It's been many years since I've gotten into a fight with somebody, but fuck, the way Nathaniel was acting around Travis made me see red. He didn't even have enough respect for Travis to listen to what he was saying.

I know it seems hypocritical since I was the one he cheated on Travis with, but I fucking hate cheaters. Despise them, have no respect for them. I know all too well what it feels like to be on the receiving end of cheating. I can't count how many times Robbie strayed in our relationship, only to get caught and swear it would never happen again.

It would always be the dumbest excuses too. He got too drunk and missed me too much. He was stressed at work and they were just there. We got into an argument, so it was my fault and I pushed him to do it. And I was pathetic and naive enough to believe him. To forgive him.

When you're in a toxic, unhealthy, manipulative relationship, it's so easy to lose yourself. Who I was before him, and who I am after him never would've fallen for his shit. Never would've put up with it. But when you're in the thick of it, under the manipulation and the false pretense of love, and you've put time into something and you desperately want it to work, it's easy to be fooled. It's easy to be played.

Never again.

And I certainly never wanted to be the person who helped someone be who Robbie was to me. So, I guess, yes, today was maybe about what he did to Travis and it was maybe a little bit about claiming Travis for myself, but it was also for me, too. For him falsely leading me into helping destroy a relationship. Because even if I've never admitted it to Travis, I was furious by the time Travis left that house. And not because I was just whacked over the head with some hideous lamp that looked like it came straight out of the 1800s, but because of my part in all of it.

Sure, Travis deserves so much better than Nathaniel, and he's better off now, but being part of the reason he got his heart broken is awful. And it's obviously a huge part of why Travis thinks he hates me—or why he *wants* to hate me.

Turning the faucet off, I climb out, wrapping myself in a towel. Nerves flutter around my stomach incessantly as my mind obsesses over tonight. I don't know what to expect, and I think that's what makes me the most nervous. Inviting Travis tonight was probably dumb. It was a way to get closer to him. To spend time with him outside of the bedroom. Cashing in on the bet to an event like the engagement party was the only way I could see him willingly spending an evening with me. My need to be around him is growing every time we hang out, and I'd like to think he feels the same, but he shuts me out any chance he gets, so I can't be sure. I'm hoping tonight will help open him up a little more. Help him see me better. See that I'm not just the guy who fucked up his relationship.

To be fucking honest, I don't understand the way I'm feeling at all, but it's becoming harder to pretend, so why the fuck not embrace it?

I probably should've told Travis about Robbie, just so he has some sort of a heads up, but when he asked me why I invited him, I froze. Admitting to him that my ex-boyfriend, who royally fucked me up emotionally, will be there and how that thought makes my palms sweat and panic rise in my chest, felt too fucking vulnerable and embarrassing to admit out loud.

So, of course, I took the coward's way out and told him nothing. It's stupid, because if anyone would be able to relate and understand what I went through with Robbie, it's Travis, but I've never talked to anybody about what happened with Robbie. Benny and Miguel, and even Doran, knew our relationship was shitty, and it ended badly, but they don't know any details. I'm more of a *suffer in silence* type.

Once I'm dressed, I throw some gel into my hair, and finish getting ready. I roll a couple of joints, figuring we can smoke one on the way there. Maybe the marijuana will help calm my nerves. I'm a fucking mess right now. My hands are trembling, my heart is racing. I fucking hate the effect Robbie still has on me to this day.

I'm not this person. The type who gets nervous around people, or who gets anxious about anything. I pride myself on being level-headed and unbothered. It's fucking baffling how one person, one relationship, can fuck someone up to the point they don't recognize themselves.

Strolling out into the living room, I grab my phone, unlocking it and seeing it's time to leave. I blow out a heavy sigh, slipping my feet into my shoes.

It'll only be a couple of hours. It'll be fine.

I walk out into the hall, take the few steps over to Travis's door, bringing my fist up to knock. It doesn't take him but a few seconds to answer. Pure annoyance radiates from him, but I still allow myself a few moments to greedily take him in. He looks fantastic with his white and black polka dot short sleeve button-down shirt and navy-blue slacks. His dirty blond hair is styled in a messy, effortless way that has my fingers itching to run through the strands, and he's wearing cologne that I've never smelled on him before, but it makes my mouth water.

"Ready?" I ask.

He rolls his eyes but doesn't budge. "Do we really have to do this?"

"Yes, *cariño*. Now, let's go."

Grumbling, he grabs his coat off the hook behind him. "Fine. Let's get this over with."

The car ride is tense and quiet. I'm not sure who's more

anxious; him or me, but we turn the music up and smoke the joint, keeping the conversation to a minimum. We pull into the long, winding driveway a few minutes past six.

"*This* is where the party is at?" he asks, eyes wide as he takes in the grounds.

"Yeah, Scottie's family is loaded," I mutter, pulling my car out front, where the valet crew stands.

The house is crowded as we walk in through the front door. The double banister staircase in front of us is blocked off with velvet rope, the white marble flooring is spotless, not a scuff in sight, and there're servers walking around with trays of champagne and hors d'oeuvres.

"This is absurd," Travis mumbles, scanning the area. "Who is she marrying? Bill Gates's son?"

Chuckling, I say, "Pretty much."

I spot Ally across the room at the same time she spots us. A smile spreads on her face as she ambles over. "Matty!" She gives me a tight hug before turning her attention to Travis. "Hi, I'm Alondra, but you can call me Ally."

Travis takes her hand, shaking it. "I'm Travis. Nice to meet you, Ally. Congrats on your engagement. You look beautiful."

Ally preens under the compliment. "Well, aren't you the sweetest. Thank you." She throws me a look that says she'll be asking about him later. I told her I was bringing a date, but didn't give her any details. "There's a bar through that door," she informs us, glancing over at me. "And appetizers are being passed around, but we'll eat in a little bit. I gotta go mingle, but have fun, you guys. It was nice to meet you, Travis."

He looks over at me, amusement dancing in his baby blue eyes. "She seems nice," he mutters. "What the fuck happened to you, Matty?" He laughs at himself for that one.

"Oh, you're so funny," I deadpan. "Let's get some drinks."

The bar is easy to find. It's in the formal living room, and despite the crowd, we're able to get our beverages in no time at all. With our drinks in hand, we make our way to the far corner of the room.

"So, is your family loaded too," he asks before taking a sip of his vodka soda.

"No," I reply with a laugh. "Not even close."

"How'd they meet? Your sister and her fiancé."

"They went to high school together."

Travis's eyes go wide. "They've been together since then?"

I nod. "Yup. She was a cheerleader, and he was the class clown. Their story reminds me of some small-town romance book."

"That's sweet, though."

"Yeah, I guess."

"How is his family so wealthy?"

I don't miss the way our bodies have naturally gravitated toward one another. We're practically shoulder to shoulder as we chat and people watch.

"His dad is the CEO of some huge pharmaceutical company." The words leave my lips the moment my eyes land on the very person I was hoping to avoid all night. My heart stutters in my chest and my throat tightens.

Shit.

What's worse, is Robbie's spotted me too, and he's heading this way. I should've warned Travis, but now it's too late. He says something in response to what I said, but I don't hear it over the buzzing in my ears.

"Mateo…" My name is spoken in a sickly sweet voice that has bile rising in my throat.

"Robbie."

"I didn't know if you'd show up." Robbie stops directly in front of me, a whiff of the cologne he always wears wafting over to us. I clench my jaw.

"It's my sister's engagement party," I state plainly, pissed at that assumption. "Why wouldn't I show up?"

"Because you're never at events our families do together anymore." His eyes drag over to Travis like it's the first time he's noticing him beside me. Every muscle in my body goes rigid. "And who is this?"

Oblivious to the tension, Travis smiles, holding out his hand. "I'm Travis."

"My boyfriend," I add in, earning a confused side-eye from Travis at the same time a wicked smirk slides on Robbie's lips.

"Is that so?"

"Uh…" Travis fumbles. It's only for a second, but fuck, I really should've told him about this beforehand. "Yup, that's right." Travis regains himself, looping his arm through mine, Robbie following the movement.

His wide grin, the one I used to find so charming, intensifies as he meets my gaze. "I didn't know you had a boyfriend, Matty."

That nickname coming from him makes me want to peel every layer of skin off of my body.

"Why would you, Robbie?" I quip back as dryly as possible. My grip on the glass in my hand is so tight, I wouldn't be surprised if it shattered under the pressure. "If you'll excuse us, I'm going to go find my sister."

Robbie's eyes narrow momentarily before he rights himself. "Of course." Turning to Travis, he says, "It was nice to meet you. Maybe I'll see you at the wedding." With one last smile that looks more like a sneer, he turns and leaves, and it's like I can breathe again.

As soon as Robbie is out of sight, Travis turns to me, his arm still linked with mine. "What the hell was that about?"

Heaving a sigh, I drag a hand down my face. "Let's get some more drinks first."

Travis looks like he doesn't want to let it go, but eventually, he follows my lead to the bar. We end doing a couple of rounds of shots, like we aren't at some pretentious rich family's house for a respectable engagement party. A couple side-eyes land our way, but I couldn't care less. As soon as we down our third round of shots, Ally lets us know dinner is starting.

This should be fun.

Absolutely no surprise to me, given the type of people Scottie's family are, there's a seating chart. Ally and Scottie sit up by Travis and me, and just my fucking luck, Robbie is across from me, only a few seats down. My body couldn't be more tense even if I tried, nor do I think I could force myself to relax either. Sweat drips down the back of my neck, lining my forehead, and my palms are slick as hell.

Travis must sense my unease and my anger because his hand slips under the table, resting on my leg just above the knee as he glances over at me, mouthing the question, "You okay?"

I nod, hating how obvious I am. I need to pull myself together and make it through this dinner so we can go home. Being around Robbie as little as possible is the best option for everyone involved.

His stare is weighted as he watches us from across the table. I try to avoid his gaze as much as possible, but like my brain has a mind of its own, my eyes flit over from time to time, rage boiling inside of me when I see him watching Travis. The urge to lunge across the table and pluck his eyeballs out with my bare hands is strong. He has no fucking business looking at him. He's *mine*.

·

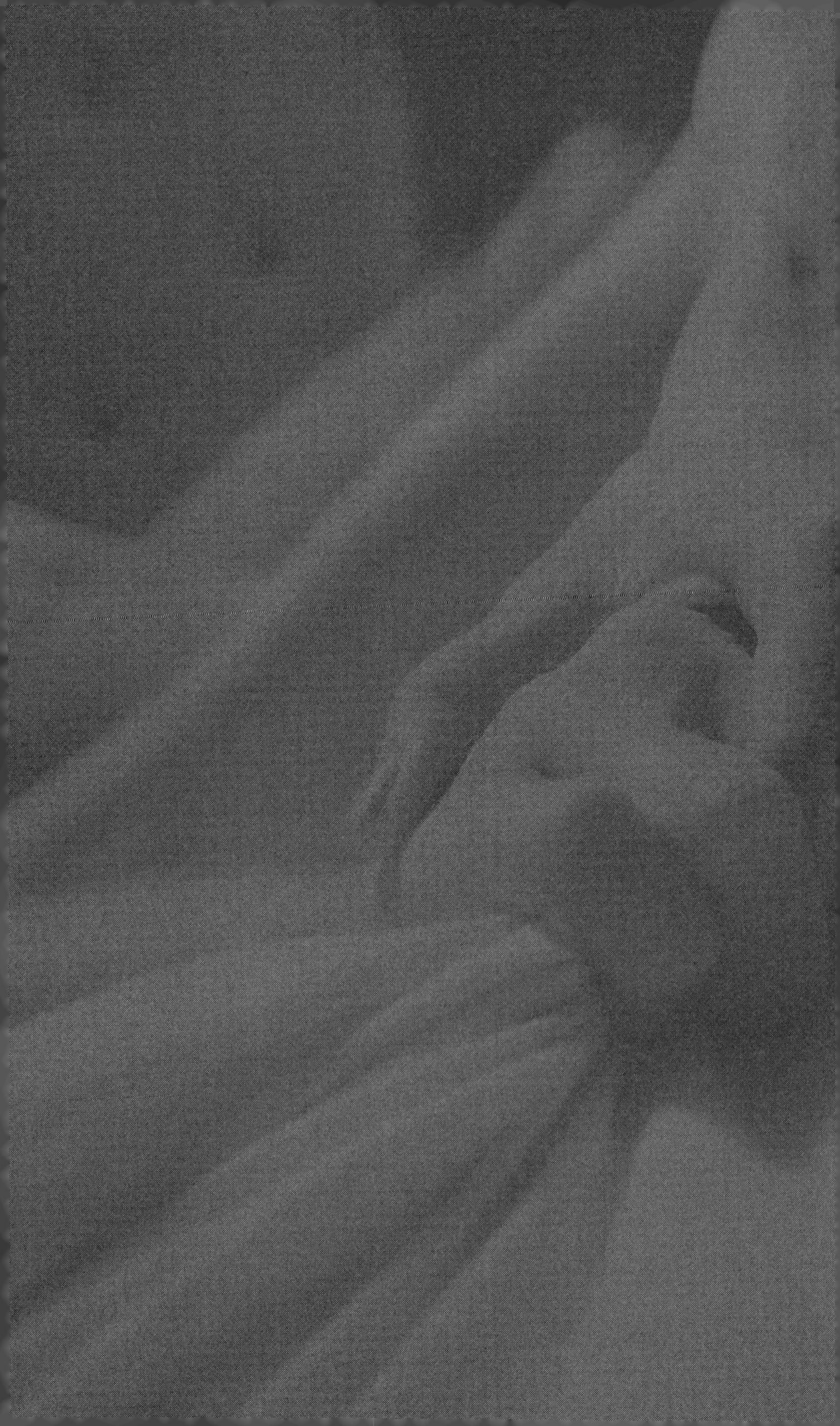

THIRTY

Travis

I'm gonna go out on a whim and say Robbie and Mateo used to date.

Mateo won't give me an outright answer, not that we've had time between eating and talking to his family, but it's the only reason I can think of why he's behaving as weirdly as he is. The way his body language shifted when Robbie walked up to us when we were having a drink, the way he's stiff and even more growly than usual, and the way his jaw seems to be permanently clenched tight.

He looks uncomfortable and unsure of himself, something I'm not used to seeing from him. It's unsettling, and I find that it doesn't sit right with me. I don't like knowing that something about Robbie puts Mateo on edge. What's even more surprising, and quite horrifying, is the fact that I find myself wanting to do something to make it better.

Maybe it's why, after we finish up with dinner, I grab Mateo by the hand and lead him to the dance floor. "Dance with me, Matty," I murmur as I wrap my arms around his neck, hauling him in close. One quick glance to the left shows Robbie's eyes on us, and it only takes a single pause from Mateo before he folds, placing his hands on my hips as our bodies sway together to the slow beat of *You Are The Reason* by Callum Scott playing throughout the room.

A smirk grows on Mateo's lips. "What is this, *cariño*?"

I shrug innocently. "Something about the way he keeps looking at you, and the way you get all agitated around him, makes me think we need to be making him jealous. And well, you put on a nice show for Nathaniel for me. Figured it's the least I could do."

An emotion I can't quite name passes over Mateo's features, his fingertips gripping onto me tighter as we continue to sway. The song is sweet—too sweet—and I'm not sure if that's the reason for the sudden shift in the room or maybe it's all in my head. Swallowing thickly, my gaze stays locked on Mateo's. The weight of his stare is overwhelming; it makes me want to squirm and hide.

His mint green eyes dip down to my lips a moment before he wets his own. "He's my ex-boyfriend," he croaks, voice gravelly. "He's to me who Nathaniel is to you."

Without fleshing out that statement, he's said all I need to know. Just like that, the image of this cold, heartless monster I've held in my head since I've met him morphs into something a bit more human. With that one sentence, Mateo's letting me see his vulnerability, even if he doesn't realize it.

I don't know any details, but I know Robbie hurt him. And that little piece of knowledge makes my blood boil for reasons I don't quite understand, nor do I think I want to try to. It makes my skin prickle and my heart race, creating this burning feeling inside of me. It makes my throat thick and my stomach twist into knots.

This flood of feelings pouring through me is the only reason I can think as to why I do what I do next.

Mateo inhales sharply when my mouth brushes against his full, plush lips. My hands move around until I'm cupping his face, and it's about that same time his mind and body seem to kick into gear. My lips part as his tongue slips inside, my insides lighting up like the Fourth of July. He tastes like the tequila he was drinking and the feel of his rough, scratchy beard brushing against my freshly shaven face feels too good.

It doesn't escape me that this is the first time we've kissed in a non-sexual way, and I know this should frighten me, but be it the alcohol in my system or the odd sense of rage I feel for whatever it is Robbie did to Mateo, it doesn't. At all. In fact, kissing him has never felt so right.

The world around us disappears—the music, the people, the way I *should* feel toward him—until it's just us, Mateo and Travis. I'm not sure how long we stand there, swaying in each other's arms, making out in the middle of this makeshift ballroom, but when we pull away, my head is dizzy and my lips are swollen. I meet Mateo's gaze dazedly, and the music and the people all come rushing back.

"Well, that was a first," he says with a small chuckle, which I return with one of my own.

"Like I said, it's the least I could do."

We pull apart, but only fractionally.

"If I didn't know any better, *cariño*, I'd say you're starting to actually like me." His smirk is flirty and sultry, and it makes my stomach do a somersault.

I roll my eyes. "But you do know better."

The grin only grows with that, like he knows just how

full of shit I am. We watch each other, swaying to the song, the moment feeling monumental in a way. Like it's shifting something between us. And I don't know how I feel about that, to be honest. Mateo's endless green eyes bore into mine, his features softening as he takes me in. I feel like I'm seeing another new side of him in this moment.

Clearing his throat, his grip on my hips tightening like he's trying to make sure I stay close, he murmurs so quietly, I barely hear him, "I didn't know about you."

My brows knit together. "What do you mean?"

"When I hooked up with Nathaniel," he clarifies, my heart pounding in my chest. "I didn't know he had a boyfriend. I never would've agreed to meet up with him had I known."

My lungs forget how to work for a moment too long, air seeming difficult to suck in as I replay what Mateo's just said. Of course, I've always wondered, but I never felt comfortable asking. But... "Why are you telling me this?"

"Because I wouldn't do that, and you deserve to know the truth, Travis."

Travis. Not cariño.

I don't know what to say back to that. The conviction in his tone just about knocks me off my feet.

Thankfully, he doesn't give me any time to respond. The song ends, and with a quick glance down at the watch on his wrist, he asks, "Ready to go?"

Giving him a quick nod, we make our rounds of saying our goodbyes. Meeting Mateo's family was... interesting. His mom was pleasant enough, but it felt like more of a *forced polite* type of way. I didn't speak with her much, just a quick introduction when we first got here. His sister is really nice. She was welcoming, and only slightly nosy. Ally's husband was cool, although, at times it seemed like he didn't have a single thought between his ears. His family was a very stereotypical wealthy family, but overall, welcoming.

And the food was really fucking delicious.

And everything I learned about Mateo tonight… This wasn't the absolute worst way to spend a Saturday night, I suppose.

When we arrive at the apartment complex and park, I wonder if the evening ends now, if we'll go our separate ways once we reach our floor. The question is answered for me, though, when I stop outside of mine and pull out my keys to unlock the door, and Mateo waits behind me, *not* unlocking his own place.

Nova races to the door, the sound of her nails, that are in need of a trim, clanking on the hardwood floor as she trots across it before I even step inside. Turning on the light, I glance over my shoulder at Mateo, who's following me like this is a totally normal occurrence.

"So, we're not done hanging out?" I ask, crouching down to pet an overly excited Nova.

"Hell no," he blurts out, kicking out of his shoes and shrugging out of his jacket. "Let's drink some more. The night's young."

Watching him with humor in my eyes, I shake my head, grabbing Nova's leash off the coat rack. I'm thankful he's not bringing up our dance confessional. I don't think I could handle it, any more honesty. "Whatever. I gotta take her potty. Wanna roll us a joint while I'm gone?"

This feels so fucking weird. *So domestic.* Us hanging out like it's nothing. My hackles are up, waiting for the shoe to drop because it has to with a guy like Mateo.

It only takes Nova and me maybe ten minutes downstairs. Thankfully, at night she's good about doing her business quickly without too much dilly-dallying, especially on nights like tonight when it's exceptionally chilly. As soon as we make it up the elevator onto our floor, I can hear it.

Music coming from my apartment filtering through the hall. And not just any music. No, *I Wanna Know* by Joe is blaring. That time I caught him singing along to that Olivia Rodrigo song at his shop pops into my head, a chuckle breathing off my lips as I stroll toward my door, attempting to open it as quietly as possible, not that he could hear it anyway over the music.

Okay, it's not really *that* loud, but the walls in this place are pretty thin, so I can hear the lyrics damn near perfectly from out here. Glancing down at Nova, she's already looking at me. I hold my index finger up to my lips in a *"shh"* motion before pushing the door open.

Mateo is sitting at my dining room table, his back to me, the rolled joint beside him as he scrolls through his phone. His body is relaxed, indicating he probably didn't hear me come in, and I hear the very distinct sound of him singing along to the song. I can't help but smile.

Letting the door shut loudly to let him know my presence, I shout, "I fucking knew it!"

He jumps, clearly having startled him, as he whips around in the chair, his eyes, already narrowed, shooting daggers at me. "What the fuck are you talking about?"

"You *were* singing along to that Olivia song in the shop that one time!"

He rolls his eyes. "Yeah, okay, *cariño*. Whatever you say."

Laughing, I look down at Nova as I remove her leash. "You hear that, Nov? We got a singer on our hands, girl."

"Oh, for fuck's sake," he grumbles. "Are you ready to smoke this or what?"

"Sure thing, Backstreet Boy. Let me grab the alcohol."

His scowl deepens as he mumbles something under his breath, heading toward the couch.

A couple of hours, a few joints, and several shots later, Mateo and I find ourselves lying on top of my bed, the lights off, and a galaxy light brightening up the ceiling as we chat like we don't hate each other.

Which, hell, maybe we don't anymore.

"So, how'd you two meet?" I ask before taking another pull off the nearly empty bottle of vodka.

Music's filtering through my Bluetooth speaker softly, the entire room a relaxing vibe.

"In high school." His voice has gone raspy since we got back to my place. Probably all the smoking and drinking we've been doing. It's hot.

"How long did you guys date?"

"Couple of years." He twists the cap back on the bottle, setting it on the nightstand beside him before staring up at the ceiling. "We met at a rough time."

"How so?" Mateo doesn't strike me as the sharing deeply type, so I'm trying to tread lightly, but there's so much I want to know about him.

He glances over at me—just briefly—but I don't miss the faint glint of vulnerability in his mint green eyes. But it's gone by the time he looks away. "My, uh… my parents weren't the most accepting when they found out I was gay. You know, strong, age-old Catholic beliefs and all that."

My heart drops for him. My mom and stepdad were nothing but loving and supportive when I came out to them.

253

"They tried sending me to this summer camp my dad's friend told him about." Mateo clears his throat, continuing to keep his gaze on the ceiling as he continues. "It was supposed to remind the teenagers of the path they should stay on. The path *God* wants us on. I realized real quick what type of place it really was, and I left before anything could happen."

"Conversion therapy?" I ask, my voice barely above a whisper.

He nods. "I was fifteen with no money and nowhere to go, so of course, I went back home. Hoping, naively, that my parents didn't really know what type of place it was. Maybe it was a misunderstanding."

I don't say anything. I don't have to.

"It wasn't," he murmurs. "Dad kicked me out right then and there."

"Fuck," I blow out on a breath. "Where'd you go?"

"My Uncle Benny's. I lived with him until I turned eighteen and could afford to live on my own. But it was right after all of this when I met Robbie. I was hurt and confused and angry. Little bit reckless. And all I wanted was for someone to see me and accept me for who I was."

"Yeah, but didn't your uncle?"

"It's not the same," is all he says.

Mateo reaches for the bottle again, taking another swallow before passing it to me. Nothing's said for several minutes. The air is tense, the energy surrounding us stifling. It's clear this is a sensitive topic for him, and a large part of me wants to comfort him.

But I don't know how, and I don't know if it's my place. So, instead, I ask, "What happened with Robbie?"

He blows out a breath, pausing before responding, like he's thinking over how best to explain. "You met his family.

They're a bunch of rich yuppies. Robbie was a spoiled rich kid who got what he wanted, when he wanted. He's not used to being told no, and he's used to being in charge. That's how our relationship was; he said jump, I said how high."

Chuckling, I say, "That doesn't sound like you at all."

"Yeah, no," he retorts, meeting my gaze for the first time in a while. "I was a lot different back then. I'd already been rejected by my parents. I needed to cling to the attention and the, what I thought was, love he gave me."

"Can relate there," I say without meaning to. "So, what happened?"

I'm waiting for him to tell me to fuck off. It doesn't come.

"Things became a lot really quickly." I turn on my side, holding my hands under my cheek, watching him as he runs a hand down his cropped beard. "He wasn't my first. I lost my virginity back before my parents even found out I was gay. But this was... different from what I was used to."

Confusion clouds my mind for half a second before it clicks. "He topped you."

I don't phrase it as a question, but he answers it as one anyway. "Yeah."

"And what? You didn't like it?"

He huffs out a laugh, but there's not an ounce of humor in it. "The first time he fucked me, I bled. Said we didn't need to use lube, that spit would work just fine."

"Shit, Mateo..."

"After that, I told him I didn't think I liked it and asked if we could switch next time. He told me if I cared about him, I'd stop being such a bitch. He'd sometimes, like after a fight or something, tell me he'd let me top him soon. Soon never came."

Mateo's body is stiff. It's clear remembering all of this is hard for him. I've never wanted to comfort him more than I do in this moment. Before I have a chance to, he continues.

"It wasn't until we broke up, and I was away from him, that I realized just how badly he gaslit me into feeling like in order to prove how much I cared, I needed to do something I wasn't comfortable with."

Holy shit.

"Is that why you're a strict top now?"

Mateo nods. "By the time we finally broke up, the thought of another person getting me in that way was enough to make my skin crawl. I couldn't do it, so I didn't."

"Damn, that's so fucked up." My chest aches for him, having to go through something like that. "So, you've never had an enjoyable experience back there at all?"

He goes quiet for a moment, chewing on the inside of his cheek. "I have," he states plainly. "By myself."

Arousal stirs in my groin. That visual, especially right now, shouldn't turn me on as much as it does. But I ignore it. "I'm sorry you had to go through that. And, uh, I'm sorry about your parents. Feeling unloved by your parent—or parents—is one of the worst feelings there is."

Mateo finally turns to meet my gaze. "You got shitty folks too?"

"My dad," I confirm quietly. "He left me, my mom, and my sister when I was little, and started a whole new family."

"Damn, really?"

Nodding, I say, "Yup. I actually had no idea what happened to him until I was in high school, and saw him at a basketball game with his new family across the bleachers. Rival team. I thought he was dead."

"Fuck, *cariño*. We're quiet the fucked-up pair, aren't we?"

He laughs, which in turn makes me laugh.
"I guess so."

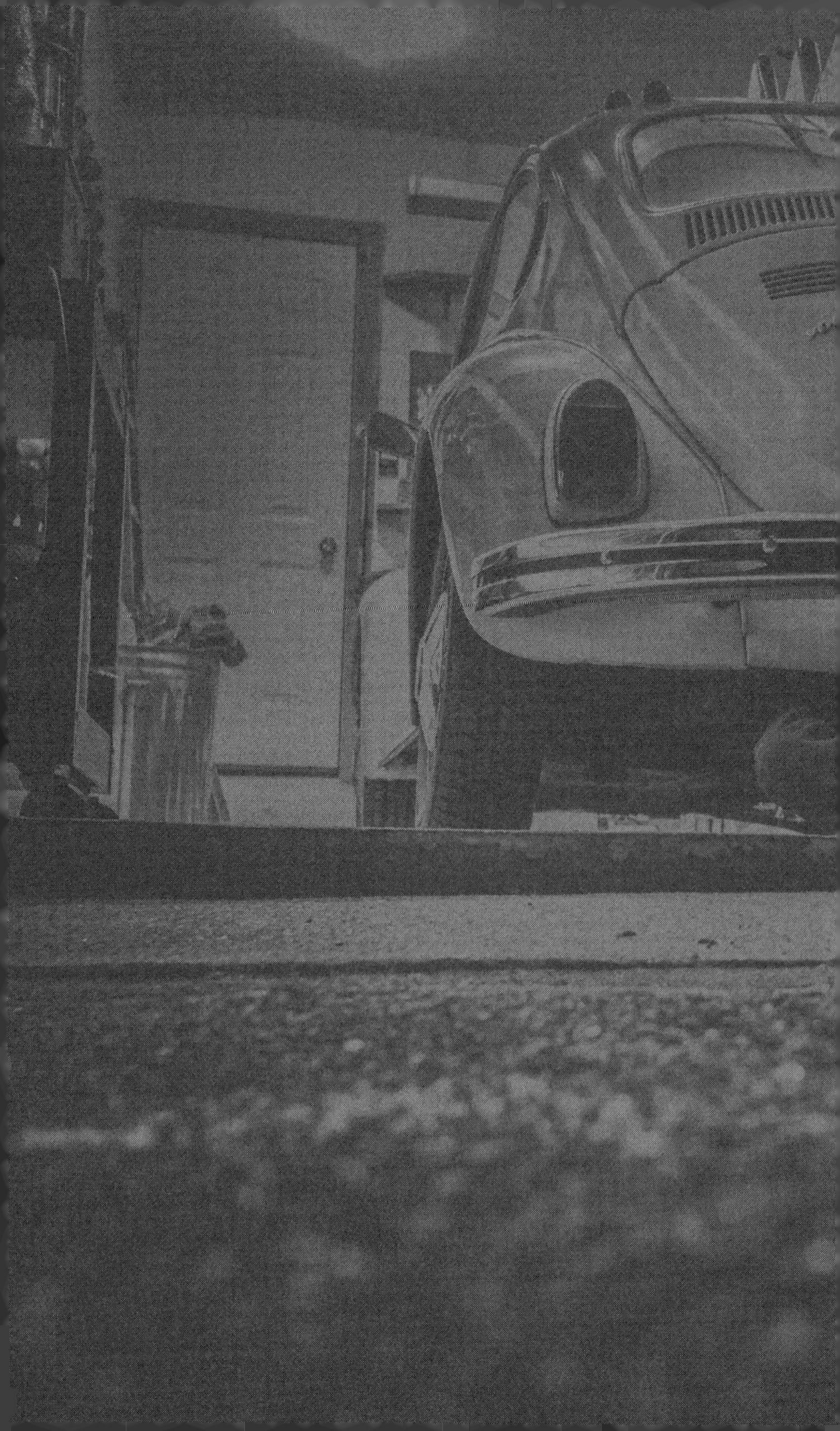

THIRTY-ONE

Mateo

It's barely eight in the morning, and I've already been up for an hour.

Travis, on the other hand, is sound asleep, mouth open, snoring, and drool spilling onto the pillow and everything. It's annoyingly cute.

After we had a surprisingly intimate conversation about our fucked-up childhoods last night, we smoked another bowl and passed out. It was the first time we've slept together without actually sleeping together. It's odd, but also… nice. Like, really fucking nice.

I just took Nova downstairs to go potty. When we got back upstairs, she was staring at me expectantly, like she was starving and couldn't wait a minute longer for breakfast. After rummaging through his cabinets, I found her food. I don't know when I became the guy to wake up and walk and feed someone else's dog. If this were anyone other than Travis, I feel like I would've woken up and gone straight home.

Now, I'm back in Travis's room, watching him as he *still*

sleeps, but that's about to change. Similar to the first morning we spent together during the snowstorm, I'm horny, and hungry as fuck for a taste of Travis. Snooping as quietly as possible in his closet, I find exactly what I'm looking for, grabbing them quickly and padding back over to the bed.

He stirs as I secure his left hand to the headboard, and by the time I fully secure his right, his eyes have peeled open and he's watching me with a sleepy, but unsurprised gaze. "What do you think you're doing?" he asks, voice raspy.

"What does it look like I'm doing?" I retort. "I'm getting ready to have my filthy way with you, *cariño*."

Travis tugs on the restraints, heaving a sigh when he doesn't get very far. "Must you tie me to my own bed using my own ties? I wear those for work, you know."

"Yeah, well, we aren't at my house where all the real equipment is, so we must improvise." Flashing him a wide grin, I grab the third tie sitting beside him, and use it to wrap around his head, covering his eyes.

"You can't be serious," he deadpans.

"Oh, but I am, *cariño*." Placing a quick peck on his lips, I bring my hand down roughly on his cheek, using it to grip his face in my palm. "Now, hush, baby, and let me take care of you."

His Adam's apple bobs on a harsh swallow, but he doesn't say anything else.

My eyes greedily rake over Travis's body as he lies before me, vulnerable and unable to move. His chest is already bare, having taken his shirt off last night, but from the waist down, he's in a pair of boxers that are getting more snug by the minute as his cock thickens behind the cotton.

A smirk pulls at my lips, knowing he's getting aroused by this just like I am.

The sleepy, throaty groan that pulls from him when my fingers tweak his tiny pink nipple rolls through me like tornado, stirring arousal deep in my balls, making me want to hear more and more of that sweet fucking sound. I bend down, running the flat of my tongue over the now erect bud before sucking it into my mouth. His skin is an intoxicating mix of salty and sweet, my mouth watering as I switch to the other one, giving it the same treatment.

Goosebumps break out all along his flesh as my tongue licks across his chest, up to his neck. My pulse quickens as his body trembles beneath my touch. He's always been so responsive for me, and I don't think I'll ever get used to it. The pads of my fingers dance along his hip bones as I pepper his throat with kisses that turn into little red marks.

Travis groans, his hips lifting to seek me out. "Fuck, Mateo…"

I love that he can't move, can't see. He's completely helpless to me and my desires. His body is wound up tight, lit up like live wire, and with every single brush of my tongue or nip of my teeth, he's that much closer to detonating. To exploding. And I haven't even got to the good stuff yet.

"You like this, *cariño*?" My fingers hook under the waistband of his boxers, tugging them down.

Travis nods, lifting his hips, his stiff cock jutting out and slapping his abs. "Touch me," he pleads.

Chuckling, I say, "You're such a needy little slut, aren't you?"

His dick is pulled taut and angry, the bulbous tip glistening with his growing arousal. My eyes travel up, taking in the rapid rise and fall of his chest, the marks on his collarbone and neck, various shades of red. His bottom lip is red and swollen from where he's been biting down on it, and his hair is in a disarray, dirty blond strands sticking up every which way.

He's such a beautiful, stunning, infuriating man.

Ninety percent of the time, he wants nothing to do with me, and I can't seem to get enough of it. From the very first time we slept together, I've felt this pull to him. This possessiveness over him. And it's only growing stronger as the days pass.

Seeing him with my family last night, seeing the way he fit in so well, and then having him notice the tension I felt from being near Robbie without me even having to tell him, only to have him dance with me. It's like he knew exactly what I needed to calm down without me having to breathe a single word of it. To top the whole night off, coming back here afterward and him listening to me as I tell him things I've never told anybody else. I honestly don't know what came over me, or why I decided to share what I did. It felt… right. Like I could trust him fully. I can pretend all I want that last night didn't change something for me, but it's a fucking lie, because as I sit here right now, with him undressed and willing for me, my chest aches with something so wholly unfamiliar, it scares me.

The longing in my bones for him, the way my mind *always* gravitates toward him lately, and hell, even the way I feel some sort of odd attachment to his fucking dog… it's so unlike me. And I feel like it should worry me more than it does, especially considering he's still firmly in the *I hate Mateo* stance most of the time. Although, maybe after what we shared last night, that'll lessen a little more.

But even if it doesn't, I don't fucking care.

I don't care if he thinks he can't stand me.

I don't care if I have to fight him every step of the way.

I don't care because whether or not he believes it, he's fucking *mine*.

Lowering my head, I run the flat of my tongue along the

underside of his cock, a shaky whimper falling from his lips moments before he bites down on his lip again. I breathe out a laugh before closing my lips around him, the salty flavor of his pre-cum exploding on my taste buds.

He's a high unlike any other. A high I never plan to get sober from.

He slides all the way to the back of my throat, his entire body thrumming with need. Spit dribbles out of my mouth, and I use it to slip a finger through his crack until I'm circling his tight, puckered hole. Working a finger in, his cock leaks onto my tongue, and I moan around his length. He tastes so fucking good.

"*Mateo...* more," he begs. "I need more. Please."

A growl rips from my throat as I pull off of him. "Mmm, what is it that you need, *cariño*?"

He whimpers, the sound rolling through me, wrapping around my being like moss. "F-fuck me," he cries out as I sit back, taking my hands completely off him. "Please!"

Travis's body is flushed, glistening with sweat as the early morning sunshine beams in through the opening in the curtains, blanketing him in a warm, angelic glow.

I'm almost glad he's blindfolded so he can't see the way I'm ogling over him.

"Lube?" I ask, my voice breathy.

Travis tips his chin to the left. "Bedside table."

My heart is racing a mile a minute, my hands practically trembling as I reach for the little clear bottle in the drawer. Sinking into him, feeling his tight warmth surround me, is suddenly all I can think about. Pouring the cool gel onto my fingers, I work him open thoroughly but swiftly, anticipation and need prickling at my nerve endings.

Once I'm sure he's well prepped, I lather up my length, lining up to his pretty pink hole. I sink inside, both of us groaning. His velvety hot channel sucks me in, gripping me tightly as he wraps his legs around my hips. His hands tug on the restraints to no avail, and he lets out a frustrated whimper that has my nuts aching.

"Goddamn, *cariño*," I growl, gripping onto his hips as I pull all the way out, sliding back home, my head dropping onto my shoulders at how fucking good he feels. "Your pretty little pussy loves my cock, doesn't it, baby?"

He cries out, his cheeks splashing a blushing pink. "Yes… fuck, yes, it does."

His admission fuels the fire raging through my veins, the heat only intensifying each time I brush against his sweet spot, causing his hole to constrict against my cock. It's heavenly, the way he feels.

Reaching up, I rip the tie off his face, his baby blues finding my gaze automatically. "My hands," is all he says, tugging against the other ties for emphasis.

I chuckle, shaking my head. "Not yet, *cariño*."

Sitting back on my calves, I lift his lower half, raising him up and down my shaft, the new angle seemingly hitting all the right spots inside of him because his jaw drops open, eyes rolling back. "Oh, fuck," he gasps. "Oh, holy fuck. Shit… *yessss*."

His body writhes as I pound into him, my name falling off his lips in a chant, mixed in with other inhuman sounds that feed the gluttonous beast in my soul. There's nothing more beautiful than when Travis lets go. When he gives himself over to the pleasure I can give him. He shoves aside all his issues, his insecurities, his qualms with me, and he just feels. There's nothing quite like it. It's a glorious thing to witness, especially when his lust-fueled eyes drink me in as I feed his greedy cunt every last inch of my cock.

I can feel myself getting close, so I decide to put him out of his misery and untie his hands. Wrapping my arms around his middle, I haul him into my lap, drilling into him from below. His arms find purchase around my neck, his lips right beside the shell of my ear as he moans breathlessly.

My balls tighten up to my body, and he feels too damn good to hold back. "Want me to come into this tight pussy?" I growl, tightening my hold on him. "Fill you up like the fucking cum slut I know you love to be, hmm? Have you feel me drip out of you messily for the rest of the day."

"Oh, God…" Travis pulls back, his soft, warm palm cupping my cheek. "Do it," he begs. "Please, Mateo. *Please.*"

His mouth crashes down on mine as soon as the plea leaves his lips. Hungry tongues clash together, swiping and tasting and professing. It's my undoing. I spill inside of him, a deep-throated groan rumbling out of me as tears spring to my eyes from the sheer intensity of the orgasm. Between us, I can feel him explode. Thick, hot spurts of cum marking my chest as he cries out into my mouth.

The moment feels supercharged, everything about it heightened. We kiss our way through both of our releases, taking and giving in equal measures. By the time we finish, we're both out of breath and utterly spent.

"Holy shit," I breathe.

Travis snorts out a laugh. "Yeah, holy shit is right."

Lying him on his back, I pull out, watching with pride as my seed spills out of him. Using my thumb, I shove it back inside, leaning down to press a kiss to the inside of his thigh.

"We should stop the games and give this a real go. What

do you say, *cariño?*" Looking back on this moment, I don't think I'll ever know what came over me or why I thought it was a good idea to blurt that out. Post-nut psychosis, maybe.

The look of part-confusion, part-horror, plastered on Travis's face would normally be funny, but right now, it has my gut shooting up into my throat, lodging itself there, making it hard to breathe.

"What? Absolutely not." He sits up, knees pulled into his chest. "This"—he indicates between us—"isn't anything. It can't be."

My heart is pounding. It feels as if my chest is sliced wide open and everything—all the muscles, tendons, guts, organs, everything—is spilling out and on display. It's unsettling, and I suddenly need to leave.

Barking out a laugh, I jump up off the bed, reaching for my clothes. "No, yeah, of course," I mumble. "I know what you mean. I was joking."

Something passes through his eyes, and he rises off the bed. "Wait, Mateo…"

"Nah, it's cool," I lie. "Hey, look, I gotta get going. I have something to do today, but I already took Nova potty and fed her before you got up."

Without waiting for a response, I bolt, regretting every single fucking thing I just said.

THIRTY-TWO

Travis

My concentration has been shit today. I legitimately haven't gotten a single thing done that I needed to at work because my mind won't stop replaying the trainwreck that was my bedroom yesterday morning. What started out as such a perfect morning quickly morphed into something I never would've pictured.

And the way Mateo hightailed out of there afterward. I can't help but feel terrible about it. Clearly, the way I responded was uncalled for, but I'd never felt so blindsided by something he's done or said before.

"We should stop the games and give this a real go." Where in the actual fuck did that come from?

It's nearly three by now, and an email I started to type two hours ago is still sitting up on my computer, unfinished. Grabbing my phone, I do the only thing I can think to do; call Xander. Surely, he'll have some good advice. Some guidance. He always has the answer.

After a few rings, it finally connects. "What's up, man?" His deep voice sounds muffled, like maybe I'm on speakerphone.

"Hey, you busy?"

"Nah, not really. Driving back to work after going to the bank. What's up?"

Giving him an extreme CliffsNotes version, I spend the next several minutes filling him in on all things Mateo, and all things Mateo *and* Travis, including our very awkward post-coital conversation that led to him fleeing my room.

"Wow," he mutters when I'm finally done.

"Yeah, wow."

Xander breathes out a laugh. "What happened to there being nothing to worry about?"

"I don't know," I grumble. "It's like the more I said I wanted nothing to do with him, the more he was there with his witchy abilities."

He snorts. "Witchy abilities?"

"Yes, Xander, witchy abilities. His dick carries magic, I swear to God. And it's like I'm incapable of controlling myself around him. *Witchy abilities!*"

A fit of laughter hits my ears, and I roll my eyes, regretting making this call at all. It sounds so stupid out loud. I sound like a lunatic. Hell, I *feel* like one.

After the laughter dies down, Xander blows out a breath. "Shit, maybe I was wrong about him after all."

My eyes nearly bug out of my head. "Excuse me?"

"I mean, maybe give him a chance. Given his past and what he admitted to you about Nathaniel—if he's telling the truth—then I think my initial judgement of him may have been wrong. He's clearly proven he's not going anywhere, and I highly doubt someone would go to this extent for something they wanted to be temporary."

I scoff, appalled at what I'm hearing. "Xan, what the fuck happened to the whole be careful speech?"

"Well, yeah." He laughs. "Of course, still be careful, but I don't think you should shove away something you want strictly out of fear of getting hurt."

"Who the hell says I want him?"

"Oh, come on, Travis." I can practically hear his aggressive eye roll through the phone. "You're not as slick as you think you are. The brief time I saw you two in the same room, you both practically radiated your feelings for one another. It's okay to admit it, you know. I know Nathaniel hurt you badly, and I know you haven't had the best luck with men in the past, but it's still okay to admit when you care."

I hate that he's right on the nose. Hate that he can read me so easily.

"You know I'll be the first to be straight up with you about a guy, Trav," he continues. "If I truly thought he was bad news bears, I'd say that. But I'm admitting I may have been wrong about him before."

"Well, fuck." Blowing out a sigh, I mutter, "I'm an asshole."

"Nothing a good ol' fashion apology can't fix," Xander offers. "I'm not saying jump into a relationship with the guy, but at least keep your heart and mind open to the possibility, if that's what you want."

"Thanks, Xander."

"Anytime, man. Look, I gotta get back inside, but call me later. Let me know how it goes."

"This is fucking stupid," I grumble to nobody but myself.

Truthfully, I don't know how I found myself here, outside

of Mateo's front door with a bag of takeout in my hand, contemplating whether or not I'm going to knock on the door or turn and go into my own house instead.

After my chat with Xander, I felt terrible for shutting Mateo down so quickly and wanted to figure out a way to say I'm sorry, and food was what I came up with, but now I'm not so sure. It feels awfully like admitting defeat, like he's going to answer the door, gloat, and laugh in my face about being right.

"Fuck, I can't do this."

Just as I'm about to turn and unlock my door, his opens, my eyes shooting up to meet his. "You do know I have a Ring cam, right?"

It's at that moment my eyes snap over to the tiny black camera right beside his door before dragging back to his amused expression. I refuse to fold or be embarrassed. Instead, I square my shoulders, lifting the bag full of food, and say, "I brought dinner if you're hungry. I wanted to apologize about yesterday."

Mateo's not quick enough to hide the surprise, but as quickly as it's there, it's gone again as he steps to the side. "Come on in, *cariño*. As a matter of fact, I'm starving."

The air smells faintly like marijuana, mixed in with the vanilla candle he has burning on the kitchen counter. He's in a pair of comfy looking black sweats and nothing else, looking like he just got out of the shower. Maybe right before I knocked.

We both dish up, taking a seat at the dining room table in silence. It's nothing fancy, just some teriyaki from down the street. About halfway through eating, he clears his throat, my heart stuttering in my chest.

"So, you wanted to say sorry?"

Glancing up, I fight not to roll my eyes at the smug as fuck look on his face. I knew he'd fucking gloat.

I nod, taking a sip of my Coke. "Yes, I could've reacted better to what you said after we had sex yesterday. It was uncalled for, and I'm sorry."

"Well, well, well." Mateo plops a piece of chicken into his mouth, studying me as he chews and swallows it. "This is a first."

"Don't be such a dick," I grate. "I didn't have to come over here, but I did."

"No, you're right, *cariño*," he admits, shocking the fuck out of me. "And while I appreciate the effort and the apology, there really isn't anything for you to apologize for."

"I do," I insist. "Because it's not just about yesterday. It's about all the assumptions I made leading up to me turning you down. I never gave you any room to tell your side, and I based my whole opinion of you on judgements. I am sorry for that."

"Well," Mateo starts, a mischievous grin tugging on his lips as he leans back in his chair, hand clasping behind his head. "If you're feeling apologetic, I think there's another way we can go about relieving your conscious and earning my absolute forgiveness."

Oh, for fuck's sake. What can of worms did I just open up? "And how's that?" I deadpan.

"Well, forgiveness should be earned… yes?"

In an attempt to fly out of my chest, my heart hammers against my ribs, a cold sweat breaking out along my hairline. *This cannot be going anywhere good. I absolutely should not be entertaining whatever this is.*

Except I want to. "How so?"

His grin is blinding. "I'm so glad you asked. Follow me."

Abandoning the rest of his meal, he stands from the table, not even bothering to see if I'm following as he heads farther into his apartment. I stand, scurrying after him, but it becomes abundantly clear very quickly where he's leading me.

The spare bedroom. AKA his sex dungeon.

Mateo opens the door, stepping inside. I'm not far behind. Similar to last time, when he flicks on the lights, the room is shadowed in a red glow. The white walls turn crimson, and everything is covered in a sensual, yet sinister feel. Chills roll down my spine as I close the door, shutting us away from sanity, standing with my back against the tall, heavy wood, waiting for instruction.

There's so much in this room I've wanted to try since seeing it for the first time. The swing was just the tip of the iceberg. My body still remembers exactly how it felt to be suspended in that swing as he fucked into me with purpose. *God, that was fucking good.*

Mateo turns to face me, probably ten feet away, the usual bright mint green of his irises looking nearly black amongst the red glow.

The Devil himself. That's how he appeared the first time he had me under his spell one room over all those months ago.

"Strip." The one word is spoken with so much authority, it has goosebumps spreading along my flesh.

"Always so bossy," I quip, not moving a muscle. Not yet, at least.

Laughing, the sound dark, he closes the distance between us until he's a mere hairsbreadth away from me. Mateo's bottomless eyes drink me in as one hand rests flat against the door beside my head, his other coming up to my face, thumb rubbing mindlessly against my cheek. "This may be new for you, *cariño*, getting punished. But let me let you in on a little secret, *mi amor...*"

Tipping my chin up with his fingers, our eyes meet. I'm hypnotized, unable to look away even if I wanted to as he wraps me up in his web, covering me with his spell. The longer

I stand here in his presence, the idea that I can keep this purely physical starts to feel more like a lie to myself than anything.

This thing between us, whatever it is, has never been *just physical*. Not even that first time.

"When I give you an order," he continues, reminding me why I'm standing here. "You obey, or the punishment will only be harder. Do you understand me?"

Swallowing thickly, I nod as best as I can, despite the unforgiving grip he has on my chin.

Mateo smirks, his eyes narrowing. "Wonderful. Now, *strip*."

This time, when he steps back, putting some distance between us, I do as he asks. First my shirt, then my pants. My gaze lifts, meeting his questioningly as my fingers pause on the waistband of my boxers. He nods, and I shove them down, kicking them to the side until I'm left standing before him wearing nothing but tantalizing desire.

His eyes drink me in, and he drags his bottom lip between his teeth when his perusal lands on my hard, jutting out cock. What I'd give to replace his teeth with my own right now. Lifting a brow, he murmurs, "You listen so well when you want to."

I bite down on the inside of my cheek, fighting the urge to tell him to fuck off.

Checking me out for a beat longer, Mateo tips his head toward the corner of his room, my eyes following the direction. "Go stand in front of the cross."

"You can't be serious," I deadpan, not budging.

"Oh, *cariño*," he coos. "You're in for such a rude awakening."

My eyes drag from his, to the black-and-red tufted leather cross sitting in the corner of the room like a fucking statement. Each arm of the cross has a set of leather cuffs attached, ready to strap its next victim to the contraption. My body trembles, a chill racing down my spine as I chance one more glance at Mateo before fumbling my way over to where I'm supposed to be.

I'm starting to regret coming here.

I don't think I'm going to survive the wrath of Mateo.

He steps up behind me, footsteps lighter than a feather, startling me. An arm wrapped around my middle, he pulls me into his body, my back against his front, as he peppers the curve of my neck with kisses. His scent wafts around me; marijuana, vanilla, and horrible fucking decisions.

His lips hover over the shell of my ear, his breath hot against my already overheated flesh. "If you're a good boy for me, *cariño*, you'll be rewarded in spades." Goosebumps pebble every inch of my body as he adds, "Now, hands up, baby. Let's strap you in."

THIRTY-THREE

Travis

This is so fucked up. A thin sheen of sweat covers my naked body, my wrists and ankles are secured to this cross using leather cuffs, and my backside is exposed to whatever fuckery Mateo is about to put me through.

I should be horrified. Embarrassed. Furious.

But I'm not.

I'm so unbelievably horny. I feel alive, like every inch of flesh is made up of live wire, my blood infused with electricity. My body is a hair-trigger, certain to go off with the barest of touches.

Rampage by gizmo is pulsing and vibrating through the speakers, the LED lights casting the room in a familiar red glow, and I can't quite make out what Mateo is doing behind me with the way I'm strapped into the cross. My heart pounds nearly as fast as the beat of the song, my hands clammy, and my dick throbbing with arousal.

The hairs on the back of my neck stand on edge, skin prickling with awareness as Mateo crowds my back, his body heat radiating against mine. "There are a few things we need to go over before getting started." His hot, minty breath fans my skin, a shiver racking through me. "First things first, paddle or flogger?"

Confusion has my brows knitting together. "What?"

He chuckles, the sound gruff as it washes over my body. "Would you prefer I use a paddle on you, *cariño*, or a flogger?"

I swallow thickly over the lump in my throat. "P-paddle," I decide.

"Lovely choice." I can feel his smile against my neck before he licks a hot, wet trail along the expanse of the area. "Do you remember your safe words?"

I nod, eliciting a growl from Mateo.

"Oh, baby, you know I need your words."

Excitement and arousal course through me in waves. "Yellow means slow down, and red means stop."

"Good job, *cariño*," he praises. "And lastly, under no circumstances are you to come without my permission. Do you understand?"

I nod again, confusion taking over. I'm not really sure I'll be in a position to come with him whacking me with a leather paddle, but sure.

"Words, Travis."

Heart thumping almost painfully in my chest, I blurt out, "Yes… yes, I understand. No coming without your say so."

"Good boy." Mateo growls the words against my neck before sharp teeth sink into the sensitive area, my head dropping back as a gasp falls from my lips. His hand skates down my abdomen, palm wrapping firmly around my stiff length, giving me a few slow pumps. "Such a fucking cock slut. So willing to do whatever you can for a little attention, hmm?"

My chest rumbles on a groan, his thumb swiping over the slick tip, smearing my arousal around. He sucks on my neck as his hand skillfully works me over, marking me before soothing the area with his tongue. My head is light, dizzy, euphoric as a cascade of pleasure and emotions floods my system.

Mateo works me right to the edge before removing his hand and mouth from my body. A whimper that should be embarrassing falls from my lips at the loss of contact, and I hear his dark chuckle behind me.

"Ready?" he asks.

I nod.

"What are your safe words again, *cariño*?"

"Yellow, slow down. Red, stop."

"Good boy." His praise sets my blood on fire. "I'm going to start with a couple warm-up ones. Two on each cheek. Just to get you used to the feel of the paddle, okay?"

Swallowing hard, I mutter, "Okay."

The heartbeat hammering inside my chest is a dead giveaway of how nervous I am. I've never done anything like this before, never having been hit with anything harder than an open hand during some doggy style.

But I've always wanted to. I've watched porn on the kinkier side before, and fantasized about what it would be like. I've always been with men who either aren't into stuff like this or who I wouldn't trust to take care of me and work with me through something to this extent.

My chest tightens as the realization hits me... I *do* trust Mateo to take care of me and work me through this. When did that happen, and why does that knowledge make me feel so confused?

Before I can think too much about the how and the why, the first strike hits me. Just like he promised, there isn't much force behind it, but the sting is still present. Heat blooms from my left cheek as I gasp from the contact. He strikes the right side next with the same force, the other two following closely after.

Mateo closes the distance between us again, one arm wrapping around my middle, his other coming up to grip my throat, pushing my head up until it's resting on his shoulder. It doesn't escape me that, like every time we wind up in one of his bedrooms like this, he's still fully clothed despite me being completely nude.

"Doing okay, *cariño*?" His rough, calloused hand wraps around my now half-hard cock, stroking it back to life, his teeth nipping my earlobe.

Nodding, I breathe out, "Yes." My eyes roll back as his wrist twists deliciously on the upstroke. "I'm doing good."

Rolling his hips into me, his erection is evident. This is turning him on. "Think you can take it a little harder?"

"Yes, I know I can." The reply is instant, a need burning inside of me to show him how much I can handle. To make him proud.

Pressing a kiss to my neck, he growls into my ear, "I know you can too."

Mateo steps back, the cool air from his absence jarring against my heated skin. My hands clench into fists and my body tenses for the impact to come. When the paddle connects with my left cheek, it's significantly harder than the first round, a stinging type of pain radiating from the entire area immediately.

A cry falls from my lips, my head throws back onto my shoulder, and even though I know I can't get free, it doesn't stop my arms from trying to rip from the cuffs. "Fuck!"

I barely have time to catch my breath before he's striking the opposite side with the same strength. My entire body is coiled tight, a throbbing ache coming from my backside that radiates through my bones.

"Take a deep breath, *cariño*." I do. "Your skin looks so fucking beautiful burning red for me," he growls a second before the paddle connects with my ass again.

And again.

And again.

Thwack... thwack... thwack.

Hearing the praise falling off Mateo's lips, his voice smooth like butter as he dishes it out, is enough to make me melt against this cross. It squeezes my chest, its effects caressing my mind, making it go all warm and fuzzy.

The sound of something hitting the carpeted floor reaches my ears moments before I feel Mateo at my back. At some point, he must've ripped his shirt off, because the slick heat of his chest rubs against my skin. His palms grab hold of my ass, massaging the throbbing globes as his lips pepper all along my shoulders and my neck with kisses.

"You okay?"

Fuck me, his voice is deep and throaty, so much arousal dripping from each word.

I nod, an odd wave of emotion taking hold of me once more, tears springing to my eyes. My throat aches, and I don't think I could get any words out if I tried.

Mateo continues to soothe the hot, stinging flesh with his hands. "So proud of you, *cariño*. You did so good. You know what that means?"

Shaking my head, I drag my lip between my teeth to stifle the sound.

For a second, his hands are gone, and I want to cry out because of it. But then... Well, then the distinct sound of his knees hitting the ground reaches my ears, and his hands are back on me, gently spreading me open, and then his breath is hot and wet against my hole, his tongue circling the puckered flesh, swiping along the length of my crack.

Before long, and before my brain even has a chance to catch up, his face is buried in my most intimate areas, and he's feasting on me like he's Jesus himself and this is the last supper. Pleasure floods my system as his pointed tongue spears through the tight muscle, and he starts fucking me with it while one of his hands reaches between my thighs, wrapping around my heavy, throbbing length.

I'm paralyzed, my arms and legs still strapped to this cross, my entire body thrumming with an intense type of need and desire. My hands itch to touch him, to make him feel like he's making me feel. The wet, smacking sounds coming from him make my cheeks flame even redder than they already are, but I can't get enough.

I need more of him.

I need all of him.

"Mateo… *please*."

My dick is so hard, it has its own heartbeat, my balls filled with lead, they're so heavy.

He pulls back, chuckling at the whimper that I can't hold back. "You're so pretty when you beg, you know that?"

"Please…"

At this point, I'm so far gone, I don't give a shit if I beg. I'll beg on my hands and knees, kissing his feet, if it means I get what I want. If it means he'll fill me up and I get to come, I'd do just about anything he asked of me. I clamp down on my lips to keep from blurting that out, though.

Mateo walks away, leaving me strapped to this damn cross,

and I hear more than see him open up one of the drawers. The distinct sound of a cap damn near reverberates through the small space, and it's then that I realize the music has turned off.

Cold, slick fingers find my hole, and he pushes a single finger inside. The way Mateo works me open quickly, with zero finesse, lets me know he's as gone as I am. It lets me know he wants me as much as I want him right now.

Which, in hindsight, really shouldn't be that surprising. He's never been quiet about how much he wants me. Mateo's not quiet about anything, really. It's me who's been quiet and closed off and in denial.

With his lips right next to the shell of my ear, voice low and growly, he says, "I'm going to fuck you now, *cariño*. You still doing okay?"

I nod, then correct myself and speak a breathy "yes, please," needing this more than he even knows.

Removing his fingers from my body, he quickly replaces them with his dick as he lines himself up, pushing inside. I gasp, and he groans, my back molding to his front once he's fully seated. He brings his arms up, hands gripping onto the same leather cuffs holding me upright as he starts to move in and out of me.

Slow, at first, but his patience wears thin, as does his restraint, and before I know it, his hips are slapping against my sore ass cheeks, and he's fucking into me with abandon. It's feral, animalistic. I love every fucking second of it.

"You like this, you little whore?" he growls beside my ear, my pulse racing as I fight to catch my breath. "You like me destroying this tight little pink cunt for anybody else?"

"Oh, God…"

The flat of his tongue runs along the side of my neck. "You

know there'll be no one else, right, *cariño*? Whether you want to believe it or not, you're. Fucking. *mine.*" Each word is spoken with a violent strike of his hips. "My lips to kiss. My body to mark. My pussy to fill. *Mine.*"

"Mateo... oh, fuck!"

Mateo's gruff, boisterous laugh washes over me. "Are you gonna come listening to me claim you, *cariño*?"

I nod feverishly. "I'm close... so... fucking... close."

With a growl, he nips at my ear. "Then come for me, *mi amor*. Show me how much being mine turns you on. Show me how much me owning you turns you inside out."

That's it. I'm a goner. Heat spreads rapidly through the base of my spine, through my balls, until I'm coming hard, completely untouched, against the front of this cross. Mateo doesn't let up either. He lets go of one of the cuffs, grabbing my chin to roughly turn my face to the side, smashing our mouths together as his tongue delves inside.

The hunger, the want, the need, all of it is potent on his tongue as it tangles and meshes with mine. It takes as much as it gives, his hips undulating into me. He grunts into my mouth, body stiffening against mine as he spills into me.

We stand there together for several moments, him still inside of me, as we both work on steadying our breathing. Eventually, he uncuffs my hands before leaning down to do the same to my ankles. I rub at both my wrists, my arms tired as fuck.

"Come here," he says, reaching for my hand and leading me out of the room and into the living room. He sits me down on the couch, leaving me for a moment, only to come back with a bottle of water. He uncaps it, handing it to me as I chug most of it in one go. Once I'm finished with it, he twists the cap back on, setting it on the side table before having me lay my head in his lap.

There's a blanket resting on the back of the couch that he grabs, covering me with it as one hand strokes through my hair, which is probably disgustingly sweaty, and the other slips under the blanket, massaging my very sore backside. Neither of us says anything during this process, but we sit there as he does this for probably close to twenty minutes.

The emotion swirling around inside of me feels uncontrollable. My eyes sting, my throat aches. I'm overwhelmed with how good his gentle touches feel. I'm overwhelmed with how all of him is making me feel right now. Eventually, my eyes get heavy and sleepy, my body more relaxed than it's been in who knows how long, and my chest swells with an emotion I can't quite place.

Or maybe I can, I'm just not ready to.

•

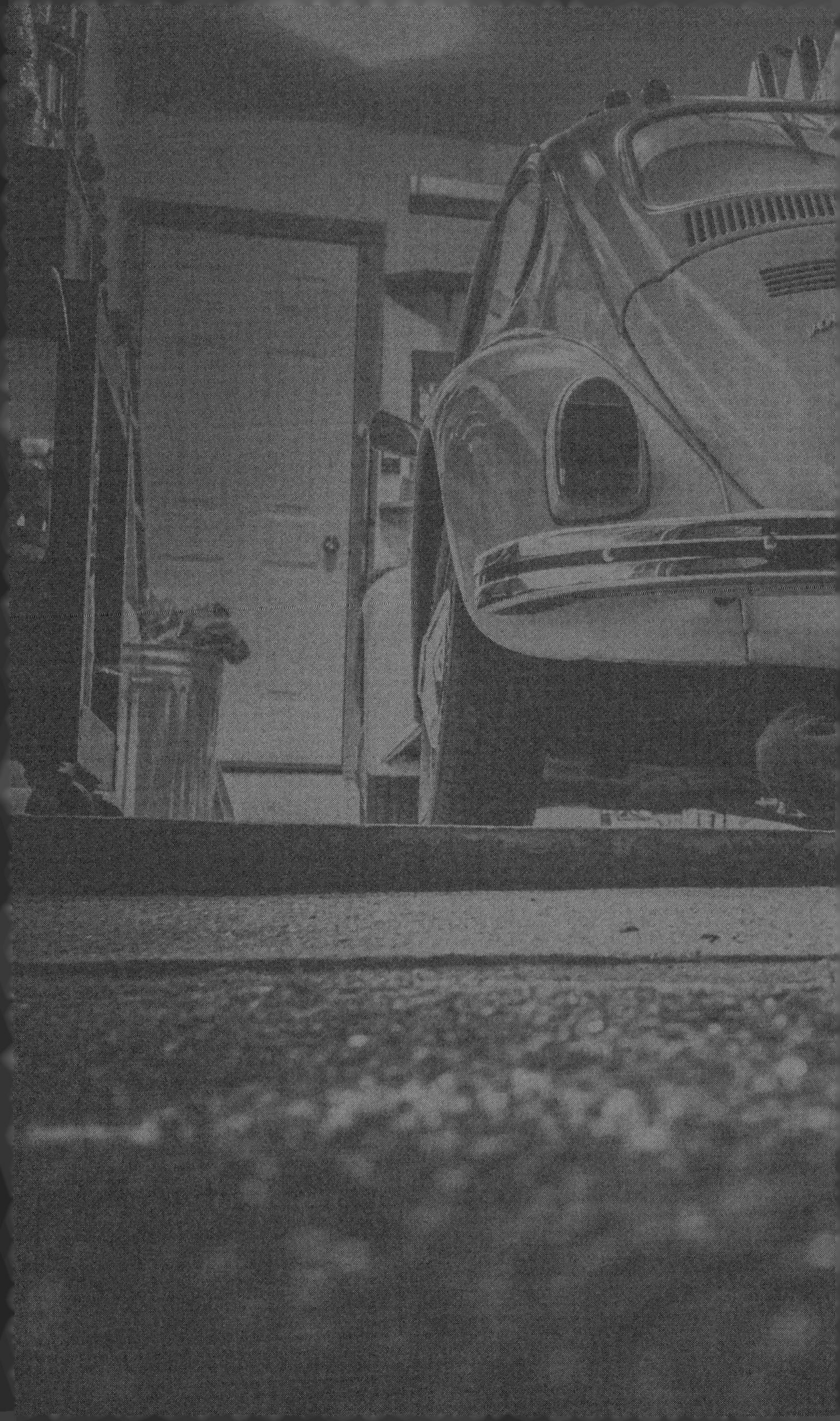

THIRTY-FOUR

Mateo

The door to my apartment creeks as it opens, and glancing over my shoulder, my eyes connect with Travis's baby blues, a grin tugging on his plump, pink lips. "Hey, *cariño*. About time your ass gets here."

"Well, I'm sorry we can't all slum it at home all day," he mutters sarcastically. "Some of us have jobs to get to."

"Oh, fuck you," I growl, turning and hauling him into me. The kiss we share is heated and passionate, my tongue slipping past his parted lips, tangling with his, and ending much too soon.

Benny's having the office repainted, so he gave Miguel and me the day off, which has been really fucking nice. Lying around in pajamas all day, watching trash TV, snacking and smoking to my heart's content, is the highlight of my week… Until now, of course.

Travis's work, on the other hand, has been insane for the past week and a half. Apparently, they're amping up to bring on a couple more high-profile clients, so we've barely seen each other.

It's been about a month since he let me paddle him against

the St. Andrews Cross. Things between us have continued since that night, minus the hate. We've started hanging out more often, doing things other than just having sex. Now, don't get me wrong, we're still having sex, but it's like he's allowing an actual friendship to form too.

I don't fucking want a friendship with him, though. No, not even close. I want everything with him, but I feel like he still has this wall up that I can't seem to tear down. As the days pass and my feelings only grow deeper, it's driving me nuts and making me desperate. I was trying to ease the bricks down, one by one, and now I'm ready to make a sledgehammer move instead. Knocking down that wall around his heart will be the only way he'll be able to see what we could be.

"What are you making?" Travis asks against my lips.

"Just some skillet enchiladas. You hungry?"

"Starving. There was a last-minute meeting this afternoon, and I skipped lunch."

Turning back to the stove, I turn the oven down to simmer. "Wanna go into my room and grab a joint from my dresser?" I glance over my shoulder at him. "We can smoke before we eat."

"Um, yes, please," he replies dramatically. "That sounds perfect."

After we get a nice buzz going and eat our body weights in enchiladas, we curl up on the couch together, turning on *Shameless*. Travis had never seen a single episode of this show until a few weeks ago, but I have opened his eyes, and now we watch it together whenever we get a chance.

Lying here with him like this feels so natural. I don't get why he won't just give in and take the leap already. Travis has got to be one of the most stubborn people I've ever met… and that's saying a lot coming from *me*.

Burying my nose in the hair atop his head, I inhale, getting dizzy on his scent. "Want to go grab Nova, and you guys can stay the night?"

He peers up at me, and I already know his answer before he says anything. "I'd love to, but I gotta FaceTime my mom tonight, and I have to be up early in the morning for a meeting with the manager of Product Development. But this weekend?"

Travis returns his attention to the TV, and I roll my eyes. He acts like he can't FaceTime his mom here, or like staying here would make his drive to work any longer than it already is.

We watch another episode and give each other head before he goes home for the night, and I climb into bed, annoyed despite the orgasm I just had.

I don't know when exactly I became the guy who was so adamant about a relationship, so pushy for that official status. It's not who I am—and I haven't been that guy for years—but with Travis, hooking up isn't enough for me anymore. I want to hold his hand in public. I want him to not only tell people about me, but do so without being all grumbly about it. I want to cook him dinner every night and sleep with him in my arms. I want to claim him once and for all as mine for the entire world to see, and not just by way of hickeys on the neck.

I've been patient, but frankly, I'm tired of waiting. It's time for me to take matters into my own hands and woo his ass.

I don't really know what that entails yet, but I'll figure it out. It's about damn time Travis remembers that I get what I want, and what I want this time is all of him. Enough of this casual bullshit.

Woo him.

Those two words have haunted me for the last three days since they came to me. Given what I know about Travis's past relationships, I know it needs to be something big to get his attention. Something to make him feel seen and special. Yet, knowing that and actually figuring out how to follow through with it are two very different things. Annoyingly, I was coming up blank, up until yesterday morning when something clicked into place.

A tidbit of information I remember Travis telling me that I could definitely use to *woo him*. Which is why I stand outside of Travis's door, early as fuck on a Saturday morning, raising my fist up to knock, with, what I think is, a great fucking plan in my arsenal.

When the door swings open and Travis appears before me, he's in pajama pants and a black tee, his hair disheveled, and pillow marks on the side of his face like he just woke up.

His brows pinch together as he takes me in. "Yes?"

"Come with me."

"Huh?" Confusion really takes over his features now.

"Get dressed. I got somewhere for us to go."

Travis glances over his shoulder, and for a moment, I think he may have someone inside. My stomach bottoms out until I realize he's looking at the clock on the microwave. "It's barely seven in the morning," he groans, peering back over at me. "I'm gonna need a little fucking more from you than *'come with me.'*"

I roll my eyes, my frustration growing. "Well, I wanted it to be a surprise, but you clearly suck at those, so I'm taking you snowboarding."

His eyes widen a fraction, and I watch as his Adam's apple bobs on a swallow. "Snowboarding?"

"Yes, *cariño*." I blow out a sigh. "Snowboarding. Now, can

we get a move on? It's like a four-hour drive."

Travis watches me silently for a moment. What I wouldn't give to know what's running through his mind. Finally, he pops his hip out, crossing his arms over his chest as he blurts out, "Mateo, I can't just leave town on a whim with zero notice. What about Nova? I can't leave her home by herself all day."

"Will you chill the fuck out?" I hiss. "I asked your sister to come hang out with her today."

He blinks hard once.

Twice.

"My... my sister?"

"Yes, you know... Charlotte."

I can practically see the wheels turning in his head, and if I wasn't so annoyed with how long he's taking, I'd laugh.

"How do you know my sister?"

Pinching the bridge of my nose, I mutter, "I got her number from Xander. Now, can we fucking go?"

"Xan—"

"Travis!"

Truth be told, I had to hunt Xander down on social media and present him with my plan, and even then, he didn't want to help me out. I had to bribe him with a year's worth of free oil changes before he'd give me Charlotte's phone number. I'd originally asked him to watch Nova, but he's heading out of town today and couldn't. Or so he says.

Travis holds his hands up innocently at me, brows raised. "Okay, fuck. Sorry. I do have to get dressed and take her potty first."

"Fine. Hurry up."

This is starting out just fucking swimmingly.

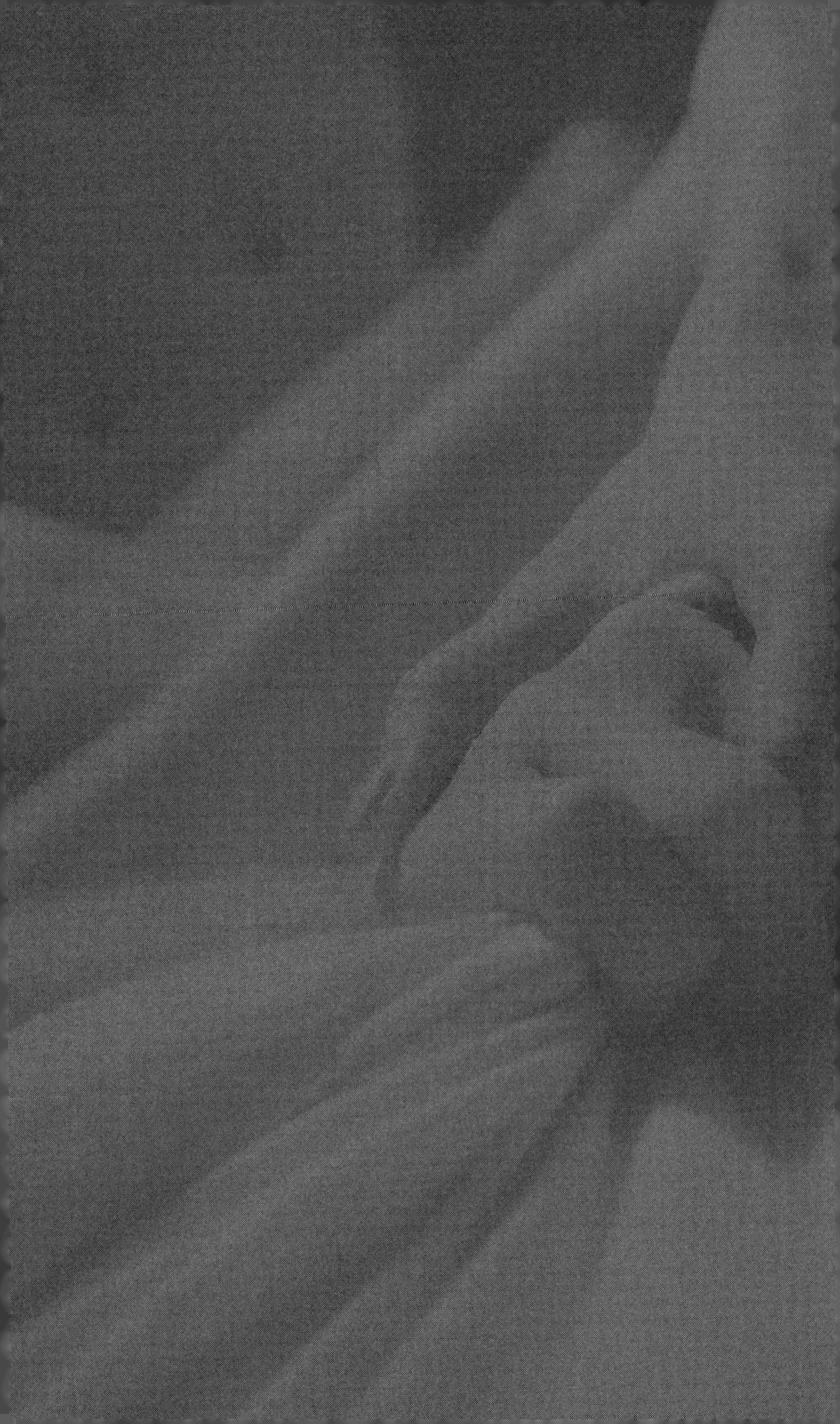

THIRTY-FIVE

Travis

Me: What the fuck is going on, Xander?
Xander: Good morning to you too. Not a clue. What you mean, dude?
Me: I am currently in the car with Mateo on our way to the pass to go snowboarding!

Glancing over at Mateo, he's focused on the road as he drives. He's got on a pair of black shades, and he's dressed comfy in sweats and a t-shirt. We took his car on this little last-minute excursion, and it smells like him. I'm practically salivating.

We've been on the road for about an hour now. Neither of us have spoken, despite me having way too many questions. Hence why I texted Xander to try to get to the bottom of this.

My phone buzzes in my hand, my eyes rolling as I take in the response from Xander on my screen.

Xander: Hell yeah. That sounds dope. Have fun!
Me: I don't fucking think so, Xander. SPILL!

He sends a gif of a little girl shrugging, looking innocent.

Xander: I don't know what you mean.

Me: Why'd you give Mateo Charlotte's number? And since when are you and Mateo on speaking terms? Why is he taking me snowboarding? I NEED ANSWERS!

Xander: 1. He asked for it. 2. *shrugging emoji* 3. Maybe because snowboarding is fun and you love it? I don't have your answers. Well, I do. But I won't be giving them to you. In fact, I'm not responding to you anymore. Have fun. Keep an open mind. Bye!

Audibly grumbling, I lock my screen, tucking the phone back into my hoodie pocket before reaching for the energy drink Mateo got me in the cup holder.

"What the fuck's the matter with you?"

His voice startles me, my head whipping to the side. "Nothing. Just… I didn't realize you liked snowboarding."

"I don't."

"What? You don't?" I balk.

He reaches over, turning the music down a little. "I guess it's not that I don't. I've just never done it, nor did it seem of interest to me."

I'm so confused. "Then why are we going?"

"Because you like it." The way he says it, so simply put, like it's the most obvious answer in the world. Like it clears up all my confusion.

It doesn't. It just gives me more questions.

"How do you know that?" As soon as the words leave my mouth, it hits me. Holding up my hand, I say, "Wait, let me guess… Xander."

Mateo glances at me from above his sunglasses before returning his attention to the road. "No, *cariño*. Don't you remember the night of the engagement party, you told me that you love going but you haven't been able to go this year with everything that happened with Nathaniel and moving, and how the season is almost over."

Holy shit.

Holy fucking shit.

I stare at Mateo. Gaping at the side of his head as his words trail through my mind on a loop. Yeah, *now* I remember telling him that. How does *he* remember that, though? It was practically a side comment in a random conversation while we were tossing back tequila shots before dinner.

My chest is all warm and tight, my pulse racing, and there's a horribly large lump in my throat making it hard to talk or breathe or do anything except sit here, flabbergasted. I bite the inside of my cheek to keep from smiling like a moron.

Why would he do this? Drive four hours to do something he's never done, never had any interest in doing, simply because I mentioned enjoying it and that I haven't been able to do it this season?

Why?

Nobody has ever done something so thoughtful for me before.

The last month or so, we've been hooking up more regularly, but it's stayed at mostly just that. I've gotten the feeling that Mateo maybe wants more than that… not that he's ever come right out and said it. I don't know, though. That thought makes me nervous. While he's shown me that he's not who I originally thought he was, and while I'm pretty sure I'm over what Nathaniel did to me, I still can't help but worry.

What if it happens again?

What if I start to fall for him, and he cheats on me?

A part of me wonders if those types of thoughts will ever fully go away, or if they're engrained in who I am now. When someone is cheated on, their way of thinking can't help but be changed, even if they don't want to be that way.

What if I really am a conquest to Mateo, and the finish line is getting me to fall for him? I don't believe that logically... but what if?

It's reasons like those that have made me keep him at an arm's length. But the truth is, I am starting to care for Mateo more than I would've liked. I look forward to seeing him. I've started finding comfort in being near him, and that fucking terrifies me. And now this? *Fuck.*

"Earth to Travis." Mateo snaps his fingers beside my head. "You alive over there?"

"Uh, yeah. Think I'm gonna take a nap before we get there. Make sure I'm nice and rested for the slopes."

I turn over in my seat, facing the window, and pretend to nap for the next three hours.

"This is so fucking stupid."

Laughter bubbles out of me, puffs of white clouds forming in front of me from how cold it is up here, as I watch Mateo attempt to stand up again after eating shit for the hundredth time in the forty-five minutes we've been out here.

One thing is for absolute certain; Mateo is *not* a natural at snowboarding. I wouldn't be surprised in the least if he woke up tomorrow sore as fuck, black and blue, from all the falling he's done.

"It's not stupid," I mutter, offering him my hand to help him get back up. "It's hard if you don't know what you're doing, and this is your first time. Cut yourself some slack."

Mateo's finally upright, and he's brushing the snow off himself, huffing and puffing his annoyance. I can't help but watch him and think how fucking cute he looks all flustered. It's not something I'm used to seeing from him, but I like it. It makes him a little more mortal like the rest of us.

We're still on the bunny slopes, barely having gone anywhere yet. Normally, when I come here, I'm on more advanced slopes, but I don't really want to ditch Mateo to go do that, especially when it was his idea—his extremely *thoughtful* idea—to come here. So, despite his insistence that I do just that, I'm here with him, trying to help him find his footing, so to speak.

"Here." I hold out my arm for him. "Hold on, and let me help you try to find your groove."

He takes the hand, attempting to stand, but loses his footing immediately, dragging us both down into the snow. I bury my face into the crook of my arm, trying to hide the laughter, but it's no use.

Grumbling loudly, Mateo picks up a fistful of snow, throwing it at me. "Stop fucking laughing at me."

He can't even get the words out without a smile splitting on his face.

"Hey!" Molding a snowball with my hands, I throw it at his head, pegging him right above his ear. "Don't throw snow at me, asshole."

I go to stand, but before I can, Mateo swipes his arm out, knocking my legs out from under me. Falling onto the snow, the air is knocked from my lungs, but laughter bubbles out of me all the same. He rolls on top of me, snow completely surrounding us, with an expression I can't quite place. It almost looks… loving. But that can't be right.

Clearing my throat, I wrap my arms around his neck. "You're kind of a poor sport, you know that?"

"Is that really all that surprising?" he drawls.

"No." I chuckle. "But if you stop being a brat for a second, I could teach you."

Leaning down, he brings his lips onto mine. They're cold, much like most of me, but when his tongue dips out, sliding into my mouth, it warms me up immediately.

Kissing Mateo never fails to make my head all fuzzy. I wonder if there will ever come a time when it doesn't. Arousal swirls in my groin, and suddenly, I'm wishing we were in a much more secluded area.

Mateo breaks the kiss much too soon, placing a quick peck on my cold and red nose before standing up—successfully this time. He offers me a hand, helping me up before muttering, "Well, come on then, teach. Show me a thing or two."

The next several hours are spent in similar fashion to before—lots of falling, swearing under his breath, nasty glares in my direction when I don't fall even when he does, but also lots of kissing and laughing. It's been a shitshow, but a fucking hilarious one. Even though he's frustrated beyond belief—clearly, he's not used to not being good at things—this has been way more fun than any Saturday I would've had planned for myself.

We're stopped at the top of the smaller slopes, taking in the view—granted, the view would've been much nicer had we been at a higher altitude, but hey, who am I to judge. Biting down on the tip of my glove, I rip it off my hand, reaching into my pocket, and grab my phone.

"Come here," I mutter to Mateo, grabbing his arm and pulling him into me. "Let's take a picture up here." With the camera app pulled up, I position the phone in front of us as I smile, and Mateo looks bored out of his mind—but I can still see a sparkle in his eye, like it's just for me. "Jesus Christ, smile, will you?"

It takes a few tries, but eventually, I snap a pretty great picture of us. Tucking my phone back in my pocket, I try not to obsess over the fact that Mateo and I now have a selfie together, and we look oddly like a couple in it. I also try to ignore the way that thought makes my stomach do a flop.

I put my glove back on, glancing around at our surroundings. "Well, we should probably return our gear and start heading back home. Otherwise, it's going to be late by the time we get back."

The first happy smile I've seen from Mateo since we got out here slides onto his lips, looking as mischievous as ever. "About that."

My brows pinch. "What?"

His grin turns beaming. It's so fucking beautiful. "I actually got us a cabin for the night."

"You did what?" I'm positive if I was looking at myself from afar, I'd resemble one of those cartoons with the eyes that bulge out of their head dramatically. "But I have to get home to Nova."

Holding up a hand to stop me, Mateo says, "I took care of it. Charlotte is keeping her overnight. She picked her up shortly after we left, and I packed you some clothes while you were taking Nova for a walk this morning."

"A cabin…" My mind is spinning, and all these new feelings are swirling around inside my gut. I can't make sense of them. I can't make sense of anything.

He nods. "Yeah. It looks pretty nice online, and even has one of those outside hot tubs." With the huge goggles propped on his forehead, it's almost hard to miss the waggle of his brows.

"Let me get this straight… not only did you surprise me with a trip to the pass to go snowboarding because I happened to mention to you *in passing* how I love to go but haven't been able to, but you also booked us a fucking cabin to stay in overnight?"

The organ in my chest is rearing up to bust out of my ribcage, it's beating so fast.

"Yes," he replies plainly. "Exactly that."

But it is. "That's... that's so sweet of you, Mateo."

My head feels light, and I don't think it's the altitude that has it hard for me to breathe. This considerate, soft side of Mateo is making it harder and harder to deny just how much I care about him. And that terrifies me.

"It's not a big deal," he insists. "And besides, you deserve it." The last sentence comes out growly, and he doesn't give me a chance to respond before he turns and attempts to make it back down the mountain. He doesn't make it far before he falls right on his ass again, though.

Forcing myself to put all of this on the back burner, I laugh at his string of curse words before going to help him up. It ends up taking us close to an hour to get back to the rental office, both of us sweaty by the time we do. Mateo's patience is shot, and we're both starving.

We decide to grab a bite to eat at the lodge restaurant before going to check into the cabin he rented. On the way there, Mateo slips his hand into mine, linking our fingers. It doesn't escape me that this is the first time we've ever held hands.

This feels so different from every other time we've spent the night together, and I don't know how to handle it.

THIRTY-SIX

Mateo

"Wow…" Travis walks into the cabin we're staying in tonight, dropping his bag onto the ground as he scans the room. "This is really fucking nice."

It is, I won't lie. There're rose petals everywhere, a couple of bottles of champagne with some chocolate on the table, and the view is killer. I can't help but laugh.

He turns, meeting my amused gaze. "What is so funny?"

"So, I kind of told them we just got married."

Travis's eyes bulge out of his head, and I lose it to a fit of laughter. "What?" he hisses. "Why on earth would you do that?"

"Look at all that free champagne we got." I snort out another laugh. "That's all because I said this was our honeymoon."

Before coming here, we went out to dinner and had *a lot* of alcohol. I'm feeling pretty toasty already, and I'd be willing to bet he is too, but who's gonna say no to free champagne?

"You're horrible." He chuckles, walking over to the table and grabbing one of the bottles.

Travis works on opening the bottle as I take a look around the rest of the cabin. I'm surprised there were any left to rent on such short notice. I didn't book this until yesterday, but luck was on my side because they had a last-minute cancelation right before I called. The view is insane, even though I can't see much right now since it's dark. The hot tub is on the back patio, and snow-covered branches are all around, making it look like something out of a movie.

Coming up behind me, Travis hands me a glass. When I meet his gaze, his baby blues are full of nerves. "Thank you," he breathes, hand reaching up to cup my face. "For everything today. It's been incredible, and it's really sweet. Thank you."

"You're welcome."

The air thickens between us as we sip our drinks. It's heavy and suffocating, but in a way that makes me want to pull him closer and wrap my arms around him. Through every revelation today, Travis has looked more and more shocked. Like he couldn't believe somebody would want to do something nice for him, which honestly, makes me feel a little stabby.

It makes me stabby because nobody has ever done something selfless and nice for him before, so when it happens, he doesn't know how to act. It's clear in the way he stiffens up and stumbles over his words that he's uncomfortable with the gestures, and that's not how it should be.

Travis deserves all the grand gestures. All the surprise trips and nights with champagne. My body may be sore as all hell, and I may have bruises forming on places of my body I didn't think could bruise, but all of that is worth it to see his eyes light up.

He takes a step forward, closing the distance between us. His hand brushes along my cheek, his mouth a mere two inches from mine as his eyes lock on mine. "Can I show you how thankful I am?" He doesn't wait for a response before he seals his lips to mine.

Taking the champagne flute from me, he sets both on the table before leading me by the hand toward the hallway that must lead to the bedroom. He doesn't turn the light on once we enter; there's enough light pouring in from the back patio that we don't need it.

Shaky, yet sure, fingers find the hem of my shirt, and Travis kisses me softly one more time before dragging the shirt over my head, letting it drop to the floor beside us. Next, he removes his own shirt before shoving my pants down until they pool around my ankles. I step out of them, watching as he pushes his down too.

It's no surprise that we're both almost fully hard by the time we're undressed. As we stand here, greedily drinking in the other, I can't help but notice how this time feels different than all the others. There's a look in his eyes as he takes me in that is new, like he's seeing me for the first time today. My pulse races under his gaze. *Something* has shifted, and I pray like hell it's a good shift. I hope when all of this is said and done, Travis can finally believe me when I say I'm into him.

I'm not one for big, grand speeches about my feelings, but I'm also not someone who says I want something when I actually don't. I will be the first to admit that getting under Travis's skin was amusing when he first moved in, and I was a bit more of a dick than I probably needed to be, but from the very first time I had his lips on mine, felt his body pressed against me, I knew he couldn't be temporary.

Travis is mine, and my feelings for him only get larger and more intense as the days go on. I need him to see that for what it is.

I need him to believe that like I need water to hydrate my body.

And I need him to feel the same.

It's been a long time—too long—since I've felt this way. Since I've allowed myself to feel this way, and I don't know how I'll move on if he doesn't.

Blindly, we make our way over to the bed. Travis positions me at the head of the bed before climbing on top of me. His erection glides against my own, and I groan into his mouth. Rolling his hips, he licks into my mouth, sucking on my tongue before moving to my throat. His hot breath and the soft press of his plush lips have goosebumps pebbling along my skin.

With my hands firmly on his hips, I continue to rock into him, a pool of our shared arousal dripping onto my stomach.

Travis works his way down the length of my body, tasting and savoring every inch of me along the way. When he reaches the mess we've made below my naval, he laps it up with the flat of his tongue, a groan rumbling out of him. He looks up at me beneath his thick lashes, the black of his blown-out pupils overtaking the baby blue of his irises.

He looks absolutely perfect, exquisite, beautiful as he takes me into his mouth. Lips already red and swollen from us making out, they stretch around my length, moisture filling up his eyes the farther down he gets.

"Look at you, *cariño*. You take me so well." Reaching down, I run my fingers through his hair as his head bobs up and down, taking every last inch I have to offer. His hand moves down to my balls, rolling and toying with them while he works me over with his mouth. It's messy; spit falling, slurping sounds filling the air. It's erotic and filthy, just the way I like it.

Before long, his hands abandon my balls, fingers inching lower. He applies pressure to my taint, his tongue swirling around my tip, my body going rigid the farther down he gets. It's right there on the tip of my tongue to tell him to stop. Tell him that he can't go *there*.

It's what I would say if this were anybody else.

But as my gaze locks on his, and I see the adoration and gentleness overflowing from his eyes, and I feel the softness in which he touches me, I find that I don't want to tell him no. I don't want him to stop.

I find that for the first time in… well, ever, I want to try.

I realize I trust Travis. Trust him to not push me past what I want to do, but I also trust him to make it an enjoyable experience for me.

So, even though every bone in my body is trying to live in fight-or-flight mode, I force myself to relax. I force my mind to shut off and let Travis guide me through this. He must notice the shift too, because he removes me from his mouth, sitting back on his haunches as he peers up at me.

"You okay?"

The question reminds me of earlier this week, him strapped to the St. Andrews Cross, and me asking him the exact same question.

I nod.

He offers me a small smile, his eyes glinting. "You can trust me, you know."

"I know I can." My voice is like gravel, my nerves wrapped around my vocal cords.

Travis climbs up my body, pressing his lips to mine. The kiss is gentle, but meaningful. It's meant to be reassuring. Comforting.

And I love him for it.

The blood roars in my ears as the thought simmers in my mind, embedding in my chest like a knife.

I… love him.

Fuck…

Putting that thought away for a different day, I force myself back into the here and now as Travis breaks the kiss and climbs off the bed, padding over to the duffle on the floor. He unzips the side pocket, pulling out a bottle of lube that I put in there before leaving my house. How he knew it was in there is beyond me.

He climbs back on the bed, positioning himself back between my open thighs. His mouth closes around my cock again, gliding down, my toes curling as he does. At the same time, he runs his now-slick fingers down through my crease.

My breath hitches, but again, I force myself to relax. *He's got me. I can trust him. Travis isn't* him.

The pad of his index finger circles my hole, the touch featherlight. It sparks something foreign inside of me. Something overwhelming and invigorating. His tongue circles my tip the same way his finger is, the paired sensation otherworldly.

A groan rumbles from my chest as I fist the sheets. Sweat lines my body and my heart is spazzing out. Emotion sears my eyes as I fight to keep them open, needing to watch him every step of the way.

Every single thing about Travis is extraordinary. The way he can't help but wear his heart on his sleeve, no matter what, despite all the heartbreak he's been through. His piercing blue eyes that hold humor, and love, and even anger sometimes. And the way he's still so soft and gentle despite the world trying so hard to make him jaded.

He's beautiful and kind and funny.

He can be sarcastic and tough when he needs to be. And he's so utterly shameless in everything that he wants. Travis isn't someone I thought I'd end up with. He's someone the old me would've walked all over. Taken advantage of. But as I lie here, his hands and mouth all over me while he takes such good care of me, it's abundantly clear that he's *exactly* who I should have by my side.

I swallow thickly around the lump in my throat, forcing myself to breathe deeply as Travis applies more pressure to his finger, slipping past the tight muscle. It's something that would've sent me spiraling a few months ago. It's something I wouldn't have even been open to.

But right here, right now, with Travis? I welcome it.

I crave it.

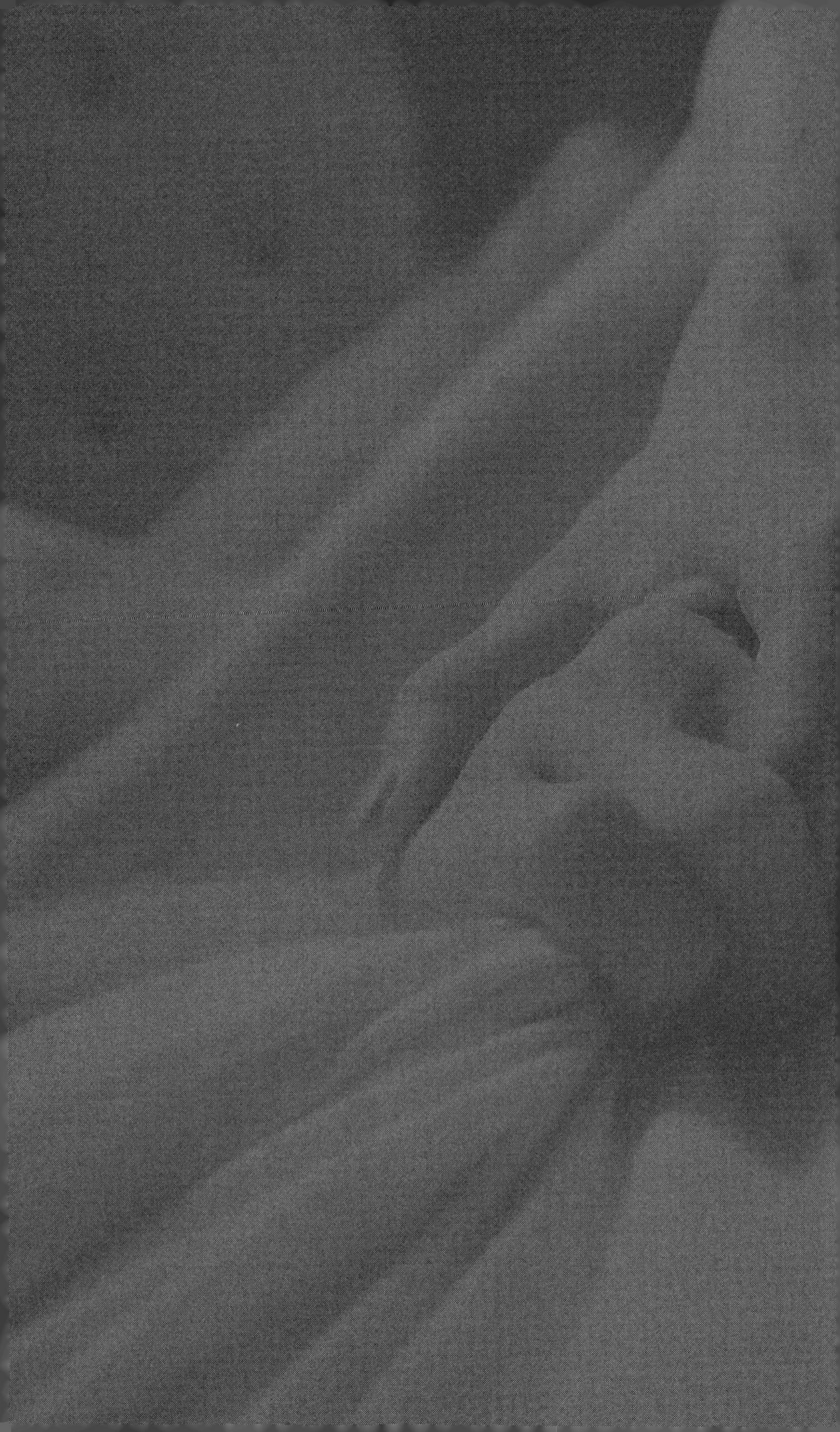

THIRTY-SEVEN

Travis

Mateo's body is trembling beneath me. The fact that I'm even in this position, and that he's putting such a high level of trust in me at all, is astounding. His vulnerability is stunning.

Everything about this day, from the very moment he knocked on my door this morning, until right now, something has changed. It's been a slow-burn change, that probably started before I even realized it, but today is the turning point. Today is the day I can no longer pretend there's nothing between us. That it's strictly physical.

As much as I've tried to deny it, Mateo has awoken something inside of me. He's given me headaches, yes, but he's also given me comfort and warmth. Without me even realizing it, he's made me feel seen and heard. This trip is proof of that. He's fought for me, despite my every attempt to push him away.

He's shown up. It's as simple as that.

And now it's my turn to show up for him. Make him feel comfort and warmth. Allow him to be seen and heard. Because he deserves to feel it all on his terms, in a way that makes him feel safe. I want to single-handedly erase every bad memory he has regarding sex, and replace them with only the good, the euphoric, the all-consuming, the mind-numbing goodness I know I can give him.

Mateo's thick, rigid length pulses against my tongue, pre-cum dripping, as my finger glides in and out of him. He's tight and hot, wrapped around the single digit, and I can tell he's fighting to remain calm, his body going back and forth between tense and relaxed.

Removing him from my mouth, my lips trail down, tongue dipping out to swipe along his sac. A full-body shiver rolls through him, and I can't help the smile the tugs on my lips at the raw physical reaction he has to me. I suck one of his balls into my mouth, humming as I do. He groans, the sound chest-deep and rumbly. It wraps around my marrow, blooming and spreading to every nerve ending.

The farther my mouth goes, the more nervous I become. I want so badly to make this good for him, and I'm half-expecting him to flip out and put a stop to it at any second. I withdraw my finger, replacing it with my tongue, spreading his legs wider and pushing them back, giving me full access to him.

Pulling back only slightly, I allow myself a moment to admire him and all he has to offer. His hole flutters under my gaze, and I glance up, finding him already watching me. His eyes are nothing more than hungry black orbs, and his thick brows are pinched, with his full, red lip dragged between his teeth.

"You doing okay, Matty?" I ask him, my thumbs running soft circles along the insides of his thighs as I hold his legs back.

The nickname makes him smile, despite rolling his eyes. "Yeah, *mi amor*, I'm good."

Mi amor. He's called me that a few times. I can't even deny how hard it makes my heart race.

"Let me know if you need me to stop, okay?"

He nods.

Leaning down, I run the flat of my tongue over his puckered hole gingerly. He lets out a whimper, the sound something I didn't even know could come from him. I do it again. So does he. I wrap my hand around his dick, pumping him slowly as my tongue continues to flick out against his hole. Making sure to get him nice and wet, I use my pointed tongue to spear into the muscle. He gasps, one of his hands finding the top of my head, fingers gripping the strands. He isn't pulling away, but instead, keeping me there.

I moan against his flesh; the taste and feel of him is too much. My hips rock into the mattress, desperately seeking friction. Hearing and seeing him fall apart for me turns me on way too much. I could easily get used to this, and that scares me.

Reaching for the bottle of lube beside him, I sit back on my haunches, flicking the cap open. I pour a generous amount on my two fingers, bringing them to his crease. I smear the cool gel around, feeling him shiver. Our gazes lock as I circle the pads of my fingers around his hole, grabbing his cock again to stoke as I apply the lightest bit of pressure.

Mateo's body tenses, and he inhales sharply. One look at him, and it's clear he's starting to spiral. But he hasn't told me to stop yet, and if there's one thing I know about Mateo, it's that he wouldn't have any problem telling me to if that's what he wanted. Deciding to trust him, I lean over, pressing my lips to his, before breathing into his mouth, "Relax for me, Matty. Let me in."

For a moment, he does nothing. His chest rising and

falling rapidly. But then, miraculously, he nods, his entire body melting into the bed as he bares down on my fingers. I slip past the tight ring of muscle, and he grunts at the intrusion, but he breathes through it, eyes boring into mine.

This moment is intense. It's overwhelming and electrically charged. It makes my chest tight and my blood heat.

God, he's fucking beautiful right now. Flushed, glistening with sweat, with a dick that's hard and throbbing in my palm.

I take my time, working my fingers into him slowly, stretching him nice and easy, while continuing to stroke his dick to counteract the burn that comes with my intrusion. He's halfway to sitting up now, his hand wrapped around the back of my neck, our foreheads nearly touching as we breathe each other in. The eye contact and the nearness are staggering. It's heady, my head dizzy.

Crooking my fingers, I graze his prostate, earning me the most delicious and sweet moan I think I've ever heard. I drag my thumb over the tip of his dick, smearing around the pre-cum pooling at the slit. He's *dripping* for me, and I love it. I'm now fucking him in earnest with my fingers, stroking him fervently as he pants hotly against my mouth.

"Fuck, *cariño*..."

"You're doing so fucking good, Matty," I coo right before he closes the distance, sealing our lips together in a searing kiss. His tongue sweeps into my mouth, showing me just how much he loves what I'm doing to him.

The kiss ends far too soon when he rips his mouth from mine, tugging on the hair at my nape as his breathing quickens. "God-fucking-damnit, I'm close," he moans.

Doubling down on my efforts, I caress that sweet button inside of him over and over as my grip tightens on his cock, wrist twisting with each stroke. He's crying out, the grip on my hair painful as I take him higher, working him closer to his explosion. Mateo's entire body trembles, his free hand grappling at my arm.

"Come on, baby," I breathe against his lips. "Come for me. Give it to me."

And boy, he does…

Mateo's hole constricts around my fingers, as a deep, guttural groan rips from his throat. Thick, hot ropes decorate his chest as his orgasm takes over, limbs twitching as his body convulses. I work him through it until every last drop seeps out and he collapses onto the bed. My dick is throbbing it's so hard, but this was about him, and I don't want to take away from that.

I move to lie next to him, but he stops me before I can. He steals my breath with his lips before uttering words I never thought I'd hear come from him. "Fuck me, *cariño*…"

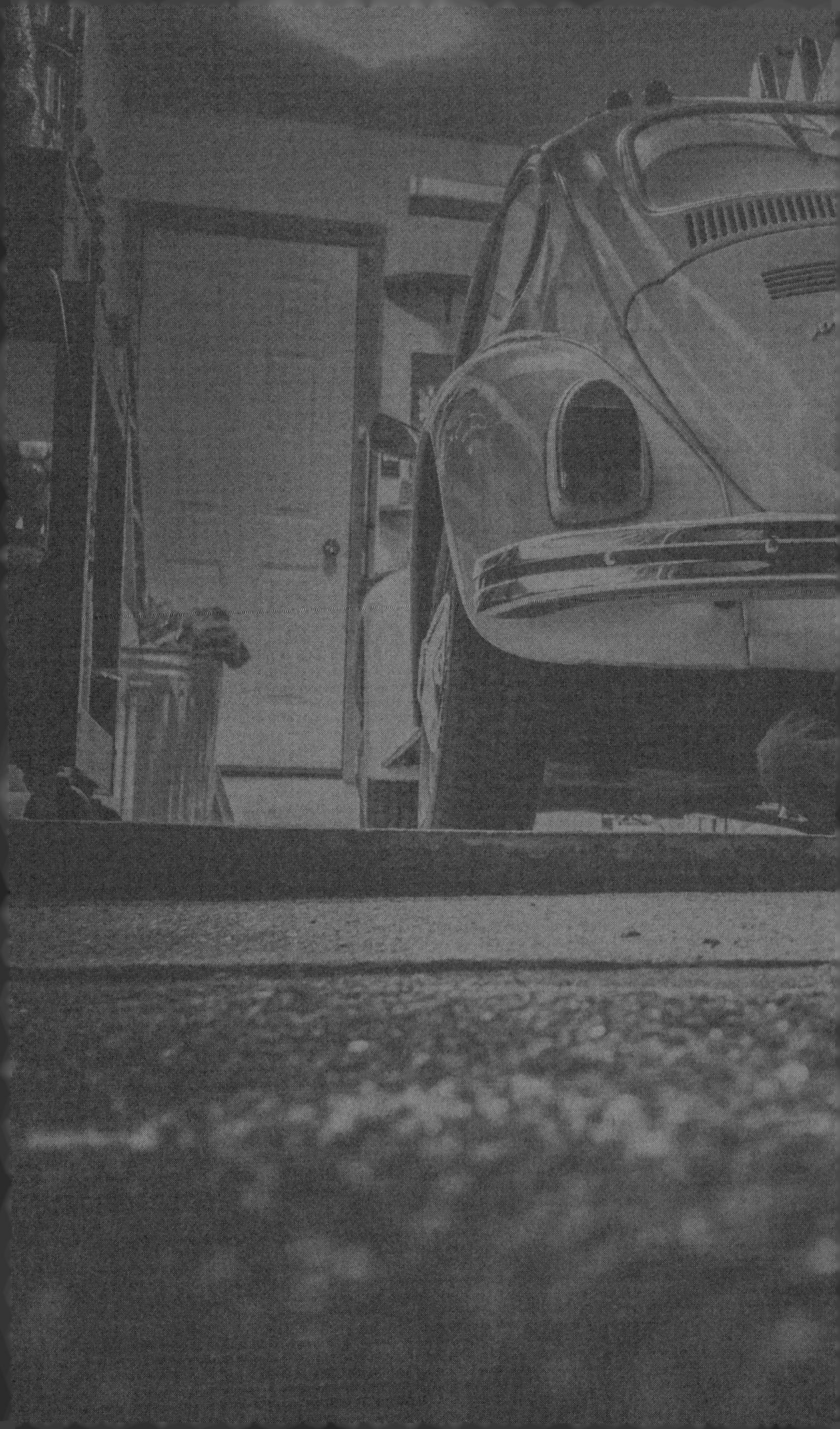

THIRTY-EIGHT
Mateo

Travis is frozen. Like I made him glitch. He's staring at me with his baby blue eyes wide, his lips parted open in disbelief, and he hasn't moved from his position above me. A chuckle rumbles out of me.

"Did I break you, *cariño?*"

He blinks a few times, tongue poking out to wet his lips. "I, uh… I don't think I heard you right, is all."

Travis is a masterpiece right now, and always. Miles of pale skin on display, I can't help but admire every curve and dip his body has to offer. Where I'm covered in ink, he's free of it; all untouched flesh. His dick is long and hanging heavy between us, a flushed, swollen pink tip glistening with his arousal. He's gotta be dying with how hard he is right now, yet he hasn't made a single move to get himself off.

Reaching up and grabbing him by the back of his neck, I haul him into me. He gasps into my mouth as my tongue sweeps inside. He tastes so fucking good. Slowly, he relaxes into my touch, his body coming down, blanketing mine, with not a single fucking care in the world that I'm covered in cum. My body is still spasming from the hardest orgasm I think I've ever had in my life. The way his one hand worked my cock like a fucking instrument while his other massaged the hell out of my prostate was the most intense experience I've ever had.

Every bottoming experience I've ever had with someone other than myself was awful. There was little to no prep, spit for lube most of the time, and it was abundantly clear that it was an experience for their pleasure, not mine.

I've done butt stuff by myself before, but the end result was never like *that*. That was fucking mind blowing. I saw stars as I came, and I thought for a second I was going to pass out. My entire body tensed and twitched, and when my release finally hit me, an insane tidal wave of pleasure rushed through my entire body, limb to limb. It was unlike anything, and I never knew it could be like that.

The kiss breaks, but we make no move to separate. It's like neither of us can get close enough to the other tonight. Our breathing is heavy, chests heaving.

"You heard me right," I whisper against his mouth. "I want you to fuck me, *cariño*."

He swallows hard, his Adam's apple bobbing in his throat. "You're sure?"

"Yes." I laugh. "Why do you look so terrified?"

"I just..." He lifts a shoulder in a shrug. "I just want it to be good for you."

My entire body warms, chest tightening, at his admission. At the sincerity in his tone. And it's how I know, without a shadow of a doubt, he *will* make it good for me.

"You will," I assure him, wholeheartedly believing that.

He nods, lip tipping up in a smile that makes my stomach

clench. Finding the lube, he applies more to his fingers, thoroughly working me open. It's not so bad since he was just knuckle deep in there a few minutes ago, but he still takes his time.

Once he seems satisfied, he pours some directly on his cock, lathering it around, and getting himself nice and slick before setting the bottle to the side and lining himself up to my entrance. My heart hammers in my chest at the feel of his blunt tip pressed up against me, the air leaving my lungs in a huge exhale.

His eyes meet mine, and the emotion pouring out of them takes my breath away. But it isn't until I give him a quick, subtle nod that he pushes forward, inching his way into my body. He goes slow, giving me time to breathe and get used to his size. He's significantly larger than the fingers he used on me earlier, but the burn and the stretch aren't so overwhelming that I can't handle it.

With Travis, it's very easy to slip into this bubble of just him and I. It's easy to forget that there's a whole world around us, and this time is no different. Travis gives us a moment once he's fully seated, and I'm already dying for him to move. To fuck me in all the ways I've fucked him.

Once his hips begin to rock into me, the burn quickly gives way to a pleasure I'm not used to feeling. It's different, but amazing. My hand wraps around him, gripping his tight, firm ass, pushing him into me farther.

Sweat beads on his forehead and his cheeks are flushed, lip tucked between his teeth as he bites down so hard on it, I'm surprised it doesn't bleed.

"Come on, *mi amor*. Give it to me harder." To emphasize my point, I wrap my legs around him, meeting him thrust for thrust.

Travis blows out a laugh, sitting back on his haunches to

pick up the pace. "You aren't in control here, Matty. You don't get to top me from the bottom. It's my turn."

I'll never admit this out loud, but hearing him call me *Matty* feels so right. I kind of love it, and I've never loved anybody calling me that. Not even Miguel, and he's done it our whole lives.

I snort. "I'm always in control, *cariño*. The sooner you realize that, the better."

Arching a brow, he asks, "Is that right?"

"You know it, baby," I quip, winking at him.

Surprising me, he pulls out, flipping me onto my stomach in one swift move. Grabbing my hips, he hikes them up, arching my back before sliding back inside me. The move happens so quickly, I have no time to react, a choked gasp falling from my lips at the sudden change in position.

Hands planted on the pillow beside my head, he covers my body as his hips roll into mine, bringing his lips right next to the shell of my ear. "You were saying?"

He chuckles darkly, and it causes a chill to roll down my spine. Despite already coming, my dick is thickening up again, throbbing as he fucks into me with purpose. A yelp is pulled from me when the sting of his hand cracking down on my ass cheek reverberates through my body.

"What the fuck!"

"That's for trying to be a toppy bottom," he grits out as he roughly thrusts into me. The humor is evident in his tone, but the dominance he's exuding is surprisingly fucking hot.

"A toppy bottom is not a term," I rebut, only a moan takes over.

Another hand to the cheek, and I cry out again. "That's for your inability to shut the hell up and let me fuck you."

"Okay, okay. Jesus Christ, who are you and what have you done with Travis?"

He chuckles, grabbing a fistful of my hair and tugging as his hips undulate into my ass. The slapping sound of our skin connecting is loud, but so fucking hot, and the easy, slick glide of his cock into my ass is erotic and addicting.

My dick is fully hard once again, hanging heavy between my legs.

Travis's grip on my hips is bruising, as is the one in my hair. I can't get enough, and based on the noises coming out of him, I'd say he can't either.

"Fuck, Mateo," he groans. "Your ass is so fucking tight and hot. Feels so fucking *good*. And *God*, you look so fucking perfect taking my cock. The sight of you swallowing me up is enough to make me bust."

I push myself back, meeting his thrusts, going out of my mind with need. The pleasure and the emotions rolling through me simultaneously are crazy.

"Oh, fuck," he breathes out as his movements get a little jerkier, and I know he's close. His grip tightens on me as he punches his hips once... twice... three more times, before he hips slam into me, and he spills his release on a deep, thunderous groan.

Once he finishes coming, Travis is careful as he pulls out of me. Using a hand to spread me open, I feel the pad of his finger circle my used hole, and then feel the pressure of him pushing that finger inside. If I had to guess, I'd say he's pushing his come back into me, but I don't look. My chest is tight, and everything feels too much right now.

I just need a minute before facing him. This was *a lot*. It was fucking incredible, but a lot, nonetheless.

Travis slides off the bed, leaving the room, only to come back a moment later. A quick glance over my shoulder shows me that he went to get a washcloth. He cleans himself off before climbing onto the bed and cleaning me up. The act somehow feels more intimate than the sex. It makes me uncomfortable.

"Come on," he murmurs, startling me out of my thoughts. With a quick tap to my thigh, he gets off the bed, heading to the door.

"Where are we going?" I ask as I follow.

"To the hot tub."

Random, but okay.

He swipes the open bottle of champagne off the table on his way out. Neither of us has clothes on—or shoes, for that matter—so stepping onto the back deck is fucking *freezing*. I've never seen two grown men jump into a hot tub so fast in my life.

"Jesus fucking Christ, this water is hot," I curse under my breath.

Travis chuckles. "That's why it's called a *hot* tub."

"Okay, smartass, you're so hilarious."

He flashes me a smirk before bringing the bottle up to his lips and taking a swig. Passing it to me, he maneuvers until he's positioned behind me, my back to his front. I take a swig of the champagne to avoid having to ask what he's doing.

Deft hands land on my shoulders, massaging the area firmly. Hot lips press down on my neck, goosebumps blooming from the touch. "How are you doing?" he asks, mouth right beside my ear.

A stupid lump forms in my throat. I have to swallow around before I can respond. "I'm fine," I manage to grit out, but it doesn't sound believable at all.

Instead of calling me out on my internal freakout that I know he's picked up on, Travis simply continues to work out the tension in my shoulders and back. It feels so fucking good. He takes his time, his hand sometimes dipping down and rubbing at my chest.

It's the first time that I've ever let anybody take care of me like this after sex. Usually, it's always me doing it. The role reversal feels odd, but it's nice. Really nice. Like maybe it's okay to allow myself to be taken care of sometimes. It's becoming clear that maybe it's okay to sometimes switch up the roles. It's okay to give up a little control from time to time. I've spent way too many years holding on to the control because it was the only way I felt I could ensure my needs were met—and protected—but maybe I don't always have to be in fight-or-flight mode.

At least not with Travis.

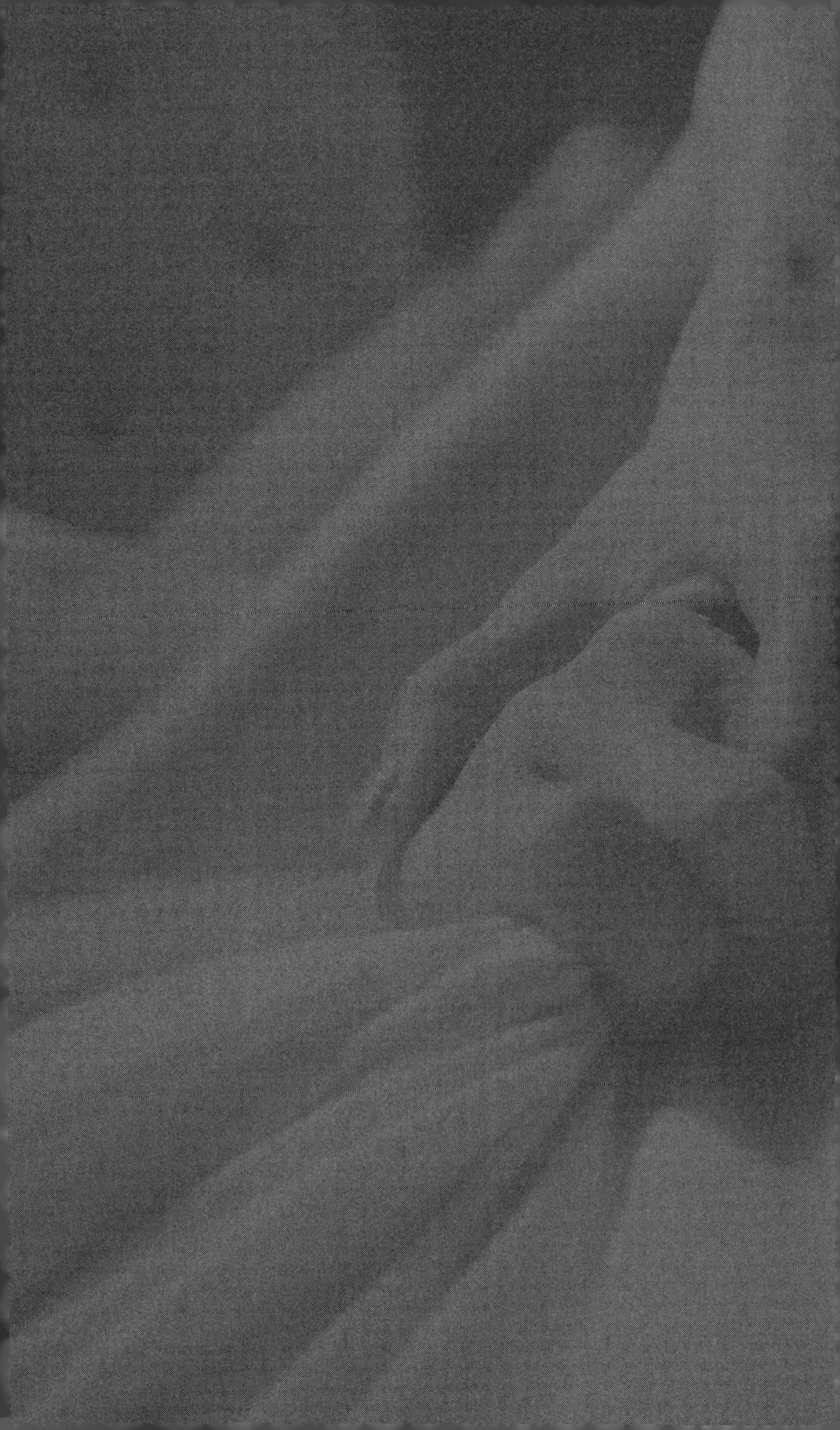

THIRTY-NINE

Travis

The contrast between the chilly air and the heated water is relaxing and soothing as my fingers work through Mateo's slightly wet hair. Exhaustion has taken over my body and mind, and it would take little to no effort to pass out right now.

But I can't seem to pull myself away from him for long enough to exit the hot tub.

I'm still in disbelief about everything that just went down. The fact that Mateo actually let me fuck him is mind-boggling. We've had some really fucking great hot sex, but tonight takes the cake.

The amount of trust I know he had to put in me to allow that to happen makes my heart race. It makes my throat constrict with emotion I've tried to ignore since meeting him.

Mateo turns around so he's facing me. "What's got you so quiet, *cariño*?"

Looking back on everything that's happened between us, from the very unfortunate meeting we had, to the snowstorm, my car breaking down, to tonight, I'd be lying if I didn't admit that Mateo has notoriously always been very upfront about how he's feeling.

He's continuously been honest.

He's continuously allowed himself to be vulnerable for the sake of being true to himself when it comes to his feelings for me.

And he's continuously, especially tonight, put an enormous amount of trust in me when it comes to his past or his emotions.

So, even though my hands are shaky, and my mind is screaming at me not to, I answer him truthfully, because if he can put his trust in me with his dark and scary, then I can do the same.

Swallowing around the lump in my throat, I say honestly, "I'm thinking about how I was so completely wrong about you, and I'm realizing how happy I am to be wrong."

The grin that pulls on his lips is flirty, but also cocky. It's perfectly Mateo. "Is that so?"

I nod, rolling my eyes, a grin of my own forming. "Yes, you smug bastard."

"So, what you're saying is, you're leaving here a fucking fiend for the way I make you feel?"

Mateo waggles his brows at me, and it's not lost on me that he's repeating the very threat he said to me the day of the snowstorm. It should irritate me, and previously, it probably would have.

But it doesn't.

It's endearing. As much as I hate to admit it, his cockiness is one of the reasons I undoubtedly fell for him. His confidence, and the way he's always so sure of himself, when I rarely am. Admitting that, even to myself, is bizarre, but it's the truth.

"You're fucking ridiculous," I say, shaking my head.

He leans in, lips pressing against mine. My body immediately relaxes at the feel of his tongue brushing along mine, my arms wrapping around his neck to hold him close. Being honest with myself, and with him, is a ton of bricks lifted from my shoulders. It's a breath of fresh air.

I couldn't even say how long we sit here in the hot tub, making out like teenagers, but by the time we break apart, both of our dicks are hard again and our chests are heaving. Neither of us makes any moves to take care of the raging erections, nor do we move to put any distance between us either.

This moment is the start of a new chapter.

A chapter I never in a million fucking years thought I'd see.

But it's a chapter I now can't imagine not starting.

Mateo pushes a stray hair off my forehead, his mint green eyes drinking me in. "So, what's this mean for you and me, *mi amor*?"

I wince, feeling my cheeks heat. "Baby steps?" I offer with a lazy shrug.

"Fuck that," he snorts. "I think this means I'm your boyfriend."

It's embarrassing how hard the organ in my chest thumps for that one word falling from his sexy as sin lips. "I don't know about *all that*," I tease.

Mateo's head throws back onto his shoulder as he barks out a laugh. "Oh, fucking please, *cariño*. I'm your boyfriend now. Better get used to it."

Pretending to get out of the hot tub, I mutter, "I take it all back. Every last word. I hate you."

Somehow, like always, we end up with our arms wrapped around each other, letting our lips and tongues say everything we need to say. Our fingers and toes are shriveled up by the time we finally pull ourselves out of the hot tub, and foregoing clothes, we climb into bed together, and stay wrapped up the entire night.

Part of me was worried I'd wake up, and the morning sun would shine regret down on me, but the regret never came.

Despite everything I had to go through to get to this moment, I wouldn't change a single thing. Every hard lesson, every heartache, every one-night stand that never went further than that… all of it led me here, to Mateo, as crazy as that sounds.

Mateo saw me for me.

He picked me.

And he continues to pick me day in and day out.

I was never a just-for-tonight.

I was never an afterthought. Or a second choice to him.

Mateo showed up, a force to be reckoned with, and turned out to be absolutely everything I never knew I needed.

I don't know how our new chapter looks, but I do know I'm excited to find out.

FORTY

Mateo

SIX MONTHS LATER

"We should skip it," I grumble while I continue to fuck with the bowtie around my neck that I can't seem to get right.

Travis is in the bedroom getting dressed. I hear him chuckle before his head pops into the ensuite. "Mateo, we cannot skip your sister's wedding." Tugging on my shoulder, he spins me around until I'm facing him before helping me with the fucking bowtie I can't get to work. "Not only are you *in* the wedding, but you know Ally would slaughter you—and me—if you didn't show up. It's going to be fine."

I roll my eyes, scoffing. "Easy for you to say."

Tonight isn't the first time my mom is meeting Travis, but it is the first time she's seeing us as an actual couple. When she originally met him, it was at Ally's engagement party as my date, but this feels different.

Travis gets the material tied together in no time before reaching up and cupping my cheeks. "It's going to be fine,

Matty. It's going to be such a huge wedding anyway, so I doubt there will be much opportunity for you two to spend any long amounts of time together." He leans in, brushing his lips against mine. "And besides, she's at least been trying lately. Maybe she won't be so bad."

I wish I held his level of optimism.

Although, she *has* been trying. I'll give her that. I don't know what caused the shift, but a few months ago, she started reaching out more. Even if it drives me nuts, she calls about once a week to check in, and even though it seems like it pains her to do so, she even asks about Travis sometimes. Old habits and ways of thinking die hard, and logically speaking, I know most of the hate came from my father, as she simply was a bystander. But it still stings that she was never there for me. That she never made an effort to understand me better—even after my dad died.

The part of me that's still the rejected teenage boy yearning for his parents' acceptance thinks she's only been making an effort because the wedding was coming and she didn't want to let Ally down. But the rational part of me thinks that would be way too much effort for one event. Travis agrees with the latter.

We both finish getting ready before heading to the venue. Travis sits in the front row with my mom, his mom, and his sister while I walk Ally down the aisle, giving her away, before taking my seat beside him.

Travis and I unknowingly forced our sisters to become friends a few months ago. Ally and Scottie were looking to buy a house, and since Charlotte is a real estate agent, we passed her info along to Ally. I've never seen two people become such fast friends. They are *always* together, hanging out, and if they aren't, they're texting back and forth. Most days, I don't know if I regret introducing them or not. Charlotte ended up finding them a house, and Ally invited her to the wedding.

The ceremony is beautiful. Scottie cried before Ally did. My mom cried. Even Travis got a little glassy eyed by the time they shared their first kiss. I'm surrounded by a bunch of saps. After the ceremony wraps up, we head to the reception, and even though I'm still feeling on edge, I'm eager to be by Travis's side again.

Because Scottie's family can never do anything normal and not over the top, they have some well-known, impressive chef preparing the meal for us. Servers in penguin suits pass out our first course as we all sit around huge, round tables. Of course, we're at the same table as my mom. It's too quiet for a few minutes, but luckily, I have a hand to hold and a stiff drink to sip to get me through.

"Camila, Ally looks so beautiful in her dress," Travis's mom, Evelyn, says, cutting through the awkward silence. "Charlotte mentioned that it was your wedding dress?"

Glancing over at my mom, she smiles, and it brightens her whole face as she wipes her mouth with her napkin. "Sí. Alondra made some changes, but it is the same one I wore on my wedding night."

"Well, it is gorgeous," Evelyn gushes. "I've gotten to know both Mateo and Ally over the last several months, and they are incredible and kind people. You must be so proud."

Her compliment squeezes something in my chest. It's true; since Travis and I decided to make our relationship official six months ago, we've spent a lot of time with Evelyn and Charlotte. Travis is close with both of them, and while I'm close with Ally, it's interesting seeing the way he is with his mom and sister.

From the very beginning, Evelyn has treated me like family. It was something that took a lot of getting used to. Charlotte has also been very welcoming when it comes to me, despite her knowing the shitty way Travis and I met. I wasn't sure if she'd like me. Although, I should've known it would be okay when she agreed to help me with Nova when I took Travis to the cabin. It's crazy to me how simply and how quickly his family has started to feel like my own. His mom was immediately accepting of our relationship, taking me in with open arms, literally. She's a hugger, that one, but I can't say I don't love it.

It's bittersweet. My whole life, that's all I ever wanted from my actual family. And sure, I got that from Ally, but who doesn't want their parents' unconditional love?

We all continue friendly conversation while we finish our meal before watching Ally and Scottie have their first dance. More tearing up ensues, and it's definitely not coming from me.

Okay, maybe a little bit, but I'm going to blame all the champagne I've consumed this evening.

The dance floor eventually opens up to all the guests, and when Travis gets up, I expect him to ask me to dance. Surprising me completely, he extends a hand to my mother, smiling down at her.

"Can I have this dance with the mother of the bride?"

Her eyes widen a little and she lets out a nervous laugh as she looks around the table, eyes finding mine. I don't even realize I'm smiling at first, but he always has a way of surprising me. After a moment, she nods, slipping her hand in his as he leads her onto the dance floor. Glancing over his shoulder, he throws me a wink.

I watch them dance, unable to take my eyes off them. They're talking as they sway together, and I wonder what about.

He even gets a laugh out of her, despite how uncomfortable she looks before slightly relaxing into it. Someone slides into Travis's seat, but I don't look away yet. My chest swells as I take him in, my throat tight with emotion.

"Is that Travis with Mom?"

Turning my head, I realize it's Ally who's joined me. "Yup."

"That's so cute." She nudges me with her elbow. "You should go dance with her next."

"What?" I hiss, glaring at her. "Not happening."

"Oh, come on," she grumbles. "It's a wedding. People set aside their differences at these type of things."

"I don't think that's true, Ally."

She scoffs loudly before standing and tugging on my arm. "You're doing it, Matty."

I don't know why I let her drag me onto the dance floor, but I do. She cuts in between them, stealing Travis and leaving me with our mother. I'm not someone who gets uncomfortable easily, but as I stand here with about a foot of space between me and my mom, I can't help the wave of nervousness that washes through me. I know how much this means to Ally, but I don't know how to let my mom in. I just don't.

Too many years have passed. Too much hurt. But… it is Ally's wedding day, and I guess I at least owe her this much. So, even though my mouth is dry and it feels like my throat wants to close up, I extend my hand toward my mom and ask, "Dance with me?"

There isn't any hesitation as she takes it, letting me pull her closer. Her eyes fill up, and something twists sharply inside of me. The song continues, and we move to the slow beat, neither of us saying anything. We both look in the direction of Ally and Travis. They're talking and laughing while they dance.

Pride fills my chest, thinking over how easily he's settled into my world. How easy it was for him to get along with my friends. My sister. How he had no qualms about meeting my mom, despite knowing what he does. It was effortless. With Robbie—who's around here somewhere, but thankfully, I haven't had to see much of him tonight—it felt easy for him to mesh in with us simply because my family already knew him because of Scottie. Not because of who he was as a person.

With Travis, he's a bright light amongst the bleakness. He's friendly and kind, and he wears his heart on his sleeve. And yeah, maybe before I saw that as a fault, before I really got to know him, but now I know it's quite the opposite. He sees the world in a way I've never been able to. And as I watch him mingle with my sister, appearing totally comfortable, I realize, not for the first or the second or even the third time, how fucking lucky I am to have him. How much better my life is with him in it. And how that man is going to be my husband one day, and nothing has ever made me as proud as that.

As if reading my thoughts, my mom breaks the silence. "He's a very nice boy."

My heart slams against my ribs as I look at her, finding her already watching me. "Yes, he is."

I can only imagine how hard that one simple sentence was for her. Just when I start to think that's the end of our conversation, she adds, "I'm glad you found someone who makes you happy, *hijo*."

Before I can respond—not that I'd even know what to say—the song ends. She leans in, standing on her tiptoes, pressing a kiss to my cheek.

"Thank you." Her voice is quiet and her eyes are glossy. She walks back to the table while I swallow down the unexpected emotion that's overcome me. Ally and Travis step closer to me, both of them grinning as Travis takes my hand, leading us to the bar while Ally goes to join my mom.

He leans into me as we wait for our drinks. "You okay?"

Turning my head, I meet his curious, yet worried baby blue gaze. Nodding, I reply honestly, "Yeah, I think so." I lean in, fusing my lips to his, letting myself bathe in the comfort he gives me before adding, "Thank you for coming with me tonight. It means a lot."

Travis smiles against my lips. "Of course. I love you, Matty."

I'll never get tired of hearing that.

"I love you, *cariño*."

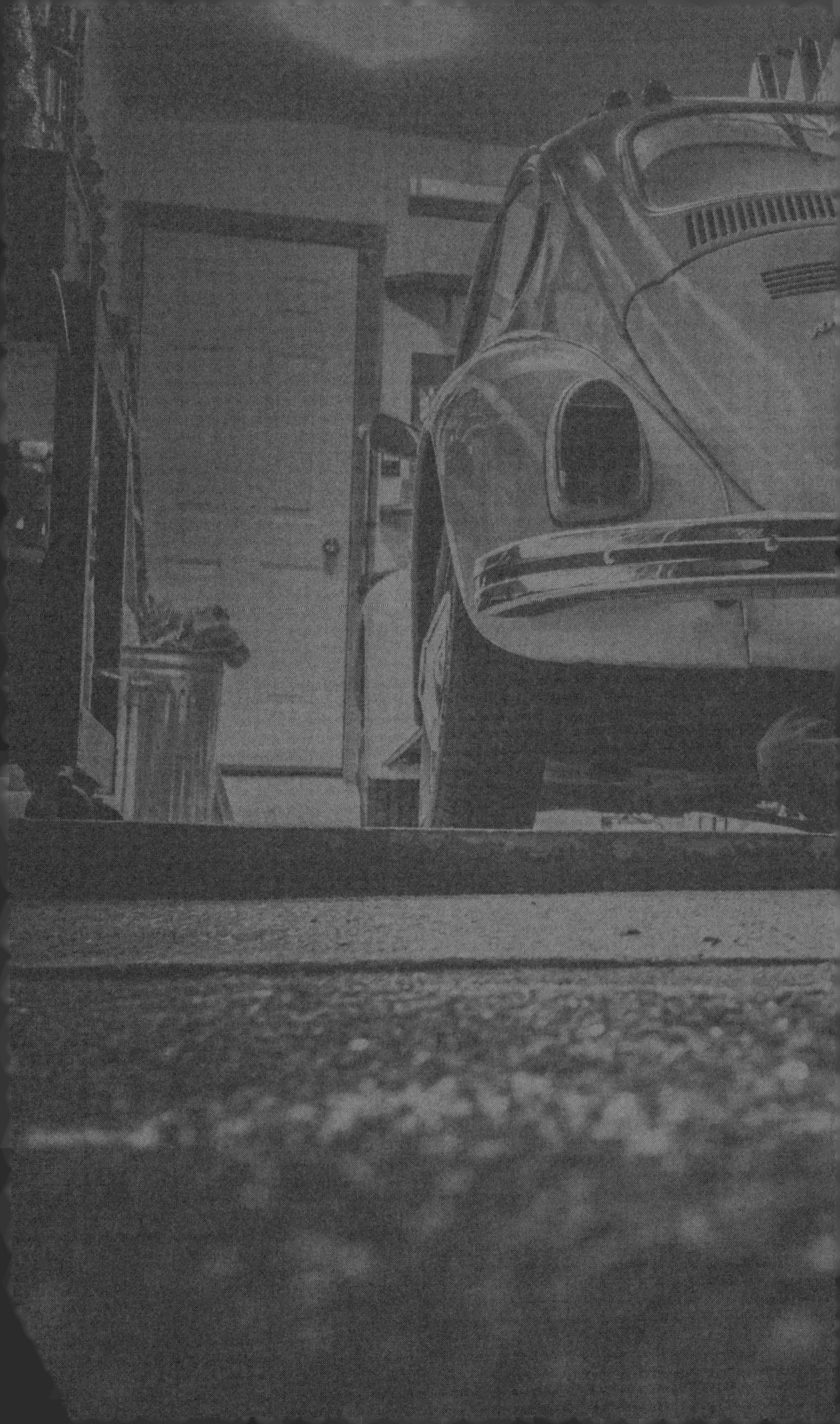

EPILOGUE

Mateo

THREE YEARS LATER

"Holy fuck, it's cold!" Travis holds his hands together in a fist in front of his mouth, blowing into them as his wild, excited baby blue eyes gaze at me while I rip my glove off and reach into my pocket to grab the keys.

Chuckling, I murmur, "Well, yeah, it's something like thirty-three degrees out, dumping snow, and we've been snowboarding for the last four hours."

Unlocking and pushing open the door, Nova greets us with a wagging tail and her tongue hanging out the side of her mouth. Travis bends down to pet her as I close the door, kicking my snow-covered shoes off.

"I still can't believe you got the same place," he murmurs.

It's our anniversary, and it seemed like the perfect opportunity to get out of town and go back to where our relationship officially started, the snow-capped cabin in Snoqualmie Pass. We've been back to the mountains several times over the last three years to snowboard and get away from the everyday life, but never back to this cabin.

The trip has been mostly a secret, as I've been planning it for the last few weeks. Travis knew we were going *somewhere*; he just didn't know it was to the mountains until this morning when we were leaving the house. And now he's practically bouncing on the balls of his feet all over again, and I couldn't contain the grin on my lips even if I tried. Surprising Travis is always kind of hard. He's such a snoop, and he hates being out of the loop, so the fact that I managed to keep this a secret until this morning is quite a feat.

"Do you want to take her potty while I get us some drinks poured?" I ask, needing him to get out of this cabin for a few minutes so I can set up.

Nodding, Travis grabs her leash, and they're out the door again.

Standing and staring at the door he disappeared behind for a few moments, I kick into gear, heading into the kitchen. Pulling open the fridge, I find the bottles of champagne and the chocolate-covered strawberries sitting in there, just as I requested. Grabbing both, I meander across the hardwood floor, somehow managing to get the French doors opened without spilling everything. Right next to the hot tub is a table that I set the items on before heading back inside and finding the last piece of this puzzle.

I strip down and climb into the hot tub, pouring two glasses of the champagne while I wait for Travis and Nova to get back. There's a slight tremble to my hands, and the fluttering in my gut almost tickles. Tonight is something I've wanted to do for a while now, but I wanted to make sure everything was perfect before I did.

My relationship with Travis over the last three years hasn't always been a walk in the park. We each had issues we had to work through, both together and separate, and I don't think either of us realized how hard it would be to learn to trust a partner again. We'd both been hurt in different ways, and a good part of that first year together was learning to work through it.

As much as I wanted to speed through every milestone and make Travis mine in any way that I could, it was important to him that we take things slow and not rush. Patience has never been my strong suit, especially when it comes to Travis, but I did it for him. About a year ago, we finally moved in together. Up until then, we were still living across the hall from one another, which seemed silly most of the time. Especially since we'd wind up in each other's bed most nights anyway.

We didn't move far—well, I didn't move *at all*—Travis gave up his lease and moved into my place with me.

This has felt like the next step for months, but I didn't want to scare him off, so I waited.

But the wait's over.

I hear the front door close moments before Travis yells through the cabin, "Matty?"

"Out here, *cariño*."

My chest tightens, the blood roaring in my ears as I watch him through the glass door. A big, goofy grin is tugged onto his perfect, pink, full lips, and his baby blues are lit up.

"What's all this?" he asks, reaching behind his head and tugging off his shirt.

Wagging my eyebrows, I tell him, "Get in. We got celebrating to do, baby."

He spots the table beside the hot tub. "Are those the

chocolate-covered strawberries from that place on fifth?"

"Yup, sure are."

Travis climbs in, wrapping his arms around my neck, and pressing his lips down on mine. Everything about him—his touch, his taste, his scent—is intoxicating in the very best way. In three years, the electric vibration that runs through my veins every time I'm touching him hasn't lessened any. Every kiss is like the very first one we shared in my apartment during a blizzard. Every time I sink into him, feel his tight warmth encompass me, it's like it's new all over again.

He's everything.

Travis pulls back, his thumb rubbing along my cheek absentmindedly as he gazes into my eyes. The smile on his face is slightly crooked, but full of the love I know he feels. "Thank you," he breathes, emotion thick around the words. "For setting all of this up, and for bringing me here again. It's perfect."

"You're perfect." My lips trail along his jawline, peppering it with kisses while trying to not let him see how nervous I am.

One hand to my chest would give away how fast my heart is racing. I've gone over how this night would go for months. Even before I knew where I would do it, I knew *how* I would do it, but nothing could've prepared me for just how fucking nervous I am right now.

"Can you believe it's been three years?" I ask against his throat as I nip at the sensitive flesh, making him gasp. The sound sending a chill down my spine.

"It's crazy, isn't it?"

Turning my head to the side, I call out, "Hey, Nova?"

Travis left the door ajar so she could come and go as she pleases. She hates being able to see us but not get to us. As quickly as her name leaves my lips, I hear her nails clank against the wood floor as she trots out here, jumping up so her front two paws are on the lip of the hot tub. Her tongue's hanging out excitedly, her tail going a mile a minute.

"Hey, pretty girl, can you go get me a beer?"

Travis rolls his eyes. "When are you going to give this up?" He laughs. "And why do you need a beer? We have champagne right here." He grabs one of the flutes, bringing it up to his lips, and he takes a sip as if to accentuate his point. "How long have you been trying to train her to do this, and she never gets it right."

"Oh, *cariño*, she'll get it soon. She's a smart girl."

"If you say so." He grins, taking another sip of his drink. "Oh, look, she has something. Probably another box or a sock or something."

For the last several months, I've been trying to train Nova to fetch me a beer out of the fridge.

Or at least, that's what Travis thinks I've been doing.

I've been training her to fetch something for me, but it's not actually beer.

She jumps up, and when I hold out my hand, she drops the box into my palm. I catch the exact moment Travis sees it, and it clicks in his mind. His eyes widen, brows shooting up, and he sputters on the champagne he's trying to swallow.

"What is that?" he asks, his voice small and kind of shaky.

Ignoring his question, I say, "You know how much I fucking love you, right?"

Travis smiles, his eyes leaving the box in my hand and finding mine. "You're joking."

"Uh... no?" Confusion clouds my mind as I watch him hop out of the hot tub and run inside. "Where are you going?"

Time stands still, the entire world fading as he comes

outside, climbing back in... with a box of his own, tucked away tight in his grip. Now, it's my turn to ask, "What's that?"

His grin is almost smug, like he's proud he pulled one over on me. He shrugs. "You first."

Suddenly, my throat is dry, my tongue like sandpaper as I fumble with the memory of what I'm supposed to be saying right now. Every single thing I practiced is gone. The blood roaring in my ears is deafening, and I'm surprised I don't drop the box in the hot water as my hands shake.

Our eyes meet, and the warmth and love and adoration pouring out of his make me melt. Wetting my lips, I decide it's sink or swim. "Travis, you're everything light and good in my world. You came bursting into my life, all sass and attitude. Not that I blame you. But from the moment I met you—okay, maybe not the *moment* because you gashed my head open—but from the very beginning, I fucking knew you were it for me. I knew I had to have you, no matter what I needed to do."

A tear falls down his cheek, but he doesn't bother wiping it away.

I clear my throat, thick emotion suddenly clogging it, but I continue even through the crack in my voice because Travis needs to hear this. He deserves it. "You are fucking everything to me. I wake up each day, thankful to be next to you. I love you beyond words, and I can't fathom walking a single day on this earth without you."

With trembling fingers, I open the box, his jaw falling open as he watches.

"Travis Edward Barnes, would you please make me the absolute happiest man alive and be my husband?"

His eyes are overflowing with tears now as they cascade down his cheeks. He wipes one side of his face with the back of his hand as he laughs. "Yes, but I was supposed to be doing this, dammit."

Travis opens the box he's holding, revealing a ring very similar to the one in mine. We glance at each other, and both start laughing.

"I can't fucking believe we both came here to propose," he gets out between chuckles.

I take the ring out, slipping it onto his finger before he does the same to me.

"Fuck, you look sexy as hell with that on," I mutter.

"I do, don't I?" He laughs before cupping my face in his palms. "I love you so damn much, Mateo. I don't have a fucking clue how we ended up here, but I'm so glad we did."

Travis is absolutely everything I never thought I'd find. He has me wanting things I didn't think were possible, and I never thought I'd find myself happy about breaking a relationship up, but when it comes to Travis, I couldn't be happier because it landed us here.

And nothing feels more right than this.

Than us.

"I love you too, *cariño*."

THE END.

Turn the page for a sneak peek at Eight Seconds to Ride, the first book in the Copper Lake Series coming January 2024

PROLOGUE
Shooter Graham

The announcer's voice booms over the loud speaker, rumbling as the crowd goes wild. "Here all the way from Copper Lake, Wyoming, a two time bareback world champ, coming from a long line of rodeo champions, Shooter Graham, ladies and gentleman!"

This is it.

The arena is booming, the crowd roaring. Energy is so high, every single body in here can feel it. Feel the win that's about to be mine.

My body is buzzing as I lower myself onto the bronco, making sure everything is just so—wrapping and then re-wrapping the rope around my glove until it feels right, adjusting the placement of my hand holding the rope—preparing for them to open the chute. For it to be my time to shine. This is the final rodeo of the year, the National Finals Rodeo. What I've worked for all year. That buckle, that prize money... it's mine. I can feel it, the low vibration coursing through my bloodstream, the heavy pounding of my heart against my ribs, the thrum of energy spreading its way through my body—from my head, through my limbs, down to the tips of my toes. It's everywhere. I can't taste it. Taste the victory like a sweet treat on the back of my tongue.

This. Is. It.

The announcer continues, but honestly, the rest of what he says falls on deaf ears as the bucking chute opens. Eight seconds… that's all I have to do, make it eight seconds. Bronc riding is something I've been doing since I was a teenager. My father was a bareback bronc rider, my grandpa, my uncles. It's in my blood, the talent. Running through my veins.

A score of eighty-five takes the title.

The seconds tick on, my bronc bucks, her legs kicking, my body jolting. The adrenaline pumps through my blood, making me feel invincible. Making me feel on top of the world. The high, it's unlike anything I've ever experienced, and when the buzzer sounds, I feel fucking good. I feel like a champion.

I don't bother waiting for the pick-up man as I jump off the horse. My chest heaves as I throw my hands in the air, shouting to the audience as they cheer me on. The crowd in here is wild, excited, every seat taken. Tens of thousands of people travel from around the world every year to watch this event, find out who the next world champ is, and for the past two years, it's been me. And when the guy over the loudspeaker announces a score of eighty-six, I know I've just become the world champ for a third year in a row.

The arena erupts in cheer, everyone raising from their seats. Cameras flash, reporters surrounding me as my team closes in on me. The next few hours pass in a blur of interviews, photographs, and other general PR shit that I hate doing.

The NFR is held in Las Vegas, which is the perfect place to celebrate a victory like this. After I finish with the mandatory shit to keep my agent off my back, me and a couple of the guys that flew in with me from back home decide to go out. Picking a place off the strip to avoid massive crowds, we wind up at a small, hole in the wall place called Juno's.

The space is dimly lit, music way too loud for small talk, and the best part, there's hardly any patrons in here. My buddy

Copeland, another bronc rider who competed tonight, heads to the bar to get us all a round of drinks while the rest of us set up the pool table. The energy between all of us is palpable. We're on a high from the wins tonight—and it wasn't just me who won either out of our group.

We toss back drink after drink while we play a couple rounds of pool, shooting the shit and overall just being rowdy as hell the more tipsy we all become. A bunch of cowboys who hardly ever make it out of their small town... we're used to getting rowdy on tour and leaving the aftermath in the dust on the way to our next stop—which in this case would be home. When we're working the circuit, we're like a pack of outlaws on the loose.

When it's my turn to get the next round, I meander over to the bar, waving the bartender over. It's gotten busier in here since we arrived, but not by much.

"You were great tonight," someone says, and when I turn my head to the left, my gaze collides with a smoldering set of honey brown eyes attached to a very attractive guy.

"I know," I reply with a smirk.

The hot stranger with the dimples and the dark brown curly hair chuckles, scrubbing a hand over his mouth. "And incredibly modest I see."

"What can I say? It's been quite a night, riding that winning high, you know?"

Just then, the bartender drops off the round of shots I ordered. Taking one off the tray, I hand it to Dimples on my left before grabbing one for myself. Holding it in the air, I toast, "To me, a three time world fucking champion."

He laughs, clanking his shot glass to mine before we both toss the liquor back. Slamming them down on the counter, we hold eye contact for a moment, the air thickening as he practically eye fucks me, the desire and the want clear as day in his . I take a single step toward him, closing the distance. Sandalwood and something rich fills my nostrils as I lean in, mouth right beside his ear as I whisper brazenly, "What do you say you help me celebrate that win?"

He pulls back, and I arch a questioning brow as I run my gaze shamelessly over him, a grin tugging on my lips as arousal stirs low in my groin. In a simple plain black t-shirt, a pair of straight legged Wranglers, and a black and gray baseball cap that looks well worn, he's absolutely my type. Spending a little bit of time getting to know him a whole lot better wouldn't be the worst way to celebrate tonight, that's for damn sure. Instead of waiting for a verbal response, I turn and make my way toward the bathroom at the back of the bar. I don't need to look behind me to see if he's following me.

I know he is.

A quick glance toward the pool table, my eyes connect with Copeland's before he drags his gaze behind me. A knowing smirk pulls on his lips as he returns his attention to me, shaking his head. I wink before he's out of sight.

The noise from the chatter and the music dulls as soon as we're behind the closed door of the bathroom. I let him walk past me into the confined space before locking the door, resting with my back against it. A flash of what can only be described as nerves pass through his features, but it's gone just as fast. He comes up, crowding me, body flush with mine, and he hesitates only for a moment before he flips his baseball cap backward and crashes his mouth into mine. Full, soft lips are greedy and hungry for me, and when I run the tip of my tongue along the seam, he parts them, letting me slip inside and take from him.

His hands come up, cupping my face as his hips press into mine, the thickening erection rubbing against my own. He groans into my mouth, the sound choked and desperate, sending a bolt of arousal down my spine until it nuzzles in my balls.

Our lips break apart and he takes a step back, eyes dark and wild, lips slick and swollen as he watches me. Fingers going to my belt buckle, I work it open before flicking the button and sliding the zipper down on my jeans. His eyes drop, tracking the movement, his Adam's apple rolling in his throat as he swallows. I shove the material down until it bunches on my thighs, pulling myself out and stroking nice and slow while he watches, my dick thick and throbbing in my palm.

"Well, what are you waiting for, baby?" His gaze jumps, meeting mine as I smirk. "It's not gonna suck itself."

He fumbles a bit before dropping to his knees. Hands coming up to rest on my thighs, he peers up at me. Even under the shitty florescent lighting, his eyes practically shimmer as they watch me, like pools of honey, lashes long and curly, lips so full, I know they're going to look delectable wrapped around my dick in a minute.

A shaky hand grabs my cock at the base as he flicks his tongue tentatively against the tip. A groan sounds from him before he takes me in his mouth. Just the head at first. He sucks and licks and sucks some more, and I let my head fall against the door, it hitting with a loud thud.

"That's it, baby…" My voice is rumbly, the desire intertwined with each syllable. "Work that pretty mouth of yours. Take me deeper."

My hands come up, fingers raking through his messy brown curls as I ease into his mouth a little more. He gags, backing off as he peers up at me, eyes filling with moisture. Such a glorious sight. My pulse races when his cheeks flush and the corner of his lip tilts into a barely there smirk.

As he starts sucking me again, someone tries to open the door. When they realize it's locked and they can't get in, they pound a fist on it. He freezes, trying to pull back but with the grip I have on the back of his head I don't let him.

"Keep going," I whisper to him before shouting to the person on the other side of the door who just banged on it again, "It's occupied, asshole. Come back later."

Returning my attention to the man on his knees, I rock my hips a little, working more of my cock into his mouth. Honey-colored eyes stare up at me, watery and bloodshot, as my dick disappears inch by inch into his hot, wet mouth. Sparks of pleasure swim through my veins watching him struggle to take it all. His body is stiff like he's unsure of what he's doing despite it being more than clear in his facial expressions and the noises he's making around my cock that he's enjoying it.

Hell, maybe the nerves are because it's me he's sucking off. Maybe he's never had this caliber of cock fed to him and that makes him nervous. Either way, it's hot as fuck, my body thrumming a salacious type of energy at his abashed presence.

His erection is thick and straining against his light denim jeans—another dead giveaway for his want. I'm dying to see it. "Pull yourself out," I instruct him on a growl. "Play with it for me."

Hands leaving my thighs and falling into his lap, he quickly does just that, like he was simply waiting for my permission, letting out the sexiest groan as soon as soon as his hand makes contact. The faster his fist flies up and down his length, the more he relaxes his jaw enough for me to fuck his face a little deeper. It takes no time at all for me to get there, my balls tightening as my body tingles, a warmth spreading and taking over.

"I'm gonna come," I warn.

He hums, slamming his eyes shut seconds before I spill into his mouth. A groan rumbles from my chest as I empty every last drop onto his tongue. Glancing down at his lap, I watch as he works himself over. I can tell he's getting close by how jerky his movements are. Taking my cock out of his mouth, he plants his hand on the tile floor, holding himself up as he pumps himself, flicking his wrist in a twisting motion.

With his glossy, hooded eyes locked on mine, puffy, red lips parted, he lets out a long, low moan as his dick explodes, thick spurts of cum covering his hand and somehow managing to miss his clothes all together. Kind of impressive actually. And hot as fuck.

Chest heaving, he reaches up to grab a paper towel. Presumably to wipe the mess off his hand, but before he can, I lean down, wrapping my fingers around his wrist and bringing the cum-covered fist up to my mouth. He watches with wide eyes as I drag the flat of my tongue along his hand, gathering his release and cleaning him off. His salty flavor explodes on my taste buds as I make sure to get every last drop, never taking my eyes off him.

"Fuck, that was so hot," he rasps once I'm done. Standing, we both tuck ourselves back into our jeans, but when my hand reaches for the door, he grabs my arm, spinning me around.

Arching a questioning brow at him, I'm unable to get any words out before his lips crash into mine for the second time tonight. It's jerky and messy, his teeth clanking against mine as his tongue thrusts into my mouth. When he pulls back, his cheeks are flushed and he smiles, looking awkward and uncomfortable.

"Uh, thanks," he mumbles.

Chuckling, I unlock the door, pulling it open. Meeting his gaze one last time, I nod and smirk. "You too."

Exiting the restroom, I find my friends right where I left them at the pool table. I watch out of the corner of my eye as the stranger with the dimples who just sucked my dick leaves the bar a moment later, but not before throwing me one last glance over his shoulder.

That was... interesting.

ACKNOWLEDGMENTS

My daughters. Always. They're my reason for everything.

My family. I'm so blessed to have such a supportive family. I'll never not be completely thankful for your love and support.

My alpha. Katie… Well, well, well. Here we are again. Honestly, what is there to say that I haven't already said in previous books? You're my true ride or die, and I'd be lost without you. I know I'm biased as hell, but you're the best alpha there ever was. Nobody could ever convince me otherwise. Whether it's helping me plot through a tough spot, listening to my wacko ideas, putting up with my millions of changes at the most random times, or simply being there to support me and my work, I could never thank you enough. I know I can always count on you to be real with me, and you're also such an amazing hype girl. I love you so big! ALSO! Thank you so much for this absolutely fucking stunning cover. You took my vision and brought it to life. I love it so damn much.

Mads. You're the best PA, such a phenomenal fucking friend, and you're Mateo's biggest fan. I don't think you realize how truly amazing it is having your support for this book. The way you hype it up and shout it from the rooftops, and the phenomenal commentary you gave while beta reading it… seriously, thank you. I love you and I'm so thankful to have you in my life.

Shann. I'm so thankful to have you as not only one of my beta readers, but as one of my closest friends. I adore you. Also, thanks for hyping up a particular scene… IYKYK.

Kenzie. First of all, thanks for putting up with me when I was straight up panicked over the dev edits on this one. You're the real MVP. I always look forward to working with you, and I know I've said it before, but you're quite literally the best editor a woman could ask for. Thank you so much.

My Smutty Buddies. The best street team ever. Thank you for all being so freaking awesome. All the love and support, all the sharing you do, and recommending my books to anyone who will listen… thank you. You guys are amazing.

My readers. I hope y'all enjoyed this one as much as I did. If you read them first in the anti-valentine novella, I hope they lived up to your expectations! Whether you're new here or you've been here since the beginning… THANK YOU!

I literally wouldn't be able to do this if it weren't for your love and support. I can't wait to share many more books and characters with y'all. Thank you from the bottom of my heart.

ABOUT THE AUTHOR

Ashley James is an LGBTQIA+ author who enjoys writing (and reading) the toxic, swoony, broody, filthy talking, red flag men. She is originally from Washington State—and no, not Seattle—but now resides in South Carolina with her two daughters and her three Sphynx kitties, Goose, Maverick, and Houston. And if you're wondering if those names are Top Gun references, you would be absolutely correct.

SAY MY NAME

CONNECT WITH THE AUTHOR

Website: www.authorashleyjames.com
Patreon: https://www.patreon.com/AshleyJames823
Instagram: https://www.instagram.com/authorashleyjames/
Facebook Group: https://www.facebook.com/groups/1654869494890217/

SAY MY NAME

BOOKS BY ASHLEY JAMES

The Deepest Desires Series
Barred Desires (Book One)
Forsaken Desires (Book Two)
Illicit Desires (Book Three)

Hidden Affairs Series
Brazen Affairs (Book One)
Storm Clouds and Devastation (Book Two)
Insatiable Hunger (Book Three)

Copper Lake Series
Eight Seconds to Ride (Book One, Preorder Here)

Standalones
Kismet
Wounded
Whiskey Nights and Neon Dreams (Preorder Here)

Printed in Great Britain
by Amazon